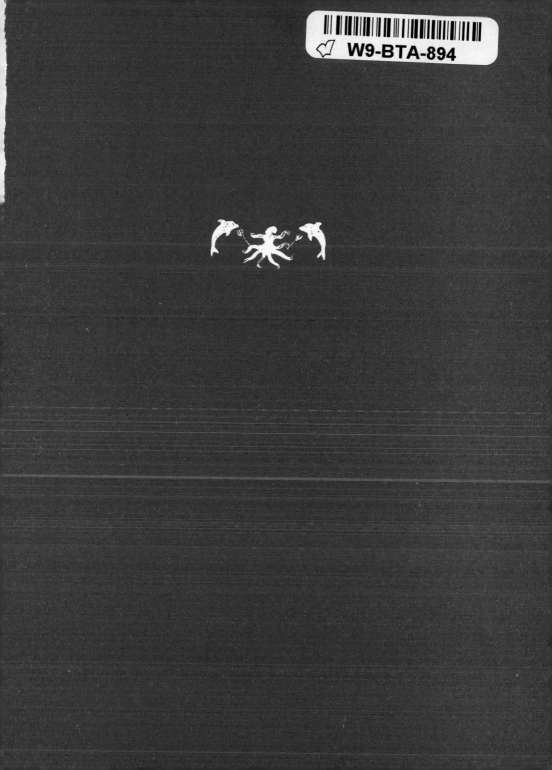

ANGRY YOUNG
SPACEMAN

© 2001 Jim Munroe

Published in the United States by:
Four Walls Eight Windows
39 West 14th Street, room 503
New York, N.Y., 10011

U.K. offices:
Four Walls Eight Windows/Turnaround
Unit 3, Olympia Trading Estate
Coburg Road, Wood Green
London N22 6TZ, England

Visit our website at http://www.4w8w.com

First printing September 2001.

Library of Congress Cataloging-in-Publication Data:
Munroe, Jim, 1972 -
Angry Young Spaceman/by Jim Munroe
p. cm.
ISBN 1-56858-208-0
1. Life on other planets--Fiction. 2. English teachers--Fiction. I. Title.

PR9199.3.M817 A75 2001
813'.54--dc21

2001042279
CIP

10 9 8 7 6 5 4 3 2 1

Book Design: Beehive
Cover Illustration: Mike Brennan
Inside Illustration: Basma

Printed in Canada

for my friends, who helped me make this book

Bubbles over Plangyo,

Where did you go?

— Octavian folk song

ONE

I had a massive suitcase dragging down one fist and my Speak-O-Matic case in the other.

"Let me help you with that," said Lisa. I pushed my suitcase at her, but she reached around it to snatch the jet black translator.

I let go reluctantly. "Careful," I said, lurching on with my suitcase.

She swung it jauntily as she walked, smirking back at me from under her messy mop of brown curls. I set the suitcase down and picked it up with my other hand.

"What do I need antigrav cells for, Lisa?" Lisa said in her stupid-guy voice as she watched me struggle. "What a total waste of money!"

I looked at the spaceport ahead and picked up my pace. "You deliberately parked the floater far away to —" A guy with a jetpack touched down between Lisa and me, cutting me off. I scowled at him as I walked through his purple exhaust, my nose burning from it.

She watched me with a smidge of sympathy. "How's your head?"

I shrugged. "Not bad, considering."

"Yeah, it was quite a party," she said with a crooked smile. "Were you surprised with how many people showed up?"

I nodded. The rooftop had been packed, new people landing every minute it seemed. I felt, again, a bubble of doubt rise, as I thought about all the good friends I had on Earth. I could feel Lisa watching me. Ahead, a rocket launched, its ignition-plume predictably lighting a burst of excitement in my chest.

"It's gonna be good," I said, staring at it as it rose. I suddenly worried about my boxes. They had been sent ahead and (hopefully) already sat in the belly of my rocketship.

We reached the whisk-away and it slid us into the spaceport. I was able to put the suitcase down for a minute and flex blood into my hand. We passed through the field and stepped off near a bunch of shops.

Lisa checked her watch. I took my Speak-O-Matic back from her, saying, "I'll take it from here."

"Sorry to get you here so early," she said. "I gotta get to work."

I smiled at her. "It's not that early." I thought about last time we were in a spaceport together, back when we were going out.

"Well, I guess . . ." she said, folding her arms and looking at me.

"Thanks, eh," I said at the same time.

"Oh, yeah," she said. "Skaggs wanted me to give you something to remember the gang by."

I put up my fists.

She laughed and fished out a moviedisk. I took it and tucked it in a side pocket of the suitcase, then picked up both my bags.

"See ya," I said, and she lifted her hand.

I turned away, trying to decide if I should go to the bar or check in first.

"Oh, and here's something to remember *me* by," Lisa said behind me, and I reluctantly turned around, hoped it would be a hug rather than a kiss.

It was a perfectly-aimed right hook, and it knocked me cold.

"Lead the way, sir!" said the luggage-droid hovering above me.

I sat up, rubbed my jaw and neck tendons. My head was really pounding now. There were a few curious onlookers, but as soon as I stood up they lost interest.

"Where would you like me to carry your bags, sir?" chirped the luggage-droid. It made my massive suitcase look infuriatingly light, bouncing there in mid-air.

"Nowhere! Drop them," I growled.

It set them down. I picked them up.

"Please deposit zero credits," it said to my back, then buzzed away as it realized the stupidity of that request.

I headed into the washroom. There was a medvac installed on the wall, which was great — it meant I didn't have to go rooting through my suitcase. I set it to medium and stood in front of it as the healing rays swept over my face. I shut my eyes (one hand on my suitcase) and smiled, thinking about Lisa. She couldn't resist giving me a pug send-off. So sentimental.

I spat in the sink — no blood — and felt my head. There was an egg under my crewcut where my head had hit the ground, but it wasn't leaky. The medvac had snapped off so I turned it on again, crouching awkwardly so it could reach the back of my head.

A Yenatian sprung suddenly over the door of the toilet stall and made me jump.

"Do not move," the medvac chastised with the voice of a grumpy nurse.

The Yenatian bounced to the door and out, his characteristically innocent eyes looking me over. I tried not to glower at him. It wasn't his fault that most of the universe was engineered for people with door-opening appendages.

The medvac switched off. I checked the spot on my head, and other than the residual numb tingle it was back to normal. I picked up my suitcase and left for the bar, with a plan to make the rest of my head numb.

☉

"Could you stop that?"

The charliebot continued polishing the shot glass. "What?"

"The polishing. You weren't doing it when I came in." They have some subroutine that gets them doing some pointless busy-work. It's irritating. "Just stop the polishing, willya?"

"Uppity human," he growled as he rolled away.

That was a bit extreme. Someone had been in here talking revolution, or at least bitching about Earthlings. The idea was that it gave each carbon-copy bar its own character, for better or worse: the bar near my place had a charliebot that spouted the annoying pretentious witticisms of its lunarian regulars.

I resisted the urge to ask what species had used that phrase — it'd just feed my own prejudices, after all. It was odd, though, 'cause bars were mostly a human thing. I looked around, a little paranoid. I couldn't see anyone, but that didn't mean anything.

"How many people in the bar, Charlie?"

Charlie's head extended about a foot on a thin metal pipe neck . . . turned one way *clickclickclick* . . . .turned the other way . . . *clickclickclick* . . . then turned his jug-eared lump of a head back to face me. From on high, he reported: "It's just you and me, buddy. No other patrons present." His head dropped down with a hydraulic hiss and he asked: "So who owes who a drink?"

When the charliebots were being test-marketed, the locals (after they got tired of mocking it and getting it to repeat various naughty phrases) started taking advantage of its sensor functions, usually with a little bet involved. The manufacturers saw this and capitalized on it, adding theatrics — a charliebot doesn't have to extend its neck to count the people in the bar, for instance — and, naturally, the follow-up pressure sell. Don't ask me how I remember clavinish facts like this, but the craven and clever tactics of business are in my blood, I suppose.

Of course, I also remembered all the times they had slipped up — asking the one person in a bar who was buying, for instance. An "if barpatrons=1 then. . ." statement would have done the job.

"Come on, don't be a cheap bastard. Our house beer is only eighteen credits, buddy!" The charliebot's hose arm extended, poised above my glass, waiting for my OK.

I sat there quietly. With sales-happy robots, no input is the best input, if you can stand it. Sometimes, they'll presume consent, and if you haven't actually ordered it . . . I sat there quietly.

Charlie started filling my glass. Like beer, silence can be golden.

"Who's paying?" he said, driblets falling from his retracting draft arm.

"The other guy," I said, watching as it paused to sense for the "other guy." There was no theatrical flourish this time, just a quick attempt to get its hose into my glass.

"Whoa, Charlie," I said as I snatched up the glass. It would have sucked it back up in a second if I had let it. The charliebot has its charms, to be sure, but when it comes to class and breeding — well, it's no jeevesatron.

It stood there for a second, processing the fact that it couldn't charge me for a drink I hadn't ordered, nor take a drink out of my hand. Then it rolled away. When it stopped, it barked a word I recognized as a curse from the ghettos of the most depraved Nebular planets. A word, incidentally, I had never used — even in a joking, over-the-top way with my friends. How was it getting exposed to that kind of language?

Jesus, I thought. *Spaceports are weird places.*

And then it got even weirder.

☉

Before I even write the next line I want to put in a disclaimer. I can't stand the thought of someone reading this and thinking "Oh wow, this guy is total xenophobic trash!" Because that's what I would think if I read the next few lines cold. This is the situation: I was totally paranoid because the charliebot was talking some serious evil-alien shit, and I was worried they were regulars. I wish it wasn't the case, but aliens often make me paranoid — not because I think they're all bad, just that I think that they have a genuine beef with us Earthlings. What with the war and all the fucked-up shit that happened. I think if I was a rough-and-tumble Neb, for instance, and I saw someone like me in a bar all alone. . .

In fact, that was one of the reasons I was headed to one of the most isolated planets in the known galaxy — to see just how non-xeno I was. But if I worried that I was a xenophobe, I soon found out that there are more virulent cases out there.

☉

Halfway through my free beer someone came in. I glanced backwards. Human.
Thank god.

He was dressed in a gray body-suit with a superfluous-but-still-snazzy collar. I wish I was the kind of guy that could just throw out "Cool collar!" to an utter stranger, but the best I managed was a civil nod.

He took a seat at the bar, ordered a gin-and-tonic.

"So," he said, in a strange scratchy voice, "What brings you to this godforsaken hole?"

Now I had just been thinking about what a creepy place this was, but "godforsaken hole" was a bit bombastic. It wasn't as if there were acid tests going on at the tables or kids skinning themselves or anything. "Well," I said, "It's a little sterile . . . but it feels like God is here, somewhere."

He gave me a guarded look.

"Maybe in the beer," I said.

He went back to his drink.

"I'm here because I'm going to Octavia," I said, picking up the thread.

He looked at me slowly. "Octavia, eh? It'd be a nice place, except for all the sea monkeys."

I froze. My grandfather would use that slur, war vet that he was, but I'd never heard it from the mouth of someone my age.

"Not that I've been there, of course. Someone like me can't afford to. . ." He made jerky hand movements meant to resemble carefree planethopping. ". . . to *flit* about any time he wants. Some of us have to *work* for a living."

I guessed he was a driver or worker at the spaceport. And he had a point. Anyone without money or a university education couldn't hope to leave Earth. All they could hope for was some lame vacation someplace like Barcelona or Tokyo, while the privileged class got to go ring surfing, or swim in the molten core of a star . . .

But the bud of sympathy quickly withered.

"Not that I'd go to that fucking . . . hole. You must be fucked, buddy."

I shrugged. Oh well, there goes civility. "You seem to know a lot about a place you've never been to," I said, speaking with a mildness I didn't feel.

"Oh, I know. I know enough. Robot, another for this poor jackass. On me."

I debated whether it was worth it as the charliebot was filling my glass. I checked the time. Still had a while.

Looking at the charliebot made me think about the free beer I'd just scammed. "Heh, you know if you . . ."

I stopped when I saw the way his eyes were locked on the glass in front of him, hovering but going nowhere. I waited to see if he would prompt me to continue and when he didn't I started to see how quickly I could drink my drink without being completely obvious about it.

Pretty quickly, it turned out, but not quickly enough.

His head swung towards me as if on a hinge. "I know enough. I had something going with one of those cold fish once."

I nodded. Lifted my glass.

"A *digital romance* is what they call it," he said, his face rippling with scorn.

I knew this was going to get nasty. "Remote" is what they actually called it; "digital" had less pleasant connotations.

"So fucking high and mighty." He pulled at the collar I had admired earlier.

Lifted my glass.

"All that bullshit about mating."

Thought it might have had something to do with that. What a prick.

"Frigid sea monkey bitch. She had some problems all right. She —"

"Sounds like you're the one with the problems."

He looked at me. Nothing in his eyes. I stared him down.

He looked back at his drink. Shrugged a little. "You'll see. Fuck."

"Yeah, I'll see, for real. I won't be some jacked-in jack-off, pulling his pud to four-second-old relays."

It was a cheap shot — two actually, 'cause if he worked here then his comm set-up *was* probably really slow — but I was suddenly dying to box this guy's ears. My resolution to leave my pugilistic habits behind were quickly dissolving in a red haze. Checked my aggrometer wristwatch — I had the time and adrenaline to crack this guy's head before I caught my flight.

I looked at his greasy hair and loose mouth and waited for him to give me an excuse.

A minute passed. Nothing. I checked my aggrometer, and my levels had dropped below optimum. Reluctantly, I got up. Grabbed my suitcase.

"Thanks for the beer, asshole," I said as I turned away.

A few steps from the door there was the familiar music of cheap bar glass smashing against . . . what was that? I turned around. Ah. Fuckwad had thrown his glass into the display of expensive liquor bottles. His back was to me, and his arms were crossed in a sullen way.

The charliebot was immobile. One of the lights in his neck switched from green to red. I heard the tally as I shoved my way through the door.

"You owe the bar 450 credits for the damages incurred."

It made me smile, but it wasn't a real smile, just skin pulled tighter.

A few steps outside the bar I switched hands again.

"Carry your bag, sir?" The luggage-droid hovered like a vulture, its claws slowly opening and closing in anticipation. I hefted my suitcase and started moving. If you slowed down or faltered, the droids were all over you. I prided myself on striding through these places without ever giving them an excuse to pounce, the cred-gobbling little bastards . . .

It was a bit of a walk, but it was good to walk off the adrenaline. I wasn't used to having it course through me unused, and I felt my jaw clenching as I imagined that xenophobic jerk back at the bar "helping" with the various species that used the spaceport. I was still amazed that I had walked away from a fight — a first for me. Not like a pug at all, I thought with grim happiness, not at all what you'd expect a pug to do.

It excited me, this new course of inaction. Maybe I *could* leave it behind.

I walked the last few steps sort of shuffle-pushing my bag into the line, staring down a droid who veered off as it realized I was in a line-up and therefore not in need of service. I watched it go, its red cap wobbling, wondering why I got so worked up. It wasn't so much the droids themselves, but rather what they symbolized —

Join the moneyed class and you'll never have to sweat again. My mom's world. I grimaced as I surveyed the line, separating the haves from the have-to-sweats. An old human sat on his trunk festooned with stickers, shifting it along every minute or so. A gray Urasan, horn-shaped lips twitching as she flicked through her pad, was attended by a droid. The only toss up was a young woman in formfitting sports gear and a large backpack. Looking closer, however, I saw the slight haze that betrayed antigrav cells sewn into the lining. Rich.

Despite it, I considered chatting her up — just to kill the boredom of waiting in line — but I couldn't think of anything to talk about beyond the health dangers involved in having cells so close to her spinal fluid.

A few minutes later I was at the counter.

"Destination?"

"Octavia." I waited for the slight, obscurely gratifying shock that I had come to expect. Nothing. Not even a raise of the eyebrows — only a flicker of the light running over the surface of her eyeballs as she accessed the file retinally.

I wondered why her indifference to my destination was so deflating.

I had decided to go for a bunch of reasons, most relating to my dislike of Earth. I chose the most remote planet I could figuring that it'd be the least like the self-proclaimed center of the universe. But over the past few months, people had responded to the news with shock and wonder: "Really? Golly, how brave of you!" and all that. I had made the decision alone, but it had been bolstered by people's gratifying reaction.

"Mr. Sam Breen. You have a week stopover on Polix." She blinked up some more data. Her lashes were lovely, and the way she stared through me to the data made her look dreamy.

"How did you know —"

"There's only one human traveller to that destination."

"So I guess you don't see a lot of people going to Octavia," I said, fishing. She shook her head. I smiled, secure again.

"I started a week ago," she said.

My smile broadened in appreciation of my pathetic neediness.

"Are you travelling with zap guns, cultural products, registered technology?"

"Yeah, my Speak-O-Matic," I said, looking at my single suitcase.

Oh shit.

"I'll need to scan it, sir."

I rewound my recent activities frantically. I had set it on the bar stool . . .

Shit shit shit.

"Sir?"

I lifted my suitcase onto the platform automatically.

"I've left it in the bar," I said. "I . . ."

Her eyes widened. "You left a . . . you should go back." She looked at me sympathetically, but I felt no satisfaction in piercing her veil of boredom. "I'll send this ahead, and if . . . when you get your item, I can register it."

She tapped my bags with a wand and they became enveloped in black plastic, then the platform dropped out of sight. I took the flight card from her and walked away from the counter. There was no point in running, I told myself, it was either there, or it wasn't.

I started running.

The frothy glass that glowed above the entrance to the bar grew bigger and bigger as I dodged luggage-droids and nearly stepped on a family of Plevs. How was I gonna teach English to kids when I couldn't even speak —

The door of the bar slid closed behind me, and my eyes adjusted to the dim light. Three humans were chatting quietly a few stools down from where the xenophobe and I had been sitting.

I walked to the stool where it should have been, hope draining out and self-loathing filling the empty space.

"Whattalitbe, buddy," the charliebot said.

"Did you see a Speak-O-Matic in a triangular case—"

"We can't be responsible for items left on the premises," it said, starting to polish a glass.

I looked over at the humans, who had heard the exchange. One of them shook her head.

A trip to the lost-and-found office revealed that items of that cost were rarely returned, and that the number of employees who wore gray body-suits numbered in the hundreds. I took a seat in the waiting area, watching families reunite and break apart.

One recently reunited family of metal triangle people sat down beside me and started tinkling to one another. Two little ones had bravely taken the chair next to me. They were swivelling towards me and talking, and my casual curiosity as to what they were saying swelled up; and was suddenly smacked down by the reality of the situation.

I can't believe I lost my fuckin' brand new Speak-O-Matic.

Suddenly the lovely tinkling became too much to bear, and I stood.

It was the longest line-up I'd ever been in in my twenty-three years, and there was a long way yet to go. In the distance I could see the glass tube that arched over the landing pads and kissed the rocket ship.

The shock of losing my Speak-O-Matic was wearing off. I was calculating how long I had worked at the foundry to earn the credits it cost: three months, I figured. I imagined pounding my friend in gray for about three months, to even the score.

A part of me, the stubbornly pug part, was grumbling: *If I had left him in a bloody heap in the first place, he wouldn't be sneaking off anywhere for a while.*

We finally turned the corner and started moving through the tube. The rocketship was this old model, but still shiny — a classic, and I was excited despite myself. The last time I went offworld, it was in a ship just like this one, and I had been amazed by the size. I had known the toy I had at home was smaller, but I had expected something just a little bigger than the family floater.

Now I was amazed at how small the rocketship seemed, in comparison to the endless line of people. How were we all gonna fit in that skinny thing?

The tube vibrated a bit as another rocket blasted off. The ignition fire whipped shadows on and off the faces of the other people in the line. Other than the occasional alien, they were mostly human — not a single Octavian in the lot. I looked back as far as I could, then forward as much as I could — nope. And it wasn't as if they were hard to spot. I guessed I'd have to wait to meet a live Octavian, face-to-face.

Not that I'd be able to communicate with them anyway. Damn it!

TWO

Hi Lisa,

Nice punch. Haven't you heard that pug is dead?

No, I'm not on Octavia yet. All us new English teachers have a week of orientation on this dinky little planet before we're flung to the stars. It's OK, though, the gravity's awesome. At the end of the day I've got so much energy left I've just *got* to go out and hit the local bar. Their most tolerable local brew, Poikapoik (means "mighty king killer"), has a kick you remember well into the next day. The illustration on the bottle is a pile of smoking bones with a crown on top, as if His Royalness has just been energy-fragged. The bartender told me that the original king was actually eaten alive, but the natives are always trying to freak us out with their cannibalistic stories . . .

Back to the gravity — cool for Earthlings, not so cool for lunarians — it's actually higher grav than on the moon. One or two of the thinner ones actually had to be sent back because of organ problems. The rest of them are just tired all the time. Between their thinness and exhaustion, when a trooper of a lunarian actually hits the bar with us they usually end up hitting the pavement, too. Poikapoik is quite a bit stronger than what they're used to.

Amongst the more predatory of the Earthlings, this was really good news. Who didn't grow up with a crush on one of the bird-boned lunarian mediastars, with their grace and thin angular beauty? (Guess that's why people are said to be "mooning after" someone . . .)

A real conversation: "Hey Julia, how'd it go with your lunarian boy last night?"

"Well, he had two whole bottles of Poikapoik . . ."

"Uh oh."

"Yeah. When we got down to it I found out it kills more than mighty kings."

Some of the lunarian women are really attractive, but they're so tired all the time — and seem a little nervous around Earthling men — that I haven't been seriously smitten. And you know how I hate that flowery, excessive way lunarians talk.

In fact, that's how I met my first friend here. There was this beeeyoutiful moonboy whispering on about something at dinnertime with, like, eight Earth girls hanging on his every word. After he said "the most atrociously designed springboots ever to grace the planet's surface" I checked my wristwatch aggrometer — out of curiosity, Lisa, just to see.

The guy next to me asked me what it was, and I tried to tell him, but the shrill laughter from the lunarian's entourage drowned me out. I watched the needle move a little closer to the red zone, then repeated myself. "It's just a wristwatch with an aggrometer feature added. It gauges levels of aggressiveness in the wearer."

"Oh yeah, that's a pug thing," he said. "My friend had one, but it was bigger and had a holo readout. Went on his chest."

"Well, then your friend wasn't much of a pug," I shot back. "The idea was that it wasn't flashy. Those morons who walked around with black eyes and idiotic gloves didn't have anything to do with the pug I knew."

He raised his hands. "Did I say he was my friend? He was actually more of an acquaintance. Sort of an enemy, really."

Matthew's the only guy here with shorter hair than me. We walk around the place like Stumpy and Stumpier, yelling "You want to get to hell, you gotta get through the burny bits!" at inopportune moments. It's fun.

Sam.

It was four in the morning when the room's speaker snapped to life.

". . .Breen Samuel, you have a call from . . . Earth, America, New York—"

"Patch it through."

Lisa's voice came through. "I'm not getting a visual."

"There's just a speaker here," I said. "You know what I look like."

"I'm imagining you with hair all flattened and pillow creases in your face."

"Exactly."

"What kind of place are you in? They have visuals on prisonships, for Christ's sake."

"Prisonships? Who do you talk to there?"

"Uh . . . never mind. My attorney —"

"Lisa, why are you calling me? Do you know how expensive it is?"

"My work's paying for it. We do a lot of business in that sector, so no one'll notice."

"Nice." I relaxed.

"By the way, what the fuck are you doing there? Anything important? Other than drinking and stalking lunarians?"

"We have classes and stuff during the day. About the planets we're going to, the culture there and that kinda crap. But we're grouped together in sectors, because it's usually one person per planet—"

"You're the *only* person going to Octavia?" There was a satisfying measure of concern and awe in her voice.

"Yup. Might be the only offworlder there. Other than the occasional tourist. So the classes are kind of pointless, because it's so general. I've been trying to get a jump on the language, though."

"Why bother? With your swanky new Speak-O-Matic —"

My stomach lurched as I remembered. "I lost it."

"Oh." There was a pause. "Sam? I'm waiting for the punchline."

"I put it down in a bar and that was the last I saw of it."

" . . . Aw, man."

"Yeah. So luckily the Octavian language is hypothetically compatible with a humanoid brain. That's about all I know so far."

"They can't send you home for not having a translator, can they?" she asked.

"No, it's not an *official* requirement," I said. The topic exhausted me, so I chose a new one. "Oh, I know why you're calling prisonships . . . it's a new boyfriend, isn't it?"

"Funny you'd say that. I gotta date tomorrow night. He's taking me to a dance recital in Persia." There was a lilt to her voice that was either excitement or crowing.

"What!?"

"That's right — you're in the theory stage, while Lisa Industries has already moved to the development phase. I'll let you know how it goes. And of course, since I's goin' out first, I actually dumped *you*."

I smiled in the darkness. "Like hell! We had a mutual —"

"Mutual's boring. As soon as I hint how delicately I let you down, and your subsequent offworld retreat —"

"I'll just get on the horn right now and tell everyone I'm snogging lunarian models —"

"But you're hopeless at lying, Sam, that's what I always liked about you." She yawned and I wondered what time it was there.

"And you're hopeless at being evil, Lisa, that's what I always blah blah blah. Hey, you know how they say blah blah blah in Octavian? Allum allum allum."

She barked with laughter. "Well, I'm glad you're learning how to be flippant in another language." She paused. "I'm going to miss allum allum allumming with you, Sam. We've hung out for what — three years now?"

I thought back to when the Prague scrap had been. "Yeah."

"Anyway, this has been a standard business call length, so gotta go. Have the widgets arrived at the docking bay, Mr. Breen?"

"They certainly have. I'm one happy customer, Ms. Kamac."

The speaker clicked. I scooted under the sheets some more and looked up at the ceiling, where the light from outside had stamped oblong rectangles.

Near the end of orientation we went on a field trip. It was with the three other guys who were going to my sector: Matthew (who I already knew), Hugh (the irritating lunarian at the table when I met Matthew) and 9/3 (a roboman who, like most robomen, scared and impressed me).

"I'm so thrilled you're coming with," Hugh said to the roboman as our shuttle shot out into the black expanse. It was the first thing any of us had said, so it sort of sat there.

"Why?" the roboman replied. His voicebox needed calibrating, it was really staticky.

"Well, what with robots being so much faster and stronger than humans," quoth the prettyboy. "It offers me a level of comfort."

The roboman's square head swivelled to stare at the guy.

I just sat there, motionless. I dared a glance at Matthew, who was also frozen, his eyes noticeably bugging.

The lunarian noticed the red lights glowing at him. He shifted uncomfortably in his restraints.

"I am a roboman."

"Precisely, that's—"

"Not a *robot*. That is *your* word for a robotic slave with no brain." His head didn't move.

"Oh. But—"

"We have a word for humans, but I do not use it . . . for politeness' sake." I half-hoped he'd say it: *fleshpots*. I'd never heard a roboman say it, 'cause usually if they did they were just about to attack you.

His head swivelled back into place with a sharp hydraulic whine.

"I'm sorry," Hugh said, his eyes downcast. "I just . . ." he trailed off, which was a good idea, 'cause I noticed the roboman's eyes flicking to red again.

"Well, I'm Sam. Sam Breen, Earthling. Toronto, specifically. It's on the N.Y.C. line," I clarified.

"Matthew Chan. I'm from Earth, too. The eastside. Asia."

The roboman and the lunarian looked at each other and the lunarian tilted his hand. The roboman said, "I am from Roboworld. My name is Nine slash Three dash Zero Zero Zero One."

"You're from the progenitor line," I said.

"Yes."

The lunarian looked confused at this, and said softly, "I'm Hugh. From Darkside."

There was a silence.

"So," I said to 9/3, "What's your function?"

Matthew rolled his eyes at my robo-savvy chit-chat. There was a pause, so I looked over at 9/3. His eyes appeared dimmer.

"I have no function."

Matthew's eyebrows lurched in surprise, as did mine. No function?!

It was a trip destined for social blunders, it seemed. We spent the rest of it in silence, watching the green planet grow from a pebble to something much larger.

🪐

Matthew had one arm around 9/3's shoulder and one around Hugh's. They were smiling and sweating; even 9/3's metal seemed to glisten. Behind them was a valley of obscene lushness, a smooth green made softer by the mist.

"OK?" I asked, amazed by Matthew's ability to put his arm around anyone for the sake of a picture.

Matthew nodded, grinning.

I pushed the button.

"Thanks, guys," Matthew said, patting them both on the back. 9/3's back rang hollowly, which awakened my old curiosity: how much of the boxy design of your average roboman was for actual circuitry and wiring and how much was for looks? I had never asked the other guy I knew, which got me thinking about him . . .

"Hey, I knew a roboman back on Earth. He was cool. He played bass in my friend's band."

9/3 didn't respond.

It wasn't bare enough to sit down and admire the view, so we were sort of standing around in this tree-circled clearing. It had taken us a good little while to get up here, so I didn't want to head back right away even though I was kind of nervous out there. Surrounded. I couldn't stop wandering in circles, pretending to admire the view like some vacationing tourist but really checking the perimeter.

Matthew finished mumbling into his recorder-pad. He saw me looking at him. "Sent off the pic to my girlfriend."

"Faithful guy, you," I teased. He had sent a five minute clip of the whole bunch of us at the bar, singing a regional song about Poikapoik. I asked him how she'd liked that.

"She said it was too expensive to be sending clips back."

"Smart."

Hugh had been listening. "I'm beginning to wish I'd brought my pad."

"I'm beginning to wish I'd brought my pad," 9/3 repeated exactly, except for a whiny buzz of static.

Hugh looked at him quickly, hurt shock on his face.

"I am making an audio-visual recording of this expedition. You may have access to it," 9/3 explained. I had thought he was being mean to Hugh, which amused me; then I realized he was being kind, which surprised me pleasantly, too.

Hugh looked at Matthew for a second. Hugh had been pretty quiet on the hike, and when I looked at him now I could see the fatigue hanging on his body. "How'd your girlfriend feel about you leaving for Squidollia?" he said, his eyes nervous but intent.

"Well, she's from there, so she was really happy at first," Matthew said, pulling a leaf off a tree. It was almost a perfect circle, its stem in the center. "As the time came closer, she was kind of bummed out. But we had already told her relatives there and everything. So I was committed for the year, anyway."

So she was Squidollian. That explained the relationship's intensity, which was very similar to Octavians in that respect.

"You leave any broken hearts behind you, Hugh?" Matthew asked.

Hugh was squatting, drawing in some dirt with a stick. "Not unless you count mine." He was tracing squares and bisecting them.

Damn. Empathy was breaking up the jealousy clots.

"Well, let's get out of this creepy place," Matthew said.

I whipped around. "You think it's creepy, too?"

Matthew nodded. "Yeah. I feel like the place is gonna grow right over me."

"What?" said Hugh. "How can you—"

"What I hate about it the most," I ranted as we started walking back to the ship, "how peaceful it looks from a distance. But when you get close up it's, like, got a million insects all over it. Totally sneaky."

"But that's the marvellous part, is how there's life *everywhere* here. It's teeming with creatures of every sort," said Hugh, his eyes wide and his thin arms moving as he spoke. "Look at this tree."

I stopped and looked. It was a tree as broad as a city transtube entrance, maybe five times as high. It was a dark brown, and every inch of it was covered with these intricate swirls. It made me dizzy to look at it.

"It's like an apartment block for the animals here."

Matthew was annoyed by this. "Oh, I understand *now*," and started off.

Hugh was looking up at it as if he wouldn't mind moving in.

"Earth used to have trees," I said to him, following Matthew. "I'm not unfamiliar with the concept."

"Have you ever climbed one?" Hugh asked, innocently enough.

Matthew shot back what I would have classed a warning look.

Hugh wasn't looking. He kept on, "It's a lot easier back home, of course. When I was young I could pull myself up with one hand."

I heard Matthew mumble something sarcastic about how *perfect* the terraformed moon was, getting worked up. It was the heat, none of us were used to it. He was quickly putting space between himself and Hugh.

I looked back. Hugh was trying to keep his bangs out of his face, blinking sweat out of his eyes. He tried to wave 9/3 ahead of him but the roboman silently insisted on taking up the rear.

"I fear I'm slowing us all down," he said with a painfully shamed smile. "You know what they say about lunarians . . ."

Since Matthew was annoyed, I felt it was OK to ease up. "*They* say a lot of crap. We're not in any hurry." I said, picking up a pebble to show how relaxed I was. "Is your teaching planet as high-grav as this?"

"No, it's about halfway between home and this."

"This is good training, then," said 9/3.

Hugh gave a rueful nod and we continued on. Before we landed the shuttle, we had scanned the planet and mapped out the easiest two-hour hike. It was hard going — while the grasses were low in this area, there was only the roughest of paths that we ourselves had made on our way up to the clearing. Each step met with some resistance; a tangle of grass, or an unseen root, or just a dip that was obscured that you had to compensate for. It was as if the surface had been randomized. I was getting a little stumbly myself, and I'm used to higher gravity. So it was hard going.

We were only half-way back when Hugh collapsed. The first time, he got up himself, smiling and bright-eyed in the way of the utterly exhausted. The second time 9/3 had to pick him up. And he picked him up entirely.

"I will carry you. You are dangerously weak."

I didn't want to stop and turn around because I knew Hugh would be mortified. I couldn't hear what he said, but got a general sense of his futile resistance.

9/3's staticky voice carried, though. "That is not a concern. I have enough energy in my atomic battery to carry 100 of you 4,504 times the distance back to the ship."

Mechanical exactitude had a way of carrying machismo to a whole new level. There's a good reason robomen heroes dominate the action movie genre.

I listened for further resistance, but there wasn't any more discussion except for the heavy steps of 9/3 and the occasional cracking of branches under their combined weight.

I sped up a little. The path dipped down for a while and then climbed back up. It was an unusual sensation, a pleasant level of exertion. I had never liked running, and walking was too easy — the slight incline was perfect. It was like finding the ideal thickness for a protein shake.

Pretty soon I was back at the shuttle. Matthew was sitting against the landing gear, no longer looking annoyed. I flopped down beside him. The landing thrusters had caramelized and smoothed out the area nicely. "Ah, flat ground," I said gratefully, feeling it warm under my hand. It had been autocooled, of course, but then the sun had got at it.

We watched the forest. I wondered about Lisa, thought about how well she'd get along with Matthew, imagined them meeting.

"Why did they send us to this overgrown rock?" Matthew said. "It's nothing like the planets we're going to."

I shrugged. "I think it's a get-to-know-your-sector-buddies thing. They're pretty serious about us hanging out with our fellow English speakers — that's why we get free travel in our sector. So we don't go nuts."

"Free travel. Still can't believe that. Too bad we're stuck with a blockhead and a moonboy."

I smirked despite myself. "9/3 seems OK. Hugh is a little irritating, except . . ."

"Except when he's extremely irritating?" Matthew said, yawning. It was getting dark.

I willed myself to argue, although I basically agreed. "All lunarians talk in that fakey-fake way. It's not his fault."

"Oh yes it is," said Matthew without thinking.

"Why did that stuff about the tree bug you so much?"

Matthew grimaced. "It sounded word-for-word like the crap my dad spouts. 'Before the rise of the bourgeoisie, Earth was a glorious garden.' Such bull. I traced our family tree back. We've been living in cities as long as there's been cities."

"Parks not parking!" I said, fist in the air. In university, I was sympathetic to the regrowth cause, but not because I wanted a forest to frolic in. It was the threat it presented to the powerbrokers that really interested me: valuable real estate turned into public land.

We had time for a spirited debate on activism and a discussion about the attractiveness of a certain female in the orientation before 9/3 and Hugh finally arrived

We heard them before we saw them, the rustling. Then I saw movement, and the glimpse of 9/3's eyelights, and then they emerged. 9/3 cradled the lunarian's wisp of a body against him. Hugh was sleeping, one hand on 9/3's chestplate. His mouth was slightly open. 9/3 was walking extra slowly so as to not wake him up. This was one strangely considerate roboman.

We quietly walked up the ramp and into the shuttle.

🪐

We were taking a break in the middle of the Emergency Situations seminar. A pretty good one, actually — this army guy described some pretty gruesome situations involving offworlders caught in the middle of wars, ecotastrophies and the like — the moral being, "Register with your planet's consulate." A bit dramatic, but effective.

"How was your cultural history class? Edifying, I hope?"

Hugh was standing beside me, sipping a cup of water.

"Not too bad," I said. "Not really specific enough, though. How was yours?"

"Similarly inadequate," he said, looking at his nails. "Everyone going to planets with dominant symbiotic species were thrown together. Very little was said about my planet, not that much is known about the exact relationship between the Unarmored and the Armored."

"Other than that the Unarmored write better love songs than the Armored," I said, smiling a little. Hugh was obviously going out of his way to talk to me, but there was no need to make it overly easy for him.

He looked at my face and seemed to be trying to see if I was making fun of him. "Yes. A lot can be gleaned from their art. In fact, most of my studies dealt with extrapolating societal norms from their verse."

"Huh," I said non-committally, thinking about how many women would love to talk with Hugh about his poetical extrapolations. As if he read my mind, Hugh suddenly left.

Later that day I sat with him during dinner. He seemed happy to see me.

"Samuel," he said with a nod. It was potatoes done lunarian style, with sweet onion bulbs, so Hugh had a huge plate of it.

"No way you'll finish that," I said.

Hugh shrugged and grinned, scooped his fork in.

"So what interests you so much about the Unarmored?" I said, determined not to let my petty jealously get the best of me.

Hugh's face lit up, and he set his fork down. "It's the extremity of the situation. They're given the choice between being stripped down to a cloud of nerve endings — the ultimate in vulnerability — or being strapped into a mechanical block, a suit of armor — the ultimate in defence."

"I find it amazing they co-exist peacefully," I said.

"Or do they?" said Hugh, pointing a finger at me. "There have been rumbles about the exact nature of their symbiosis ever since the part the Unarmored played in the war. But to me their governance is less important than their symbolic value. Defenceless and free, or armored and trapped? Isn't it a delicious analogy for the social mask every sentient being chooses?" He lifted his hands up as if to frame the question.

I shrugged. I doubted many people would enjoy being a delicious analogy.

9/3 sat down, foodless of course. "That sounded interesting," he said. Ever since Hugh had fallen asleep in 9/3's arms they had been close. Go figure.

"Just talking about the Unarmored," Hugh said. "The only thing I'm an authority on."

A group of lunarians walked by and waved at Hugh. He waved back distractedly, looking around. "Where's Matthew?" Hugh asked. "We could have our whole sector crew here."

"He went bowling with a bunch of people. To that place we passed on our way back from that green planet."

Hugh's eyes widened. "The one with the bowling pin carved out of a meteorite? Blast, I wanted to check that out."

"It's gotta be two meteorites stuck together. It's too huge," I said.

"He said he wanted to send a picture of it back to his girlfriend," 9/3 said.

After a moment, Hugh said cautiously, "I know very little about relationships on your planet, 9/3."

"There are no relationships on Roboworld. Officially."

"Officially?" I asked. "So there *are* relationships."

9/3's eyes blinked assertion.

Hugh said, "I met a roboman who seemed to travel endlessly. He talked about being involved with an offworlder. He said he didn't want to go back to Roboworld."

"Really?" I said.

9/3 said, "It is unacceptable for a roboman to have singular emotional congress with another. Those who do are said to be defective, and treated accordingly."

Defective. That made me feel a little sick.

Kalen passed by at that point, one of the Earthlings with an eye on Hugh. "Hey Sam. Hugh." We nodded, Hugh scraping up the last of his potatoes. "Lunarian style," Kalen pointed out.

Hugh flashed her a brilliant smile. "Right you are."

Kalen patted 9/3 on the head. "Hi 9/3-0001!"

"Hello."

"See ya later," she said, and sauntered off.

No one said anything, the clinking of fork against plate being the main sound. 9/3 finally broke the silence.

"Flirt."

THREE

"Do you realize there's a low level hum coming from your torso?" I asked him, finally.

We had been waiting for a full hour, and that weird hum had been there the whole time.

"Oh. Sorry," 9/3 said. "I did not notice that."

I felt bad, snapping at him like that. "It's my nerves. Just a little worried that our co-teachers haven't shown yet."

"I am, too. That is what caused the sound — it is an imperfectly muted warning alarm caused by stress."

Huh. I didn't know robomen got nervous. Sometimes it's hard to remember that there's a human brain swimming around in that iron case. Not that that made them human, exactly, but it looked like some things still held true.

The transfer spaceport was quite dead, which was good. It was a small place and I didn't think I could take Montavians crawling all over me. There were a lot of them, but not enough for their famed different-concept-of-personal-space to kick in. Montavians and Octavians passed by in equal numbers.

The Octavians, naturally, were of particular interest to me. They lay on their sides on their floating platforms, their bodies insupportable in the oxygen atmosphere. They were soupy bags of flesh, a single tentacle raised to the controls. I stared at them openly, thinking that this spaceport may be the last place that I could look at them as aliens. Soon, I'd be the outsider.

9/3's nervous hum started up again. I looked at him and it stopped instantly.

I chuckled. "Hey, 9/3, if you had Richardson in front of you right now, what would you do?" 9/3 had been suspicious of the co-ordinator's competence since the beginning, and now that he had warning alarms going off because of him. . .

The roboman's arm stretched out and a flame-thrower nozzle protruded past his tri-pincers. The pilot light popped on like an exclamation mark.

"I would think of something," he said.

I barked a laugh. 9/3's static-tinged voice suited his low-key dry wit perfectly. The people passing by were staring openly at us now, veering away, and you couldn't really blame them. When 9/3 retracted the nozzle, the people-flow straightened out.

"I have already filed reports with the four most relevant agencies."

"Good," I said. "You can add my name to that letter."

There was a pause as he did just that, his eyelights going offline briefly.

The loudspeaker spoke in a language I couldn't understand, but some nearby Montavians cocked an ear. "Ah, Montavian," I said wisely.

9/3 looked at me. "It is good you have been studying. Without a translator, you will need it."

"Thanks, pal."

"I have heard that some co-teachers have a very low level of English and must rely heavily on the translators."

Nothing good would come out of my mouth, I knew, so I clenched my teeth.

"Why are humans so inefficient?" 9/3 pondered.

"Why are *blockheads* so fucking *blockheaded*?" I exploded. Twenty-eight hours on a ship, and now this crap?

9/3 looked at me, and I stared back at him.

"I did not mean you," he said.

"Well . . . you don't even know it was Richardson's fault," I said. "It could be your host."

"It would have to be both our hosts, then."

"Yeah," I admitted. Fuckin' Richardson. Probably on the vapors when he made the arrangements, the goddamned . . .

"Maybe," 9/3 said slowly, "they do not recognize us."

I snickered. "Yeah, we're kind of hard to spot."

"Ha ha," 9/3 said. 9/3's laugh always cracked me up, so we were in the middle of a laughter avalanche when our hosts finally showed up.

They were the only Octavian-Montavian pair I had seen, so I waved on a hunch. They waved back in the slightly loose way that people from non-waving cultures do.

We snuffled and chortled our way to a full stop by the time that they got across the room. Maybe it wasn't the most professional, but it was better than catching us while I was spouting xenophobic slurs or when 9/3's flame-thrower was activated.

I checked my watch. Dead on the hour. I looked at 9/3 and his eyes flickered, his way of nodding.

"Richardson gave us the wrong time," he grated so that only I heard.

"Very glad to meet you," my Octavian co-teacher said, after positioning his platform so his head faced my way. He lifted his head a few inches, with great effort. "I am Laz Cha Zik. You may call me Mr. Zik."

We had split off to meet our hosts privately. I heard 9/3 address his co-teacher, a tall Montavian (almost 3'6") in another language. The munchkin looked relieved.

I fought an urge to apologize immediately for not having a translator, and instead just introduced myself and stuck out my hand. Mr. Zik's tentacle waved out and slapped into my hand. It was dry, but there was a slight stickiness that I had been warned about.

Luckily. Because if I didn't know that it was from micro-suction cups, I would have obeyed my instincts and wiped my hand on my pants. Wars have been started for less, and it would certainly make for a less-than-auspicious beginning to a working relationship.

"So . . ." said Mr. Zik.

9/3 and the munchkin were talking a mile a minute.

Mr. Zik smoothed his head crest, then said, "Shall we go?"

"Sure," I said, turning to 9/3. He was setting the Montavian on his shoulder. The Montavian smiled at me and fiddled with something behind the roboman's head. 9/3's neck hissed briefly.

"So, I'll uh, give you a call," I said to 9/3, wondering what in the hell was going on.

The Montavian clambered back to the ground. 9/3 lifted his head off and handed the cube to his co-teacher. "Yes. I will stay in touch," he said, from the tiny man's arms.

The Montavian nodded to us and left with 9/3's head. 9/3's body sat for a few more seconds, then stood up and walked in the opposite direction.

I looked at Mr. Zik and said, "Weird!"

He took a second to process it, then said: "Yes."

We walked through four entire docking bays before we found it. They were smaller bays than at an intergalactic spaceport, but weren't by any means small. Mr. Zik tried to keep his platform at a regular speed, but kept shooting ahead.

"How was your trip?" he asked.

"Kind of rough. I drank too much coffee and so I couldn't sleep."

"Ah," he said. "Coffee." He made a hissing sound. "Drinking coffee makes me . . . jumpy?" He looked at me.

I didn't know what he was asking me.

"Is that right?" he asked. "Jumpy?"

"Yeah, that's right, jumpy." I said authoritatively. The teaching had begun! "They had hoses on the ship where you could get any beverage you want, so I drank too much. I love coffee."

Mr. Zik nodded. We stopped in front of a large gold saucer. "There is no coffee on Octavia," he said, perhaps sadly.

"Oh," I said, certainly sadly.

Mr. Zik pushed a button somewhere on his person and there was a bleep. The ramp started to lower.

"This is a nice saucer. I haven't seen rocket thrusters on a saucer before." I pointed to them, two large chrome pipes right below the back window.

Mr. Zik paused on his way up the ramp. "No," he said. "They aren't rocket thrusters. They're . . . thrusters."

"Another . . . kind of thrusters?" I fished.

"Yes!" He continued up the ramp and I followed him. "I'm sorry, I don't remember the word for the kind of thrusters." He made the hissing sound again, which I decided was probably a laugh.

"That's OK," I said. "Your English is very good."

"No," he said. "It's very blad."

The cockpit had been rearranged to facilitate the platform. He moved in close to the control board and his tentacles swept out across it in a languorous way. We were airborne in half the time a human would need to take off.

"Wow," I said, as we manoeuvred through the asteroid belt that surrounded the station. "Having eight appendages is really useful!"

He laughed softly, his head still on its side, watching the viewscreen. "It is useful for driving . . . not so useful for walking."

"Well, knowing how to walk isn't very important for people on Octavia. Most humans can't swim very well."

He watched the viewscreen and said nothing. I waited for a while, to see if the conversation was paused or finished. I knew there were questions I should be asking, but I was so tired my brain felt like there were cables cut in it, the frayed ends sparking. I looked out the window and thought about how good it would be to get some sleep.

Traffic was really light, just the occasional saucer passing us every couple of minutes. Saucers were very popular here; they never really sold well on Earth because the first models were all manual control and got the rep as being death-traps before the fully automatic ones came out. But I always liked them — one of my best friends in high school had built one from scratch, pretty much, for shop class. He had to keep it at school, though, 'cause his dad was a bigot who thought that driving anything without a motor meant you were an alien sympathizer.

"I went on a road trip in a saucer once. My friend Pete was a really good pilot."

"Why did your friend fly a saucer?" Mr. Zik asked.

"Why? . . . Uh, well, they're really cheap. A lot of students get them because they don't need fuel and you can fit a lot of people in them."

He nodded. "I see."

I thought about telling him about how the young people also like how it pisses the xenophobes off, but decided against it. "A lot of my friends swear by them. Do you know that phrase?"

"Yes. 'Swear by them.' "

"Yeah, they think they're more reliable than floaters."

Pause. "Yes. More reliable. More efficient, too."

It had become quite busy, saucers on every side. Gold was most common, and the rest were silver. It was an odd feeling, because I was used to floater traffic with only the occasional saucer thrown in. As well, the guy behind us was really close. I was about to mention it when I noticed we were just as close to the guy in front.

"Sit down and connect your seat blelt," said Mr. Zik. "We are ablout to enter the stratosphere."

I did just that, thinking about how pleasantries disappear with the stress of speaking another tongue, and suddenly noticed something.

All the signs in the saucer, down to the little seat-adjuster, were in English.

"Why are the signs in English?" I blurted.

"They are made for explort," said Mr. Zik. "We will reach the entry ploint in four, three, two, one, now."

The gravitational shift felt like a too-tight halter-top. The idiot behind us got even closer and I was sure he was going to be up our ass. I was alternately watching him (his outer shell was starting to glow with the heat of re-entry) and squeezing my eyes shut (they always give me problems during gravitational transitions) so I guess I looked a bit frenzied.

"Are you OK, Sam?" Mr. Zik said worriedly.

I wrenched my head to point it at him. "Uh . . ." I said, staring at the Octavian. The grav did funny things to his skull-free head, pulling back the skin of his face against soft cartilage. His eyeholes were huge and cavernous, his mouth grew larger.

"Are you sick?" he asked. "The gravity will blee normal soon."

His head returned to normal as the gravity lessened, but I could still see it.

"I'm fine, really. I was just shocked . . ." I stopped. What was I gonna say? That he looked a bit like a monster?

"I am sorry. The gravity is very . . . plowerful."

"Uh, yeah."

"I am very sorry."

"No problem, it's my fault."

He slapped a few controls. "Are you ready?"

I nodded. We dropped like a rock, aerodynamics eventually turning us sideways. It was hard to gauge how close we were getting to the water, because we were approaching the landless side of Octavia so there were no landmarks to gauge our distance or speed. The viewscreen was a solid blue-green for twenty minutes.

As soon as we hit the water the thrusters came on. Bubbles whooshed out of the pipes behind us. "Ah, *hydro*thrusters," I identified.

"Yes," Mr. Zik said. "Hydro. I forgot. My English is not so good."

I shook my head no.

The saucer traffic was just as tightly packed underwater. We were headed down in a diagonal, but there was no scenery to speak of this high up. I tried to keep my eyes open but the drone of the hydrothrusters eventually had their way with my exhausted self, and I nodded off.

I had an anxiety dream about being torn apart by aliens with squashed-skull faces, and woke up a little contemptuous of my subconscious's lack of imagination. We were level now, and were going through what looked to be a small town.

"Where . . ." My mouth felt weird. My whole face felt weird, actually. "What?" I moved my arm around and watched Octavia's atmosphere ripple faintly.

"I filled the cablin with our water. I was told it was easier for humans to adjust to our atmosphere when they sleep. Are you OK?"

"Yeah, I'm fine," I said, breathing in the water oxygen, in and out, in and out, letting it fill my nose and lungs. I had only panicked once, back in orientation, and that was because I was still feeling the side-effects of a chemical cocktail Matthew had made for me the previous night.

I looked at Mr. Zik, upright for the first time. The points of his headcrest bobbed slightly and were much healthier-looking than when they had been strands hanging limply over his platform in the oxygen atmosphere. The platform had been tucked out of sight somewhere and Mr. Zik reigned supreme from his cockpit chair.

My feet felt funny, and I realized I was wearing cotton socks. Odd that I would remember to water-treat all my clothes but the socks, but I didn't mind the discomfort — it drove home the fact that I was somewhere very different.

"Where are we, exactly?" We were passing the buildings too quickly to see anything but ribbons of colored light.

"We are in Plangyo."

Plangyo. I had first seen the name four months ago, on my work contract. It was hard to believe I was actually here. I stared at the viewscreens with a new intensity.

Mr. Zik, noticing this, slowed down. Storefronts selling unknown products represented by mysterious colorful pictures. A building with a crest on the gates and a guardhouse that could have been an army base or city hall. A block of apartments, with kid-sized saucers tied to the balconies.

We turned into a small apartment building and parked. Mr. Zik lowered the ramp and gracefully left the saucer with a kind of skipping lope. I stood carefully and followed, hanging on to the handrails and getting my sea feet, appreciating the reversal of our comfort levels.

Most people I talk to back home are under the painfully ignorant assumption (painful for me too, since these people are my friends and I expect better from them) that the atmosphere of Octavia is the same as the oceans of Earth were before the draining, except you can breathe in it. And I have to say, "No, look, it's got stronger gravity. It's almost exactly half-way between swimming and walking." Really, though, it's incredible how much Earthlings don't know.

I was walking so slowly that the ramp started to retract before I got to the bottom. Mr. Zik started fumbling for his key chain but I jumped — enjoying my slow movement through the atmosphere — and landed on my feet, socks squelching.

He led me into the apartment and turned the light on. There were a few pieces of furniture there, which I was happy about, because we were warned that we were guaranteed an apartment but not necessarily furnishings.

"I'm sorry, blut I must go now. Tonight, I will come black and help you clean the aplartment," Mr. Zik said.

I wandered into the bedroom. The bed was a simple single, but that night my wearied brain couldn't have seen a finer object.

"Tonight I will be asleep. In that bed." I said, pointing demonstratively.

"Yes, of course, you are very, very tired," said Mr. Zik, and his hiss-laugh. "Call me for anything, even a small thing." He left, pulling the door shut behind him.

I took off my clothes and was in bed before they had floated to the floor.

☄

"Flsfjhas lsfheriheu fjshflahdoe Sam Breen. Fheoi ejkthjad goirteoi gdkgjvn?"

Underwater! drowning! I'm fucking drowning! I frantically started swimming for the surface.

My flailing got me about three feet in the air before I remembered where I was. I floated back to my bed, weighted by shame and blankets.

"Flsfjhas lsfheriheu fjshflahdoe Sam Breen. Fheoi ejkthjad goirteoi gdkgjvn?"

Quick, what was it? How do I say yes? *What's Octavian for —*

"En," I said, screwing up the intonation completely.

The vidphone lit up the room, and an Octavian's face started to fade in.

"Visuals off, visuals off!" I yelled, pulling my sheet up to my chin. Was it even Mr. Zik?

"Uhh . . . falfje elrelj," said the person on the screen. The vidphone image faded out.

"I am sorry," Mr. Zik said. "Did you wake up?"

"Yeah, it's OK. What time is it, anyway?"

"It's nine o'clock, Plangyo time."

I set my watch, something I'd avoided doing since I left the orientation. I was going through so many systems, some that didn't even keep time, that there had been no point in doing it before now. I noticed the needle on my aggrometer had registered my waking terror.

"Your luggage has come. It is outside."

I started pulling on clothes. "Right now?"

"Yes. Can I come to your aplartment?"

"Uh . . . I guess so."

Pause. "Is it OK?" he asked.

"It's fine, come over," I said, smoothing out my blanket.

The speaker clicked off without a good-bye.

I went to my front door. The windows were letting in a blue-green light, and my suspicions were confirmed about just how dirty the living room was.

When I opened the door, a line of droids buzzed in.

"Ido?" they said, in turn. They each carried a box of stuff, and I recognized the scrawl on top as my own. "Ido?"

Ido?! What was — oh yeah! "Where?"

I tilted the box of the nearest one so I could read it. *Kitchen Crap.*

I pointed towards the fourth and last room in my apartment. I was a little scared to check it out, considering how nasty-dirty the rest of the place was. I pointed the other droids on their way.

Other than the little trails of bubbles they left, and the fact that they had metal tentacles instead of arms, they were pretty standard-issue droids.

Or so I thought. One of them, on their way out, brushed my sleeve — and didn't apologize. Not in any language. That was surprising.

A noise from outside distracted me. I looked out the window. Mr. Zik was getting out of his saucer. He hurried to my door.

He surveyed the scene. "Good," he said. "I was worried you would have trouble."

"Oh, no," I said. "They said 'ido,' and I knew that meant 'where?' "

"Very good, very good." He looked around, then quietly ordered the droids to do something. They all pulled an attachment from a small compartment in their backs and used it to clean the floor.

"Great!" I said. "I didn't know they could do that. Droids on Earth are a lot more job-specific. They can only do one job," I clarified.

Mr. Zik nodded. "Octavia was very ploor until this century. We could not afford too many droids."

I happily watched the little guys go about their work. I had been wondering how I was going to go about cleaning in an aquatic atmosphere, and now I didn't have to bother.

Mr. Zik just stood there. I didn't know why he had come over, exactly, and I couldn't ask him without feeling rude. "I'm going to look at the kitchen," I said to him, pointing at it. "I haven't seen it yet. I went to bed right away last night." I put my hands together and rested my head against them in the mime for *sleep.*

Mr. Zik didn't react, just followed me. I realized how stupid it was to mime for a person who obviously understood English perfectly. Also that I had no idea of how Octavians slept.

The kitchen was pretty much like an Earthling kitchen. Mr. Zik floated by me and started opening up cupboards, two or three at a time. In one of them, he found a bottle. "Ah, Zazzimurg!"

"What's that?"

"It's a . . . tea. Traditional Octavian tea." He shook it and watched it settle, opened it and sniffed it with his stubby nose. "And it isn't too ripe."

"Let's make some," I said, eyeing its dark brown color with caffeine lust.

While he busied himself with that, I rifled through the cupboards. There was quite a bit of stuff there, although most of it didn't have any English on it. "What's this?"

"It . . . is a kind of Octavian flour."

I picked up a box with a cartoon chimp on it. The green chimp looked halfway between insanity and ecstasy. I angled it his way.

He laughed. "Ssss-sss-ss. Candy. For children." He was holding the teapot with one tentacle, the kettle with hot water in another, and the bottle of distillate in another above his head. With the end of that tentacle, he unscrewed the cap and tilted the bottle.

The distillate came out in a thick brown stream, moving with unnatural slowness, arcing towards the teapot. Then he started to pour the boiled water, which came out equally slowly, gleaming carved silver. After he stopped pouring the distillate and before it entered the pot there was a second when it was a stream unconnected to anything, like a bent rusty bar.

I watched it, mesmerized. I knew liquids would look different poured through a soluble atmosphere, but I never imagined it'd be so beautiful. Mr. Zik had put the bottle away and shut the cupboard by the time both streams had entered the pot. He sealed it, breaking my gaze, and set it down on the counter. I stared at it like it was a genie's lamp.

"Is that . . ." I mumbled, "is that a ritual?"

Mr. Zik was putting the kettle away. "Ritual? No," he said. "It is just making Zazzimurg."

One of the droids came in and said something to Mr. Zik. He nodded and the droid bobbed off. I wondered why it hadn't talked to me. Was it programmed to favor Octavians? That was illegal, but possible . . .

"What are your plans for today?" he asked me.

"Um, nothing really. No plans." Other than cleaning this place from top to bottom, unpacking . . .

"Would you like to go on a trip?"

"Uh . . . sure?"

"Wonderful." He waited a second and looked around the kitchen. "Can I use your vidphone?"

"Yeah, of course."

He turned on the vidphone and spoke with another Octavian, one wearing a rainbow colored bandanna who gesticulated a lot. I poked through the cupboards.

Something was happening in my brain. I was able to note an outlandish bandanna on an Octavian without it registering how odd that was. Now that I did register it, though, the first thing that came to mind was how hilarious my friends back home would find it when I told them.

And that wasn't quite right either.

We had been on the bus for four hours before I cracked.

"When will we arrive, Mr. Zik?"

My voice was very conspicuous. Four people looked and a half-dozen more wanted to. It wasn't as if I was the only one speaking — there were two guys up near the front who were really loud, and attracted no looks despite their volume.

Mr. Zik told me that we'd be there in two hours. I didn't ask where *there* was.

The seats were really quite appropriate for human dimensions. After four hours, however, the differences became more significant. I wondered how 9/3 was doing in the land of the munchkins. 9/3 didn't have to worry about leg cramps, mind you. The image of 9/3's body walking headless through the spaceport came to mind, and I made a mental note to call him when I got back.

If I got back. It was Friday, and I figured there was a good chance of getting back for Monday. But for all I knew, I wasn't scheduled to start work until the following week. I really didn't know anything. What prevented me from asking was one of the things they had taught us at orientation.

"With many cultures, you'll find that their concept of duty is far more important." This was from a tall thin man just back from a year of teaching. "For instance, the Squidollians take being a host very seriously. Amongst a group of friends, they'll take turns being host — and the host pays for everything, arranges everything, takes all the credit and blame for everything. And being an offworlder means that you'll probably never get the honor of being a host." A happy murmur went through the room.

"Yeah well, it cuts both ways," he said. "You'll never pay — and you'll never really belong. Anyway, have some faith in your host. Often offworlders badger the host with questions about everything, and this can be taken as a kind of insult — 'cause you're basically questioning their ability as a host. Here — on Earth that is, not *here* here, I think I'm home already — saying someone's a bad host is kind of a joke. There, it's . . . not."

"Are you uncomfortable?" asked Mr. Zik.

"No, it's not so bad," I lied. "Maybe I can put my legs out here . . ." I stretched them out in the aisle, watching for a reaction. A little girl, who was playing with a little human doll, looked at me and then back at her doll. She seemed to make a connection, but stayed quiet about it.

But why was the doll not shaped like an Octavian? I watched how the girl played with it: moving the doll through the air in the slightly wavy way Octavians moved, using its legs to pick up things as often as the arms.

There wasn't anything in the orientation against asking toy questions, so I went for it. "Mr. Zik, aren't there Octavian dolls?" I nodded towards the girl as I said it.

He nodded. "Yes. The human dolls are very popular. More popular."

"Huh," I said. No further conversation ensued. I may have gotten the impression that all Octavians were closed-mouthed but for the two polar opposites of Mr. Zik at the front of the bus. And in fact, the whole bus refuted the idea that Octavians were the same — there was every shape and size.

Every Earthling has seen a beautiful Octavian model — her shapely upper torso ending in suggestively undulating tentacles, her mysteriously pupil-less eyes and an upswept headcrest — but she bore little resemblance to the people on the bus. Closest were the two giggling schoolgirls, make-up-less and plain, who kept looking back at me. The old man two seats over was terrifying to me, his head a withered old balloon and the soft skin that ridged the top of his head lined with purple veins. And there was a middle-aged guy in a suit and tie who was so fat even his tentacles moved sluggishly. Despite his appearance, the round crackers he was eating made me think about how hungry I was.

I watched the scenery in an effort to take my mind off my stomach and my bladder. The huge pink and gray columns of rock and the scrub brush were good for about thirty minutes before I started thinking viciously intolerant things about people who didn't have bathroom breaks.

The bus headed off the main throughway.

"Great!" I said.

"Yes, we will stop to use the toilet. Are you hungry?"

"I'm starving!"

Mr. Zik stared at me blankly.

"I'm not really starving, I just feel like I'm starving."

"Ah yes," he said. "Starving. Ssss-sss-ss."

A second after I said "starving" I had been worried he would take it as a criticism of his hosting, but evidently he wasn't that sensitive. I relaxed a little.

We piled out of the bus and I headed towards the bathroom with an icon of an Octavian with thick tentacles (thinner tentacles and cocked head indicated the female) and I got into a booth. Poised on tiptoes, I whipped out my johnson and let it fly.

It was easier than it would have been in an oxygen atmosphere. I'd say about 80% accuracy. 85%, even. Not bad for a first try. And I wasn't the only one to have missed the hole in the wall today, either — why did they make it s'damn small? But compared to a lot of alien toilets, this one was only mid-range challenging. At least it stayed stationary.

I left the booth, washed my hands and walked out, hearing a few indecipherable comments and laughter in my wake. I found Mr. Zik outside the restaurant and we went in. There were a couple of policemen eating soup over a small table, their zap guns holstered. They stopped eating to watch me walk to the counter.

When the counterman turned around, Mr. Zik pointed to himself and said something. Then he pointed to me and said something else. I smiled uneasily.

"Sligllgy blick?!" asked the counterman, his eyes wide..

"En, sligllgy blick. Koogeem." Then they laughed together.

"Koogeem" meant "offworlder." I smiled and nodded, repeating my mantra: Trust your host, trust your host.

The counterman prepared the food and brought it to us, two plates of seed-speckled seaweed, red dumplings and other vegetables that I didn't recognize.

"Oh Kay?" said the counterman when he gave it to me.

At first I thought he was speaking Octavian, but then I figured it out and nodded.

"OK!" he confirmed, and the policemen behind us laughed.

I kept telling myself that I was lucky to be on a planet with human-suitable food, even if I had to eat a lot of it by Octavian standards. I took my fork out of my pocket and started eating.

I knew this would cause a bit of a stir. We had been warned that a fork may be mistaken for a weapon and so it was best to start eating with it immediately. The policemen made gestures towards it and looked to be deciding who should ask me about it. I ate quickly and kept my head down.

"They think your fork is very interesting," Mr. Zik said.

"Really?" I said, eating faster.

I was just trying to buy myself some time. I'm not going to dwell on it, but Octavians are messy eaters by our standards. We've all heard the stupid sea-monkeys-in-a-posh-restaurant jokes, and there is an element of truth to them.

One of the policemen, in an endearingly bashful way, sidled up to me. I kept eating. Then he said, "Can I . . . food-tool?" His friends were watching intently.

Mr. Zik said something to him. The policeman quickly slurped the remaining food off of his tentacle-ends and then held one gleaming one out. I scraped the last bit of food into my mouth and gave him the fork.

His friend, mouth ringed with soup-stain, came over to get a look at it.

"Fork," I said, pointing at the silver utensil.

"Fork?" he said. I confirmed. He said "Gheithih fork, eoituihvv slork!" to his friend and Mr. Zik laughed, too.

"It sounds like a word in Octavian," Mr. Zik said.

I nodded.

The policeman feinted at his friend with the fork and his friend jumped back.

I waited for their fun to be exhausted, wondering if I'd ever get it back. How much would it cost to get a new one sent here?

Now he was using it to pretend to eat from an empty plate, though it seemed to be more to get the feel of it rather than mock me.

I belched quietly, realizing I had hardly tasted my dinner in my rush but that one of the vegetables had left a pleasant aftertaste. Mr. Zik finished his food and put his plate to one side. They saw that as a sign and handed the moist fork back to me. I took it with the tips of my fingers, which would have been rude if they had understood it as a slight.

"Good-bye," I said.

The one who had first approached me stuttered out a good-bye, much to the amusement of his friends.

The saucer's acoustics seemed to be designed to amplify the noise-sound Mr. Zik made.

I looked back out at the countryside and tried to reconstitute my shattered daydream. Scenery of this sort was new to me: the gray hills of coral rock sparsely dotted by pink and green bushes were a sharp contrast to stimulus-rich Earth. Every half an hour or so we'd pass through a town, a welcome rush of people and buildings, and I'd scour them for a bizarre storefront or a mysterious activity that would keep my mind busy until the next town. Because the space between each town was so long and empty, the trip reminded me more of space travel rather than any trip I'd taken on Earth.

We were headed for the surface. Mr. Zik and his friend Mr. Oool had promised something "very interesting" and "wonderful" there. Mr. Oool, who we had met up with last night, was having no trouble sleeping despite the occasional bump and noise-sound. What I had mistook as a bandanna on the vidphone was actually traditional Octavian garb — the multicolored scarf went around the neck and also entwined itself around all eight tentacles. Often Mr. Oool would chew on it thoughtfully, which I suspected wasn't traditional.

We passed over a whole row of the green bushes, and their vines stretched out to us in our wake, wiggled and floated back down to the ground. Small round forms that had been scared out by the sudden animation went back under the bushes. What were they? I was about to ask Mr. Zik about them when I was struck with the regularity and the abundance of the bushes.

"Are these . . . farms?" I asked him, incredulous.

He nodded. "Octavia makes all its food on Octavia."

I almost said what I was thinking — too bad — when I realized there wasn't any embarrassment in his admission. How outrageously inefficient! I thought to myself.

"That's why . . . no coffee," said Mr. Zik with a smile. "Sorry."

"No, don't apologize . . ." I said, thinking to myself: *The only reason we have it is because people like Mom keep the Neb slave planets producing it . . .*

Mr. Oool came awake with a hacking cough. "Hello," he said.

"Good morning," Mr. Zik and I said in tandem, and then we all laughed.

"Are we to the destination?" Mr. Oool said. We had been travelling for two hours already — on Earth, we could have done a world tour. It was a real conceptual puzzle: Octavia was half the size of Earth, and yet felt twice as big due to the transport systems and the low population density.

"We are very close. You are like the child, I think," said Mr. Zik to Mr. Oool. "Always ask, to the destination? To the destination?"

Mr. Oool had a laugh twice as big as his body merited. "Ftehui iruet faeiu?" he said in a whiny voice, poking Mr. Zik in the neck. "Ftehui iruet faeiu?"

"Are we there yet?" I guess-translated, and Mr. Zik confirmed it.

Making an impressed noise, Mr. Oool asked me if I spoke Octavian. I laughed and shook my head. "You have a translator?" he asked.

My good humor shrank under this cold reality. "No," I said, watching Zik from the corner of my eye. He didn't react for a second, then he did.

"At home? You have?" he said, looking at me directly for the first time this trip.

"No," I said, looking out at the town we were bombing through.

No one spoke.

Mr. Oool took his scarf out of his mouth. "So, you learn Octavian. No problem."

"Yes," I said, foolishly grateful. "Yes."

Mr. Zik's face was expressionless. A few seconds later he made the nostril sound, and my heart jumped because I thought he was going to say something.

A few minutes later he parked and we got out. It was exceptionally bright and humid at this elevation, and there were quite a few people milling about. Mr. Oool immediately went to buy us bladders of iced Zazzimurg tea at a concession stand, and then we went through the ornate gates.

"The Line," pronounced Mr. Oool, pointing up at the lettering on the gates. It was only then that I noticed the sky. When you look up on Octavia, you usually see an indistinct gray-blue haze, with no discernible horizon. But suddenly, the horizon was there, a few feet from the top of the gates. "Wow!" I said, starting to point but then, feeling dumb, let my finger drop. It was just the Line, after all.

We walked a bit more into the park and came across a titanic statue of an Octavian in bleached coral rock, some of its tentacles unfurled to the ground and some of them lifted to where the water met air.

Where breathable water met unbreathable air. It made me dizzy to think about it. Mr. Oool and Mr. Zik simply began loping up the nearest tentacle, and I followed them.

"When you say 'Don't mention it' what does it mean?" asked Mr. Oool, his eyes bright, handing me a bladder of iced tea.

"What?" I asked, looking away from the kids playing on the uplifted tentacles to meet his eyes.

" 'Thank you.' 'Don't mention it.' You know?"

I looked at Mr. Zik for guidance but he was in his own world, sucking at the corner of his bladder.

"Oh," I said. "It's like, 'You're welcome.' "

"Same-same?" he said, his blue-black eyes fixing on me. "No difference?"

Well, there are certain nuances and connotations — I thought, and stopped myself. "Uh . . . well, no, there is a small difference."

He waited. A kid hanging on to his father's back yelled something at me when they went by on their way down.

" 'Don't mention it' means that it is a very small thing, too small to say thank-you for," I said, warming up a little. "It is more polite."

"I understand," said Mr. Oool, and he looked like he did.

"That's an excellent question," I said, meaning it.

Mr. Oool laughed and slapped Mr. Zik, repeating the word "excellent." Mr. Zik responded with something that made Mr. Oool explode with mirth. I was glad to see Mr. Zik had a sense of humor, even if I didn't understand it.

We crossed onto the second tentacle — this one was a little thinner, only about four people could walk abreast — and I made sure I was near the middle. It made me a bit nervous, even though I knew that a fall from this height wouldn't kill me unless I died from embarrassment. An old Octavian couple passed by and said something that made Mr. Zik look at them sharply.

"What did they say?" I asked.

"To know the time," he said. I glanced back, caught them staring at me.

Now that we were close, I had trouble taking my eyes away from the Line. It was a giant wavy mirror that stretched over the entire world. I could see, distorted but distinct, the three of us walking together — or rather, the smooth slide of the two of them beside my jerky bipedaling.

We got to the tip of the tentacle. The Line was perhaps four inches above my head, a reflection of my face etched in silver. It looked faintly absurd, my average flattened features on such a gorgeous canvas, but I couldn't look away. My neck muscles were beginning to complain about the constant tilt, so I looked around at the other three tentacles that were raised up to The Line.

All had kids on them who pushed their tentacles into the Line's surface. Their parents, having done the same as children, watched on passively, indulgently. The surface gave, stretched astonishingly, but didn't tear. One stone tentacle was so close to the Line that the children mashed their faces against it, their soft heads twinned and intent. I wondered how my more solid skull would fare.

I reached out my hand and pushed the metallic rubber, gently at first, and then pushing all the way to the wrist. The surface enveloped it, warm, yielding, and when I stopped pushing it ejected my fist. I looked over at the stone tentacle closer to the Line and wondered what would happen if I stood up there. Would it stretch to accommodate my whole body to the waist? Would I be able to see the sun, the surface — nothing but water? Or would the Line press against my eyeballs and blind them?

"Is it bloring to you?" said Mr. Oool. "Too bloring, I think," he said to Mr. Zik.

"No, it's not boring, it's very interesting," I said, in a daze. What would happen if I broke through? Found myself on the other side? Could I get back? Would I be stranded?

"Is interesting to children. Keeds," Mr. Oool said.

I touched the Line again, slid my fingertips across it and watched the lethargic ripples. "On Octavia," I said. "I am a child."

FOUR

"So the cool thing is that Mr. Zik apologized for them." I had just recounted the story of the fork-curious police.

"So he knew how gross it was?" said Matthew from the vidphone.

"Yeah. 'His tentacles were not clean.' I didn't expect it. But then, Mr. Zik's a rare gem. No evil drunk like the guy you have for a co-teacher."

"He's not evil. He's just real irritating. He's kind of sweet. And he *really* wants me to like him."

I went to sit down on the couch — way down, since most Octavian furniture was close to the ground. Matthew looked around the room, or as much as he could from the vidphone. "So as you see," I said, sweeping my arm across my boxes, "I haven't had enough time to unpack any boxes. We left on our fantastic voyage twenty minutes after they arrived, and got back . . ." I checked my watch, "forty minutes ago."

"That's all I've had energy for," said Matthew. "Unpacking. I haven't even seen the town yet. Well, a little at night."

"Oh — I almost forgot," I said. "How have you found the whole see-through-walls thing?"

"Not too bad. I had kind of psyched myself up for it. They actually stare a lot less than you'd think — when it's part of the culture to be so open, people really respect privacy in a strange way."

"Huh. So you don't feel like you're in a zoo?"

Matthew adjusted the pillow he was sitting on. "Not really. Because I can look at any Squidollian in their home, too. And they really only *stare* when I'm on the toilet or eating. Especially eating, which they've got an endless fascination for."

"So have you got a normal toilet?"

Matthew arched his eyebrows. "Yes, I got an *Earth-style* toilet. It's very *ab*normal for Squidollia —"

"Yeah yeah whatever," I said, embarrassed at my faux pas. "We'll see how you talk if you gotta crap in one of them sideways johns."

Matthew looked pained. "Already have. We were in the goddamned bar till seven in the fuckin' morning!"

"Drinking the whole time?!"

"Yeah."

"Both nights?"

"No. I begged off at three last night, after learning the joys of ralphing into a sideways toilet. Through liquid atmosphere."

I laughed. "Nice!"

"I don't find it a big deal at all. The liquid air thing. I'm used to it already." Matthew ran his hand through the atmosphere quickly and left a trail.

"Same here," I said.

"So tell me about this trip you went on," Matthew said.

"Naw," I said. "It'll take too long. I'll tell you when we get together. I'm . . . still kind of absorbing it all now."

Matthew yawned. "OK. Man, I can't believe I'm yawning. I got up four hours ago."

"You're screwed. Don't you have to work tomorrow?"

Matthew smiled. "Nope. Triumph Over the Hurtful Days."

"What?"

"It's a school holiday to commemorate the long Squidollian struggle for freedom."

I rolled my eyes at his pious tone.

"I feel very strongly about it, especially since it means I get to sleep in —"

"Bastard!" I looked at my watch. "No wonder you're so damn chatty. I have to get my work clothes ready for tomorrow. They're probably all wrinkly."

"All right," Matthew said. "I'll get in touch with the other guys and we'll meet soon."

"See ya."

Matthew nodded and the screen winked out.

I started pulling boxes open, looking for my clothes.

♄

I was tricked out in a suit and tie, my hair slick from the shower. I looked at myself in the mirror. I tried to convince myself I looked like a Venusian gangster, but I didn't buy it.

Checked the time. Still ten minutes until Mr. Zik was supposed to arrive. I would have liked to leave right away, to be swept along with the constant demands and distractions that come with the first day of anything new. Instead I found myself getting reflective in front of my reflection.

My genetically bestowed square jaw and heavy eyebrows gave me an authority I despised. My broad shoulders made me look good in a suit, and I hated it. It wasn't the first time I had donned the uniform of the ruling class — but it was the first time I had done it voluntarily.

I knew it would drive Mom crazy if she knew. She had made some fairly big concessions in an effort to keep me on Earth.

She even went offline while she discussed it with me. I was used to talking to her as she scanned the net retinally, watching the light flicker in her eyes and the rapid blinking as I talked about the political demonstration I went to or the band I saw the night before. She would frown and her voice would sharpen if I mentioned anything that may have threatened my profile graph — she knew nothing about my pug scraps, until the end — but usually she would respond with a vaguely positive murmur.

"Samuel," she said, a few days before I left. I was trying to get a sandwich together in the kitchen before I met up with Skaggs in Paris, so my head was in the fridge. I could tell it was serious, though, from the tone of her voice.

"I'd like to make you a final counteroffer." Her arms were folded, and that's when I noticed she was offline.

The last counteroffer, through her assistant, had also warned me that it was the *final* one but I didn't bother pointing that out. I did try, you know. "OK, let's hear it," I said as I cut the bun open in my hand.

"Use the cutting board for that, hon," she said, distractedly. "There's an entry level position in the media conglom. Low stress. No physical presence needed. Fifty hours a week, but most of that just on call."

"No suit or anything, huh?" I said, chomping into the bun, holding my hand under it to catch the crumbs.

"Just for the prelims."

I scowled a bit, pretended that really disturbed me. Mom rolled her eyes.

"I don't think so. Thanks anyway."

She shook her head. "Open file, recruit: Breen, Samuel." Light danced across her eyes as she accessed my file, adding to the angry sparks there. "Mark it closed. Erase file."

I smiled. That was dramatic, since she could have done it by blinking rather than voice. "How are you doing with the new school crop?" I said pleasantly.

"Better than ever," she snapped, still online. "Who in their right minds would turn down a conglom job?"

"This Urasan spread is just delicious," I said, my mouth half-full.

"And you know that . . . offworld job doesn't qualify you for any of the trust fund—"

"Oh, I know. Why don't you do something with it?"

"I can't invest frozen money, Samuel. The market is *so good* right now. There would be four or five investments that would be just *perfect*."

The look on her face was frustrated misery. It was a look that wouldn't have been out of place when Jane left, or Grandpa died, but it hadn't been there in either of these cases.

I decided to cut to the chase. "You know I don't want it," I snapped.

"You don't want to be out of debt?"

"I don't want money that was made from planetary renovations. The slave planets —"

"Oh, stop that — that neo-abolitionist nonsense was fine for your university days, but they're over now."

I had finished my sandwich and walked out, saving my rage for the scrap that night.

In front of the mirror, waiting for Mr. Zik, I wondered how much the Urasan spread cost on Octavia. Or if the green delicacy was even available. And if my mom would ever get worked up about anything other than a missed business opportunity.

I saw Mr. Zik's saucer pull up, and I went out to meet him.

"You look very handsome," he said, his tentacles rippling with pleasure.

"Thanks," I said.

☄

I nodded and smiled, trying not to wince every time the old guy looked at me. His eyes were traced with red and white cracks. He said something, and I was sure he was asking about my translator.

"Supervisor Lok would like you to be very welcome," translated Mr. Zik.

Supervisor Lok was sipping his tea, unfortunately opening his mouth to do so. I thanked him in Octavian.

He nodded, looking out the roof. There was a dome window that looked quite expensive. I looked up at it again. We sat in silence for a few minutes. I glanced over at Mr. Zik, who was incredibly nervous. He kept smoothing his headcrest down, and glancing between the two of us. I felt a little sorry for him, and tried to answer the ugly little man's questions properly.

I sipped at the tea. It was woody with an unpleasant sweetness.

The office of the supervisor was plushly furnished, and didn't look like a lot of work got done in it. I looked over at the supervisor, who was calmly drinking his tea, and felt a surge of dislike for him for the anxiety he caused Mr. Zik. He wasn't doing anything to encourage it, from what I could see, but neither did he try to lessen it.

The supervisor said something else, holding forth for a few sentences, a tentacle poised in the air.

"He said that you are an important part in Octavia's . . . desire to become more galactic," Mr. Zik told me.

I nodded, and waited for the rest. Nothing. Was he a redundant blowhard, or was Mr. Zik choosing what to tell me? Not that I necessarily wanted the long version — I had heard the party line already. To remain/become competitive, planets had to learn the tongue of trade: English. Only a few could afford the expensive English-translators, and most Earthlings were contemptuous of non-English speakers anyway, so the solution most planets gravitated towards was a . . . .blah blah blah. Allum Allum Allum.

Mr. Zik was staring at me, his tentacles bunching and unbunching. For his sake I delivered the appropriate response.

"Teaching English to your citizens will give your planet a commercial advantage. It's a good investment."

Mr. Zik translated, making it two or three sentences long.

Mr. Lok stood, offering a withered tentacle to me to shake. I did. He said something to me.

"You are a very handsomebloy, he said."

I smiled at Mr. Lok, who fixed those awful eyes on me, and tried to reciprocate. Honestly. "Your . . . office is very comfortable."

"Good-bye," Mr. Lok said.

After we left, Mr. Zik said, "I didn't tell him what you said ablout the office."

"That's OK," I said, smiling at a person with files that we were passing. "It was pretty meaningless, anyway."

Mr. Zik looked thoughtful.

"It was unimportant."

"Oh, I see," he said. "Ssss-sss-ss."

We walked out of the school board building and I almost asked him why he'd been nervous, but it felt like I would be implying that he was stupid or cowardly for being so. So we got into his saucer in silence.

Soon the gates of the school came into sight. My stomach leapt, and I was surprised by my own nervousness. The building was white, with glints of windows.

"Is that it?" I asked.

Mr. Zik nodded.

We parked and passed through the gates. There were children around the entrance who moved aside to let us through. They had brooms and bags.

"Zik oewiru, eoit fljnt fadntr he?" one called.

"Kllletnroj fldaj rnui Sam Breen, English oewiru," Mr. Zik said brusquely.

I looked back at them and smiled. That started everyone talking at once.

"Hello!" someone said.

I looked back and said hello.

This prompted a few squeals and a couple of follow-up hellos. I didn't respond, since we were almost out of earshot. One of them said something that made Mr. Zik's head swivel.

He didn't respond to it, but to me he said, "They are the blad students. They must clean up the ground."

I looked back at the bad students and they looked like they were already talking about something else. Ahead, a few windows went up and curious heads stuck out, their tentacles sticking out over the windowsill.

Mr. Zik walked smoothly and calmly through the halls. I followed, feeling clumsy with my two-legged gait. The groups of students twined their front tentacles and bowed to him, and some of them even made this polite greeting to me. He said something that sounded friendly without being chummy. Was this the same Mr. Zik who had been shaking with terror twenty minutes ago?

He turned into the staff room and glanced back to make sure I was there. I straightened my tie, yanked on my cuffs, donned a blinding smile, and walked into the room.

FIVE

Hi Lisa,

"Welcome to Plangyo. Are you a criminal?"

So yesterday I'm going about my business. Not doing anything out of the ordinary, except I'm taking a little more time than usual to buy my vegetables since they have physical currency here (5 Beeds = 1 Intergalactic Credit, I feel rich!) and I can't read the signs and I've never seen a double-barrelled cucumber . . .

No, I'm *not* complaining. Just explaining why I was holding up the line. I had to put everything on the counter to pull out a handful of beeds and for some reason people thought that was really funny — Octavians don't often run out of hands, I suppose. I was probably blushing to beat the band (archaic English idiom I'm using to make you feel dumb) and when I did get a handful of their damnable (though admittedly quite lovely) spherical currency out of my pocket two dropped to the ground.

The laughter stopped suddenly at this point and I still don't know why. Were they at first amused by my awkwardness, but then shocked and moved to pity at this proof of how extreme my clumsiness was?

I handed the correct amount of beeds to the cashier (there was a read-out, luckily) but before I could go crawling for the dropped balls (now rolling away) the female behind me in line picked them up.

I put out my hand and smiled, trying like hell to remember Octavian for thank-you. She had them sticking to the suckers on her tentacle. She looked at my hand for a second, and then put them on the counter! She actually swerved around my filthy human hand to do it!

I scooped up the two beeds and looked at her, dumb-struck. She had dipped her tentacle into her purse and came out with beeds running along its length, one for each sucker. Then she sort of twined it with the cashier's tentacle for a second and the cashier deposited the money into the cashbox. All I could think was: she wouldn't *drop* something into my hand, but *twining* with a stranger was just fine.

Then she pushed by me to leave. After I stared a few daggers into her back I checked my aggrometer — surprisingly, a few notches below the red zone.

I got my double-barrelled cucumber and turned to leave, and some budding comedian spits out "Hokay-thank-you-come-again" to the merriment of all assembled. This cut me free — I felt the giddy light-headedness of white rage.

Balloonhead, as you call it. I swayed there for a second, looked at my double-barrelled cucumber and reminded myself of a few things: Octavian atmosphere made a fastball punch into a lob. Octavian boneless physiology made a lob punch rather ineffective. Which, as you know, is one of the reasons I chose Octavia in the first place.

By this time, the people in the store had gone about their business — having tired of staring at the freak clutching the cuke — and my aggrometer needle had stopped rising and started sinking.

And that was just the beginning.

So a few steps from the store this cop comes up to me and says, or rather gestures, that I should come with him. I had this sudden paranoid flash that I had broken a law by dropping a beed, like how it was illegal on some planets to desecrate the flag, and that I had been reported. Of course I hadn't thought to even register with the Earth consulate, even though I had had plenty of time. (And no, I still haven't.) So we get to this little police booth — the rather sinister crest above the door involves several snaky looking creatures — and go inside.

There's a fat Octavian inside there, looking mighty pleased with himself. That's when he welcomes me and asks me about being a criminal.

Before I can say anything he busts out laughing, a few bubbles even coming from his nostrils. "Joke, that I thought of!"

"How proud you must be!" is what came to mind, but dry wit doesn't suit this atmosphere. Doesn't suit it at all. Instead I said, "That is a very funny joke," in a tone that *sarcasm* doesn't begin to describe.

Nauseatingly, this puffed him up even more, and he immediately said something in Octavian (except for "criminal" "joke" "very funny") to the guy who had brought me in. I watched the little guy's face and his nervous smile and noticed he only had one little snake pin on his collar to fat-boy's five.

"Und's English, very good!" the little guy said, more to his beaming boss who didn't even refute it — quite unusual, most Octavians I'd met were very modest. I gathered that I had been arrested to give Und an English lesson.

"What are the snakes for?" I asked, determined to get something out of this.

He looked at me, his mouth slightly agape. "Snakesfor?" he repeated, the crest above his eyes furrowing. The little guy said something quickly in Octavian and my host dismissed him with an undulate of his tentacle.

I pointed to the silver pin on his collar once the underling had left. "Snake," I simplified. "Why?"

"Ah," he started. "Me, Mr. Und." He counted the pins. "One two three four five. Five very good! He, Mr. Plon. One. One not good." He laughed.

Yeah yeah, I thought. Rank-proud fuck. "No, I mean . . ." I pointed to the snakes on the police crest on his chest.

He laughed again. "I see! I see!"

His eyes narrowed with the effort. "Before," he finally said, waving a tentacle over his shoulder. "Snakesfor . . . help Octavia."

I couldn't be bothered pressing for details. "I see," I said, forcing a satisfied smile. Then I stuck out my hand and said "Glad to meet you. Good-bye."

It was pretty much as easy as that, although he made me promise we would go drink ujos, the local poison. When I walked outta there I instantly felt better — I wasn't gonna have to call up Mr. Zik to get me out of jail, at least, and I knew it would make a good story for you.

Anyway, Plangyo — ah Plangyo. Known primarily for having the best cucumbers (not the double-barrelled one I was buying, but a gray-skinned sister) and very little else. Unless you count me, the only resident offworlder, the right to whom they won in a lottery. They actually won the right for three years of teachers, of which I am the second — Plangyo's the testing ground for the Octavian English program, which has progressed to the point where every kid is capable of yelling hello.

I had been led to believe that the planet was had been pretty much levelled during the I.G.W. but it turns out that the west side of the planet and the major cities got the brunt of it. Farm towns like these still have a lot of the traditional coral houses, although Mr. Zik says that most people prefer the rounded apartment blocks.

Evidently, one of my predecessors complained about the rounded floors — the Octavian's suckered tentacles allow them to use a bit of the wall space, as far as gravity will allow — and so I live in the only "flat" building in town. Pretty boring, although it's about three times the size of your place. Sorry, downtown girl, had to rub that in — no more crouch showers for Sammy-boy!

I'd kill to live in one of the traditional ones. Mushroom-shaped, beautifully colored, and growing right into the ground. Mr. Zik says that poor people live there, because anyone who's anyone wants to live in the modern and convenient apartment buildings. Phooey.

There's so much space here, it's unbelievable. It takes me a solid fifteen minutes to walk from my apartment to the school, and there's a total of seven houses and one small apartment block on the way. Most of the houses are on huge plots of land, not because they're shamelessly rich but because they grow food there. It's wonderful, getting to walk so much — there's something about walking that lets me think, just like my jetpack flights did on Earth. Must be the movement.

Actually, I think I'll go for a walk right now. Night isn't too bad for walking around, because it never really gets pitch black. The mushroom houses look amazing against the deep purple twilight.

Seeya,
Sam

☄

"It is Octavian cookie," said one of the teachers, proffering a bowl of chunky green diamonds. I took one.

"You are handsomebloy," she said.

"Thank you," I said. I put away my pad. I had pretty much been writing letters all morning — after I was formally introduced, I was shown to my desk and left alone. Not ignored, in fact people watched me constantly and smiled when I caught them, but no one had talked to me until now.

"What do you teach?" I asked slowly, biting into the cracker. It was very salty, and I had been expecting sweet, so I had to contain a wince.

"Me? I teach . . . science. Science teacher." She smiled. "Yes." She said something to the teacher sitting beside me that got a laugh.

"Your English is very good," I said. I took another cracker. They weren't bad now that I knew what to expect.

"Sank you," she said. "You are very different from Jessica."

"Who?" I said, thinking even as I did so that the name rung a bell.

"Jessica. She was the last teacher here."

Ah. I had seen the name on the class schedule across the room. I looked back at it, all written in Octavian except for the past teacher's name spotting it here and there. I had felt a silly twinge of hurt pride that my name hadn't been put up in its place.

"She half-human. You all human," the science teacher said. "You bletter teacher, I sink."

I smiled, even though it was bullshit. There were plenty of people of mixed species at the orientation and they spoke English as well as me.

"Jessica very good friend me."

49

"Where did Jessica live?"

"Same apartment."

"The whole time?"

The science teacher furrowed her brow. She had the sheen of oil on her tentacles that older Octavian women wore, and her features were made-up in Earthling style. (Octavian faces being already quite humanoid, the make-up mostly consisted of darkening the hairless ridges above the eyes and shading the cheeks so as to de-emphasize the slightly different angle of the cheekbones.)

"Did Jessica complain about the apartment?"

The science teacher shook her head and shrugged. "I don't . . . sink I understand."

Mr. Zik glided into the staffroom, a book curled in one tentacle and a mug in the other.

"Time to go," he said, taking a sip. "Ready?"

I nodded, but what I was thinking was: *There's no steam coming from that mug. I won't be able to stare at the steam curling from my coffee cup for a year.*

I had already stood up and put on my jacket on automatically when the science teacher's awkward stance yanked me out of my odd funk.

"It's . . . very nice to meet you," I said, smiling and waving perhaps too enthusiastically. But I would have felt like a jerk underdoing it, since she was the only person who went out of her way to be nice.

Her face lit up and she waved a loose wave.

As we left the room for my first class, I scanned the other teachers. Instead of the intense surveillance I expected — some part of me expected to be caught before I could impersonate a teacher — they were all going about their business. Getting ready for classes themselves, writing stuff down, and in one oldster's case, drifting off to sleep.

I imitated Mr. Zik's regal bearing as nearly as I could, staying close in hope that his teacherial aura would encompass me as well. Out in the hallway, a cluster of girls turned to us like sunflowers. One of them, tall, wore a bow on her head. When we turned the corner to the stairs she called out "Hello!" and her comrades giggled and hooted.

I looked back and waved. She buried her face in her tentacles and the giggling intensified.

"You are very plopular, wow," said Mr. Zik with a smile.

On the ramp to the second floor there were boys playing with a yellow ball that disappeared when they saw us. Mr. Zik said something mild to them and they scattered, flowing down the ramp.

"The science teacher is very nice," I said.

Mr. Zik nodded. "Yes. Her husband is a news-teller."

"Oh."

"Her name is Mrs. Pling." He slid open the door with a flick of his tentacle.

Pling, Pling, Pling I repeated to myself as the class saw me and started to froth over like a test beaker. Luckily, Mr. Zik was a stabilising agent.

"Good morning," he said to the students, a few of which were still running about the room to their desks. One student was cleaning the board, an expectant smile on his face. I heard someone gasp, "Handsomebloy! Oh!"

I smiled and smoothed out my tie. Mr. Zik said something in Octavian. The class laughed. One girl asked Mr. Zik something, plucking at him.

"Ask him," he said with a smile, pointing at me. She buried her head in a tangle of tentacles and made an embarrassed-alarmed sound: *waah!*

The boy cleaning the board handed the brush back to me with four twined tentacles, his eyes wide and grin infectious. "Thank you," I said, relieved that I didn't have to mumble through the Octavian translation — in fact, this being English class, I *shouldn't* speak Octavian.

"This is Sam Breen. He is from Earth. He will blee your teacher." He nodded to me.

It seemed to me like he had already used all my best material. What else could I say in simple, easy sentences? What the fuck was I thinking? Teaching? Me?

"Hi!" I said, smiling as broadly as human physiognomy would allow.

"Hello!" said forty unreasonably excited children.

If I had my goddamned translator I . . . I what? What would I say to them, even with a translator? It would be a good prop, I suppose, something official to fiddle with . . .

Write something on the board drifted up to my consciousness, perhaps from orientation.

I took off my blazer to buy some time, and the female part of the class made a siren sound like a line graph, rising and falling, against a solid giggle background. A little alarmed by this, but completely without a response, I turned to the board. As I picked up a black marker and wrote my name, I tried to figure out why taking off my blazer had that kind of effect. Octavians didn't wear pants, just a loose multi-armed shirt to cover their chests, so it was kind of hard to know.

I turned to face them and the class laughed at me. I looked at Mr. Zik, and he was poking at buttons on the side of the board. He nodded to the board, which had changed my handwriting into proper characters — proper Octavian characters, the ones that were closest to the English letters. Then they squirmed back to what I had originally.

"Sorry," said Mr. Zik. "It is automatic."

I looked back at the class. "My name is Sam Breen," I said. "Repeat. Sam,"

"Tham!" they repeated enthusiastically. I guess I *sounded* like a teacher . . .

"Breen."

"Bleen."

Hmm. I looked at Mr. Zik, but he was gazing benignly out at the students.

"Sssssss," I hissed, failing to keep a faint smile from my lips.

Amidst giggles, they repeated.

"Sssssssam."

"Sssssssam."

All right! I gave them the thumbs-up.

"Brrrrrrr," I said. They repeated, but it came out wrong. "Brrrr," I repeated, this time wrapping my arms around myself and shivering. They repeated, again poorly, some of them also miming shivering. I realized that I had no idea if Octavians shivered with the cold.

"Breen," I said.

"Bleen," they said.

Mr. Zik looked at me. "It's very hard."

I nodded and gave up. I turned to the board and started to draw a circle.

"O," someone called out, just as I started to color it in. When he realized his mistake he ducked down in his chair, and the boy next to him whacked him with a tentacle.

If I can't think of anything else, they're obviously up for a game of Identify the Letter.

Out of the corner of my eye I noticed a map on another wall.

"Ah," I said, leaving my crappy drawing and striding fake-confidently over to the galactic map. I pointed to a planet at random.

I looked out at their rapt, spellbound faces and was temporarily speechless. God, it was scary! Was I *that* fascinating?

"Is this Earth?" I asked.

"No," "No!" "Nooo," and "NO!" pelted back at me.

"Right. *This* is Earth," I said, pointing to Mars. I watched them expectantly.

Eventually, "No!s" started coming.

Mr. Zik hiss-laughed. "You are lying." He had taken a seat at the teacher's desk, and I was glad he was relaxed.

"Psycho!" someone called out.

Choking back a laugh at this weird bit of vocabulary, I asked "Where is Earth?" As I said it I realized that Earthlings at the same age wouldn't have had a spit-on-the-sun's-chance of identifying Octavia.

I chose the first tentacle that shot up and a fat kid marched up to the map and poked my home planet, then marched away.

"Very good!" I said, and the kid raised a few tentacles in victory before he thumped back in his seat.

I traced the route between Earth and Octavia, a little amazed at the distance myself. "It was a long trip. A long trip," I said, emphasizing with my outstretched arms.

The kids were looking at each other. Mr. Zik translated, also stretching his limbs. I looked at him and nodded wisely, as if I understood exactly what he said, and when he said something that made the class laugh I smiled indulgently.

"How did I get to Octavia?"

They looked at each other. Mr. Zik stayed silent this time.

Oh dear. I repeated myself.

"Rast weeka," one boy called out.

Was he swearing at me? I wondered.

"Yesterday," a girl at the front shyly said.

Oh.

"Not when, *how*," I clarified. I wrote both words on the board, for no good reason, then crossed out *when*. "How? How did I get to Octavia."

No response.

I mimed driving a floater. "Did I *drive* from Earth to Octavia?" I goose-stepped down the aisle of desks and back to the front. "Did I *walk* from Earth?" They laughed, but didn't answer.

Fuck. What was I doing up here? I started imagining returning earlier-than-expected to Earth, Mom's smug smile waiting for me . . .

"Rocketshipuh," a thin boy at the front said.

"Yes!" I said, pointing at him. I ran to the map. "I took a *rocketship* from Earth to Octavia." I made the sound of a rocket as I traced the route. The class laughed, some imitating the sound.

I held up the marker. "Draw a rocketship," I challenged.

The kid next to the thin boy pushed and whispered at him, and the thin kid got up slowly, watching me as if he was cornered prey.

He took the pen with twined tentacles and wrote on the board: R o C k—

"Nonono," I said, shaking my head. Some wag in the back repeated it. The thin boy flicked terrified eyes on me. I smiled and took the marker back. He got back to his desk as quickly as possible, muttering something to the laughing boy beside him before burying his head.

"Draw a rocketship. *Draw*."

I shot a look over at Mr. Zik, who was scratching his ear. "They know the word 'draw,' right?" I asked, trying not to stare as the tip of his tentacle seemed to slide unnaturally deep into his ear canal.

He nodded, looking unconcerned. "Draw a rocketship," he repeated.

"Ah!" a girl exclaimed, jumping up and then seeming to regret it. I held out the pen and tried to make my face more encouraging than desperate.

I was tempted to pretend she was right, regardless of what she did — to give up trying to communicate would have been embarrassing for everyone — but I was worried about how Mr. Zik would react.

When she started to confidently sketch the upright bullet, complete with landing fins and tiny portals, I slowly exhaled. She looked back at me and I nodded her on.

When she finished I gave her the thumbs-up sign. "Very, very good." There was a short series of popping sounds coming from somewhere but I decided to ignore them.

She rushed back to her desk, her face a beacon.

I looked at the drawing and drew a stick figure sticking improbably out of a window. I pointed to it and said, "Sam Breen," then pointed to me to drive the point homer than home.

Laughter. I scribbled beneath the fuselage and made the taking-off sound. More laughter. I minimized my smirk, mostly brought on by how lame I was, but found myself genuinely fed by the laughter. Who needed sophisticated humor when you had childish shenanigans?

I started to erase the board, thinking frantically for something else to do. The few things they taught us about actual teaching had all but vanished from my memory. I was running out of things to erase . . .

I could hear Mr. Zik talking to a student with the part of my brain that wasn't scrambling. "Sam? She has a question."

I turned around and put a friendly smile on my face.

The same girl who had drawn the rocketship stood up. "How . . . old are . . . you?"

"I'm 23 years old."

There was a murmur of translation, so I wrote the number on the board for good measure. The class gave that funny up-and-down 'wooo' of approval. I looked at Mr. Zik, a little confused at it.

"You're young," he said. "That's good. Young teacher."

Another boy put up his tentacle. I nodded to him, but he was really looking to Mr. Zik. He stood up and grunted out, "Do you . . . like Octavia."

"Yes," I said enthusiastically. "Octavia is beautiful." I remembered the Octavian for beautiful and said it with gusto. They were impressed, and so was Mr. Zik.

"Oh very good," someone called out.

A couple of girls stopped giggling long enough to beg Mr. Zik to ask me something. He refused. They looked at me and went back to beg Mr. Zik some more. He was laughingly adamant. Finally they turned their fearful eyes back on me and one of them blurted out: "Girlfriend?"

Through the sudden deafening noise, I attempted to clarify with Mr. Zik: "Do I have a girlfriend?"

He nodded, calling out something that reduced the noise level.

"Uh, no," I said to the girls, and they were happy with this answer. Indeed, all the girls seemed to like this answer. What the hell were they planning for me?

Mr. Zik fielded a question in Octavian and translated it. "They want to know if you would have an Octavian girlfriend."

Uh-oh. Loaded question. "Um . . . I don't know," I said, choosing the safest and (coincidentally) the most honest answer. I doubted it, given the problems I had communicating.

He translated for them.

I braced myself for the next question, which I was worried would be if I liked younger women. Since I doubted he'd be asking me that, I relaxed a little when the fat boy's hand went up. I shouldn't have, though.

Mr. Zik gave him the nod. He stood up and seemed to rally his energy, then blurted it out.

"Can-you . . . sing-a-song?"

I laughed at first, and then realized how excited everyone was getting. "Sing-song! Superstar!"

Forcing a smile to climb onto my face, I checked the clock. Mercy, I begged, please . . .

No mercy. There were ten minutes left at least.

I looked at Mr. Zik, who had a look of pleased anticipation. "They want you to sing a little song," he said.

"Uh huh, yeah I know." I licked my lips. Thought fast. Thought *mean.*

"Tell them," I said, "That I will sing a song . . . after *he* does." I pointed at the little bastard who had asked me.

After listening to Mr. Zik, he looked at me and pointed his tentacle at his chest, as if to verify.

"Yes, you," I nodded with a mild smile, feeling triumphant and guilty at the same — *the kid was smiling. The little —*

He got to the front, a little shy, but still with that plump grin. "English?" he asked me.

"Whatever, English or Octavian," I said, still stunned.

He listened to his classmates suggest songs, and he shook his head a couple of times and then decided on one. He put two tentacles together and pulled them apart, making a popping sound, and the class did it with him, making a rhythm section.

He sang very well. I leaned against the board, watching this kid belt out the pop song or whatever it was with flair and confidence. He even had this little spinning dance move that shot his tentacles out so that I had to move or be hit. The only thing wrong with his performance was that it was too fuckin' short.

After the popping applause had stopped (and I had learned that you can't clap in a liquid atmosphere) they looked at me expectantly.

"Teacher sing-song!"

I looked at Mr. Zik, then at the clock, then at their shining happy dreadful faces. I had never sung in public. Tough enough to do that. Now my cleverness had made it even worse.

Now I had to follow a killer act. And I didn't know any spinning dance moves.

Well, at least in this atmosphere they won't know I'm sweating.

SIX

I bellowed for the waitress.

Hugh looked at me, his face shock-smashed.

I looked mildly back, shrugged, savored his outrage. I recognized the vintage — it was the same I had produced when I was new.

The waitress arrived and I ordered more beer and snacks for us in Octavian. She understood what I was saying right off, which was gratifying.

"Fuck, Mr. Fluent over here," said Matthew.

"It's just restaurant-Octavian," I said. "But I've been picking it up."

"Did you have to yell like that?" said Hugh, still scandalized.

"It's what you do here," said Matthew. "Same on Squidollia."

I continued. "You can't just catch their eye. It's hard at first — but I actually kind of like it now. I feel like I'm getting away with being rude."

One of the other tables bellowed for more.

I gave Hugh a "see?" look. He still looked disgruntled.

We had just got there. Matthew had been there for an hour already, came here straight from the rocketship — he was into his fourth or fifth beer and he was more intent on checking out the clientele than watching how pissed off Hugh was. I had started it, but then he just made it worse.

"S'pose the Unarmored have a *subtler* way of doing it," Matthew said distractedly.

Hugh finished his beer in a quick draught. "I wouldn't know," he murmured.

"Whattaya mean," I said. "They must have taken you out?"

"Yes," he said, rolling his glass back and forward between his palm. "But I'm not with the Unarmored. I'm with the Armored."

"What?!" Matthew and I sputtered. Oh man, I thought. Hugh had been dying to meet the Unarmored. What a blow.

"They tested me before I entered the atmosphere. Turned out, by their estimation, that I was better suited for armor than stripping."

"But you weren't actually going to — like, get stripped, were you?" Matthew said, a rare look of worry on his face. "It's irreversible, isn't it?"

"No, I wasn't planning to . . . but who knows?" Hugh lifted a slight hand in the air and let it drop.

We sat and drank in silence to ponder this massive fuck-up in our minds. How crazy was that — everyone knows lunarians were like, Earth's Unarmored.

And Hugh was almost uncannily so. A table of Octavians laughed inappropriately across the room. There were maybe four sets of couples there, some of which were actually touching each other. The big city certainly was different than Plangyo!

"Where is the big guy, anyway?" said Matthew, his eyes following a female Octavian's admittedly hypnotizing trip to the bar. My fascination ended when she opened her heavily made-up mouth and brayed at the bartender, but Matthew's didn't.

"Might not be so big, now," I said, thinking about how the roboman's body and head had parted ways at the spaceport.

Matthew's head swivelled. "Whattaya mean?"

I shrugged slyly.

The order arrived and I dug into the twisty snacks. "Man, I love these things," I said, ignoring Matthew. "They're hot!"

"Seriously —" Matthew started. I noticed a smile on Hugh, and he noticed me noticing.

"9/3's mounted his head on a small mobile unit with treads," Hugh said, spoiling my fun. "You know how the Montavians feel about big folk."

"How'd you know?" I asked Hugh.

"When I called him to tell him about us meeting. Don't say anything about it. He has no idea how strange —"

"That's probably why he's late," Matthew said. "It must take a long time to . . . roll anywhere."

I had an image of him as a tiny tank, buzzing obliviously through a crowd, but I was distracted by someone's hip knocking our table.

Hip?

I looked back.

"9/3!" I blurted. "What the fuck!"

On the top of this perfectly normal human body was 9/3's bread box of a head, staring back at us.

Hugh opened and closed his mouth. Matthew yelled for another beer.

"What's wrong?" 9/3 inquired, taking a seat. I watched as he placed his slightly hairy forearms on the table in an unnervingly natural way. His nails were dirty.

"We thought you were a tankbot, that's what's wrong," Matthew said, looking a bit annoyed. "With treads and shit."

"Ah. No, that would not have been appropriate for this meeting. It would have been foolish."

The beer came and 9/3 made a fist, then used his other hand to pull it out of his arm. It popped like a cork and came clean out of the socket. He set it down on the table and picked up a mug of beer. He held his fistless arm upright and poured the golden liquid into the empty wrist.

Hugh laughed. "Marvellous!"

I looked at the hand on the table. It was still fisted, and wobbled back and forth a bit because of the uneven surface, and when it wobbled towards me I could see the gleam of metal inside.

"Whoops," 9/3 said as his arm cavity foamed over. It slid down his arm to be soaked up by the roll of his plaid shirt, since of course he couldn't slurp it up. I had a weird flash of Hugh leaning over to do so, but of course he didn't.

9/3 clicked the fist back into his hand and wiggled his fingers alive. "I borrowed this body from one of my teaching aides — Theodore."

"You're pretty open minded," I said. "It's so . . . humanoid."

"Yes," said 9/3, almost sadly. "My . . . friends would be shocked and disgusted. But they didn't understand why I was happy to leave Roboworld, either."

I picked up a mug of beer and Hugh did the same. I raised it to 9/3. "A toast to the rebels," I said.

"Hear hear," Hugh said.

"Where's *my* fuckin' beer?" said Matthew.

"You've got a head start on us there, bucko," I said. "Reign it in. I don't want you wreaking havoc on *my* planet."

Matthew looked at me with the floating eyes of the Already Tanked and said, "Gotta take a piss." He left.

"So does it absorb it all at once, or does it feed the alcohol slowly into your brain?" I asked 9/3.

He held up his arm and showed it to me. "You see those spots there?" he said, pointing to a few small dots. "When they go away, I am ready for another."

"Really!"

"No." 9/3 said. "Ha ha ha. They're just freckles. Ha ha. Gullible fleshpot."

Hugh let out an astonished hoot.

"Fuck you, blockhead," I laugh-blustered. "You ain't so tough without your goddamn flame-thrower."

"He's still got the laser eyes, remember that," Hugh said.

"Oh yeah. I was just joking." Took a sip of my beer. "Spare parts motherfucker."

"Ha ha ha. Actually, I cannot power the laser without my body. I am completely helpless. Ha ha ha."

I cracked up.

Matthew returned, an anticipatory smile on his face. "What?"

"He called me a gullible fleshpot!"

"What?!" Matthew said.

"Yes, and I am completely helpless. Ha ha ha."

We cracked up again. That fucking laugh is unbelievable! I looked around the table, amazed that a month ago I had hated Hugh, feared 9/3, and had just met Matthew.

I was also amazed by the attention that a noisy table of offworlders got without half trying. A cook, or maybe the manager, was framed in the kitchen door. The couple closest to us moved their chairs slightly to get more table between them and us. No one else at our table seemed aware of it, so it may have been a case of host anxiety. I wondered, would I blind myself to this if I could?

"They think I look like Sean Plynn," Matthew was saying. "Can you beat that? Soon as I get into the classroom, it's 'Sean Plynn, You are Sean Plynn.' "

We all laughed. "He's not even from Earth!"

Hugh shook his head with mock grief. "I'm afraid I don't see the resemblance."

"Thank god for that," Matthew spat, "Prettyboy."

"And how," I said, clinking glasses with him. The clink was muffled and echoey. "Next time they accuse you of being some lunarian flit you just show 'em some muscles." I whacked my biceps.

9/3 looked down at his own muscles, flexed them. "Muscles are a poor substitute for steel."

I snagged a waitress and ordered more beer. Once that was done, I held my hand up to cover my view of 9/3's head. "You know, you look OK like this — like some kind of Neb farmboy — or like this," I moved my hand so I couldn't see the body, only the head, "That's fine too. But together," I whipped my hand away and said slowly, "You-look-like-a-total-*freak*."

9/3 shrugged, holding those too-human hands aloft. "Why? I do not understand your complaint."

I looked around. Matthew was doing the hand trick I had done a moment earlier and Hugh wore a mild smile. "Am I wrong?" I asked.

"It's just disturbing, is all," Hugh said. "It's not that much more unusual than a human brain in a robot body, which is the entire population of Roboworld. It's just an extreme example of seeing someone with a hat on who never wears it or vice versa." Hugh looked around. "Frankly, we're all freaks, and I don't think *they* can tell the difference between us. What I find hard to understand is why the Montavians would want such a large android."

"He's an Earthling model," said 9/3. "They use it for English class and . . . other exercises."

Smirks all 'round. When the talk turns to androids, can sexual innuendo be far behind? And would we have it any other way?

Oddly enough, it was Matthew who saved us from that particular predicable conversational black hole. "So did you sing?" he asked me, his beer mug not quite hiding a sneaky smile.

"Sing?" asked Hugh.

I told them the story.

"Green Earth Forever?" Matthew hooted.

"It was the only one I knew by heart!"

"A little controversial," said Hugh.

"They didn't understand the words," I scoffed. "You kidding me?"

"And there was no chance of them recognizing the tune," Matthew said.

"Yeah, I made sure of that." I looked at Matthew. "What'd you sing?"

"Sing?!" he made a dismissive sound. "No way. I was ready. When they asked me I said it was against my religion to sing. The kid who asked looked ready to hang himself."

"So you knew about the singing?" I sputtered. "Fucker! Why didn't you tell me?"

"Ah, I knew you'd do fine," he said with a grin.

"Actually, I got a standing ovation," I said proudly. "I think it was the somersault I did in the second verse that won them over."

Hugh looked at Matthew. "An experience you've missed out on."

The beer arrived and 9/3 popped his fist out on the table. The waitress squealed in amazement. 9/3 spoke to her in Octavian, his Speak-O-Matic built in. She had a plate of fruit as well which I knew we hadn't ordered. She pointed to it and spoke, saying a word that I knew and loved: free.

"The fruit is free," 9/3 translated. "It is to thank us for drinking here."

"I knew that," I grumbled. "So did you guys bring your translators?"

Hugh and Matthew shook their heads. "Too risky. You know how expensive they are out here?"

I shook my head, morose. I didn't want to know.

"You'll be OK," Hugh said. "You've obviously got a knack for learning languages."

I thought about Hugh's recent let-down and took heart from my comparative good fortune. And I *was* picking up words with a surprising ease. I had actually been avoiding learning, still pissed about losing the damn thing . . .

"I forgot my translator in my apartment when I went to the store for some juice," Hugh said, "*repugnant* protein juice, the staple of Armored food, and when they gave it to me I'd forgotten how to say *thanks*. I felt like such a . . ." Hugh's face was pruney from the memory, "such a . . . typical human, no manners at all. It was the first time in a long time I'd felt shame like that."

We drank quietly for the first time that night. Then 9/3 said, "The far table says that Matthew looks like Sean Plynn."

"Ask them if they wanna fuck," slurred Matthew, not looking up from his beer.

"Ha ha ha. No."

Matthew sighed.

I gave the girls a long look, and was impressed to see that they didn't bury their heads in their tentacles.

"Well, that's a good thing about not having a translator," I said gamely. "I now have a good excuse for being alone and loveless. Plangyo's not exactly a fashiontank, either."

"They all go to big cities like this for university," said Matthew. "But have you met your workshop teachers yet? Some of mine are awfully cute . . ."

"I'm supposed to get them next week," I said.

"Let's not talk about work," said Hugh. "I'm drinking to forget." He looked over at 9/3. "I got stuck with the Armored."

9/3's arms jerked. They talked about that for a while.

I looked at Matthew. He was staring right at me with a wicked grin.

" . . . .I even told them I did a paper on Unarmored culture, which was embarrassing, because it made me sound like some kind of groupie . . ." Hugh was saying.

"Let's go whoring," Matthew said to me.

The conversation stopped. Hugh looked at me, his eyebrows raised.

Matthew got up and stumbled for the door.

"I'd better . . ." I thumbed towards him. "I'll meet you guys back here?"

I gave them a handful of beeds for our beer and took off after Matthew. I pointed the suspicious waitress in their direction, and noticed 9/3 patting Hugh's hand in commiseration, already deep in conversation.

I pushed the door open (and I really had to push, the liquid atmosphere felt like a stiff wind against it) and Matthew was standing there, hands on hips, looking down the street like he was directing a movie.

He turned around to look up the street and saw me. "That way looks good to me."

I looked up at the sign, and tried to get my beer-addled brain to lock on this location. I took note of the clothing store across the way and the small cart selling dubious-looking food, and we walked off together towards the dark and steamy.

I had noticed two identical clothing stores and three carts before I had even figured out what I wanted to say. I didn't want to seem like a sanctimonious jerk.

"I thought . . . um . . . you were pretty dedicated to . . . your girlfriend."

Matthew looked at me, surprised. "I am. What, just 'cause I'm looking for a whore now doesn't mean . . ." He looked at me sharply. "You're not one of those monogamy freaks, are you?"

"Well, no," I said defensively, "not really." But there was something about the exclusive couple that did have a forbidden fruit appeal, perverse and selfish though it was . . .

"Man, I'm hungry. Those snacks just didn't do it," Matthew said.

"Yeah, same here," I said, a little relieved not to have to talk any more about it. We stopped at one of the carts and got some breaded fried things on sticks with yummy red filling.

"You know that guy Simms? Who was on our floor during orientation?" asked Matthew, his mouth full.

I shook my head.

"The guy with all the back implants," he said, and I nodded. "Well, he got a Neb outpost planet, and he keeps getting offered flesh to eat."

That was shocking. "Has he reported it?"

"S'hard to enforce the law there, I guess." He shrugged, throwing the stick in a garbage can. It took a few seconds to float to the bottom.

We were definitely in a different area — whether or not it was likely to have hookers wasn't something I could judge. There were more offices, but also a few rowdy bars.

"Anyway, about the whore thing: I figure, you know, she's never going to know. So no one gets hurt." He looked over at me.

"How would you feel about her doing that?" I said.

"She wouldn't. Because she's Squidollian. But if she did, and I didn't know . . ." he shrugged. "Then I wouldn't know."

"OK, but it's not really fair, because you really can't see it happening. Who's your best friend back home?"

"Wing Lau," he said.

"OK, so what would you do if you found out Wing was having an affair with her?"

A bunch of guys foamed out of the bar in front of us. One of them had his tentacles all over a girl, but still had the time to gawk back at us. He yelled something at us everyone else found really funny.

"That's different," Matthew said, his face troubled. "That's more of a betrayal. Plus everyone knows."

The guy in front of us said something else in our direction.

"Shut your fucking pus-hole!" I advised at a high volume, feeling adrenaline rush in to replace the energy yelling had expended.

Matthew's eyes popped out. "Sam, take it easy."

"I'm kind of in the mood for a fight," I told Matthew by way of explanation. "I haven't scrapped for *weeks*." Half the group ahead of us were hurrying to get away, half were lagging behind. The wise-ass was staring at me. "What you looking at, chump?" I called.

"I suppose it doesn't matter much what I actually *say*, huh?" I said to Matthew, enjoying his discomfort. Perhaps whoring wasn't to my taste, but there were other parts of the night I was well acquainted with. "Yea, verily," I bellowed at the wise-ass, "'Tis better to *give* than to *receive*!" I looked at Matthew. "That's the kind of accent the English pugs would use," I said, educationally.

"Man, they're slowing down . . ."

I smiled, folding up a nice fist to give the wiseass's weak chin, and walked straight for him.

"Hello," said one of his companions, with his tentacles twined in polite greeting. He was wearing glasses.

"Hello," I said dourly, feeling my righteous anger start to soften and droop.

"My friend, he is drunky. He is so sorry."

"Damn," I said.

Matthew offered Glasses a hand to shake.

Drunky had gone to join his maulfriend who stood with the other girls a little ways ahead.

"Shall we go?" Glasses asked.

I shrugged. When you don't know where you're going, any direction's good as any. I shoved my hands in my pockets.

SEVEN

I pulled the door closed behind me and inserted the card-key. It took me a second to find the slot in the dark. It gave a reassuring "click" and I slipped the card into my pocket.

As I walked out, I realized that if I lost it, I could not get into my own apartment. How strange. I stuck my hand to feel if it was in a deep enough pocket, enjoying the bumpy texture of the key as I did so.

When Mr. Zik had given me the key originally, I had flipped it over, thinking that a password for the apartment's security system would be on it. But all it had on it was a scribbled note in Octavian.

"Key?" I had said, wondering if it was a language thing.

Mr. Zik had taken it from me and walked outside the apartment. I had followed. He had showed me how the key worked, locking it with deliberate slowness, then opening it.

I had nodded, smiling, feeling like an ass.

"Very old fashioned," Mr. Zik had said with his hiss-laugh. With incredibly casual speed, he passed it through a series of tentacles to hand it off to me.

I fingered it, thinking about how Mr. Zik was so apologetic for every difference between here and Earth, as if I didn't come here expecting it, wanting it. Even having to fumble in the darkness, because the apartment lights had to be activated by a wall switch, was a novelty.

Outside it was twilight, but not as dark as the apartment hall. The atmosphere was a green-blue, and for some reason the motion-ripples were more visible than at any other time of day. All moving things radiated.

I walked along the road away from the town. A saucer passed by overhead, so close that the wake swept some road debris into my hair. The saucer was trailing a round disk full of some kind of vegetable. I brushed the debris out — just some coral sand and weeds — feeling ambivalent about the close call. But when I saw a path winding away from the road, I was glad of it.

Just as I left, another saucer whipped by. This one — maybe because it was a fancy model with tinted windows — whipped up my ire as well as the debris. But how-close-is-too-close is a cultural norm, I told myself, and my anger dissipated with the hydrothruster's bubbles.

Most people assume that, because I was a pug, the first thing I want to do when angered is duke it out. Most pugs I know are less rash than your average person. If anything, I've learned to focus my anger and choose where to channel it.

In a way, that's what pug is about — the choice. Most people never even consider that there's a way to react to injustice other than retaining a vengeance vendor; that they can do something more direct about their situation than hire someone to slander-by-the-hour. It's a rare animal that's more misunderstood and misrepresented than the pug.

The path led between two fields of the cucumbers Plangyo was known for. "Agnay," the Octavian for it, came unbidden to my mind. I had been rather pleased by the speed with which I was learning vocabulary. Mr. Zik had given me a children's book and then a collection of Octavian songs to translate.

I was humming one of them, the one about the splendors of the Kyung hot springs, when a flash of ripple caught my eye. Out in the field, an old Octavian woman raised herself on her tentacles and stared at me. I thought suddenly —

Holy, this old woman is still working while the privileged offworlder has the leisure to stroll around her town —

My guilt blurp was cut short. Her mouth, revealing the few gray teeth she had in her wrinkled head, let loose a nasty cackle, and she grabbed a person working a row over with her tentacle and jerked her up.

"Koogeem!" she laughed, pointing at me with a jab. The other person, an old lady with a blue head-covering and a cucumber still in her tentacle, stared dazed at me. The first woman started singing the song I had been singing, more for her friend's benefit than mine, until the friend started to smile.

I smiled at them weakly. The woman sung more of the song with a bray to her voice that translated easily. My smile disappeared. The other worker went back to her picking and the original lady kept staring at me and calling things at my back I didn't understand.

Yeah, we offworlders sure are funny, I thought sadly, staring at the ground as I walked.

The path had been made by something with heavy treads, and my light footfalls didn't leave prints despite the soft surface. I heard a light bubbling behind me but I didn't want to look in case that hag was still staring at me. But instead of it coming from somewhere in the fields, as I had assumed, it was a small vehicle on treads that was suddenly behind me. I let it squeeze by me with its cart of gray cukes and the old man operating it didn't look at me, but called out his thanks in Octavian.

I was surprised and, for some reason, touched.

Watching him move off to the transport saucer, I noticed a quick dip in the path caused a cucumber to float off the cart and fall to the ground. When I got to it, I picked it up. The skin was a little sticky.

The transport saucer was set off to the side of the path, and at first I thought that it had set down on the cuke field. But as I got closer, I saw that there was an area cleared for the huge round ship — of course there was. For some reason, though, I had a stupid notion that massive saucers set down wherever they liked, that if they could destroy something in the process it was all the better. But that was probably because I had only seen saucers of this size in war clips.

Now I was well under the lip of the saucer, and I looked up at the angular Octavian characters stencilled there — it looked like a serial number. The landing ramp was down and the conveyer belt was dragging up loose cukes. I wondered why they didn't have boxes and then, looking at the rounded hull, realized why. The old man was putting tentaclefulls of suckered cucumbers onto the belt when I approached him.

He looked up at me holding out the errant vegetable to him. He looked at the loaded belt, then back at me. I smiled, lifting the cuke a little to indicate he should take it, suddenly wondering if I was making a rude gesture. His blank stare didn't help. The noise of the belt was a little unnerving.

I pointed back to the path. He smiled suddenly, his weathered cheeks bunching.

"No," he said, waving his tentacles. He pointed at me, then mimed eating.

"OK!" I said, bowing to him.

"OK!" he said, then said something else.

Listening to the river of words rush by, I grabbed the word "big" but nothing else. I dumbly nodded and stuttered out a thank-you.

I walked home. I tossed the cucumber up in the air as I did, sort of juggling it, but it floated down so gradually that it forced me to slow down. I let myself into my apartment with the key-card I had not lost and went into the kitchen. I had already had supper but I cut the cuke up anyway. I didn't have any of the sauce they usually served the cucumber in, so I sprinkled some salt on it. It was a little bitter.

Octavian schools have architecture very similar to schools on Earth, angular and square, so I was often lulled into a false sense of familiarity. Then when the little tune for the next class would play, I'd get up from my desk, walk down the hall and turn for the stairs — and find none. The ramp made perfect sense in a school of tentacled kids but it still surprised me daily for several weeks.

I'd pause there at the bottom of the ramp and let it sink in that this was another planet because the alien children capering around me wasn't enough. Then I'd angle my feet slightly and walk up, making sure I didn't step on any tentacles. It wasn't until I was in the capital city of Artemia that I saw stairs again, a thin strip beside the wide ramp — a pleasing reversal of the Earth bias for bipeds.

Today I noticed it especially because I had to climb two flights of ramps. Usually my classes were with the younger grades on the second floor, but this afternoon I was in for something different.

I almost knocked — then I felt stupid. The teacher doesn't knock. Even if he's twenty years younger than his pupils. I slid open the door.

I walked in to the room, where three teachers sat, two men and a woman. They were mostly chatting to each other, and not staring expectantly at the door, which was a relief. "Hello," I said with a smile.

Everyone said hello back, except for a thin old man, who rose. "We extend our greetings and thanks to you," he said clearly.

This got a laugh, and I made an impressed face. "I appreciate that."

One or two nodded, and the thin old man translated for those who didn't: "Ajgjlhru appreciate ladrlejkj; I *appreciate* that."

I tried to take a seat at the side of the table, but was waved to the head by the attractive young woman. A stout male pulled out the chair for me, and this was also funny. Octavians simply slid onto the chair and perched there, so this was a human gesture.

"Thanks," I said.

"I saw in movie," said the stout teacher.

"It's very polite," I said. "Very good."

"Sank you," he said, practically glowing.

Most of the exchanges during these workshops were held over a hum of constant murmuring as they discussed amongst themselves what the hell I was saying, mixed with a good deal of chuckling.

"My name is Sam Breen," I said, prompting one or two people to start their recorders. I blinked as the camera scanned me. "I am from Earth."

"What area of Earth are you from?" said the thin old guy, lifting his tentacle in a questioning way.

"What part of Earth am I from?" I said. "Well, I'm from a place called Toronto."

There was a mumbling as people absorbed this. The young teacher asked me if "area" was incorrect, and the thin old man looked at her suddenly.

"No, area is correct," I said, impressed by her sharpness. "*What part* is just . . . more usual."

"More common," the thin old man said to the group, reasserting himself. "Plart is difficult for Octavians to say."

I nodded. "I understand. OK, for every question I answer I'm going to ask you a question. OK, could you tell me your name and your hobbies?" I asked the old thin guy, mentally registering that I was saying OK way too much.

He cleared his throat. "My name is Mr. Nekk." He placed a withered tentacle on his chest as he said this. "My hobbies are reading English blooks and exploring the caverns of Octavia."

I nodded, deciding against putting him on the spot by asking what book. I expected that with his eagerness I'd find out soon enough.

The young teacher who had asked about "area" asked about my age with a smile.

"I am twenty-three," I said.

"That's very good," she said. "Young teachers are good. The students like you very much, I think." The others nodded.

"Yes, but you're older than me," I said, shaking my head. "I feel like a total — I mean, it is very strange that a teacher is younger than his students."

"You are . . . plerfect English teacher," said the chair-puller. Mr. Nekk tried to elaborate, but the chair-puller continued. "Bleecause . . . you native speaka."

Mr. Nekk nodded his agreement and I smiled modestly.

I looked back at the woman who asked me the question, and decided to test her knowledge. "And who do I have the pleasure of speaking to?"

She looked blankly at me for a moment and then laid a tentacle on her breasts. I nodded, a little too eagerly, my eyes dipping. She said slowly, as if not sure what I asked her: "My name is Mrs. Ahm."

She had obviously just guessed at what I had asked her, but that was part of learning a language, too — it was amazing how quickly she inspired excuses.

"My hobbies are exploring caves and taking care of my baby."

Damn. She was married. Octavians never had children otherwise. Damn damn damn.

Then, as if reading my mind, she asked, "Do you have a girlfriend?" I would later pinpoint this as the point at which my lesson plan went out the window.

"No, I don't," I admitted.

"I introduce!" exclaimed the stout guy.

"Do you think that Octavian women are very beautiful?" asked Mrs. Ahm.

"Well . . ." I started, noticing her proper pronunciation of "b."

"Octavian women are ugly," pronounced Mr. Nekk, scratching an earhole that looked like a wound. "Especially in the country. Earth women are . . ." he strained for a synonym, "more pretty."

"Prettier," I corrected, but his glassy eyes didn't seem to absorb this.

"So you think Earthlings . . ." Mrs. Ahm said, fixing me with her pure blue eyes.

"No, no. I was just —"

The stout man said something in Octavian and everyone laughed.

"I think," I said loudly, "that there are ugly women and beautiful women on every planet in the universe."

"Nebula too?" said the stocky man, but I decided to ignore this xenophobic comment.

"I have seen many very beautiful Octavian women since I have arrived," I said, looking at Mrs. Ahm.

The stocky man pointed three tentacles at her and asked, "You think she —"

"What is *your* name?" I inquired quickly. Subtle flirtation was apparently impossible.

His tentacles dropped. "My name is Mr. Kung." He pointed his tentacles at Mrs. Ahm again, less aggressively, and opened his mouth to speak.

"What are your hobbies?" I said.

"Uhh . . . my hobbly . . . exploring caves. Do—"

"Exploring caves is very popular in Octavia," I said to the group at large. Then to Mr. Kung, "Do you have any other hobbies?"

"Other? Uhh . . ." he floundered, and the others suggested things in Octavian. Mrs. Ahm's suggestion got a big laugh.

"Uhh . . . drinky," Mr. Kung said, miming it. "I like to drinky."

"Do you like ujos?" I said. This got me big points, and Mr. Kung nodded enthusiastically. "I . . . love ujos!" he exclaimed. He seemed to have forgotten his earlier question in his enthusiasm.

"Have you tried ujos?" asked Mr. Nekk.

"Yes," I said, nodding and giving the thumbs-up sign. Even without digits of their own, all Octavian's recognized this sign. They seemed to want more, so

I gave them more. "It's *very good* rotgut liquor."

They caught only the emphasis, and happily nodded their agreement.

"Ah . . . Mr. Sam, I have a question," began Mrs. Ahm. "Where is your translator?"

"I don't have a translator," I said.

This caused a fair amount of consternation. "Why not?" she asked.

"I want to learn Octavian," I said, gussying up the half-truth as a grand proclamation.

"It is impossible," said Mrs. Ahm.

"I know it is very difficult. I will study very hard."

She said something to Mr. Nekk.

"No, it is more than difficult. It is not plossible," he said. "Because . . . the language has sounds that only Octavians can make. In our mouth."

"Oh," I said.

Mr. Nekk made a sound, a kind of a low bubble sound. "The word for delicious in Octavian is ijofwejo," he said, the last syllable of which had that sound.

I repeated it as best I could but the group just laughed. "There are sounds in English which are hard for Octavians to say," I said, instinctively wanting to even the score but feeling petty for it. "Like buh, or puh."

They nodded. "It is very difficult but not impossible," said Mr. Nekk. "Octavians can learn English perfectly but humans can not learn Octavian perfectly."

Well la-dee-da, I thought somewhat sourly. "Let's practice the B sound," I said. "Bad. Repeat after me."

"Blad," everyone said.

I noticed something weird. There was a slight movement around their lips. I repeated it again, and watched closely. "Bad."

"Blad," they said. When they said it, a few bubbles leaked out of the corner of their mouths. Trying not to stare, I pointed at Mr. Nekk. "Bedpost."

"Bledploast," he said, bubbles rising at the B and the P.

"Bust," I chanced, pointing at Mrs. Ahm.

She licked her lips, her tongue surprisingly tapered. "Bust," she said, only the tiniest of bubbles escaping.

"Perfect!" I said. I asked her to repeat, and she did, but I admit I did it just so I could stare at her lips a little longer.

I looked at Kung. "Bastard," I said.

"Blastard," he said, bubbles the size of eyeballs floating up.

By the end of the two hours, I had avoided as many questions as I'd answered, but they seemed happy.

"You will go to drinky?" said Mr. Kung as we left the school. "My saucer?"

I looked around at the three other teachers. "Will we go to have a drink?" I said, amazed at how stilted my speech had become.

Mr. Nekk said, "Regretfully I cannot. I am old and sick and my blody does not like to drink."

"How about you?" I said, looking at Mrs. Ahm.

She smiled. "Oh no, I must go home. My husband, I must make dinner."

"Women, no," said Mr. Kung.

Oh great, I thought, but went with him anyway. After a formal good-bye from Mr. Nekk and a cute wave from Mrs. Ahm, we bubbled off out of Plangyo to what Mr. Kung described as a "not nice place."

When we got out of the saucer, I noticed some girls about my age passing by — and they noticed me. One of them, tall and lovely, called out to me as she floated gracefully by: *you handsomebloy.*

I smiled, stunned, and Mr. Kung said, "University," he said, oblivious to the girl's comment, pointing out some nearby buildings. Then he led me away from the beautiful girls to a small hole-in-the-wall restaurant.

It was a traditional building, a small cave of black-and-white coral. There were no chairs, and we sat down in the slight indents in the floor beside a small table. He called out for the waitress and presented me. She reached out and pulled at the fingers on my hands.

We all laughed.

When she went to get our ujos, I said, "Do you know her?"

He nodded vigorously, jowls shaking. "Here I am . . . famous!" he said.

"A movie star!" I said.

We drank for an hour or two. Once again he brought up the topic of women, with a slyer look than he had had at the school.

"Introduce!" he said.

I was tempted, but uncomfortable with the idea. Somehow I doubted that he would know any women like the ones who had passed by outside the restaurant; and the idea of being indebted or entwined with this man was also unappealing. At one point, he had gestured at the waitress and curled two tentacles in front of his chest — it took me a second to translate it: *nice tits, eh?*

I hadn't really made any firm policy on whether I would be fraternizing with the natives, but I figured it was really unlikely. The chances of finding an Octavian gal who knew English beyond *hello* were pretty low, and living in cucumber town whittled them down even further.

But not, as it turned out, down to nothing.

EIGHT

We floated down the tunnel. The density of the atmosphere this far down was pretty intense, every breath a conscious one.

"You guys OK?" I said.

Matthew gave me the thumbs-up and Hugh nodded.

"Let me know if your lungs fill up with water and you die," I said.

Laughter. "Your Octavian caves ain't shit," Matthew said. "You try some caves on my planet—"

"The coral is incredible," Hugh noted. "I can't believe you're not down here every day."

I took a look at the coral, with its swirl patterns and its infinite tiny holes. "There's a saying here about something being so hard to find or rare that it's like it was hidden away in one of these pores. Mr. Zik told me that."

"Oh he's a fount of wisdom that Mr. Zik," snarled Matthew. "But I'll bet he doesn't teach you swear words and drinking songs."

An old Octavian couple wearing cave-exploring goggles surprised us as they came around a twist in the tunnel. It was pretty narrow so they flipped upside down and climbed on the roof. The man grinned at us and called out a polite greeting, but his partner gave us a guarded look.

"Talking about drinking songs," I said. "Mr. Kung and I got too drunken last week." I explained who he was. "He ended up on my back, hugging me, singing 'Intergalactic Harmony' — well, every other line of the song, anyway, filling in sometimes in Octavian." The tunnel narrowed and I worried that it would only be Octavian-sized.

"That sounds nice," said Hugh. I guessed contact with the Armored wasn't often physical.

"It *was* kind of . . . touching in an absurd way. But he let it slip that he had a mistress, which kind of disturbed me. 'I am very sorry but I have two wives.' That he would cheat on his wife was one thing, but that he would pretend to be sorry about something he was actually bragging about —"

"Fuck, I'd love to have an affair," Matthew said.

"Aw, man . . ." I said.

Hugh looked at me curiously.

"Well, I mean, his girlfriend's at home being faithful," I said.

"Yeah, but she's not going to know anything," Matthew shot back.

"And second, sex stuff here is really serious. Because of the eggs and stuff."
I really knew almost nothing about it as I had no practical need for the knowledge.

I picked a tunnel at random. Supposedly they all led to the same place, anyway.

"Why'd you form these biases, anyway?" Hugh said. "I mean, Matthew obviously follows situational ethics, which is pretty normal."

"You callin' me normal, moonboy?"

"But is there something in your past—"

I wasn't about to get into how my mom cheated on Jane. I shrugged. Had that turned me monogamist?

"Hmm," Hugh said.

"Shut up," I snapped. "Fuck. The tunnel's getting too narrow." I turned around. "Unless you're soft-boned Octavians in disguise, we're gonna have to try the other tunnel."

We started back, this time with me taking up the rear. "Mr. Zik says that one of the tunnels is human-sized."

Matthew mumbled *Mr. Zik* and made a derisory noise that sent a flurry of bubbles from the side of his head. They rose faster than the bubbles usually did topside.

"So have you made any progress on your philandering scheme?" I asked, interested despite myself. Hugh looked back but before he said anything Matthew answered.

"OK, so there was this guy who was teaching in my town last year, right? A lunarian, and so of course he was quite the bag of briskets amongst the ladies of the town. A bit of a rep that way. I get his apartment, as usual. He's left it pretty messy but with enough good shit in there so that I don't mind cleaning it up."

"What'dya get?" I asked.

"A talking pot and a pillowpat. He wasn't really being generous — he couldn't use them anywhere else because the Squidollian power outlets are different from everywhere else. Fuckin' pain in the ass. Anyway, I'm cleaning out these drawers and one drawers got nothing but, like, tins of opened chewing tobacco and a jar of spit."

Hugh curled his nose.

"I just figured the previous guy — call him Tim — took up the habit and didn't really like it. 'cause almost all the tins were pretty full. I just left the crap there 'cause I didn't need the drawer and I didn't feel like cleaning it up," he shrugged. "I forgot about it."

We came to the fork in the tunnel and took the other choice. I prayed that it'd be the lucky one, and I hadn't wasted the afternoon for the three of us. It was interesting how much pressure I felt to be a good host. Octavia was rubbing off on me.

"So one day after my class with the adults one of the teachers offers me a ride. I say OK, even though it was close by. I was hoping for a ride other than in her saucer, get me?"

"How did she ask you?" Hugh said, untouched by Matthew's crudity.

"Pretty casually," Matthew said. "But when we got in she got really excited, saying that the other teachers would be mad because she got extra time with me. But off we go and we stop off at this corner store. She gets out and comes back with a big bag. Then we go to my place."

A group of three schoolgirls appeared suddenly, and two of them twined their tentacles and bowed, using the honorific word for teacher. I responded in Octavian.

"Your students?" asked Hugh.

"I guess so," I said. "They're the right age."

"No giggling?" asked Matthew. "No hello? Those can't be schoolgirls."

A slightly echoey *good-bye* was heard behind us, followed by bubbly laughter.

I looked at Matthew. He nodded, "Better."

"So you're back at your pad," I prompted.

"Yeah, so once we're inside she immediately passes me the thing she bought at the store. It's soap for the washing machine, which is kind of useless since I get all my stuff laundered — I mean, it's so cheap — but it's a tradition to bring a small gift whenever you visit someone, especially the first time."

"Same thing here," I said, nervously watching the roof of the cavern get lower as we kept walking. I looked at Hugh. "What about—"

He gave a bitter laugh. "Are you kidding? God forbid the Armored spend even a moment doing something . . . inefficient."

"I don't know," Matthew said. "It seems kind of a silly ritual. It's not like you have a choice, it's not like spontaneously giving a gift."

Right when it looked like we were going to have to duck, the tunnel widened. I was sweating a little, although it was hard to tell.

Hugh touched the side of the tunnel. "It's . . . smoother here, I think."

I looked around. "Yeah, I think they may have widened this part artificially.

Go on, Matthew."

"So I notice there's something else in the bag," Matthew continued. "It's this little tin of chewing tobacco. I take it out and she sort of laughs like she's ashamed. 'It's a bad,' she says, taking it from me. I'm like, I don't care, so she breaks open the tin and goes at it."

"She chews?!" I said, surprised. I'd never seen women chewing on Octavia. "Isn't it a taboo?"

"Big time," said Matthew. "I was kind of excited about it because I figured, if she'll break one taboo . . ." he let his lascivious smile finish his thought. Eye on the prize, our Matthew.

"Just going into a man's apartment alone is pretty odd, isn't it?" asked Hugh.

"Yeah, but I never really thought about it. Until she starts talking, between spits: 'This is the first time I've been in a man's apartment alone since I married my husband.' Spit. 'My husband is a very good man but I am not in love with him.' Spit."

"My husband doesn't understand me?" Hugh guessed.

"More or less, eh?" Matthew laughed. "She's totally nervous. Her tentacles are twitching and her skin is cycling from red to green to white. For some reason I found this really attractive. I mean, she's not that hot — my girlfriend's way better-looking, for instance . . ."

I had to stifle a grimace.

" . . . so then she says. 'But my husband knows I am here. He . . . he trusts me.' Then she looks at me, suddenly. 'I must go now.' And she gets up and jets out. I'm left standing there, staring at her bubble trail and then I pick up the tin, close it, and put it in the same drawer where all the other ones were. Then it dawns on me that I was probably just one in a series," he said, looking more amused than rueful.

"Was it Old West brand?" I asked.

"No," he said, "Balloon Flower."

"What a lovely name," Hugh said, "Oh — here we are."

The tunnel ended with a well-worn exit. The hole was pretty small, but we would all be able to fit through it, one at a time. I opted to go first.

"It's a bit of a drop," I said, sliding my legs through feet first. "But a real Earthling won't even feel it."

Hugh said something in response but I had already swung myself out into the unknown. It was only about twenty feet, but the density of the atmosphere increased so sharply that it actually slowed me as I floated down. I had a full half minute to appreciate the scenery.

It was a massive cavern lit by glowing moss, the far wall speckled with dark holes. The roof was a craggy blue and the walls were green. It had the feeling of a secret; so far down and hidden from even the most powerful eyes on Earth. Anything could happen here.

I touched down, then sat. It was a little unnerving, how close it felt to zero grav. But I could feel my lungs working harder, and this grounded me. Matthew landed, and walked over to the edge. "Wow," he said. "I can't even see the bottom."

He looked up, and I followed his gaze. Hugh was free-falling, his eyes opened anxiously and his arms spread as if he was trying to slow his descent. His hair floated above his head like a blonde halo. Even as it impressed me, it irritated me, this endless pose he struck.

Fuckin' lunarians.

"Get away from the edge, man, you're making me nervous," I barked at Matthew. If he was to fall any further down he'd drown slowly; I didn't relish the idea of communicating that to Mr. Zik.

"Breathe!" Matthew called to Hugh.

Hugh started to. His body convulsed a little. He landed on his knees on the ledge and hiccuped violently.

"You gotta breathe evenly all the way down."

Hugh nodded, patting his hair back into place.

I mimicked him. "Ready for your close-up?"

Matthew laughed.

"So prettyboy," I said, "anytime you want to work off a little steam," I said powering a punch through the molasses-air, "you know, mix it up pugilistically, let me know, OK?"

Hugh looked at me with confused eyes. "You mean . . . fist-fight?"

Matthew said with a smirk, "Yeah, you knew Sam was a pug back home, right?"

"No, I didn't," said Hugh. He looked kind of hurt, and I felt my trusty blowtorch rage sputtering into death. "You know, (hic) my family would have been much happier if I had been born looking like you, Sam (hic)."

My aggrometer needle jumped to life.

He saw my twisted lip and went on. "I don't talk about it much," Hugh said apologetically, "But my parents are really well-off. Obscenely so, really. And everyone on the moon is beautiful, since the main industry is media. So . . . plain people stand out."

"What about the tourists?" asked Matthew.

"They're busy being milked in the hospitality zones," Hugh said. "The propaganda about it being sealed for disease prevention is nonsense. The truth is that people like my father's father wanted plainness to be the mark of the idle rich." He fiddled a little with the dials on his wristphone. "This is my mother."

We looked as the small image flickered and sharpened, a gray pinched-mouth old woman.

"Wow," Matthew said, "Mom's pretty ugly."

"No, merely plain," he said. He fiddled some more. "Dad, on the other hand . . ."

I looked away before the image was fully formed. Matthew gaped at it.

Hugh's brow raised, a pleasant arc. "Dear old Dad's majestic ugliness means that no one mistakes him for a working man. Naturally," he said brusquely, tapping the picture away, "I was a huge embarrassment to them."

There was so much rawness in that admission I couldn't meet his eye. I looked out, instead, across the cavern. On a nearby ledge I could see an Octavian couple fanning out round sitting disks, their picnic basket at the ready. She, slim and pretty — he, rotund and funny. Their laughter reached us a few seconds after it left their mouths.

"Hey look," Matthew said, pointing up. From a tiny hole there slid a chain of Octavian schoolgirls, tentacles linked. Each new too-big body emerging was a shock, a magic trick, and the chain spun and giggled and then suddenly stopped. At the top, a boy held onto the ledge and ignored the whiny pleas that he let go. I couldn't see the expression on his face, but I imagined it would be a mischievous grin.

"How can he hold them up?" Hugh said.

"It must be the density," I guessed.

Then the chain disconnected and the individual girls floated down, their tentacles spreading out to slow them like clothless umbrellas. The whines stopped and it was silent for a moment, as they fell, and we watched without a word.

The boy remained stuck at the top, with the one girl he was holding flailing her tentacles at him. He let her go, then dropped himself.

"I thought she was gonna ink him," said Matthew.

"Well, I understand it's kind of rude. The equivalent of farting on someone."

Before the boy hit the ground, one of the girls let loose a big ink cloud that he couldn't help but hit, then skittered away.

Hugh and Matthew looked at me.

"Well," I said, "they *are* farm kids."

Now that they were closer, we could hear them speaking. I strained to interpret what they were saying. One of the girls was saying how boring Earth was.

"They keep saying Earth," said Matthew, picking up pebbles and throwing them through the air in a superslow arc. "Are they talking about us?"

"Mr. Zik told me the nickname of this cavern is Earth 'cause of the green bottom and blue roof. I don't think they've seen us." Our ledge was slightly lower than theirs, though plainly visible. "They have a different name for us, anyway. Koogeem."

Hugh was lying on his stomach, staring at the Octavians with a half-lidded gaze. The boy was running after the inker and the other girls protected her.

"Nice, emotional play. Octavians must be fun to teach," he said, leaning his head against his hand with a sigh.

"Yeah, they're OK," I said. "The Armored must be well behaved, at least."

"Well, their armor adjusts them if they're not," Hugh said. "But it's so awful. Their pale little expressionless heads stick up from their armor like mushrooms. There's this one boy who cries all the time. No sound, just his eyes streaming constantly. One day I asked him why he was crying and he said that he wanted to be stripped like his mom."

"Oh man," Matthew said. "That's shitty."

"His suit immediately put him to sleep, and another teacher came in to carry him out. He told me not to worry." Hugh turned his head away, his voice thick. "He said it was . . . normal."

"Sounds like we've been discovered," Matthew said. I could hear *Koogeem Koogeem* in the distance, but I couldn't take my eyes off Hugh. His body was shaking a little, and I didn't think it was the hiccups.

Matthew, oblivious, walked over to the edge of the ledge and gave the crowd an expansive wave. He was immediately paid in excited screams. While he was faced away I leaned over and patted Hugh on the shoulder. "'Sokay, man."

He stiffened at this. "Don't you want to punch me anymore?"

I felt a little bad. I shrugged, but he couldn't see that. He sat up and rubbed his face.

"Hello!" one of the girls yelled.

"Hello you foxy babes!" Matthew responded.

Hugh snorted.

"Matthew, what the hell, man, I gotta work here."

Matthew turned around. "Don't worry. Think of what it would translate as." The boy bellowed a hello that sounded like a threat and Matthew ignored him, tired of the sensation he was creating. "So weren't you ever tempted to become a big-time mediastar, Hugh? Just say fuck your snobby family and make some serious creds? That's what I woulda done."

Hugh nodded. "I wanted to be an actor for a while. But not because of the money — I've always been rather stupid about money, really — I thought I'd find . . . people like me. I grew up on the Slackwater comedies, the arch humor and the genuine feeling of the characters."

I nodded. I liked them, although their relentless refinement started to grate after a while.

"So I ended up getting into the school where the Slackwater actors actually trained. And the people there were beautiful," he shook his head, "so darkly beautiful. I walked through the school on my first day and my feet never touched the ground."

I noticed the couple with the picnic basket were having trouble pouring tea, the Zazzimurg glinting across the cavern. I saw Matthew looking at it too.

"Gotta piss," he said, looking around. The ledge was pretty stark, no cover at all.

"Don't do it here," I said, looking across at the kids. "It'll just be this big cloud at this density."

He made an annoyed noise. "Ah, I'll just go back up to the tunnel." He started climbing the wall, pulling himself up by his hands. It looked rather impressive.

When he got high enough to make me nervous, I looked back at Hugh. "I gather your first impression of the school didn't last, eh?" I said.

Hugh shrugged. "On my second day I talked to them, and found them aloof. I was discouraged, naturally, but this was to be expected."

"You couldn't expect them to just accept you easily," I said.

Hugh nodded. "I found my manner put them off. I had a bearing and poise that I shouldn't have been able to mimic until second or third year. They suspected I had received early training, and I didn't want to reveal my high beginnings. So I developed a . . . reputation. People fell silent whenever I was around."

He sat up. "It went on for weeks. It was fairly torturous. I wanted to be loved by them, after all. One of the women there was brave enough to indulge her curiosity about me and we became involved. She was extremely beautiful and extremely dull, and at first I thought it was this latter quality that made her throw in her lot with me — she had nothing to lose, being the dimmest of her peers."

I glanced up at Matthew, now using hands and feet to climb slowly towards the hole, less cocksure than when at a lower density. I smiled at his needless caution. "Go on," I said, waiting for his story to roll past another ten beautiful but undeserving women.

"There was a Roman-nosed rival for her affections. This finally made me worth talking to. He took to insulting me, to mocking me. It was appalling," he said, looking down intensely at the ground.

"Sure," I said.

"No, it wasn't *hurtful.* It would have been one thing to be cleverly put down, to be nicked by *bon mots* or . . . incisively sliced. But these were comments of the crudest calibre, utterly infantile. Comments unworthy even of our friend Matthew, there . . ."

I smiled. Matthew was wiggling his way into the hole high above, his legs kicking, looking like the wall was eating him.

"And people laughed like these brutal banalities were the height of wit. There was something horrifying about those sculpted lips pushing out such pedestrian nonsense. Of course, I had no response. I was destroyed, socially. But more significantly, my hopes of finding common souls were destroyed."

"Hmm," I said, thinking about my more successful quest for tribe.

"I became a ghost walking around the school. The conversations didn't die on my approach, and so I got to listen to vacuous stupidities which simply deepened my gloom. Nattering about clothing without talking about aesthetics; they discussed scandal after scandal, but never ethics; drinking and self-destruction without nihilism; sport without catharsis."

Above us, Matthew reappeared and jumped, curling himself into a ball. I realized that Hugh was speaking differently than he would have if Matthew was here.

"I quit before the first semester was over, and gave up the idea of finding my people for a while. Then a friend of mine told me about the Unarmored looking for English teachers . . ."

Matthew uncurled himself in a sudden explosive move and landed.

" . . . they just seem like angels to me, you know?" Hugh said, looking at me with sad eyes.

"Yeah," I nodded.

"You talking about Octavian hookers again?" Matthew asked.

I smirked. "Right in one."

Matthew looked at Hugh. "You and 9/3 should have come along with us that night in the big city."

"Yeah, what did you end up doing, anyway?"

"Not too much . . ." Hugh said.

"So what did the big guy say when you called him?" said Matthew. "What was his excuse for not coming?"

Hugh scraped some gravel into a pile with the flat of his hand. "He didn't give one. He's kind of mad at me."

I blinked. "Really?"

"What for?" Matthew said, his eyes narrowed.

"It's . . . complicated." Hugh said, his bangs falling over his downcast eyes.

Matthew made an annoyed noise and looked at me. I shrugged.

"So do you guys have plans for the break yet?" Matthew said.

We talked about it a bit — it was still a ways away, but it was pretty exciting to talk about the planethopping we could do. Every so often I'd catch Hugh looking into the distance, but his melancholy didn't inspire my usual irritation. I thought about him explaining to his terrifying father why he wanted to go to teach English to the Unarmored, and conversations dropping away when he entered the room. His bird-bones seemed more fragile than irksome to me then.

NINE

"Gunge forbly?" I said, staring at the little prick.

He looked to his friends, who covered their gleeful anticipation with their tentacles.

"*Gunge forbly*?" I said, approaching the kid's desk. He bowed his head, his head crest dipped, but I could tell by his face that he wasn't really all that sorry.

I hated punishing them, but I wasn't gonna be called the unpleasant smelling peelings of a sweet potato. I looked at him severely and made the gesture that meant *come with me*. It's a kind of patting of the air — obviously, the curled beckoning finger means as little to them as the expanding of tentacle suckers means to me.

The class was more attentive than it had been all period, of course, as the boy slowly glided to the front. Some of the other teachers would grab the offender by their tentacles and whack the child against whatever surface was available.

It wasn't the violence that I disliked — I knew better than most that in the right context it could focus a discharge that was quite healthy. But this was institutionalized violence, always directed against the powerless for "their own good," and it left a bad taste in my mouth. So I had my own tricks.

I took the blackboard brush in one hand and spun the skinny brat around with the other. Then I patted his head with the brush, making a small black cloud — not unlike an ink cloud. Surprised laughter ensued, and I pointed the foul-mouthed boy back to his seat. Defeated and humiliated, he trudged back, waving his tentacles around his head to get rid of the cloud.

I continued the lesson, asking the students "What Number Is It?" going up and down the rows to make sure that the smart kids didn't dominate the class.

"Et."

"Eight."

" . . . Et."

"Eight." I looked out at the class, and said it in the *repeat after me* fashion. "Eight."

"*Et.*"

The bell sounded, and I smiled. Last class of the week. I looked down and put my things on top of each other, unnecessarily, but it's the body language that matters. "Bye," I said and waved.

"Bye teecha," bellowed the boy who annoyed me earlier. I ignored him, as I've come to ignore everyone who thinks English sounds better yelled, but I allowed myself to be stopped by a girl with an Intergalactic Cool Youth sticker on her recorder. She gave me a tiny gray creature, carved from coral, and a tiny smile. I thanked her, told her it was beautiful. Her tentacles twitched nervously, and she seemed to want to say something.

I pointed to her sticker. "I.C.Y. are very good!" I said.

Her eyes bugged out. Her friend, excited by this, said, "I.C.Y . . . .Octavian pop group."

I mimed someone playing the synthitar. They laughed. "I.C.Y . . . .Number One," the original girl said quietly.

I took my leave then, having thoroughly proven how cool I was.

Back in the teacher's room, Mr. Zik was waiting for me. "They have called ablout the toilet," he said.

"Great!" I said.

"Let's go," he said with a little bit of a question in his voice.

I was a little surprised. It was the middle of the day, and I usually had to kill time at my desk.

"No more classes for you and me," he said, "ssss-sss-ss."

We got our jackets and left, making a detour at the principal's office. He was listening to the newsfeed and staring into space when we interrupted him. Mr. Zik cautiously told him about the toilet, and the principal made something that sounded like a joke about human strangeness. I pretended to understand nothing, telling myself that I would put up with any number of dumb jokes to be free of the insanity that was Octavian plumbing.

"So, you have been in Plangyo a month," said Mr. Zik as we left the school. I automatically headed towards his saucer but he redirected me. "It is quicker to walk." He removed his tin of chewing tobacco from his pocket. "Bad hablit, I know."

"Has it been a month already?" I said. I watched him unscrew and lift the lid in a smooth movement, a little transported by the grace of the alien everyday.

Just outside the gates of the school there were a few boys who found our sudden presence alarming. They ducked into a store. Mr. Zik ignored them, and, I noticed, quickly put his tin away.

"Mr. Zik, I wanted to thank you for being such an excellent host. The time has gone fast because you have made it very easy to adapt to life here."

A smile lit up his face and he glanced at me shyly. "It is my duty. Duty is very implortant to Octavians."

"You have done more than your duty, I think."

He shook his head, still smiling.

We walked by a field of cucumbers, two or three old folk working away. A saucer bubbled by overhead from the school's direction.

He laughed. "Vice-principal leaves early too."

The bubbles rained down on us.

"Today a student called me 'gunge forbly,' " I said.

"He is a blad student," Mr. Zik said with a laugh. "Very blad. Did you hit him?"

I wondered if Mr. Zik hit his kids. It was hard to imagine. He told me once, during a beating that had happened in the teacher's room that it was OK because Octavians didn't have bones. I told him the punishment I meted out. "I saw how they hated being sprayed with ink, in the caves."

Mr. Zik nodded. "You are very smart, I think. And your Octavian is very good!"

I shook my head, aping his modesty. I *had* been ripping through my lessons, but what else was I supposed to do at night? I wrote all my letters during the day.

"Gunge forbly is not a polite word," he said, and we laughed. "Who taught you?"

"Mr. Kung," I said. He had given me a pretty thorough lesson in profanity — the majority of the words leading back to the tentacle that was used as a sex organ, *oogma*. I had found it interesting that it was just a tentacle until it was being used for sex.

"Last time, Mr. Kung was the host for the English teacher."

"Really?" I said. "I am more lucky, I think."

We suddenly were in the market, stalls to each side. It was the weekly market day, and thick-skinned farmers watched me with grimness or joviality. I tried to understand what they were calling out but I couldn't decipher their accent.

"They are surprised to see you," said Mr. Zik.

I could pretty much predict what my presence would do to school boys and girls, but the responses from the old folk ran the gamut from friendly to astonished to terrified to furious. I wondered if they were mad about the war — but I had been told it was mostly city-folk that had been affected by that.

A woman tapped my shoulder and put a piece of fruit in my hand. It looked like an inside-out pomegranate. I tried to hand back the beaded fruit, but she curled her tentacles back in refusal. With a gaptoothed smile, she said something I didn't understand.

"She says it is no cost," said Mr. Zik. "Free!"

I looked back at her with a smile. She was looking elsewhere, her eyes in the free float of senility. I thanked her loudly enough for all to hear.

Mr. Zik nodded at the woman who ran the restaurant where we often went for lunch. She was sitting in the curled up way of relaxed Octavians, but raised herself to greet Mr. Zik in a politely formal way. Mr. Zik didn't live in Plangyo — he lived in a nearby city — but he was known in the town, since he had taught their children for almost ten years.

"You are respected in Plangyo," I said as we left the market.

Mr. Zik blinked and said, "I am a teacher."

We arrived at the post office, and went in. I had already been here a few times, to send letters, and I bowed a greeting to the nice lady who had helped me on those occasions.

Mr. Zik spoke very quickly in Octavian to her, making a large box shape with his tentacles. She made an *ah* sound of realization (perhaps a universal word) and slid to the back room.

"It was sent from Artemia."

I nodded. That was a relief. It would have been embarrassing if they had had to ship it from off-planet.

"It is the only Earth-style toilet on Octavia, I think," said Mr. Zik.

The toilet came out of the back, hauled on its antigrav disk by a strapping young lad with acne. It sat there like a throne, white and sparkly. I quelled an urge to hug it.

Mr. Zik signed for it with a press of his tentacle (the thin one used for you-know-what) and we were off. It slid through the door with an inch to spare. I looked back to wave at my friend, but she was already back at work.

Outside, Mr. Zik adjusted the strap so it went across his chest.

"Can I help you pull?" I said, when I realized we were going to drag it home.

"No. It's easier for one plerson," he said, starting to walk towards the market. The toilet seat bounced up and down, so I walked beside it and held the lid down with my hand. It made me feel like I was doing something.

We came to the market. I could see Mr. Zik was a little winded, breathing hard. I thought of pushing from behind but I had my fruit in one hand, and I couldn't put it in my pocket. I wished I had thrown it away before all these farmers were around to see.

I felt like a total ass, toilet lid in one hand and inside-out pomegranate in another, jogging behind Mr. Zik. And how must he feel, dragging an alien shitter through the public market like some kind of service-issue droid?

We passed the restaurant, where the woman still chatted with her friend. Passed the vacuously grinning old woman, lifted my fruit to show I hadn't even considered throwing it away. Passed through the entire town, who, instead of the hoots of derision and hilarity, remained as composed and nonchalant as I have ever seen. Even knowing some of the language, Plangyo remained indecipherable to me.

I looked at the back of Mr. Zik's head as he chugged along, tentacles pulling the body that pulled the disk. *Powered by 100% Hi-Octane Duty*, I thought in amazement as we headed for home.

I'd finished dinner and did all the studying I was going to do. I was sanitizing the dishes, at a bit of a loss, sensing loneliness in the other room waiting for me. Then I remembered the moviedisk Lisa had given me before I left.

It was still there, in the side pocket of my now-empty suitcase. I set the size to 50%, popped out the center and tossed it towards the center of the room. It floated to the floor so slowly that I thought for a second that it wouldn't land with enough force to activate, but then the familiar rays of light shot out from the edge and my room was suddenly populated by three-foot-high people.

" . . . mind if we record this?" Skaggs was saying to the young blond kid. "It's Sam's first scrap, eh?"

The blond kid shrugged, looked behind him at the other people he was with. "Ye want a record of the worst arse kicking you ever got, it's fine wi' us." I saw myself tentatively raise a hand to the group.

A guy came through my ceiling and landed heavily on his boots in the midst of the two gangs. He flicked off his jetpack and pulled off his goggles. His brogue cut through the exchange of insults starting to fly between the two groups. "We've got a guid twelve minutes before the next skyeye sweep. Noo weapons or biomech implants are present." He shucked off his jetpack and set it aside, continuing despite a decided lack of attention. Insults were flying, anger was rising. "Noo biting. Noo kicking. Noo bloody mercy."

Two or three fights broke out at this point. Skaggs threw a wild punch at the blond kid, and it barely skinned her. She came back with a solid blow to the solar plexus.

Little Sam was sort of standing there, a half-smile on his face, bouncing up and down on my toes and shyly looking over at the Scottish pugs.

I sat down to watch it, fascinated despite myself. I had always been a little contemptuous of the idea of recording the fights, but here I was. I looked at my younger self — who was checking his brand-new aggrometer, waiting for the needle to red zone of its own accord — and recalled that moment with an incredible clarity.

I had felt like a total idiot. Lisa and Skaggs had convinced me to come, and I had been quite fascinated by the idea. But the reality of it left me standing awkwardly in the middle of a seething, pounding, cursing mob.

I leaned forward and changed the disc to 30%. The whole rooftop became visible, and pretty much everyone had paired up except me. I could actually see Skaggs shooting concerned looks back at me right until he got a haymaker that made him pay attention. Lisa was focused on taking down a guy about twice her size. I was watching her, concernedly, and then she looked over at me and waved.

I couldn't hear it on the recording, but at the time I remember hearing her nose crunch under the big guy's rock of a fist. He laughed a snorting laugh as she fell on her ass, holding her hand under her spurting nose. "Ach, the wee lassie canna fight!"

Guilt and rage combined to rocket me at the guy, throwing punches at his chest and face at the same time. He weathered my flailing attack and then casually boxed my ears. As I reeled back in pain, he tilted back his head and laughed. Lisa, her face streaked with red, had a fist waiting for him when he finished. One that sprung up from the soles of her heels and totally clocked the big guy.

"Reet you filthy pugs," said moustache man a second later. "That's it. Two minutes for medvac."

Lisa took my arm and led me over to the line-up. People were casually chatting, the Scottish and Canadian accents had vanished along with the hostility. Accents weren't a foolproof way to tell enemy from friend, but visual indicators were too risky.

I set the moviedisk to 75% and turned up the volume, to see if I could hear what people were saying.

Lisa was letting the blood flow freely from her nose, leaning forward so it didn't get on her shirt. She was really excited about knocking out that big guy, because the Scottish pugs were notoriously hard. She grabbed my arm and said that she couldn't have done it without me. I beamed foolishly.

"One minute," the moustachioed man yelled. I zoomed back out, to see several people fire up their jetpacks and take off like shaky dragonflies. The big guy and other knockouts were getting medvac treatment by people with hand-held units. After most people had been under the lamp, I was struck with how normal and average everyone looked. Those ridiculous jackets and bully-gloves being sported nowadays went against the entire —

Ah, the hell with it. It was all a lie, anyway. I leaned forward and popped the center back out and I was alone in my room again.

🪐

"Hey, little guy," I said to the resident of Plangyo least likely to speak English. He was a small creature that resembled half a walnut shell, if a walnut had hundreds of tiny tendrils to whisk around back alleys on. And was about a human handwidth in diameter.

I was back in the same place where the market was, although now, being night, I was the only person around. Well, the only big person.

I held out my hand, wished I had something to offer him. He faced me, floating there, but didn't move towards me. His eyes were round and white and the black pupils floated all over, independent of each other.

I didn't know it was a he, really. I didn't know if it ate anything. I stood and walked on, boggling at the fact that there was another species co-existing with the Octavians, and this was the first I'd heard of it.

I was looking in the window of a store that sold kid stuff — all your basic Intergalactic Cool Youth needs met here — when the little dude shot past me. He used a propulsion system as well as the tendrils, but the pressure was so low — him being so small — that bubbles didn't even form.

He went down an alleyway, and I was tempted to follow. Maybe his home? His speckle-shelled little offspring would approach me, cling to my shoe in the manner of the unkicked. I would prove myself worthy of trust.

I paused, looking after it, and then I remembered that I was on another planet. The Starscouting rule about dark alleys and avoidance of them seemed to apply. What would I do with a half-shell friend I couldn't talk to, anyway?

I looked up at the surface-sky. There were no moons or other celestial bodies, obviously, but the wan purplish-gray light was wonderfully foreboding.

I thought about how I would love someone to come by and throw a punch at me so we could battle it out right here. I imagined the big Scottish pug, who I'd never seen after the first scrap. There were even boxes and shit to throw. It would be so great.

Mrs. Ahm lifted my tie in a finely-tapered tentacle and admired it. "It is a very nice color." (It was a steel gray. Well, Earth steel gray. Here, steel was more of a black.)

I might have mentioned how I admired the unnerving blue of her eyes. Hell, I might have caught up her tentacle and caressed the row of tiny suction cups which were said to be so sensitive. I might have, but then she said:

"I will have to buy one for my husband."

I shrugged. "They can only be bought on Earth," I said, continuing to eat.

The older teacher returned from the washroom and settled back into her spot with a smile. I couldn't remember her name despite it being, I knew, a short and common one. I smiled back, guilty.

Mrs. Ahm said something quickly to her, motioning at my tie, using the words for Earth and only. I was hoping that they wouldn't flip it around to see the Made on Octavia tag. "This is a great restaurant," I said distractingly.

"Sank you," said the older teacher. "It is very traditional."

It was pretty fascinating. The room was small and cave-like, if you were used to caves with windows. The floor was covered with a soft lichen that glowed, providing the light, and instead of sitting disks there were shallow indents where the lichen was mostly rubbed off.

"I wish that my apartment was more traditional," I said.

"I like the modern apartments more," said Mrs. Ahm. "I am modern woman."

"Why do you like the modern ones better?"

Mrs. Ahm crinkled up her nose and tore up some lichen with her suckers. "This smells bad."

"It does?" I said, lifting up a snuff to my nose. It faded once plucked, but didn't smell.

"When it gets older it does," said the older teacher, adjusting her hat. She had an old-lady hat with flowers on it. "But she should not say that." She batted Mrs. Ahm lightly. "It is very important to our history."

Mrs. Ahm's eyes widened. "You know? The story?"

"*His*tory," the other said.

"Well, about five hundred years ago . . ." Mrs. Ahm started, then immediately consulted with the other teacher. A young, bored looking woman came in and removed empty dishes from the table. I didn't rate a look, and I pitied her for being so self-involved that even a freak didn't entertain her.

"So," Mrs. Ahm started again. "We had a war with monsters."

I nodded, so well trained that not even a smile crossed my lips. *It's those monsters again, izzit?*

"The monsters lived in Playgi, and at night they came to Artemia and killed everyone!" Mrs. Ahm made an explosive movement with her tentacles.

The older teacher was looking at my fork, which was sitting on the table.

"Everyone?" I said. "All?"

"No . . ."

When Mrs. Ahm was looking for a modifier, the older teacher reached out tentatively for my fork. She looked at me and I assented with a nod.

"Almost everyone," Mrs. Ahm said excitedly. Then she noticed that the other teacher's attention was elsewhere, and she faux-snapped at her in teacher-tone to *Pay attention!*

We all laughed at this, and I felt really happy to actually get an Octavian joke. They looked at me and I proudly explained that I also told my students to pay attention. "How did you stop the monsters?"

"The farmers planted lichen everywhere. Many many farmers died. Then the lichen grew . . . and started to . . . bring light," she said.

"Glow," I said.

She nodded, but I don't think she knew the word. "Then the monsters couldn't hide in the dark. Then the soldiers killed them."

The older teacher smiled. "Farmer's War."

"Yes, we call it Farmer's War."

I nodded. I tried to think of a comparison to something on Earth — the *yes that is like our* . . . syndrome — and came up blank. The only war that mattered was the one that essentially brought about Earth's ownership of the rest of the galaxy. The one that brought me here.

The one that was still going on, in a way.

"Shall we go?" proposed Mrs. Ahm. "Class will start soon, I think."

In the front room of the restaurant, the elder teacher pointed out a painting on the wall. "Monsters," she said.

There was a group of dolphins there, facing a group of Octavians, but I didn't see the monsters. "Where?"

She poked one of the dolphins.

I walked out a little dazed. "Are they all dead? The monsters?"

"No," said Mrs. Ahm. "They hide on the west side of the planet."

"Small," said the other. "A small amount. Is not too dangerous."

As we left, I wondered how many species lived on this planet, anyway. What was the history of those little half-shell creatures? Had they fought against the Octavians too? Or were Octavians monsters to them?

We took the saucer back to the school. I had agreed to be a special guest in Mrs. Ahm's class in exchange for a lunch at a traditional Octavian restaurant. It had come up during a workshop when I said that many people took me to an Earth-style restaurant because they thought I'd like it better.

The two women were talking about a fellow teacher they called stupid-fat-man — I took it to be a nickname — and the upcoming holiday. Mrs. Ahm wanted to go to explore a certain cavern, but she couldn't for some reason I couldn't understand. Her baby was involved.

I really enjoyed eavesdropping, especially when it wasn't about me. I didn't feel it was dishonest, since I used enough Octavian during the workshops that it was pretty obvious that I was progressing rather quickly. Finding I had a talent for it was an unexpected surprise, akin to finding something you need in a junk drawer. My spoken Octavian was still child-like, mind you, and it kept me humble.

"Do you understand?" asked Mrs. Ahm, who wasn't driving.

"A little . . . why can't you go exploring?"

The elder teacher made a surprised sound. She didn't go to the workshops, so expected me to be totally ignorant. I was only partially ignorant now — although this class today would prove how far I had (or hadn't) come.

"I need someone to protect my baby."

"A baby-sitter," I supplied.

We arrived at the school. I looked around, quite interested in seeing the differences between it and my Plangyo school. If anything, this town was even more remote than mine (well, "mine") and it was famous for a method of boiling vegetables. I decided that that was lamer than being famous for an actual vegetable.

We rushed straight to class, bypassing the tedious introductions to everyone in the staff room, and the class had obviously not been expecting me.

The girls froze. I slid the door shut, and turned to face them. I smoothed out my tie and said hello.

All hell broke loose. A kind of wailing started up, a keening that grew to an almost unbearable pitch and then dropped back down. A girl stood up and screamed *Ohmigod* and collapsed back to her seat, her tentacles flung over her head.

Mrs. Ahm raised her hand with a tolerant smile and told them to begin the class. Everyone sat down.

One tall girl sat and then rose. She told the class to pay attention. Everyone was quiet. Then she told them to bow. They did, in sync.

"Hello," said Mrs. Ahm. "Will you sing a song?"

That was odd, I thought, since the singing was usually reserved for the end. *Oh well, here goes nothing . . .*

A girl got up and made an entry at the control panel, and music started.

That's not the song I want to sing — I thought, then the girls started to sing. I noticed some of them read from their recorders.

"Do you like this song, Sam?" asked Mrs. Ahm. "It is very popular on Earth, I know."

I nodded. It was a song by the Zylophonix Corp. It sounded funny, though. "What clone group was this recorded by?"

She gave me a worried look. "I think . . . it is illegal."

I realized she was serious. I felt a moment of exhilaration at the idea that Octavia was so remote it was even outside the copyright planet sweeps.

"Don't tell my principal," she said.

"Oh, no," I said, listening to the girl's sweet voices mangle the lyrics. I decided not to tell her about the interstellar tribunal on bootleggers, and boggled at the idea that she was risking her life for a teaching aid without even knowing it.

What kind of planet made rules about the songs you can sing? The same one that copyrights its language, then makes it the universal tongue of trade, I guessed. I felt a surge of hatred for Earth, and imagined my home planet blowing up and breaking —

"Are you Pan Venrugie?"

Who? One of the girls was standing. It was question time, I guessed. I hoped my anger hadn't been visible on my face.

"I am Sam Breen."

"Maybe . . . you are the brother of Pan Venrugie," she said, pronouncing the

P sound as so few Octavians could. "The actor."

I imagined explaining that I preferred to spend my spare time punching people in the face rather than watching the latest mediastar implode. "Sorry," I said.

One of the girls activated a small holo from her ring, and held it up for me to see. Pan (I assumed) did a little dance, and from the ghostly rendering I could see absolutely no resemblance. However, we both had legs rather than tentacles, and so I was the closest person to Pan they'd ever see in real life.

I suppose I should have nodded and smiled. I shook my head. "Pan is from the moon," I said, "where all the bird-boned mediastars are made." I pointed to myself. "I am from Earth, where the *real* people live."

Glancing at Mrs. Ahm's creased brow, I mercifully simplified. "Pan lives on the Moon. Sam lives on Earth." Which wasn't true, but it was understandable, and I was rewarded by a good percentage of nodding heads and *ahhs*.

I told them All About Sam. I got them to guess how long it took on a rocketship to get to Octavia. I told them how I loved Octavia. I told them how I had a friend on Montavia who was a roboman, and got them to draw a roboman on the board. I told them any silly shit that came into my head, as long as it was simple, as they gazed at me adoringly and scrambled to answer my questions. That ate up half the class.

Then, when most other teachers would have let the students ask questions for the rest of the class, Mrs. Ahm told them that there were questions on their recorder-pads based on my little talk. Whoever answered the most questions, she said in Octavian, would get a kiss from me.

This introduced a volatile chemical into an already unstable compound. They started asking questions in English and frantically inputting.

"Do you understand what I said?" she said innocently.

"I hope you win," I said, equally innocently.

"Oh! Only the students," she said. She hit me on the arm. "You are bad," she said, but smilingly.

Why was I flirting with a married woman? I wondered idly. It had just come out of my mouth. I had listened to Matthew's schemes of infidelity with a scorn . . . an interested scorn, mind you. I supposed that forgetting my Speak-O-Matic was one of those blessings in disguise — learning the language kept me out of trouble, anyway. That jogged my memory.

"So will the students want me to sing a song?" I said casually.

Her eyecrests spiked. "You?"

I shrugged. "OK."

She immediately asked the class and the keening began, chatting amok.

I went to the control panel and punched in 66945.

The song was called "Full of Happiness," and it was clear by the stunned looks on the girls faces that they couldn't quite believe they were hearing the beginning chords of their favorite famous hit pop song.

"This is a song by I.C.Y.," I said, eliciting a piercing scream from somewhere in the back.

I had been practicing the Intergalactic Cool Youth song for the better part of a month — ever since I had been asked by the kids in Plangyo to sing a song. The only tricky thing about it was that the song used both the echoey *thac* and the *op* sound which, as I had been warned, were impossible for Earthlings to make.

But about a week ago, I had discovered that tapping my front tooth with my fingernail made the echoey *thac* sound. And a couple of silly whacking combinations later, I made the echoey *op* by lightly slapping my cheek while pursing my lips in an O shape.

So I sung the song for them, and my heartfelt rendition made them squirm with adoration. My sound-substitution made them scream with laughter.

I thought it was funny. I didn't *intend* to change Octavian society.

The only hint I had was when it was over, I looked over at Mrs. Ahm and saw her worried face. She smiled quickly, but there had been fear there.

TEN

Outside the bus station was one of those half-shell creatures, scooting around the garbage. I crouched near it and held out my hand, talked to it. Its tail snapped nervously as it spun around, its eyes floaty. I took a step towards it and it shot off down the road.

I heard laughter from the station. There was a group of kids watching me. I straightened up and wished I was going somewhere else.

The station was an old structure, mostly coral with steel reinforcements added. I entered it with a neutral expression and looked briefly at the kids laughing. They weren't my students — a few years older, but still no more than fourteen, two boys and two girls. I sat down, catching the words "dirty" and "Earthling" out of their conversation.

Letting my expression harden, I focused on the signs directly across from me. *Something something open door* said one; *Artemia express hour-something*. I told myself it was better to learn the language, even when I had to put up with bullshit like this.

Some joke involving "garbage" was told. A taboo involving the little half-shell creatures, maybe? The idiots didn't know what a wonderful thing it was to have more than one native species; how humans studied the species that had once lived on their planet with reverence and feelings of loss. What a nice thing it was to think that you could share a planet, learn from each other! Not that the half-shells wanted anything to do with me, I thought, feeling my expression grow colder.

When the lepers run from your touch, now *that's* alienation.

I was ready to bridge the intergalactic gap with a right hook — the cold fury had crept its frost over my better judgement — when I realized they weren't talking about me any more. I looked at them. The boy who was talking loudest, a tow-headed short kid, seemed to be focused on a somewhat pretty girl who wasn't paying attention to him.

I'd have been a much better pug if not for this empathy thing (Fast fists, cold heart/That's what sets a pug apart).

I looked around at the other people in the terminal. An old woman watched me, a bag of cucumbers hugged to her chest. A middle-aged guy with a suitcase. And beside me, on the bench, was a stunning young Octavian woman.

I looked away, shocked. *Was I in Plangyo? Who was she? When could I look back at her without being too obvious?*

There weren't any beautiful girls in Plangyo. Almost all the youth that showed any promise left, either to go to university or get a job in Artemia. That was probably it. She was probably visiting her parents here or something . . .

I looked back again, rubbing my eye in a ruse. Her eyes, a rare silver, were fixed on the ground. I looked back, stared at the ground myself. I wished I hadn't seen her. What could I say in my laughable Octavian? Why would she want to talk to me any more than the half-shell had? She had probably seen me scare it away, I realized, but didn't laugh at me because she had more class, she had more intelligence . . .

The tow-headed kid was suddenly in my face.

"Whassup, whassup-whassup-whassup?" he said, bobbing his head at me, raising two tentacles.

His face was blotchy, his eyes were wild, he couldn't even dance. He bounced up and down on his tentacles as if they were springs. Why was he dancing?

"Whassup, whassup-whassup-whassup?" he repeated.

I finally recognized the line from an Intergalactic Cool Youth song, the chorus of which was in English — What's up — and probably was the only thing he knew how to say in my language.

The other kids were tittering nervously, but this was a little too much even for them — and they were the town bad kids. I looked over at the pretty girl, but she was staring at the ground even more intently. I couldn't believe I was letting this little jerk make me look stupid in front of her, I wished I could make him ten years older and —

"Whassup, whassup-whassup-*whassup*," he said, this time a desperate shouted challenge. I closed my fists and thought about how I was going to find out how punching a boneless face would feel when I heard the hiss of the bus's landing gear.

"Are you going to Artemia?" said the pretty girl.

I nodded dumbly. *She was talking English.*

"Come with me," she said. I did.

As we got on the bus, she turned back to me and smiled shyly.

I showed my ticket to the driver and he pulled away, unconcernedly barking the bus on a bump of coral as he pulled away. I almost stumbled into the girl.

As the bubbles started to obscure the back window, I looked back at the tow-headed kid and took a petty satisfaction at the jealous twist of his face.

And she spoke English, I thought with a barely concealed rush of joy.

She sat down and patted the seat with a tentacle. I accepted her invitation.

I waited for her to say something. She didn't.

"Are you —" I started.

"How —" she started.

We laughed. "You go," she said.

"Are you from Plangyo?" I asked.

"No," she said. "I . . . have part-time job. In Plangyo."

"Oh, I see," I said, realizing that I was again speaking Octo-English. "I am a teacher at Plangyo Middle School." Irritatingly, I also automatically avoided contractions.

"Yes, I know," she said, and giggled. "My students tell me. You are Mr. Sam?" she said, cautiously again.

I nodded. "You have students?"

She nodded.

"Are you a teacher?"

"Yes, I am a part-time teacher. Nayundi Private School, you know?"

I didn't.

The lady with the bag of cucumbers made a horking sound with her mouth. A quick cursory glance around revealed a bunch of straining ears and averted eyes.

"Oh," she said, a little surprised. "Some of your students go Nayundi."

That was news to me. "Are they good?"

"Some of them. Some are very loud. One is in love with you, I think." She laughed.

"Ha ha," I said, looking at her sadly, thinking how absurd she must find that as an adult Octavian. She looked straight ahead and composed herself after her laughter, calmness flooding her face. Then she looked at the side of a tentacle and I realized I was staring.

I looked away just as she looked at me. "Do you know the song he sung? The bad boy?"

"Yes," I said. "Intergalactic Cool Youth."

She gave a little jump of surprise and delight. I felt a foolish grin on my face. "Yes! I.C.Y.! Pop music. Is he famous in Earth?"

"No," I said. "But my students love I.C.Y.."

"Yes," she said. "All Octavian students, I think."

"Do you love I.C.Y.?"

"No, not love . . . just like."

I nodded. We sat in silence for a while. I pretended to watch the landscape. I was thinking about things to say to her, simple questions, but all that was coming to mind were ruminations about the kitsch appeal of offworld music acts. Then I was depressed that even with this obviously intelligent woman I was unable to have a decent conversation.

"Blun Kipp, do you know?" she said, her silver eyes bright and alive and fuelling me up.

"Ah . . . no. Is he a musician too?"

"Yes," she said, her brow furrowing. "But not a pop musician. He, ah," and she broke out into an operatic soprano, throwing her tentacles up: *lalalaLa!*

"Oh," I said, looking into her serious eyes, falling in love. "Opera."

She blinked.

"He is an opera singer," I said.

She nodded, smiled.

I looked around to see if the other passengers had noticed her solo. No one was staring. I had yet to understand the exact nature of Octavian conservatism.

The bus stopped and hissed. I wondered if she was getting off, but she didn't make any moves to. I looked around and tried to see any differentiating characteristics, but other than the name of the town, I couldn't. I read out the name.

"Good!" she said. "You can read Octavian?"

"A little," I said, with feigned Octavian modesty. All Earthlings were assumed to be outrageously arrogant, so I thought I'd counter it.

"Oh," she said. "A little." She sounded disappointed.

I had outsmarted myself.

Fuck modesty. "Well," I said quickly. "All."

"Good!" She was back to her original level of enthusiasm. Then her eyes narrowed slyly. "How about —" and then she said a word with one of the impossible sounds.

I repeated it, using the thumbnail trick to compensate.

I was rewarded by a flash of delight and surprise. She said the Octavian word for *wow*, then said it in English. "Wow!"

I was happy that she wasn't as disturbed by it as Mrs. Ahm had been.

One old guy got on the bus. He was swaying — an obvious ujos victim. He traded some unpleasant words with the bus driver, and even more unpleasantly, crawled into the seat in front and started staring at us.

We sat in awkward silence for a minute. "He is very old and ugly," I said to the girl in English.

She laughed. "You are right."

He muttered something at her, low and nasty. Her expression changed not a whit, her bearing dignified. I was proud of her and I didn't even know her name.

"His breath smells bad."

It took her a second to unravel this, and then she cracked up. She slapped me playfully, her suckers plucking lightly at my wrist as she did so. It was unexpectedly erotic, but it may have had something to do with the fact that it was the first female contact I'd had in months. The old man shook his head again and then turned his disapproving alcohol-soused eyes elsewhere.

I started to wonder if she'd be on the bus all the way to Artemia. I wondered if it'd be too forward of me to buy her a juice at the rest stop. "Where do you go to university?"

She named a nearby town. "Molko. I am studying to be an English teacher. Like you. I get off the bus at next time." She looked at me. "Why do you go to Artemia?"

"I go to meet my friend," again pointlessly stultifying. "At a spaceport."

"Oh! Very exciting!"

Not nearly as exciting as meeting you, I thought. "Yes. My friend is very interesting. He is a roboman."

"Wow!" She started crawling all over me, which was not as nice as it sounds. I tried not to wince as she crawled over my groin to the aisle.

She held out a tentacle and I shook it. "Good to meet you," she said.

"Yes!" I said.

She strapped on her knapsack.

"Maybe some time we could have a drink together," I said.

The bus stopped and she jerked forward a bit. "Yes," she said. "Maybe!"

I locked my smile in place. Wondered as I waved good-bye if I should have asked her a direct question, if I had loused up the entire thing with native speaker vagueness. And how I didn't know her name or a way to contact her and now I couldn't even remember the name of the school she worked at—

The bus started again and my common sense kicked in. If she wanted to have anything to do with me, she wouldn't have any problem finding me. I was the only guy with legs on the entire planet.

I had agreed to meet 9/3 half-way. "Half-way" turned out to be this meteor in the middle of nowhere.

A meteor, I saw from my porthole in the rocketship, that was utterly barren of anything beyond the transfer station. The rounded dome stood out on the pocky skin of the surface like the ugly pimple it was.

Fuck. Why didn't I suggest the Bowling Ball? 9/3 liked that place, and it's just as close.

The rocket thrusters kicked in and we touched down. I booted it so I could get ahead of the Octavians and their platforms. I got into the chamber with the first group, and the Octavian atmosphere was evacuated with no fanfare.

Unfortunately, it was with so little fanfare that I had been breathing in at the time and had a lungful of the old stuff. I choked it out, coughing noisily, but some of the Octavians were also having a hard time. One of them hadn't positioned himself properly above his platform, so he had settled half-on, half-off, a pile of insupportable flesh. I spat out the water, amazed at how little there was for the trouble it caused, and started breathing the brand of air I had been weaned on. My lungs didn't like it. It felt like white fire.

The bay door hissed open and the four or five platforms around me hummed to life, their antigrav units kicking in. The guy who had fallen half-on half-off didn't raise at all, despite the green glow under the platform and his frantic tentacling of the keypad. Before he sped off, the guy beside him told him something that had him up and running before long. He probably had it set to the lighter-grav Octavian atmosphere.

I walked out, the platforms passing me. I didn't blame them for rushing — I wouldn't have wanted to dawdle in a place that made me look like a bag of soup. My muscles were a little sore, so when the guy who was having the problems knocked into my thigh I gave him a more dangerous look than perhaps he deserved.

He apologized in Octavian, pulling his joystick sharply away. His head was on its side, looking anxious, and only the tip of one tentacle moved. He managed to manoeuvre around me.

9/3 was waiting at the exit gate — I could see his head above the crowd. As I got closer, I realized that's all there was to 9/3. His head.

I tried to appear unimpressed. "Hi."

"Hello Sam," 9/3's head said.

"Why no body? The android have a hot date?" I asked.

9/3's head tilted off to one side. "Why do you ask? Did you like it?"

"Uh," I said. "It was OK."

9/3 paused, and then said, "Bodies are too much trouble."

I looked at him curiously. "What do you mean?"

"Where do you want to go?" he asked. We were currently in the flow of traffic, as another chamber emptied.

"Oh, gosh," I drawled, "I don't know! There's just *so many* great places to choose from."

9/3 turned towards a food kiosk. "There are seats over there," he said.

I shrugged and we headed to them. 9/3 didn't care about seats, or even meeting in person — he would have been as happy speaking over the phone. I was the one who needed to get off of Octavia. I was the one with all the demands, so I decided to drop the subject.

It was a Montavian kiosk with a consequently very short robot server. On its tin can body it had stickers in several languages, *Intergalactic food served here!* alongside a baffling icon. Taking it at its word I asked for Earth-style beans and rice, and was met with a cheery blank stare. A second or two later it chirped that it didn't have that, but perhaps I'd like to try the Montavian version of the dish? I sighed and acquiesced.

9/3's head hovered between the stool and table, finally settling on the latter. I reached around it for some salt and after I used it I set it on top of 9/3's head.

"How are you doing without your translator?" asked 9/3.

I responded *not bad* in Octavian.

9/3 laughed. "Ha ha. Your accent is good."

"Really?" I said. Octavians had told me that but I never really believed them.

"Yes. Too bad it's impossible for humans to pronounce all the sounds."

I centered the salt shaker on 9/3's head, so it looked like an antenna. "You're sure about that?"

The server droid came back and gave me some water. It noticed the salt shaker and replaced it on the counter. "Do not abuse the condiments," it said without a trace of cheeriness. "Salt is precious."

"Ha ha." 9/3 said. "I knew that would happen. Salt is a very important commodity on Montavia."

I vaguely remembered some history lessons about salt mine wars on Montavia.

"Try to steal it," said 9/3. The droid wheeled around. "Uh oh. Ha ha ha."

I snickered. "OK, it's kind of dumb, but I can do the two difficult sounds. I was learning this song by an Octavian pop group—" and I did the lines *You catch my hand I will get up, I give you happiness*. (It rhymes in Octavian.)

9/3 processed that. "89% of the population would understand that."

"Really?" I said. Statistics had a way of bolstering my confidence.

"And you use your mouth to make those sounds," 9/3 continued. "So once your vocabulary is large enough you can register as the first offworld speaker of Octavian."

"Huh!" I said, imagining a ceremony involving medals and kisses.

"Of course, there will be repercussions," 9/3 said. "It will change Octavia's cultural status."

"Oh?" I mumbled through a mouthful of food. That sounded complicated.

"At the moment, because the language is believed to be unique, certain cultural activities that would otherwise be illegal are permitted. And some sites are funded by the Earth Council."

I nodded, remembering Mr. Zik saying something about Earth in connection with the giant statue at the Line between water and air. I had dismissed it at the time, assuming that Mr. Zik was mistaken — yeah, right, the selfless Earth Council was giving money away.

"Who is your teacher?" 9/3 asked.

"You're looking at him," I said. "Mr. Zik loaded my pad up with a full tutorial, and I've been working at it most nights. Beats staring at the wall or running up long distance bills."

"Really?" he said. "Your vocabulary base is probably pretty small, then."

I nodded, untruthfully.

"A few memorized phrases," he said, and my pride rankled. "It is just as well. I would have to register you immediately otherwise."

I nodded silently, happy I had kept my mouth shut. With 9/3 I knew that thought and action were near-simultaneous.

Out of the corner of my eye I noticed something way taller than the rest of the Octavians around us. I looked over and saw what I first took to be a humanoid, but then realized it was a pair of glinting steel legs with a glass bubble torso. Inside the bubble was an Octavian.

"Wow!" I said. "Neat!"

9/3 looked over — that is, his head floated up, turned, and set down again. "Yes. They are Squidollian walkers. The bubble is filled with the user's natural atmosphere. A Squidollian visitor had one with a translator built in."

The legs loped on, moving quickly and fairly dexterously. "With English?"

"No." 9/3 said. "I said it was Squidollian. It would be far too expensive for them to mass produce."

"I thought the Squidollians were very prosperous."

"Since the Intergalactic Trade Commission adopted English as the official language, they have been less so. And the copyright fees on translators outside the Earth colonies are deliberately prohibitive."

"Deliberately?" I said.

9/3 snorted, a static buzz. "Of course. In fact, after the war there was an attempt to designate Roboworld as non-English. It would have meant we would have had to pay to speak our native tongue."

"What?!" I said. That was news to me. "That's just xenophobic bullshit! You've got human brains!"

"Yes. It was bullshit." It was funny hearing 9/3 swear. "Once it was proven that the brains that we grew in the biovats were actually more purely human than Earthling brains — statistically, because of your interspecial mixing — the Council dropped their case."

"I never even heard of that," I said, revolted by the profit-mongering. "No wonder robomen hate Earthlings."

"Robomen don't hate Earthlings," he said — I thought out of habit. But then he added. "Many robomen view the Earthling as a little brother who refuses to grow up. Earthlings are even referred to as Little Brothers, in slang. The plans of the Council were not generally known on Roboworld, anyway. My special interest has always been intergalactic relations."

"I thought information was . . . heavily monitored on Roboworld," I said, not wanting to say *censored.*

"All stimulus deigned to be superfluous is restricted," he said in a matter-of-fact way. "When I was not assigned a function, my access to various things was increased."

"Yeah?" I said cautiously. "I always wondered about that. Did you decide to come out here because you didn't have a function, or . . . ?"

"I was sent by Central Authority," 9/3 said. "Robomen do not do things simply for experience, as Earthlings do. As strange as I am among robomen, I would find that purposelessness to be extremely unpleasant."

The stream of Octavians had been replaced by a stream of Montavians, the tiny little men marching in the opposite direction, their little metal boxes swinging from little fists.

"So . . . do you think you were sent because of the relations between the two planets? Montavia and Roboworld?" I didn't want to seem like a total dummy — a total Little Brother — and I knew there was some connection between the two. What was it?

"Perhaps." 9/3 said, watching the stream of munchkins. "The Montavians make the best tools in the galaxy, and we buy exclusively from them."

That was it. Tools.

"I believe I am the first roboman to ever live on Montavia. The children run behind me in the streets."

"Same here," I said, grinning.

"They run with their small toolboxes, and if they catch up they start to disassemble me."

It was funny. It was awful. Awful funny. My face reflected both, simultaneously.

"Ha ha," said 9/3, and I joined him.

I always had a good time with 9/3, as different as we were. It made me think about how narrow my social sphere had been at home. "How old are you, anyway?"

"51 Earth years," said 9/3.

"Man, we're so different," I said. "It's amazing we get along so well."

9/3 paused. "Yes."

The door that I had come out of opened again and released a wave of Octavians into the opposing stream of Montavians. It just looked to be bad timing, because the Montavian wave was nearly finished, but neither group wanted to pause. I immediately tensed up, oddly protective of my prone Octavians in the midst of the pushy munchkins.

Sure enough, one of the Octavians was knocked off his platform and disappeared below my line of vision. None of the Montavians were stopping, and a few seconds later they were all gone. The Octavians, heaps of weak flesh that they were, couldn't help him. I got up and ran.

I slowed to a walk, thinking, *I shouldn't interfere, I don't really know what's going on.* Behind me I could hear an alarm go off at the kiosk and remembered the stolen food in my gut. I started running again, as the chamber door opened and more Octavians came out.

I ignored the alarm and dodged my way to the center of the stream. He had his tentacles on the platform and was attempting to pull himself up, the platform tilting with his effort. He wasn't getting stepped on, as I feared, and I lifted him up — so light! — and set him on his platform. It was a little embarrassing to be cradling an adult, and I could only imagine how he felt.

He turned his head to look at me and said thank-you in Octavian. I told him it wasn't worth thanks (the polite Octavian response) and he took me at my word, speeding off. I escaped the stream with only one minor collision.

I went back to the kiosk where 9/3 waited. "Did you pay?" I asked.

He nodded. "Just in time. The droid was powering up its stunner."

I had been hit by one or two of those in my day. I laughed weakly. "Thanks."

9/3 said, "You reacted very quickly."

I thought about how, back in the old days, I could be asleep when I got the call. Forty-five seconds later I'd be flicking the ignition on my jetpack. Seven minutes after that my boots would hit the ground where the scrap was, and I would be in there cracking jaws no more than a minute later. 0:08:41 was my record.

It was amazing how quickly you could react, when you believed in something strongly enough. Even if that something wasn't worthy of belief.

The kiosk droid came up to me and treated me like a new customer. When I waved it away, still deep in reverie, the stool hissed to the ground. I attempted to sit in another one and it collapsed too. 9/3 laughed, until the droid cleaned the counter and pushed him off. He fell halfway to the ground before his antigrav kicked in.

"Have a nice day," said the droid.

I stood there, arms folded, looking at 9/3's bobbing head.

"And you thought this place was boring," he said.

ELEVEN

I felt a little nervous asking. It was like questioning the floor you're standing on.

"Why did you want to learn English?"

Mr. Kung glanced at Mr. Nekk and poked at an earhole. Mrs. Ahm got that intent look. There was always a pause, and I'd taken to looking out the window in a pensive pose.

It was a tough question, and not just language-wise. I didn't expect Mr. Kung to suddenly realize his whole life had been playing a small part in a colonial conspiracy, and break down crying. I had my own reason for asking. I thought it might give me insight into Jinya, the woman I had met at the bus station. She had called my vidphone when I was on the meteor with 9/3. I had no idea what she wanted — for that matter, I didn't know what I wanted.

"I was . . . skilled at English," said Mr. Nekk. "When I was young, English was very fascinating."

I was again impressed by Nekk's vocabulary. I got up and wrote *fascinating* on the small board. Above it I wrote *very interesting*.

"Fascinating means very interesting," I said. Kung and Ahm nodded, Kung more energetically and untruthfully. "Fascinating," I said in the repeat-after-me voice.

"Fasnating," they said. Nekk didn't repeat, just sat there in a smug way.

"Why did you want to learn English, Mr. Kung?"

"Fasnating, too," he said, continuing his tradition of answer-theft. I idly wished *too* was more difficult to say.

I looked at Mrs. Ahm, who was formulating an answer. I realized I was impatient, that I really hoped to learn something.

"English is very modern. I am a modern woman. I think."

Jinya thinks of herself as a modern woman, probably.

Kung said in Octavian that modern women are good to—

"English!" I snapped.

"Sorry."

"Are modern women strong women?"

Ahm nodded cheerfully. "I think!"

"Are women more interested in English than men?" My eyes wandered back to the window, where a line of students had intertwined their arms to form a long line. Other kids were climbing from one end to the other. Before I could figure out why, Mr. Nekk set his words out in front of me.

"English is very plopular with Octavian women bleecause it is good for teaching. Women teachers are very respected."

I shrugged. "Men teachers, too."

"No," Mr. Nekk said, repeating it to Kung in Octavian. Kung shook his head. "Teaching is the blest job a woman can get," he said. "Blut men can do bletter jobs. Men teachers are not respected."

Kung said *less important than wallens* in Octavian.

"Yes. They mock us," Nekk said, his face bitter. "They say we are no better than the wallens, garbage eaters." Wallens, Mr. Zik had told me, were the little half-shell creatures I had spotted in the alleys of Plangyo.

This was pretty interesting. It made Mr. Nekk's annoying bossiness seem a little desperate, a way of salvaging some dignity — and Mrs. Ahm's cuteness seem a little affected, deliberate.

I looked at her. She nodded. "It is very difficult to be a teacher."

So Jinya was ambitious enough to compete for the best job on the planet. Out the window, the line came around in a circle and tightened until it was a huge pile of kids.

"What are they doing?!" I said.

Kung looked and said a word I didn't know.

"A game," said Mrs. Ahm.

Kung got up, suddenly active. He twisted two of his tentacles together and pulled them. They stretched an unpleasant amount. Then he released them with a cavalcade of pops and his tentacles flew out. Then he pointed at the kids.

I looked at them. I looked back at him.

"Stress," said Mr. Nekk.

"What?" I said, baffled.

Mr. Kung enlisted Mr. Nekk, who tentatively offered up his skinny frame for a demo. I was willing to drop it but obviously Kung wasn't — his eyes were alive.

"Is it like an Earth game? Football?" I said.

"No," Kung said, intertwining arms with Mr. Nekk.

"It is a war test," said Mrs. Ahm. "To practice for war."

Kung waved his arms, whipping around Mr. Nekk until I feared for his spotty gray appendages. Suddenly there was a tearing sound — I was sure it was Nekk getting dismembered, but it was the sound of suction cups popping in a series.

"I win," said Kung, looking at me hopefully. "OK?"

I looked back at the window. Now the line of kids was an undulating snake. I couldn't see any possible relation.

"Oh, I see," I lied.

Kung made a satisfied grunt and sat down. Mr. Nekk just sat down.

I didn't want to bring up the war, but Mrs. Ahm's mention of the game being practice for it tempted me. I hedged a little. "The game is traditional?" I pinched myself for slipping into simplespeak.

"Yes, we stopped the monsters with that game," said Ahm, also entwining her smooth and lovely tentacles.

I suddenly imagined sucking on one of them, suction cup on tongue, sex fantasy shrapnel, and pinched myself again. "Are the monsters," I held back *extinct*, "all dead?"

"On this side of Octavia, yes," she said, a little guarded.

"You are lucky to have so many native species alive," I said. "Dolphins, wallens . . ."

"We love wallens," said Mr. Nekk. The others laughed. It was a little confusing — trash eaters in one breath, and this in the next. Was he actually attempting sarcasm?

"Delicious," said Mr. Kung, fucking up even the simplest English words.

"What do you think?" said Mrs. Ahm, with a funny smile

"About wallens? I think they're cute."

"No," Mr. Nekk corrected. "About Octavian Sokchu tradition."

"I don't know much about Sokchu," I said. Specifically, all I knew about the high holiday was that we got the day off.

"We eat wallens," Mr. Kung said, opening his unpleasant maw and shovelling in imaginary food.

I chuckled a little. "You eat *with* wallens," I corrected, imagining a kind of interspecies banquet that had some kind of history behind it.

"No," said Mrs. Ahm.

I looked at Mr. Nekk. "We kill them. We cook them. We eat them," he clarified.

"Oh," I said, my head spinning a little. "Well."

I looked out the window, but there were no students to distract me. I tried desperately to think of anything other than their little bodies piled up on a platter, tails hanging dead over the edge.

"It is very . . . shocking?" Mrs. Ahm said, her eyes shining, it seemed to me, psychotically.

"Yes." I said, the stun wearing off and anger rising. "It is disgusting. I think."

Mrs. Ahm's eyes dropped.

Mr. Nekk looked at me, coolly. "It is an Octavian tradition."

"It is not very modern," admitted Mrs. Ahm with a shrug.

Yes, I thought. *Eating smaller and stupider species than you because you can wouldn't be in the "modern" category.* I thought about Kung's delicious comment and felt my hands curl up in that familiar way. *They want to be savage? Let's be savage, then . . .*

I thought about Jinya's tentacles tearing apart flesh and chewing it, and was overcome by a sick tiredness.

"The wallens were the allies of the monsters, who killed many Octavians. Millions. Sokchu is our day of freedom."

I checked the time. Still a lot left. I didn't want to talk about it. I didn't want to hear about the history right now, though I was interested, because hearing about how clever their generals were would give me an even worse case of moral indigestion.

Oh, how righteous you are. What's a little flesh-eating in the face of Earth's past? At least they're just eating them, not suffocating them slowly with an alien culture.

The seconds ticked on and nothing was coming to me. My growing embarrassment struggled to stifle my outrage, and, despite outrage being a weightier opponent, embarrassment won. I was surprised, but the brain's a funny ol' bean.

"Um, so," I said. "Mr. Kung, what are you doing this weekend," I asked. I already knew the answer, so I challenged myself by thinking up responses in Octavian.

"I go drinky," he said with a small laugh.

"*Me too. I go to an offworlder party.*" Where I hoped to meet people who didn't eat other people, I thought grimly.

They made appropriate surprised noises at my Octavian. Mr. Nekk made a correction and I thanked him, calling him teacher. It had the impossible pop sound.

Mr. Nekk was shocked. He spoke very quickly to Mrs. Ahm, who basically said *I told you so.*

"I. . .it is not real. . .language," Nekk floundered, his vocab coming up short.

"It's a trick," I admitted.

"Trick, yes," said Mr. Nekk. "Not real." He seemed to be saying it to himself more than me.

I was gratified to have unsettled him, but a little annoyed at myself. I had been keeping my proficiency kind of a secret — it let me eavesdrop easily, for one. And I still hadn't decided whether I wanted to find out whether, officially, my tricks were real or not.

Mr. Kung continued, having not really followed the rest. "And I go to Artemia."

I looked at him and he was beaming, a childishly sly look on his face.

I had had enough.

"Your second wife lives in Artemia," I said slowly. "Are you going to have sex with her?"

His grin dropped so suddenly I swore I heard it thud. He looked at his two colleagues, who averted their eyes.

Class ended early that day.

"We also have some hot mulled wine," the hostess said.

"Oh, I'll have that," I said happily.

"I'll take a beer," said Matthew, sneering at me.

9/3 said nothing, looking around the kitchen. He realized the woman was looking at him and watched her until her smile started to wilt.

"The wine sounds nice," said Hugh, and her smile strengthened again with that.

She busied herself and we all stood around her kitchen, looking stupid. Matthew folded his arms, tilted back to look at 9/3's ass. 9/3 spoke.

"Your decorations are quite tasteful," he said.

The hostess beamed. Hugh beamed too, for some reason. She gave us our drinks and waved us towards the rest of the party, such as it was. At the moment it consisted of us and the husband and wife who lived here.

"Let us take-a-seat," I said, when the husband followed his wife into the kitchen. I realized too late that I was still speaking slowly and put my head in my hands.

Matthew, naturally, couldn't leave it alone. "Oh Kay Tee Cha."

"IguessIcantalkasfastasIlikewithyoujerks," I said.

Matthew cupped his ear. "Uh . . . can you repeat?"

We sat down on the couch, 9/3's female android body's legs crossing smoothly. I wondered if he had practiced that.

"I hate this first-nerds-at-the-party thing," griped Matthew.

"I scheduled the trip so as to allow for a one hour margin of error," 9/3 responded.

" 'Margin of error,' " snorted Matthew. "Whattaya gotta talk like a machine for if you've got a human brain? Or that is, you claim to have a human brain," he wisecracked, taking a swig of beer and staring at 9/3's (admittedly fabulous) breasts.

Hugh's nostrils flared. 9/3 started scratching the back of his head, which was unusual.

They didn't seem ready to deal with Matthew's obnoxiousness, so I took up the slack. "Ah, shaddap. You were the one who—" I started.

"Whatever, wineboy. Enjoy your delicate bouquet," Matthew said, waving his hand and looking towards the door.

I was, actually, quite enjoying the cinnamonny drink. The steam curled and twined towards the ceiling like a ghost's DNA chain. I hadn't seen steam for months.

I heard the hinge squeak open but I didn't look until 9/3 said, "Matthew."

Matthew, focused on sucking all the yeasty goodness from his bottle of Neb Beer, eventually looked over.

9/3's head swivelled right around so that we could see that he had opened a hatch in the back. The top half of 9/3's head was a glassed-in box, within which was an unmistakably human brain.

"Aw, shit," said Matthew, looking away.

I stared. When was the next time I was going to get to look inside a roboman's head? The lower half of the head was packed with multi-colored wires. And through the glass box they led into, I could see the glowing lights I knew to be 9/3's eyes.

He spun his head around and looked at Matthew. 9/3's laughter had an echoey hollowness that disappeared when he clicked his panel shut.

"It's so *big*," said Hugh, with a strange look on his face.

9/3 shrugged. "It has the same mass as an average human brain. There is slight swelling due to the wire implants. Of course, it is much bigger than Matthew's, because of the amount of cells he has killed with beer. Ha ha."

We all laughed at this, and it was good timing because the hostess was just answering the door.

So it sounded like a little bit of a party, anyway, when the three people came in. Two guys and one, much to my surprise, rather pretty Earthling. While the hostess fussed over them, I muttered *now we're cookin' with gas* to Matthew and got an *Amen, brother* back.

She made a beeline for Hugh, naturally.

"Are you Hugh?" she asked.

"Why, yes," he said, looking mildly surprised.

"Introducing the galaxy-renowned Hugh Davidson!" said Matthew, rolling his eyes, as pissed as me.

"We're from the same planet!" she said excitedly.

He seemed to push back into the couch. "You're Christina?"

She nodded. He smiled weakly.

"You're from the moon?" said Matthew, insultingly dubious. She was attractive, sure, but it wasn't the kind of delicate-creature-beauty one found in female lunarians.

She shook her head.

"Christina teaches the Unarmored," said Hugh.

Ah.

"Hugh teaches the Armored," said Christina to one of her companions, a perfectly white bullethead android. He made a gesture with his shoulder too delicate to be called *shrug,* and said in a soft, cultured voice, "My condolences."

Hugh gaped.

"Sid is one of my students," she said. "He's riding an android for the night." I liked the way that she put that, disliked the way she patted the android's shoulder.

"Being a cloud of nerve endings," he pronounced, "does not suit travel."

"So what's it like, teaching the Armored?" she asked, sitting down.

I rose immediately and walked into the kitchen. I didn't want to hear Hugh answer that any more than I would want to watch him walk over broken glass.

Our two hosts were sitting at the table together, chatting happily. They sprung up as I entered, guilty in their solitude.

"Thanks so much for inviting us all," I said.

"Oh, it's our pleasure," she said, him nodding along. He was a stocky Earthling with short gray hair on a lumpy head.

"Do you entertain much?" I probed.

She looked at her husband. "A few times a year. It gets lonely out here."

I nodded. It had been a bit of a walk from the rocket we had rented, and we had remarked on the bleakness as we crunched our way, fully spacesuited, to the domehome.

"This is really good wine," I exaggerated. She immediately lifted the angular carafe and filled my glass. "Cinnamonny. And you worked on Squidollia last year?"

"Yes, for the last two years actually. We liked it there." She looked at her husband, who nodded confirmation. "We met Matthew when we went back to visit."

"Kids like him," the husband said, grinning unjealously.

"Young teachers very good," I said, and they chuckled.

I admired the steam from my wine again, relishing its ephemeral ascent. "Did you —" I started tentatively. "I mean, living on Squidollia, it's got the same water atmosphere as Octavia, did you find you missed the steam?"

They smiled. "It's the little things you miss," he clichéd, but somehow it was a considered, even wise, thing coming from his well-worn face.

She said, "Now I miss the feeling of waking up in the morning in Squidollia, and the shock and panic that gives way to the realization of where you are, why you're breathing water, that you're going to live after all."

"That happens to me, too!" I said. "I thought I was just a novice."

"It's hard to beat the survival instinct," he said. "Kathy woke up with a start every day we were there."

"Oh, but it certainly gets you awake," she said.

I grinned. "Beats an alarm clock."

They laughed. His was a hearty one I liked instantly. I liked them both, actually, and it felt mutual. It was odd, because I would never have met them back home, two twice-my-age geezers with no shiny attributes. Now I was so happy to talk with them I felt drugged.

But maybe it was the wine.

The other guy who came in with the Unarmored andy and the Earthling entered the kitchen and put some bottles in the fridge.

"Still on that yak milk, eh Ewen?" said the host.

"Yep," said Ewen, leaving the kitchen without making eye contact.

Sparkling conversationalist, I thought. "Is he a teacher?" I asked.

She nodded. "Yes. He started with us. Odd boy. Think he might be sweet on the girl in the overalls."

"Lucky her," snorted the host.

"Ewen's a bit . . . socially challenged," she said. "Came out here when we did. We figure he likes teaching because no one really notices what an oddbod he is."

I nodded. "Yeah, there were a few strange ones in our bunch too. Kind of a last chance thing."

"He teaches Cottellians. He actually volunteered for a second year with *Cottellians,*" the host said, his voice low amazement. It *was* hard to imagine choosing the dim-witted puffballs out of the whole galaxy of species.

"John figures he's found a way to copulate with them," Kathy whispered, covering her mouth with a hand.

"You can't imagine there's a lot of interesting conversationalists there," I said. "Maybe that's what he likes, though."

"I can only assume that's the case," said Kathy. "Not the most challenging of teaching positions. Unlike John here, getting quizzed by his students on vocabulary and grammar."

John nodded. "And frankly, I had to fake it on the grammar. My grammar, when I write something, is fine, but it's totally intuitive — I can't explain *why* I do something."

"So are you a writer?" I asked, finishing my wine and setting the glass down. "Is that what you do with your days out here?"

"Well, I'm writing the audio for a video game triptych," he said. "Nothing terribly interesting, I'm afraid. A friend of mine wrote the game, and Kathy's sculpting the objects for it."

"Wow, that sounds really hand-crafted," I said, impressed. I had never heard of anyone generating a game bit-by-bit.

"Hi," said the girl with the overalls. "Which way to the yak milk?" Her body tilted with the question, a contrived movement I found annoying and sexy.

She was directed to the fridge, where she fetched a bottle for herself. She fiddled with the cap in anxious fingers, a nervous type, but not moving towards the door. She reminded me of Lisa, somehow.

"You remind me of my friend, somehow," I said, the wine having weakened the artificial boundary between thinking and verbalizing.

"I find that the longer I'm away, the more likely that anyone human reminds me of someone on Earth," she said.

"What part?" I said too abruptly, feeling like a junkie. "What part are you from?"

"Chicagotown," she said.

"Toronto," I said. "We're practically neighbors!"

I basked in the warm glow of fellow Earthlings and wine and repressed an urge to ask John and Kathy where they were from. Why not save it for another time?

There was a silence and Christina took a healthy swig of the unhealthy liquor. "Your friend, Hugh," she started, "isn't the happiest of guys, is he."

"Well," I said, shrugging, "he's upset that he didn't get to be with the Unarmored," I said to all three listeners.

"Yeah," she said, a distant look in her eyes. "I just thought it would be interesting," she said. "I didn't know there would be other applicants."

"It's not your fault," I said, with a broader grin than applied. The impact of the wine was making me think of an Octavian folk rhyme: *Oh trickster wine/ you make my tentacles flail/ you make me fall on my head.*

I wondered what it would be like to visit the Unarmored world on weekends, what her overalls would look like all bunched up beside the bed.

"You have a lovely kitchen," said Christina, apparently on an entirely different wavelength. "The instafood oven must save time."

"Oh, it's very convenient. We had one on Squidollia and now I can't imagine life without it," Kathy said, patting it fondly.

John walked over to the wall panel and poked a few buttons. A buzzing started from overhead. The lights dimmed. "Wait 'til you get a load of this," he said. "Those ceiling panels? They're actually Opaque-tastic Glass." The buzzing stopped. He punched another button, and the glass cleared like a mist.

And we could see the stars. I tilted my head back. After a few seconds, I could see the pattern of an attacking dwarf.

"Wow," said Christina, "isn't that something."

I saw a constellation that looked like a saucer. "Yeah." I look a deep breath, thinking about being in a dome in the middle of nowhere under these twinkling drops, with nice and interesting folk, people who didn't eat people smaller than themselves. I let my breath out.

After a few minutes the Unarmored and Hugh came in together. They looked at the stars with us for a minute, but then resumed their conversation.

"Ideas are artificial, at a basic level," murmured the Unarmored guy, tilting his bullethead.

"That's exactly it, exactly," said Hugh.

It wasn't so much the pretentious drivel but the way it immediately captured Christina's attention that made me leave the room.

9/3 and Matthew were still on the couch. Matthew had his back to me, turned around and speaking intently to the roboman.

"Why not?" Matthew said.

"Why not what?" I asked, sitting down.

Matthew's head swung in my direction. He had a funny grin, and he took a swig of beer. He slowly sat back. 9/3 sat there, his pretty arms crossed and his eyelights unreadable.

I waited. Matthew shrugged and tilted the bottle back again.

I leaned forward. "Did he . . . ask to have sex with you, 9/3?"

"No!" yelled Matthew, his face painted scandal scarlet. "Come on!"

I leaned back, relaxed. "What was it, then?"

"I just wanted to see his tits," said Matthew.

I stared at Matthew, amazed. He kept defiantly meeting my eyes and looking away. 9/3 remained silent. How would he feel about that?

I swallowed the bitter dregs of my wine. The door opened and two guys walked in with a case of Neb beer.

"Kitchen's in there," Matthew said, chinning towards it. "Neb drinkers welcome."

"Thanks, man."

"Robomen don't . . ." I started, shaking my head, "You trying to get him declared defective?"

"Oh, shut up," said Matthew, rolling his eyes.

"Maybe I am defective already," said 9/3.

I need another drink. I got up and went to the kitchen. Hugh and the Unarmored guy were ensconced in the corner, Christina was getting talked at by one of the guys who had just come in. Kathy took my cup right away and as I was waiting for it back I noticed something familiar about the way that Hugh was leaning in and touching the Unarmored's hand. It was the same way he had been with 9/3 at the Octavian bar a few weeks ago, before Matthew and I left on his quest for whores.

Maybe I am defective already.

Kathy passed me a full cup. "Sam here works on Octavia," she said to the man who'd come in with the case of beer.

"Is that right? Just stopped off there myself. Quaint little place," he said, with a knowing grin I disliked immediately.

TWELVE

"He was rude," I said to Mr. Zik a few days later.

"Was he from Earth?" Mr. Zik asked. "Earthlings are very plolite."

"I don't know if he was," I said. "But he was stupid," tapping my head with a scowl, "and too loud."

"Not normal Earthling, I think," said Mr. Zik. "More bleer?"

I consented.

He called out to her as she passed. She stopped, most of her tentacles laden with platters, and continued on after giving me the once-over.

She was young and pretty by Plangyo standards, and the restaurant was flashier than the one Kung took me to, but not entirely Earthified. True, the place did have an English name ("The House") but the pictures on the walls were of Octavians rather than offworlders.

The waitress came by and dropped a bladder of beer on the table. I snatched it up and squeezed out a glass for Mr. Zik.

"You know how to use the old-fashioned style?" he said, after thanking me.

"Of course," I said. "*I am an Octavian.*" We laughed at that.

It had taken a few tries to get it to work, but the plastic bags of beer — or any liquid — made more sense, and not just due to the liquid atmosphere. All you had to see was one Octavian struggling to lift a pitcher with a handle made for human hands to show you that.

But in big, modern cities like Artemia, more restaurants used pitchers than didn't. It was infuriating.

"One of the rude offworlders told me that there was a special restaurant in Artemia that used forks." I didn't care to add that he had gone on to imitate the trouble his fellow diners had had. Only on an alien planet could you be proud of speaking your native tongue and knowing how to use a fucking fork!

"Very strange," said Mr. Zik. "Is he . . . was he visiting Octavia?"

"Yes, for a week." And for that he felt like he was an authority on all things Octavian. "He was making fun of — do you know 'making fun'?"

Mr. Zik's pale yellow eyes wandered. "Like a good time?"

"No . . . uh . . . mocking," I said, unable to think of anything simpler, though *defaming* and *ridiculing* popped uselessly into my head.

"Yes, mocking. He was mocking you?" Mr. Zik inquired, deftly rolling the bladder into his tentacle and squeezing me another glass.

"No," I said. "He was mocking Octavians. I wanted to punch him." Luckily Matthew had seen the needle on my aggrometer and had dragged us out of there. 9/3 had come with us, after asking Hugh if he was coming. Hugh stayed.

Mr. Zik blinked.

"Punch," I said, throwing one slowly into space.

"Ah yes," said Mr. Zik. "Earth-style fighting."

I nodded. Octavian fighting was, naturally, more fluid.

"But . . . it is very old fashioned?"

I thought about getting into the whole history of the pug movement, how it sprang up in opposition to the prohibitively expensive and ineffective vengeance vendors — then how I'd have to explain how the vendors got that way . . . I looked at Mr. Zik's smiling, slightly drunk face and changed the subject.

"You are working very hard these days," I said. Mr. Zik had been making charts, adding up rows of numbers, and rushing back and forth between his desk and the principal's office. I hadn't wanted to disturb him, so I kept to my letter writing. "Are you done now?"

"Yes," he said. "That's why . . ." he pointed to the glass, "drinky."

"Oh, that's why we're *drinking*," I corrected. It was fine for Kung to sound childish, but Mr. Zik deserved better.

"It is my job to send the marks to the high schools," he said.

"Why is it *your* job?" I asked, automatically defensive for him.

"Every teacher has an extra job. Some stay on the weekend to guard the school. Mr. Ent does the schedule."

Of course, I had no extra duties. I was also spared having to give out grades. I was spared a lot of things, I thought guiltily, then I remembered the gym teacher and my temper flared.

"What about Mr. Blok?" I said, thinking about his indolent strolls through the staffroom, his stupid-but-well-received jokes. He never seemed to be busy. "Is it his job to annoy the teachers?"

"Annoy? Ssss-sss-ss," Mr. Zik said. "No. He is to discipline the blad students."

My mood darkened. On the few occasions I had stayed after school I had seen it in progress, this "discipline." A student would have all eight appendages stretched out at once, secured in what looked to be a painful position. I didn't know for sure — I didn't know Octavian physiology to know what was painful, but I know it well enough to know that the position left the sex organs exposed. They were usually crying, either from the pain or the embarrassment, as Blok's reedy whip of a voice came down again and again. "*Worthless! Shame to your parents! Lazy! Shame to Octavia!*"

"I hate Blok," I said.

Mr. Zik looked alarmed. "Mr. Blok is your blig brother."

I shrugged. Mr. Zik was watching me, worry plain on his face. There was no point in pursuing it. It went too deep.

"Shall we go . . . another place?"

"Sure," I said. We got up and before I could get my hand in my pocket Mr. Zik had paid for it, passing the beeds to the young waitress. It could have been a sensuous act — the sliding of tentacles certainly looked so to me, in my tipsy state, except that the waitress was looking in another direction and calling out an order to the kitchen as she did it.

"Thanks," I said.

"Don't mention it," said Mr. Zik, grinning like he meant it.

"Wow, we're drunken," I said.

"Yes," Mr. Zik said. "I must go to washroom."

"Me too," I said.

On our way there, I ignored my general principles against humanization and prayed for Earth-style toilets. I needed to take a shit and it wasn't something I was very good at.

I opened the stall door on the wall-toilet and did my business. (I remain vague because no matter how strongly people press for details — in the name of cultural edification, naturally — I am invariably stopped before I get a full sentence out.) Mr. Zik was gratefully not one of those males who need to talk while in the john, and waited patiently outside the door.

"Every time I use an Octavian-style toilet," I said, as we left the restaurant, "I am more grateful for you giving me an Earth toilet."

"Ssss-sss-ss," said Mr. Zik. "No, is not me, is the school bloard . . ."

I cut him off with a shake of my head.

Outside, it was cool and dark. It felt like a different season than the one I had arrived in. I started thinking about the fact that planets with different orbits and species with different sleeping patterns had had to conform to Earth time. Usually, it made me mad, but tonight it made me almost teary.

We walked along the street. A lot of the places were closed, one of the places was selling human dolls. Everything's the same. Earth has bullied everyone into being like it. I felt like I had come here to bear witness to the fact that Earth was everywhere, and what was more, Earth was *welcomed* into the houses of —

"Shall we go sing-song room?" asked Mr. Zik.

I looked at him. He was smiling as if he had asked nothing untoward, a normal suggestion for a night on the town. My mood neatly inverted from crashbound into soaring. "*Tremendously marvellous,*" I said in Octavian.

We swung into the sing-song room on a cloud of joy. (My jubilation at Octavia's unassailable alienness was amplified by the alcohol as much as my prior misery had been.) Mr. Zik booked a room, and a young boy escorted us there, looking askance at me. It was a small room with two or three places to sit — I wondered if there were smaller rooms, perhaps a stall, for just one songster. He stared at me until Mr. Zik closed the door on his slack-jawed gaze.

I was disappointed at the selection. "No Intergalactic Cool Youth," I complained.

"Your favorite pop group," said Mr. Zik with a smile, removing the microphone. "My daughter, too."

"You have to sing, first. Your favorite song."

Mr. Zik nodded. He sped through the selection and chose something from the Traditional section. He made a few adjustments at once on the panel, obscure level changing that showed a casual expertise. The first twangs of the song started. "It is very old," he said apologetically.

"Good," I said fiercely, "I hate *modern.*"

He looked at me with the perplexed fondness that characterized our relationship.

Then he started to sing, slowly enough so that I was able to translate.

Bubbles over Plangyo
Where did you go?
When you were here before
You promised us more

I have mentioned Zik's sunken face and thin lips. He wasn't handsome, by his world's standards — never mind ours. I had never seen him sing before, but I would have imagined it would have been a reflection of his shy speech. It was not.

The dish is empty of food
Our hearts have drained
Beyond this life
What is there?

I sat there, glad I had not sung "my favorite song" first. It would have been insulting. Between verses, Zik looked into middlespace as if he was adding it all up in his head.

> *Hopes for our minds*
> *Dreams for our spirit*
> *Food for our body*
> *Bubbles over Plangyo*

As the last few plaintive twangs faded away, Mr. Zik came back, slowly.

"That's a very beautiful, sad, song," I said. "You sing it very well."

"Thank you," said Mr. Zik, "I am not a good singer."

"Why is it your favorite song?" I asked for lack of being able to articulate, unable to take my eyes away from his face.

"It is a very famous song," he said, looking at the microphone in his tentacle. "During the war with the dolphins, there was a battle near to this place. The soldiers who were not killed saw the blubbles from far away, and they came to here."

"They thought the bubbles meant that there were people here."

"Yes, but there were no pleeple here. Very sad story."

What happened to the soldiers didn't interest me particularly. But why Mr. Zik was so moved and transformed by this song did. Was this a moment of indulgent melancholy or a peek beyond his social facade? Was he, at his heart, a sad man? I felt unreasonably close to him.

He offered the microphone. I took it, reluctantly. "They do not have my real favorite songs."

"Yes, only plopular songs, I know," said Mr. Zik, forgiving me.

I looked at the selection. I searched for just one song in English that wasn't about rocketships or girls. The bouncy "Got me a Saucer (but I ain't got you)" almost tempted me, but it was like using belchy cola to chase a bittersweet liquor.

"Stupid songs," I said into the mike.

"Shall we go?" asked Mr. Zik.

I nodded.

I walked Mr. Zik to the bus station. He stepped into a phone booth and spoke to a blurry image I assumed was his wife. He always called his wife. I wondered what their courting had been like. Had he sung to her?

We went to the same bench I had met Jinya at. I sat in the exact same place. "I met a girl here," I said, immediately a little embarrassed at my outburst.

Mr. Zik nodded politely, but made no inquiries. A comment like that made on Earth would obviously mean *I met an attractive female on whom I've placed unreasonable hopes. Will you ask me about her so I can revel in delusional fantasies?* But Mr. Zik was completely unaware of that, for Earth can sell her music and language and entertainment, but some of the neurotic nuances were lost amongst the stars.

I thought about that, a grin pasted on my face, and leaned back on the bench. Mr. Zik took out a chew of tobacco and looked towards the road.

Mrs. Pling and I walked up the ramp to the second floor. It was a test day.

She had to wait for me at the top. "You tired?" she asked.

I nodded. I started to tell her why in Octavian, but noticed the half-dozen curious students listening in on their way by, so I tried in English. "Mr. Zik and I went drinking."

She looked blankly at me.

I mimed it.

"Ah, drinky," she said, and laughed. "Ujos?"

"No. Much beer," I said, rubbing my head.

"When too much drinky, we say," she switched to Octavian, *"The movie is stopped."*

I thought I misunderstood, but then I realized she was describing passing out. "In English, we say a blackout."

"My husband, blackout, all the time," she said with an unconcerned laugh.

"Oh," I said, as we walked into the classroom. *In English, we say* alcoholic.

The class met my unexpected appearance with the usual stunned mayhem. I smiled and stood there, watching them settle down, which they did with unusual speed.

Two kids were still standing and Mrs. Pling wrapped a tentacle around each of their necks and tightened. One she actually picked up and slammed into her seat. The other one she dragged to the front and released a torrent of abuse on. Then he was sent back to his seat with a stinging slap to the head.

The rows were silent and attentive, and Mrs. Pling surveyed them sourly for a moment. She called out for the leader of the class, and a tall boy sprang up. *"Why do you shame me in front of a junior teacher?"* she yelled in Octavian. His head drooped *"You are a bad leader,"* she said.

"I am very sorry," he said, genuine misery on his face.

I stood there feeling slightly ill. How much of this was my fault, caused by my presence? How did she change so quickly, from giggling at me for showing up to work hungover, to this?

Mrs. Pling punched a few buttons and the test started. I strolled around, watching them choose answers to multiple choice biology questions. One girl looked back anxiously at me as I peered at the diagram of an Octavian. Ah, so the sex organs *were* located where the tentacles met! I started thinking about Jinya, and our date tonight, when Mrs. Pling pulled my sleeve.

I tensed up, worried that I was going to get a smack, but she was all smiles. "Go to black," she said, pointing to the back of the classroom.

I nodded, pleased for any direction.

"Junior teacher go there," she added, by way of explanation.

I failed to keep the scowl from my lips. I got to the back, swivelled, and looked anywhere but towards Mrs. Pling. I didn't believe she did it on purpose, out of spite. It was this goddamned Octavian hierarchy that seemed to be soaked into everything, slapping everything into order.

It wasn't that I minded being told what to do, it was more the feeling that I was expected, as an inferior, to do it unquestioningly.

I looked at Mrs. Pling now, moving proudly down the rows, a handsome woman despite her age, and tried to imagine what she'd be like confronted with an abusive, irrational drunk husband who dragged her out of bed after midnight demanding food to be made for him. Would she submit grimly? Would she be jokey and good humored? I couldn't guess.

The girl beside me sighed and put her test down. I recognized her from one of my English classes — her misshapen boulder of a head and her profoundly stupid gaze made her quite memorable. I had yet to get her to say anything in English, but I still liked her.

Once, out on a walk through Plangyo, I had passed her and two older black-eyed folks I took to be her parents, resting from cucumber picking. Despite my smile, they had stared and said nothing, three silent lumps. I had been feeling particularly lonely that day, and this almost pushed me to flat-out misery.

Then the little girl remarked in Octavian: *He is my English teacher. He is a very nice man. He doesn't let the boys hit me.*

I didn't look back, because I wasn't supposed to understand. I couldn't help grinning, though. The stupid girl, so stupid she didn't know to smile when someone she liked walked by, justified all my hours of studies. More than anything else that happened, this was my real reward.

So obviously I didn't want her to quit a test ten minutes in. I tapped her pad questioningly. She glanced up slowly, with a goofy smile, then quickly back down. I didn't know how to say *pick answers at random* in Octavian.

I walked away, guessing it wasn't the first or last time she'd flunk a test. By this time another boy actually finished his test. I knew him, too, from my classes — he was one of the best students. His English handwriting was better than mine. He looked at me and winked. There was something annoying about that, but I winked back. He called up a comic book on his recorder-pad and started reading.

He was destined for university, maybe even in Artemia. She would be a cucumber farmer, if she didn't kill herself in the machinery. I wondered how they felt about each other, or if they thought about each other at all.

"English comic blook," Smarty-Pants said, showing me soldiers with projectile weapons and shields. "war comics."

"Good," I said, glancing at Mrs. Pling to make sure that speaking wasn't inappropriate junior teacher behavior. She smiled back.

Judging by the amount of brow-crunching and frowning, it was a fairly hard test — time was going quickly for them. For me, though, time had stopped. All I had to do was walk around and look official. I wasn't concerned with catching people cheating, which may have been a welcome distraction.

I was at a bad angle, so I couldn't see what the stupid girl was doing at first. I knew something was going on because I could see her boulder-head moving from side to side. I strolled to a better vantage point and saw that she had two painted rocks curled in her small tentacles. She was moving them up and down, closer and further away. What the hell was she doing?

I tried not to move or draw attention to myself since I was sure she would stop what she was doing as soon as she saw I was watching. I looked at her face, and saw her lips moving occasionally, moving the rocks at the—

Oh, I see. She's playing. The stones are little wallens or whatever.

I felt really dumb.

I looked up and realized Mrs. Pling saw her too. But instead of throttling her, she just looked away. Mrs. Pling was sad, I realized, and I wanted to tell her that it was OK, not everyone has to ace the test, not everyone has to succeed. But I suspected she would look at me as if I was speaking a foreign language.

�🪐

Hey Lisa,

Sorry it's been so long since the last letter. I've been trying *not* to write, actually, since I thought it might force me to live in the *now*. But earlier today we had a "special lunch," and I don't *want* to be a part of the now, or on Octavia at all. . .

We had flesh for lunch. There's a small creature that lives on Octavia who, due to some old war grudge, is beaten to death (because the terror makes it more delicious, I am told) and cooked and eaten on certain holidays. And because I am a special guest they tried to give me an extra large serving. When I refused, I couldn't keep the revulsion off of my face, and I felt like I was criticising the entire culture. Mr. Zik, my co-teacher and guardian angel, looked miserable.

Mulla mulla mulla.

So I'm glad to hear that you've decided to oppose the renovation of Minnora. At least one of us can do something — I feel completely powerless here, that anything I say or do is completely negated by my being an ignorant offworlder. "Renovating a planet" is just powerbroker-speak for making it economically compatible with Earth — it doesn't seem nearly as ruthless when it's done by remote control. I've seen my Mom bring down native governments during breakfast, and then express concern that I'm not eating well enough.

Unfortunately, I don't have any contacts you can use. Maybe someday I'll be able to stomach it for the length of time it would take to insinuate myself deep enough to do some damage, but don't hold your breath.

Your second question: I would stay the hell away from Skaggs, and you know why.

My romantic prospects are, on the other hand, much better. Remember your prediction that I'd come back with an Octavian wife? It may yet come true. I've got a date tonight with a lovely, lovely silver-eyed young lady with the finest set of tentacles in the sector. So here's the story:

I met her in the local bus station. We talked a little — her English was really good. I never expected her to call, but she did. She actually tracked me down. The first time I wasn't in and she left a cryptic message saying that she "had so much to talk to me about." The second time, I was just doing some studying — I think I may be up to the proficiency of a five year old! — and I answered, assuming it'd be a wrong number. (I get them often enough to know the Octavian for "You've made a vidphone mistake.")

When her face coalesced before me, I swear, there was a joy shock-bomb in my chest. Her face went from unsure to a smile in nervous gradients. And she did, in fact, have a lot to talk to me about. The conversation was easier, in that sense, than it would have been with a reluctant Earthling.

Most of the questions were about Earth. The best thing was when she asked how many kids, on average, Earthling families have. "One-and-a-half," I answered. Then, on a whim, I added, "One has no legs." There was a second, and then she laughed! She *laughed*, Lisa! It was a pretty lame joke, I know, but nothing beyond slapstick had worked until then. The humor barrier has been broken! I repeat, ladies and gentlemen, the humor barrier has been broken!

So I have hope for this. And my hope, as well as being a bright and shining thing, has also a sticky and glistening side. In other words, I am also harboring evil lusty thoughts. At one point, we discussed the biological complexity of a liaison between human and Octavian, as to whether or not the rumors were true or just another archaic half-truth perpetrated by exotic erotica. I recall, as I am sure you do, my blowing it off at the time — it was hard to imagine being intimate with someone who I couldn't banter with.

But now, things have changed. I have found myself peering fruitlessly at the diagrams on my student's biology tests. I could, of course, do a search myself, but I'm worried about being monitored.

Since you're interested in all things pervy anyway, I figured I'd ask you to confirm or deny. Can a human and Octavian go at it?

My future is in your hands,
Sam.

An Octavian female stood before us, a small planet emerging from beneath her tentacles.

"She is making birth," said Jinya.

"It looks very painful," I said.

She laughed and hit me. "No! Is not real. She . . . is mother to Octavia . . . all Octavia."

I nodded and we wandered on to the next sculpture. It was a wallen playing with a dolphin.

"Enemy," she said, poking a tentacle at it.

I looked at the dolphin at different angles, trying to divine an element of evil to it. Nothing, not even big teeth, just that half-grin that humans once found so appealing.

"Many young people come here with their sweethearts," she said matter-of-factly.

"Oh," I said, unable to tell if that was a hint. She had suggested we come to the sculpture garden near her university dorm, and I had agreed to it — I would have agreed to anything. This was admittedly better than just anything, a public park with pretty cool sculptures: my first exposure to Octavian art.

The garden was an obviously good choice for a date. There were lots of opportunities for side glances, and the sea vegetal brush provided enough concealment for a brief touch or even a quick kiss.

She was wearing an Earth-style frock that I found really sexy — maybe because I was used to seeing people wear pants with it. It had a pocket in the front between small breasts that I just wanted to rub and push and rub.

We stopped in front of a blob with a square cut into it, me behind her. I glanced at the sculpture for a second and then looked at the back of her head, neck, shoulders. I was fascinated most by the wave of her crest flowing down the back of her head, how much the delicate ridges looked like hair. I imagined tracing a wide ridge with the pad of my smallest finger — would she shrink from my suctionless caress?

"Stupid," she said, whipping around and catching me not looking at the sculpture. She smiled a small smile with downcast eyes, and her tentacles rose to cover her neck. "I don't like that sculpture."

"Me too," I said.

Her tentacles slipped down eventually, as did my embarrassment. As they slipped past her pocket, she stopped suddenly.

"*My wallet is gone*," she said in Octavian.

I made concerned noises and expressions. We went over to a bench and sat down.

"Yes," she said, with calm resignation. "I think it is stole."

Octavian pickpockets were notoriously good, for obvious reasons.

She made an *oh well* shrug with a smile, then stood up. "Let's go!"

We walked to the next sculpture. I couldn't help but grin. "You have a very good attitude, I think," I said. "Most people would be very unhappy." I mimicked crying, and she laughed.

"No," she said. "It is stupid. Maybe I will get it back." She spotted something down the way. "Oh! Sam, come on. Hurry up. It is my favorite one." Her tentacle swung out and wrapped around my arm, right up to my armpit. I squeezed it gently as she pulled me along, mad grinning. The tip of her tentacle twitched and tickled like crazy, and her with no possible clue she was tickling me.

THIRTEEN

"Where do you want to go?" the Octavian travel agent asked.

The client said, "I want to go to Earth."

"Oh, very good," said the agent, her head bobbing in enthusiasm. "The Earth is good cost now." (I wrote down: Earth fares are low now.)

"That's great!" said the client, her incredible nervousness making the lilt to her voice more manic than happy. "I am very poor."

A few of the English teachers laughed at this, although it was obvious the student playing the client had no idea of the intended humor. I noticed Mrs. Ahm looking at me, and I broadened my smile.

I had been pretty sure these were her students — the Earth references and the high level of their English (hitting their P's) were tip-offs. I looked over to the vidphone where Matthew's bored head floated.

There was a paper cut-out of a rocketship brought out, and the client-student held it in front of her. Being concealed seemed to increase her confidence, and she practically yelled: "3-2-1 Blastoff!"

"Farewell!" said the agent, waving her tentacles human-style. "Bye-bye! Take care! See you! Good-bye!"

The skit ended and there was polite popping-applause. Mrs. Ahm noticeably relaxed. Her two students made hastily for the exit, and three boys trooped in.

"Welcome to Plangyo," they shouted together. I glanced at Matthew, who was already smirking. I deliberately avoided looking at the teachers.

I wrote: Too loud.

"We-have-a-proud-filling-about Plangyo," said Tallboy.

"There-is-many-good-things-Plangyo-like-cucumbers," said Middleboy.

"And-caves," said Shortboy.

"SHUT UP," yelled Tall and Middleboy.

Matthew laughed, incredulous, and Mr. Kung beamed back. That figured.

"Plangyo-bloys-are-good-to-fighters," said Tallboy. I started to zone out, looking down at my pad, wondering where to start criticising. I could feel Kung's eyes on me like heavy, meaty things.

Shortboy earned the ire of his betters again. "SHUT UP!"

I started thinking about Jinya. I wondered if she had competed in these speech contests when she was young. Probably. If she was here, she would watch these bizarre displays and get something utterly different from it — a nostalgic charge, perhaps, seeing herself in the kid who played the travel agent. It was a little depressing how different my perception of it was from hers.

"SHUT UP!"

Matthew was, guessing by the angle of his head, writing away, a little smile playing on his lips. *What the hell was he writing? Maybe it was a letter. I wonder what's taking Lisa so long to write back — maybe she was freaked out by the idea of me having sex with an Octavian.*

Sliding my gaze along the floor, so as to not catch the eyes of any of the teachers, I admired Mrs. Ahm's tentacles. They were a little thin, maybe, but had a lovely color to them. I imagined holding them in my hands, sliding all the way up to—

"SHUT UP!"

This time Shortboy got poked in the eye by the other two, and then he ran out of the room. It looked like it actually hurt. The remaining two boys bowed, and, flushed with pleasure, left the room to applause.

The principal stood up and told the teachers that the two judges would be left alone to choose a winner. Mr. Kung, despite being the least capable of it, translated this into English. Then everyone left, Mr. Kung making jokes with the principal, Mrs. Ahm giving me an expectant smile.

"She's a sweet one," said Matthew from the vidphone when the room was empty.

His voice was coming in a bit crackly so I adjusted the knobs.

"—over there?" he said.

"What?"

"So you couldn't get them to fly me over?"

I snorted. "They were saying you should be audio only, at first."

"Jesus, the Octavians are cheap."

I felt defensive. "They're just not rich Squidollian bastards, is all. So did you talk to 9/3 about the holiday?"

"Yeah." Matthew scratched his chin. "Blockhead's in. Dunno about Hugh, though. I can't fuckin' wait to get out of this soup and catch some warm breezes."

I nodded. I missed the wind, and we had specifically chosen a destination with a breezy climate. "So the travel agent one is the winner, right?"

"No way! The Shut Up one. As I've written here: 'For pure entertainment value, Shut Up can't be beat. Four stars.' "

I rolled my eyes. "For pure idiocy value. The fucked-up thing is that the words they mispronounce are the same ones their teacher mispronounces. The guy chumming it up with the superintendent. And there's no way he wrote that skit."

"Which one did the hottie write?" he asked, eyebrows raised in a simulacrum of innocence. "The travel agent one, maybe?"

"Maybe," I said, smiling. "But it *was* the best one. The last one was the worst, man! Even the first one was better. At least they seemed to know what the hell they were saying."

"So do you think it'll get you laid?" Matthew said. "If you fix the contest?"

"I'm not fixing —" I thumped the desk. "You're *lucky* you didn't get flown in, asshole."

Matthew laughed. "Oh, like I care. Travel agent it is."

"Good," I said.

We sat there for a moment.

"How long do you figure we have?" Matthew asked.

I shrugged. "Let's just wait till they come back. Any news from home?" I asked idly.

Matthew frowned. "Stuff from my girl . . . oh, and this crazy message from my dad. Telling me not to travel."

"That's weird. Why not?"

His signal hissed a little. " . . . no reason." He got an annoyed look on his face. "As if I'm going to say, 'Uh, OK Dad, if you say so.' "

"You don't get along so well?"

"He's a freak! He's been fighting for lost causes all his life. He's missing three fingers 'cause of pissing off the wrong people."

Matthew looked more vexed than I had ever seen him. "Lost causes?"

"Yeah. My great grandfather, too — it skips a generation, thank god. Great grampa was messed up in the ASCII wars. He actually died as an anti-English terrorist, if you can fucking believe that."

"Anti-English, eh? Put that on your application form?" I could see shadows lurking outside the door, but I ignored them.

Matthew shook his head. "Idiots. I don't even know how the hell he found out I was going anywhere."

"Maybe he's hooked up into some spy network," I said, smirking.

Matthew was still agitated. " 'Don't go on vacation, Matthew. You'll enjoy yourself and forget to ruin your life like me.' " He was pointing at the screen with a two-fingered hand. "Can you believe that he tried to teach me old Chinese languages when I was young and impressionable?"

"Really?" I said. "He knew them?"

"No," he said. "He had bootlegs. But at the time, it was a serious offence. Stupid, stupid risks . . ."

"I should try to learn Chinese — I've already learned Octavian, practically." I patted down my hair in an insufferably self-satisfied way. "And I'm going to be perfecting it with a fine young miss tonight."

His face smoothed out immediately, as I intended. "Well well. Sampling the local talent, are we? Well, good luck."

The shadows outside the door were looming larger. "I suppose we should let them in."

"Sorry about freaking out, eh," Matthew said. "Talking about my drunken ass of a father will do that to me every time."

"I'm glad to see you freak out," I said, walking over to the door. "Gives me something to use against you."

🪐

When I arrived, a minute or two late, they were laughing together. She and he. I did the best I could to keep the sudden nauseating dip in mood invisible.

"Oh, Sam!" Jinya said, jumping up. Her glowing face, her happy beautiful golden face that would never be mine, shone welcome. "This is my senior, Surrong. He wanted to meet you very much."

Surrong also smiled hugely, and stuck his tentacle out. "Hi how are you? I am fine." When I didn't shake hands immediately, he collapsed into his seat again and covered his head with his tentacles.

I took a seat.

Surrong muttered *I am a fool* in Octavian. Jinya shook her head.

Mostly to impress her, I told him he wasn't a fool.

"You speak . . . Octavian?"

"A little."

"In universary, I study Englishee," he said, and the big brown eyes I had previously assessed as threateningly handsome became openly childlike.

"Univers*ity*," I gently corrected.

"Yes!" he said. "Universary! I am her senior," he said, looking at her in a decidedly superior way.

Jinya sipped her tea with a small smile, looking into the cup.

"Her English is better than yours," I said, and of course Jinya understood it first. "She is *your* senior, I think."

He sat there and looked embarrassed, and I felt a little bad.

"Surrong's written English is much better," said Jinya.

"Yes!" said Surrong, puffing up again. His changeability was alarming. "Muchee bletter!"

The way they were sitting together — a matching pair, so right for each other — wiped me out.

"*Tell me your family story,*" I asked Surrong dully, an appropriate question to ask a person you've just met on Octavia.

They laughed a little. "Accent is strange," she said into her tea. "But good."

"*My family is very rich. My mother is a housewife and my father is a businessman.*"

Surrong looked out the window as he said this, so I chanced a look at Jinya. She was still staring into her cup. Her demure behavior was even more appealing in contrast to his chafing arrogance. Could she really *like* this jerk?

"*What type businessman?*" I asked.

He said something I didn't recognize, but that had the word for metal in it.

"Stocks in metals," said Jinya. "You know?"

"Yes!" I said.

"*You are from New York City?*"

I nodded. "*I am from Toronto. It is a . . .*"

I turned to Jinya, "Suburb? Do you know?"

She shook her head and took out her dictionary. A waitress came by and I ordered some tea. "Sam Breen," she said as she walked away. I smiled and nodded. I had never seen her before.

Jinya pinpointed the word and Surrong nodded. "I see!"

I nodded. "Toronto is a suburb of New York."

My tea came. The waitress, beyond the call of duty, poured me a cup. The casual beauty in which she made it describe an arc across the table was counterbalanced by the dirty looks she gave Jinya. "English teacher," she said, pushing out the words from between her thickly painted lips.

I nodded nervously. Jinya looked at me. "You know her?"

"No."

"What ablout the family," said Surrong.

"My mother is a powerbroker," I said. "I have no brothers or sisters."

"Yes, very good," said Surrong. "Powerbroker."

"No, it's bad," I said. "I think."

"Why?" said Jinya.

"It's boring," I said, and they laughed.

"No . . . Make much money, not bloring," said Surrong.

I picked up the dictionary and looked up a word. "*Unethical,*" I said in Octavian.

The waitress looked over, then said something that made her friends laugh.

"*Unethical,*" repeated Jinya, a funny smile on her face. "Sam is very interesting," she said to Surrong.

I liked her more and more.

"*Unethical* OK, but . . . make much money good!" he said, his face desperate and confused, as if he thought it was just a language misunderstanding.

"*What is your favorite sport?*" I asked.

His face cleared and he was sunny again. He slapped his tentacles on the table. "Soccer!"

A lot of crap had accumulated on my desk so I was sorting through it when I heard the ring.

"*Audio only,*" I called out, trying to puzzle out an ad flyer that had the Octavian words *blind* and *wealth* juxtaposed with a smiling model.

"That you, Breen?" Matthew called out from the speaker.

"*Retarded waste-of-skin?*" I called out.

"I can tell it's you, fuck. You think your accent's that good?"

I smiled. "Let's hear you. Speak to me in Squid, baby."

"Etiujwtfjsdlgj," he said. "It means idiot-loser."

I laughed. "What a coincidence! I just called you that in Octavian!"

"Thought it sounded familiar," Matthew said. "So how did the speech contest go?"

I thought about the fact that Kung had to have another teacher tell him that he didn't win. His look of befuddled surprise actually made me warm to him, while Mrs. Ahm's smugness took her down a notch in my estimation. "Um . . . OK. The riot police didn't have to be called in. Thanks for helping out."

"Beat putting up with my brats in person."

"Sure. Make sure I get flown in for your contest."

"See what I can do," Matthew said.

The droid entered the room, moving slowly as it tried to clean the room. I say tried because its metal tentacles didn't seem to ever get right into the corners. I sighed with frustration.

"What?" Matthew said.

"*Video on,*" I said. Matthew solidified and looked where I pointed. "It can't get into the corners because it's built for a normal, cornerless Octavian house. Do you know how fucking hard it is to clean by hand? Shit just floats everywhere. I fucking inhaled a dustbunny — dustfishy — yesterday."

Matthew laughed. Behind him I could see through his walls and across the street, where Squidollians passed by. "What you up to?"

"Not much, just going through junk mail. Lazy Sunday. You?"

"Recovering from last night. Went out with this guy from the town. I think he's a pimp." Someone on the street behind his head stopped and peered in. He was looking straight at me, it seemed.

I looked back at the Squidollian. Eventually Matthew looked back, then shrugged wearily. "Yeah," he said. "I know."

Dustfish didn't seem so bad, suddenly. Matthew turned off the visuals.

"Doesn't it drive you crazy, the see-thru walls?" I said. I had taken to answering the phone audio-only because, otherwise, wrong-numbers tended to call back — with their friends. Free entertainment!

"Eh, there's always night time. You adjust."

When I looked back at it, I realized I had read the ad wrong — it actually said *Blind Youth*, not *Wealth*. It was interesting how similar the two words were in Octavian. I tore out the word for *Youth,* along with the model's silver eye. It made me think of Jinya.

"I had my first language lesson with that girl I was telling you about."

"Did you come to an   arrangement?"

"Yeah," I said. "We're meeting again on Monday for a lesson."

"Where at?"

"My place." Before he said what he was bound to say, I took the conversation in a different direction. "She had this guy with her this time — her senior — but I guess I passed, because she called me this morning to suggest my place for our next meeting. And he's not coming . . ." I put the eye on an ad for a jetpack so it looked like the jetpack rider had a giant eye for a head. " . . . I actually asked her if he was."

"Good," Matthew said.

"No man," I said, "No it's not. I shouldn't care." I put the eye above the jetpack guy and now it looked like the moon. "I . . . I mean, what's the best scenario here? I fall for a girl who I can only communicate imperfectly with. . ."

"Who can you communicate perfectly with, Sam? No one, that's who."

"Yeah, but . . ."

"Seriously. I got a lot of grief for going out with Ranni. Guys calling her a war bride and shit. People figured the only reason I was going out with her was because she was pretty. That's why I started going out with her, sure, but . . . there's more."

He paused. I didn't say anything.

"I'm not going to get sappy, but there's more. Her parents —"

He stopped. I turned towards the speaker, wishing I could see his face.

"I just think it's great, is all," Matthew finished. "If this girl likes you, don't fucking analyze it, man. Just . . . ride it. Ride it for all it's worth," he said, switching into lecher mode.

I thought about her tentacles wrapping around my legs on the upstroke. "That's another problem altogether. You know about copulation and Octavians . . ."

"That shit?! That's pre-war stuff. This is modern Octavia. There's some kind of suppressant they use now. Look into it . . ."

I barked out a laugh. "Oh yeah, I'm gonna ask Mr. Zik tomorrow, 'I'm planning to have sex with one of your women and I was wondering . . . ' It's not like I'm hanging around with the town pimp."

"I don't know for sure if he's a pimp," Matthew said. "I just *hope* he is."

"How can you say that shit, man," I said, "A second after talking about Ranni?" I was about to say *so tenderly* but I wanted to keep it light.

"Yeah yeah."

"Maybe I'm the weird one. It just seems wrong. It's probably got to do with my mom. She cheated on her girlfriend of about twenty years, who practically raised me, to go out with this jackass who dumped her after a month."

"It just doesn't seem wrong to me," Matthew said. "I don't tell Ranni because I know her feelings would be hurt, not because I feel guilty. Fuck, I *wish* my mom had broken up with my dad. It would have been great. Instead she just sat there and took his shit."

"Huh," I said, rolling up the jetpack ad and holding it over the incintube, waiting for the intake to pull it from my grasp. When it did, it looked like it was flying away. "You know what I wish?"

"That you were fucking that girl right now?"

"Well, other than that."

"What?"

"I wish I had a jetpack."

"Me too," Matthew said sincerely. "With this atmosphere you could make an atomic cell last like two months. Twice as long as on Earth."

"And they're pretty cheap, too. Doesn't make any sense though. It'd cost way too much to ship back after I'm done."

"Maybe you'll be staying longer than you think."

I laughed. "Just so I can get a jetpack? Don't think so." I thought about the way Jinya had giggled when I asked if she was coming alone. *Only me*, she said. *It is OK?* I smiled. "Don't think so," I said again.

"I heard you the first time," said Matthew. "And I didn't believe you then, either. Did you have one at home?"

"Yeah. Just a single-thruster one, though."

"Knew it," he said. "You pugs and your jetpacks. Polish it every week?"

"Pretty much." My stomach was growling. I checked the time and found out why, got up and wandered into the kitchen. "But I wanted to leave all that stuff behind, anyway. Strip myself clean of the . . . old."

"Why?" Matthew asked from the kitchen speaker.

I threw some food in the last clean pot. "Well, it doesn't mean anything here. I wanted to be open to new stuff, I guess."

"You brought your aggrometer . . ." said Matthew.

"Yeah, well, most people just think it's a watch." Part of me was uncomfortable about talking about this, especially with an outsider. But part of the change I imagined was about being friends again with people who weren't pugs.

"You know, right before I left, I noticed they were selling pre-stained pug jackets—"

"Yeah yeah that's great," I said, turning on the stove with a sharp twist. "I'd rather not hear about that kind of shit, OK?"

There was a pause. "OK."

"It's just not a casual topic of conversation to me, is all. Sorry."

I stared into the pot, stirring it, feeling the silence like an indictment of my intolerance. Why should I care if they were making pug into a joke on a planet a million parsecs away?

"Oh! Hey, so — holiday plans!" said Matthew. "You're still up for planethopping, right?"

"You bet," I enthused.

"Man, I been thinking about that. I haven't been on a holiday for almost ten years. And that wasn't even really a holiday."

"Where'dya go?" I said, lying on the floor and looking at the roof. No video had its advantages.

"Well, we were *supposed* to go to the rings. Saturn. But when we get there, Dad gets all excited. I thought it was strange, 'cause he was always an unhappy bastard. But instead of going out surfing, we stayed in our rooms until night."

"You were in an orbiting station and didn't go out?"

"You thought the trip to Octavia was boring — try being eleven and trapped in a room without windows, thinking about how you could be having fun on a glider instead of staring at your spazz of a dad."

I laughed.

"So we go to sleep, and Dad gets us up in the middle of the night. My mom is worried right away, 'Oh no not again.' And I know something's wrong because he's rubbing his finger stumps which he only does when he's nervous."

"Like . . . were they scabby or . . . ?" I had never seen a wound heal naturally, and I had an unsavory image in my mind.

"No, they were medvac'd. He just refused to get replacements. He was just being an idiot."

It occurred to me that there was probably more to it than that. "So something's up, and then . . . ?"

"Yeah, we're all just standing there in the apartment. My sister was really little at the time, so my mom was just carrying her."

"You have a sister?"

"Yeah and she's a real hot snog thanks for asking. Anyway, the door stands open and there's one of the Unarmored there in one of those bullethead andy bodies, like the one at the party."

"Really!"

"He just motions us to follow, with that creepy smile. I'd never seen one of the Unarmored before — just heard about them in the war news, how there was fighting between them and the Armored. I was for the Armored 'cause they had the coolest tanks. This one looked just like the guys on the news, with the dumb little capes. Do you remember?"

All I could remember was the famous clip of the group of the Unarmored meeting a phalanx of Armored, the one where the Unarmored with the egghead lifted his hand and the Armored fell like dominoes. "I think the capes were supposed to be a representation of their real bodies, all wispy and gossamer."

"I thought they looked wimpy. Anyway, the Earth Council had declared the conflict stabilized by this point and so it was confusing to see this guy in . . . uniform, I guess. And he was looking at me real closely when we were sneaking away. He was talking to my dad but he was looking at me."

"So did he whisk you away in his ship and teach you the secret Unarmored handshake?"

"No, we didn't get into a ship at all. We all suited up and stepped outside. He had access to an airlock — could have done some serious damage if he wanted. In fact, that's what I kind of thought we would be doing. It made more sense than us going to this nice Floatel — Dad was always raging about people going on holidays and stuff. It made me feel really sick. Why was my dad such a maniac?" He paused.

"And?"

"I was thinking about all those nice things and people getting sucked out into space . . . then the airlock closed. I felt better, but still shitty. The rest of them had started flying towards Saturn."

Something clicked in my head then, something about the war and Saturn. Something about it being impossible to keep under surveillance.

"They were coaxing me to follow but I just had my arms folded and was just floating there. They were upside down to me, and they looked pretty stupid that way. That made me feel a little better. Of course, it was just a matter of time before I fired up the boot blasters."

"It had boot blasters?" I said, instantly envious.

"Serious boot *and* palm blasters. Crazy thrust. So I caught up with them, passed them, pretended I knew where I was going. I wanted to lead, I didn't want to remember they were there, I wanted to be alone rocketing across the galaxy. It was such a sweet suit. Fully loaded. Weapons. Whoever these guys were—"

"Weapons?"

"Yeah. Offline, of course. Lucky for Dad."

"So you get there—"

"Well, the Unarmored guy tried to keep up with me at first but I kept pushing harder, until he just gave up. He kept us on course, right into the gaseous layers of the planet. Eventually we came to this ship—"

"A ship *inside* Saturn," I said, disbelief frank on my face. "That's impossible for a number of reasons. Is this story going to end with 'and then I woke up'?" He had had me going until then.

"I didn't know it was impossible, so I didn't ask."

"What kind of ship was it?" I quizzed him.

"I don't remember," he said after a moment.

"So this Squidollian agent you were with—" I said.

"Unarmored," Matthew corrected.

"Well, at least you remember your lies," I said. "And your dad was missing how many toes?"

"Fuck off!" bellowed Matthew.

I laughed and laughed some more.

Matthew turned the vid on, gave me the finger, and turned it off again.

"Anyway, I don't think we'll be going to Saturn, if that's what you're hinting," I said.

"You know where we should go?" said Matthew, sounding composed. "Pleasureworld 33!"

As Matthew talked on, weighing the pros and cons of the different possibilities — i.e., the likelihood of getting laid vs. the likelihood of getting killed — I felt grateful to have Matthew in my sector. I realized I had spent most of my life hanging out with people who had the same opinions as me, and when their opinions changed we could no longer stand to be around each other. But with Matthew, our differences were blatant, and yet we tried to figure each other out, and made excuses for each other. Our friendship was the answer to a mathematical equation, and we worked backwards from there to find the question that fit.

After we said our good-byes and I had my dinner I peeked at the time tentatively. It was earlier than I had hoped. The evening stretched in front of me and I knew only a few hours of it would be occupied by studying Octavian. So before it got any darker I lit out for a little wander.

I locked the door and walked out. I stood at the road, looking one way then another, having nowhere to go. Just standing there, thinking about how time had become a burden. Then, by habit, I walked towards the school.

I tried to remember when I had been too busy. In my last year at school I spent all my time doing pug stuff, in secret. I was ridiculously busy, but also, I remembered, ridiculously happy. I had just started going out with Lisa. Discovery ended it all.

"Teecha! Hello!"

I turned towards the sound gratefully. I had reached the school on automatic and there were a bunch of students on the field. I lifted my hand to wave and felt my Earth identity slide off my shoulders. I am an English Teacher.

"Hello!" I called back, stopping.

The game paused for a bit as they watched me watch them, and then some impatient boy yelled at them to start. They did, and after a second I realized they were playing soccer.

That is, they were playing with a soccer ball and following the general rules of soccer. But the game they were playing was an entirely different thing than it was on Earth. The ball was completely concealed beneath one boy's tentacles, so it was a bit of a shell game just figuring out who had it.

He moved slowly towards the goal, while his opponents slipped tentacles past his guard until one finally yanked it out, like the cork of a bottle, and immediately passed it off in a smooth rolling movement.

This guy opted for speed and held the ball aloft in one tentacle and skittered like crazy for the other goal. I approved of this method rather than the stealth of the first boy so I hoped he'd get it in. The goalie prepared himself by hanging from the top bar and spreading his tentacles to a surprisingly wide extent. The star shape reminded me of a Christmas tree decoration, and it was so striking I nearly missed seeing the shot.

The boy on the breakaway passed the ball between his tentacles in lightning succession and flicked it with an audible *pop!* at the corner of the net. The goalie snapped closed on the ball, suddenly an oblong ball himself, and floated slowly to the ground.

The boys made the routine sounds of failure and victory and I called out, "Very good!"

They seemed to remember I was there, and one of them said, "You play . . . socca?"

Surprised, I shook my head. I declined politely in Octavian and they laughed, either because I was speaking Octavian or because I was a teacher using the honorific for the students. I put my hands behind my back and strolled on.

But before I had even left the school yard in the distance, I turned around and went back.

"Can I play soccer with you?" I asked.

"OKOK!" sassed one boy, flicking me the ball. I trapped it with my foot and reared back for a kick. It flew in an unsatisfyingly slow arc back to them, black over white over black hexagons, but they made impressed noises. A boy pulled the ball to him and idly did a circuit of his tentacles in under a second.

"I will be goalie," I said. They looked back at me blankly.

"*I will . . .*" I thought for a second, "*Ball-stop-man.*"

They laughed and said the Octavian word for goalie.

"In English, goalie," I said.

One of the kids muttered in Octavian that it wasn't class time.

I looked at him. "*True.*"

His eyes widened with distress. One of his friends whacked him in the head. "Sorry teecha."

I got into net. I hung for a second from the top bar, and they laughed. Then they started to take shots. But they were soft shots, their eyes always watchful for the disapproval of the teacher, and it was hard to miss them. Once, when some mud from the ball got on my shirt, one of the students rushed to wipe it off.

The boy who had been impatient to start finally got his turn, he came at me with appealing ferocity and thrust it between my legs. The boys responded with guarded enthusiasm.

I went to get the ball and then gave it to the boy. "Number One soccer player," I said. He thrust four victory tentacles in the air.

"Good-bye," I said.

Several of the boys twined their tentacles and bowed, a few bellowed "See you," and some did both.

FOURTEEN

Jinya looked around, a small smile on her face. I waved her in, and she pushed through the door frame in the Octavian way.

"Welcome," I said.

"Thank you very much," she said. "It is very good. Very modern."

I shrugged, decided against telling her about the difficulty of keeping a modern apartment, complete with corners, clean. I had been doing it by hand with a small sieve for the last few hours.

I went to sit down and she followed suit.

She picked my pad off the table. The pad was blinking.

"You have someone . . . a message," Jinya said, and passed it to me.

I felt all important and accessed it. It was from Lisa and I read the first few words automatically: *So you're planning to fuck a . . .*

"Ha ha," I laughed nervously, thanking the fates it hadn't been on sendthru mode.

"Who is?" Jinya smiled, wanting to be in on the joke.

"A friend," I said, watching the ribbon tied around her headcrest float. It was silver, and matched her eyes. "She is hilarious," I said, saying the word slowly.

"Ah, I know." She said excitedly. "My friend Junghee is hilarious, too. She gives people names, very good names . . . fasfessfas, you know?"

I shook my head.

"Bean-husk," she said. "But it sounds very funny in Octavian. *Fasfessfas!*"

I could hear the individual words now. "Do you have a nickname?"

"She calls me Moon," she said.

I thought for a moment. "There's no Octavian word for moon," I said.

"English nickname, because I love English!"

I nodded. I could see that her tentacles were restlessly sliding along the table legs.

"Also because . . . my face is fat, like moon."

"No!" I said. "Your face is . . . perfect!"

She smiled, and lowered her eyes. I realized that, instead of the vague flirting that I would have done back home, I had been perfectly straightforward. She circled her face with the tip of her tentacle. "Like moon."

From my bedroom door there came a few thumps. I tensed.

She looked up, "Sometimes I eat too many snacks. I study for test, and eat many snacks . . . is bad. Junghee said, 'Stop, Moon!' Is good!" She laughed.

"Beautiful like the moon," I said.

"No!" she said. "Junghee is hilarious," she said, tasting the word. "She is good friend."

"She is *a* good friend," I said, unable to stop myself.

"Yes, right, *a* good friend," she said, taking her recorder out of her bag. "We start?"

I nodded.

The thumping on my bedroom door began again. I pretended to ignore it, but this time Jinya turned around. "What?" she said, turning her silver eyes on me.

I shrugged and adopted the teacherly tone, "What did you do today, Jinya?"

She smiled and settled in her chair. "Today, I went to my university. I study English very hard."

Thump thump thump. *Shit.*

"What is that . . . sound?" she said.

"My droid is broken," I said. "What else do you study today?"

"Droid?" she said.

I nodded. "What else—"

"I can fix," she said, getting up.

My first thought, even before thoughts of trying to stop her, was *she knows how to fix droids? Wow!*

It was hopeless anyway, since she was opening the door before I even got up. Octavians move fast, especially when cutting in line and following their curiosity.

The wallen shot out, saw an Octavian, and shot back in.

Jinya looked at me, her eyes wide in perplexity. "Not a droid."

"I was . . ." I balked at saying *lying*, despite its accuracy, "joking."

She looked at the wallen. "How?"

The wallen, scared of Jinya, got behind the door and pushed it closed.

"Yesterday, I went to play soccer," I said. Jinya came and sat down, watching me closely. "When I came home, he followed me."

Well, with a bit of coaxing.

Jinya nodded. "Just . . ." She made *shoo! shoo!* movements with her tentacle.

"No. I like him. He's cute."

Jinya laughed at this. "Wallen is not cute! Wallen is ugly!"

"To me, he is cute. To Earthling." I felt like an idiot. I didn't even think he was that cute. I just wanted to see if they were sentient or not. Now she was looking at me like I had been eating out of the garbage and calling it "tasty."

Her smile faded. "You have . . . I think . . ."

I felt a sinking, all the dumb hopes I had for her sinking into the pit.

I looked at her. "I have what?"

"You have . . ." She looked up something on her pad. I didn't look, presuming it was going to be *brain damage.* The wallen started banging on the door it had closed.

"You have . . . kindheart."

I stared at her and felt a grin tug at my lip.

"Many Octavians think you . . . crazy. I think you have kindheart. Just me."

My smile was too big to keep on my face. "I don't . . . I am not kind-hearted," I said. "I am a scientist."

Jinya made the Octavian sound for confusion.

"I am studying the wallen," I said.

"No!" she said, slapping my wrist. "You are kindheart." She looked around. "Your droid is broken?"

I shook my head. "No, it — actually, it *is* broken." I took her to the washroom and called it out of its cubby hole.

When Jinya caught sight of the toilet, she started laughing. "Oh! It is a surprise! Earth-style?"

I laughed, amazed by the fact that I was having so much fun. Not only was I laughing at toilet humor, but the simplest possible toilet humor — the object itself being funny.

"It is so difficult," she said. "I tried, once."

"It is very easy," I disagreed. "Octavian toilets are too difficult."

Jinya was looking at my droid, spinning it around. I told it to clean the corners and Jinya immediately saw the problem.

"Yes!" she said, and opened up the droid's back panel.

"How do you know how to fix droids?" I said.

She pushed in its eyes and its headcap popped open in its hinge. "My brother taught me. He works at a . . . I don't know the word. Owenfgv."

"Where they fix droids?"

"Fix? No," she said, thinking. "The birth of droids."

"Where they make droids."

"Yes!" she said. One of the droid's metal tentacles shot out to hit the corner.

She flicked a dipswitch inside its head.

"A factory."

"Factory," she repeated.

I wondered if he worked on the line or designed them. "Does he . . ." I mimicked putting a droid together, "Or . . . does he," I mimicked drawing them and thinking.

"He's an engineer," she said, looking back at the droid.

"Oh," I said, feeling stupid.

I watched her tinker for a few more seconds. *"Do you want tea?"*

"Yes, please," she said. When she looked up she noticed the pug moviedisk sitting a few feet from her. "Oh!" she said, and stretched a tentacle to activate it.

I went into the kitchen and started making tea, listening to the sounds from the other room. It was in the middle of a particularly vicious fight. It was in a warehouse in Moscow, during the height of the whole pug thing — there was a band playing and someone had brought a crate of oranges. I vividly remembered the orange I had eaten after that fight, how it stung the shit out of my busted lip but how I was too thirsty to wait for the medvac.

> *Because they say we can't — we will*
> *Because it's our spirit they're trying to kill*
> *The violence we make is ours*
> *Fighting gives us powers*

What was amazing was that despite everything that had happened since that fight, the song still hit me in the gut. I stood there, watching the kettle, until I heard Jinya's voice.

"Sam?"

I felt like I'd been caught at something. I felt mad at myself for not being proud. I felt too defensive to move, covered in scales.

"Oh, Sam!"

It was her alarm that broke me out of it. I walked into the room, where Jinya was watching me pound someone who just refused to go down. My fists were slick with blood and I was wearing a calm smile.

"What is?" she said. She was sitting beside the open droid, her eyecrests high.

I knew this would never work.

"It is a . . . game," I said.

She shook her head. "Too violent."

We watched for a little while longer. I started to get some punches myself, and Jinya winced. "Oh!"

"After, we medvac," I said, trying to smile. "Violent, yes, but no consequences . . . you know?"

She shook her head. Her concerned silver eyes reflected a tiny Sam punching away. She reached out and turned it off with a slap. She turned back to the droid.

The kettle was beginning to boil. I went back, thought about trying to communicate how we felt that Earth was a violent place, but it was Sadism With a Smile, Remote Control Killing and all we were doing was tearing the mask off of that, reflecting that.

I made the Zazzimurg and brought it in to her. The wallen was banging against the door again. I opened the door and it sped away into the night. She watched it go, and I could see her trying to fit my kindheart into the maniac she'd just seen.

"Very strangey," she said, sipping.

I nodded. "Is it OK?"

She looked at me, silent, then at the moviedisk.

"I mean the tea," I clarified.

"Oh, yes. Is good."

She continued to sip. The shine of her distant eyes reminded me of the Line, the place near the planet's surface that I visited with Mr. Zik and Mr. Oool. The silver mirrorskin of the world that I could push my hand into but never get through.

"That's just it," said Hugh. "There's nothing to do. This is the dullest place in the universe."

"No restaurants?" I said, intrigued despite his best efforts to entirely dismiss the Armored side of the planet.

"They take it intravenously," he said, his lip curling. "Through a socket in their armor."

"Hmm!" I said. "Let's go!"

Hugh and I walked down the street, the street being magnetized tracks that the Armored stepped onto and were whisked to and fro. The space between the buildings and tracks didn't amount to much, especially when you considered we were wearing bulky spacesuits without helmets. Mine was a cheap bubblesuit, too, so the slightest tear would mean I'd be exposed to an atmosphere which did naughty things to your lower organs. It wouldn't be fatal as long as it was brief, but it would be extremely unpleasant.

So I was quite relieved to reach the building named FOOD. A customer stepped out (looking satiated, I thought) and stepped onto the track. His head jerked back with the immediate acceleration and, even more wince-worthy, he didn't bother righting it. I watched his rectangular body go off, and thought how much more human looking 9/3 seemed than the Armored, even though their heads were exposed.

We walked through the doorway. "Are there no doors on this planet?"

"Businesses are expected to be open all the time."

I seemed to remember hearing something about the Armored work ethic from Intergalactic Studies classes. "That's convenient," I said.

"Yes, well," Hugh said. It was a large white room with recesses in the walls, a few of which contained Armored people, all facing the wall. "The hours are good, but the goods are horrible."

We stood there for a second. "They look like they're taking a piss," I said, sotto voice, hoping that they had average humanoid hearing.

"That's about the attention they afford to eating," Hugh said.

I nodded, wondering if I was really hungry after all. My stomach burbled, and Hugh looked at me. "I wish I had some solid food to offer you, but my next shipment won't come in for a week. I was pretty depressed last week and I . . . binged."

"No, don't worry about it man," I said wandering to one of the empty recesses. "This'll be fine." I waved my hand in it experimentally. A rod about a finger-width shot out and, finding no one to impale, slowly returned.

"My hunger has suddenly disappeared," I quipped to Hugh, who was going through one of his suit pockets.

Hugh laughed for the first time since I had arrived. I relaxed a little. I had turned Matthew down — and the two offworlder parties he was going to — because I had wanted to see what Hugh's planet was like. And I had been wondering about Hugh ever since our conversation in the caves.

"You should have an adapter in your pocket, too," said Hugh. "They think of everything." He held the adapter close to the rod-hole and it shot out and sealed. I found mine and did the same in the neighboring alcove, the hose from the adapter trailing into my suit.

An old guy left his alcove and rolled towards the door, his head watching us but his body not pausing. Like a child being carried away by his parent, the old guy's eyes were locked on us — even as he left, his head turned nearly all the way back.

"What — how?" I sputtered. "How can he turn his head — aren't there normal humanoid bodies under the armor?"

"Oh, there's normal humanoid bodies under there," Hugh said. "The neck ligaments have been 'loosened,' I'm told." He tapped a place on his upper arm. "You feel a disk thing under the fabric?"

I felt for it and found it.

"Now push it till it clicks."

There was a quiet snap from his, then mine.

"Slide it around a little . . ."

"Ow! Fuck!" I said.

"It's found the vein," said Hugh. "*Bon appetit.*"

We sat down on the floor, careful not to sit on our hoses.

"So," I said. "Sounded like you had personal knowledge that there were humanoid bodies under there. Checking out the Armored pornography?"

Hugh shuddered. "I haven't been, although I'm certain it exists."

"Where doesn't it?" I agreed.

"I've been intimate with someone here," Hugh said. "Although it didn't involve any actual contact." He flicked his hair back and pulled his knees to his finely-sculpted chin. "I'll call her Marion. Her hair was too long, well past her ears, and that was the first clue. Then she tried to talk to me in the street. We talked a lot. We would have these frank conversations in the middle of crowds and no one paid us any mind. I thought it was because they respected people's privacy. But eventually I realized that sexuality has no meaning here. It was like discussing shoe sizes in front of an Octavian," he said, waving to me.

I nodded, touching my arm anxiously. I hoped it was working.

"But Marion was strange. Marion wanted something. So we opened Marion up."

"And?" I said, trying to see the answers in Hugh's troubled face.

"I was amazed, first of all, at how easy it was. On one level. She lay down and unlocked herself. I just had to lift off the lid, which required all my strength, but still — I would have thought myself incapable of it. It was a coffin . . ." He shook his head. "I don't know. Her body was smooth and pale, innocent of any muscle. Nothing I haven't seen before. But then she raised her trembling head . . . to look at herself for the first time." Hugh shook his head. "Then she dropped her head back down, a stricken look on her face. It was heartbreaking."

"What did she—" I started.

"That's just it, I don't know. I touched her hand, as lightly as you would touch a bird, and there was a second — I guess it took a second for her to register what the sensory input meant — and then she started to scream."

"Holy fuck," I said.

Hugh nodded. "Oh yes, she screamed until I had returned the lid of her sarcophagus to its original state. Then she righted herself, and left, and I haven't seen her since."

"What a place for a lunarian to end up," I said, shaking my head.

Hugh glared at me. "Oh yes, us with our voracious sexual appetites. That's not a myth perpetuated for profit. Not at all."

"No, that's not what I meant," I blustered, "it's just a cultural thing . . ."

"Poppycock," he said. "Why do you think I requested to go with the Unarmored for? Because I lusted after a cloud of nerve endings?"

I thought about the intense conversation he had been having with the Unarmored riding the bullethead andy when we left the party, and shrugged.

The meter in Hugh's alcove *snicked* and then so did mine. "Are we full?" I asked.

He snorted. "No, check out the gauge. We're 1/4 through. Weren't the appetizers scrumptious?"

I smiled. "Could be worse. It's a little sterile, I suppose, but I can think of several planets where it's worse. The Urasans, I understand, don't chew . . ."

His face lit up. "Yes, have you seen it?"

I shook my head.

"I visited Urasa two years ago. They tossed entire potatoes down their gullets! And with such gusto!"

I raised my eyebrows. I would have thought Hugh would find lack of table manners disgusting.

"And they don't have grinding teeth. Just jaws. You can certainly see them tearing into the flesh of another animal. Which they did, you know, as recently as 200 years ago."

That reminded me of the wallens. "No, I didn't know."

Hugh nodded. "Oh yes. The four-legged species barely escaped extinction." He seemed to be fascinated by the subject, but not repulsed. "It's amazing, isn't it? That people considering themselves civilized could tear another people apart and actually eat them? And no one saying anything to stop it?"

"Well, it's a tradition," I said awkwardly. "It's not like —"

"Hello, Hugh," said an Armored person, looming suddenly before us. "You are enjoying some meals, I see."

"Hello, Mr. Samworth," said Hugh, his smile slowly leaving his face.

Mr. Samworth's head lolled to one side, his eyes stricken. He smiled suddenly. "You have a friend, I see."

"Yes," said Hugh, visibly sighing. He introduced us. "Mr. Samworth is the English teacher at my school."

The Armored's block spun to face me.

I had a sudden flash of Mr. Samworth, opened-up, twitching and pale. I couldn't help it.

"Where are you from?" he asked me.

"Mr. Samworth," Hugh said, "remember when you asked me to tell you if you were being rude?"

Samworth spun back to Hugh. "Yes," he said, forcing his head into a very floppy nod that would have put me off my food . . . usually.

"We are trying to have a private dinner. Private."

"I see." Spin. "It was good to meet you Sam. I am sorry I cannot shake your hand. Hee hee."

There was something so scripted and forced to this that I couldn't bear to look at him. I mumbled something.

He rolled out. Hugh stood to check the gauge, then slumped down to sit.

"He's kinda creepy—"

"*Thank* you," said Hugh, grabbing my shoulder. "Some days I wonder if it's just me."

"No, he's creepy," I confirmed.

"I have to work with him all the time. For the first two weeks he would say the thing about not being able to shake my hand *every day*. Finally I had to tell him that he could only say it once, to a new friend only."

"What is it with his mouth, too? Why does he move his lips so strangely?"

"They all do that. Half of my lesson is spent trying to get them to move their lips in a normal way."

He looked glum. I tried to cheer him up. "Hey, where did you hear about Chez FOOD, anyway? I like the way it's entering into my bloodstream so evenly with just an occasional dash of air bubbles . . ."

He smiled wanly and put his chin on his knees. After a moment, he lifted his head. "I've been trying to access them. It's not like I haven't tried. I tried first with someone I thought was quite like the Armored, then with Marion. It's been futile, though."

"Access them?"

"Emotionally, I mean." He squeezed his nutrient hose. "Back on the moon, it was like . . . people's locked doors fell open at my touch. Here . . . it's like they don't have doors. Maybe not even windows. I can talk to them, some of them, but I can't communicate. They're too different."

I thought I knew what he was upset about. "But you *could* communicate with the Unarmored . . ."

"More than that," he said, his eyes piercing me. "I could learn from them. Their music, their art — it's all about breaking down people's barriers."

"Do you ever think that they'd disappoint you?" I said. "Just like the people at the acting school?"

"That they'd be petty and crass?" he said. "That's —"

"No, not disappointing in the same way," I said. "You said they could teach you something, I just think that's—" I shrugged.

"That's what?" he said, softly.

"I don't know." I shifted. My butt was getting sore from sitting on cold metal. I felt kind of bad saying it, because what did I know? "I just think you would find they weren't the answer to the riddle."

"Well, I'll never know now," said Hugh.

"Yeah, you may as well set your zap gun to self-destruct," I said.

He looked at me. "Is that an Earthling saying?"

"No, just something a friend of mine used to say."

"Hmm." He looked at me. "And what about you, how are you enjoying life under the sea?"

"It's pretty good. I really like my host teacher. And I've met this great Octavian girl . . ." I didn't look at Hugh, fearing a knowing look, " . . . she's really smart and she actually fixed my droid."

"Is there romance in the air — I mean, water?"

I shrugged, thinking about her stunned silence to the pug fights.

"If you had your way, would there be?" Hugh lightly probed in a way I would have found impossible.

"It's hard to think about clearly," I said. "Because I don't know how much of this is my loneliness talking. I was trying to think about what I'd do if I was back on Earth, but I can't."

I looked at Hugh. He had his chin back on his knees again. "Are you lonely?" I asked.

"Yes," said Hugh. "You know, I am. And I'm not dealing with it well at all."

Mr. Zik and I walked out of the school together, melding into the stream of students leaving.

"Good-bye teecha!" came at me about a dozen times. I responded with cheery good-byes! in English until we came to the exit gate, at which point I switched into Octavian.

"*Oh, your Octavian is not very good,*" said one bratty kid.

"*It's better than your English,*" I said, and was rewarded by a swell of raucous laughter from the swarm.

One girl, linked into a giggly vibrating three-girl chain, said dreamily, "*He is just like an Octavian.*"

I just smiled. Mr. Zik said, "Is he your bloyfriend?"

They translated, the girl who had spoken covering her face and keening in mortification. Her friend said, "*My* bloyfrienduh!"

"*You are too fat to have a handsome boyfriend,*" said one boy with an I.C.Y. cap.

"*You are too skinny, Scrap-of-Nothing,*" she said.

He moved towards her with a tentacle lifted, but Mr. Zik stopped him with a word. A friend grabbed his headcrest and shook it.

We were passing by the small store. A kid came out of it with a stick of candy poking out of his mouth and pointed at me, ran back in to get his friend, then they sprinted over to us.

After they had squashed and slid past our entourage they just looked at me until the kid with the candy smacked the other kid. Thus prodded, he said "Mr. Sam . . . Jinya?"

I thought he was trying to say something in English and failing. I gave him a puzzled look.

"Jinya . . . you?"

"Do you know . . ." Mr. Zik started for them.

"Do you know Jinya you?"

Ah. I nodded. "*Yes, she teaches me Octavian.*"

"She . . . my teacher . . . too!" he said, pointing to himself. "OK!"

"OK!"

"*She is so pretty,*" said the kid with the candy stick.

I didn't react, looking serenely ahead with Mr. Zik.

"*Jinya's face is too round,*" said one of the chain-girls with a sour look.

"Does she work at the private school?" Mr. Zik asked me.

I looked at him, I guess to see if I could detect any hostility or worry or anything on his face, but there was nothing visible. "Yes. She wants to be an English teacher, like you."

"She is lucky to have met you," he said. "You are the best way to learn English. Very lucky."

I wondered about that.

When I walked in, she was cleaning the blackboard. Three tentacles quickly made short work of the day's lessons.

"Oh, Sam!" she said when she saw me. "You are so early."

I checked the time. "Yes. Sorry."

She straightened one desk. "No, is good. I am finished. I am junior teacher," she explained, looking around the room, "so I must clean the school."

"Too bad," I said. "In my school, the students clean." To teach them discipline, Mr. Zik had told me when I asked him why it wasn't automated.

"Because it is public school. This is private school." She tapped her head with a tentacle in a very human gesture. "I forgot. Today I must clean the desk. Oh . . ." she looked at me sadly. "I do not have time to have a lesson today, Sam."

"That's OK," I said. "You told me you might not have time."

"I must go from here to straight-catch-a-bus," she said, saying the phrase all at once. "Is right?"

"I must go straight from here to catch a bus," I corrected, feeling a little frustrated because I couldn't tell her why it was, only that it was. "Did you learn catch-a-bus from your class?"

"No, from you," she said. "You are better than class."

She opened up a closet and took out a box. I watched her, imagining for a moment her bragging to her friends how she had a great English teacher that she didn't have to pay at all. The thought was black oil spreading in my brainpan.

"*What did you do at school today?*" I asked.

"No Octavian," she said, waggling a tentacle at me.

We had agreed to that before, and at the time her explanation that I could speak Octavian to anyone on the planet had seemed reasonable.

"*But I like the Octavian speech,*" I said.

"*All right,*" she said amicably. "*One of my students said that you were her favorite teacher.*" She opened the box. Inside was a cloth that she proceeded to clean the desks with.

"Really?" I said. "Why?"

"*She says you are gentle and funny.*" She rubbed the cloth against a block in the box, and went back to the desk.

"That's nice," I said, failing to keep a smile from my lips.

"*Because you don't punish the students, you are very popular.*"

I smiled even wider. To distract myself, I looked in the box for another cloth. It was very gratifying to hear that — that my popularity came out of a deliberate stance rather than the fact of me being an entertaining oddity.

"I surprise you don't punish," Jinya said, rubbing her cloth on the block. "Because on the moviedisk, you hit, hit, hit." She was facing the board, so I couldn't see her expression.

"I don't like to hit kids," I said. "Because they are defenceless."

She looked at me, cloth in hand. "No defence? I see." She went back to her cleaning. "Is good reason why."

I rubbed my cloth on the block, and started to clean a desk full of love notes to various mediastars.

She stopped cleaning for a second. "Sam, what plans do you have on weekend?"

Matthew had told me about an offworlder Halloween party. I was planning to go as a Comet Pirate. I even had the laser cutlass. "There is an offworlder party I am going to."

She looked disappointed. "Oh."

I erased a poor drawing of a saucer from the desk. "Why do you ask?"

"Because Saturday is a special romantic day for Octavian youth. There is a pop song. You know? Is famous."

I shook my head.

"*The time is now/ to harvest your dreams . . .*" she sang, then giggled.

I shook my head, smiling.

She bobbed her head, "*Because tomorrow, tomorrow/ all lies dead.*"

"I like that song," I said, because I did. "But I've never heard of it. Is it

Intergalactic Cool Youth?"

She shook her head. "No, no. Is twenty years old? About."

"So it's a special romantic day because of the pop song?" I said.

"Right!" she said with a big smile. "Is too bad—"

"My plans are not important," I said shamelessly.

"Oh?" she said.

"I will stay in Plangyo this weekend."

"Oh, good!" she said.

I went back to my desk cleaning. I looked at her sometimes, when her eyes were on her work. Her smile matched mine: a goofy one that died sometimes, only to spring up again.

We cleaned desks for a few minutes. "*I love Jinya,*" I said.

"What?" she said, looking at me, silver eyes wide.

"Someone wrote it on the desk," I said. "I was just reading it."

"Where?" she said, coming over.

"Oh, I erased it," I said. "Sorry. Some crazy student."

"Yes," she said, going back. "Crazy boy."

I left the door open a crack, in case the wallen came back, calling behind me to activate the droid. I heard his vacuum powering up before I had walked out of earshot.

I checked the time. It was late, much later than we'd planned.

"I'm sorry," Jinya had said on the vidphone. "My teachers wanted to go out to celebrate the Special Romantic Day. They did not have men." She had laughed merrily at this unfortunate situation.

"I think the restaurant might be closed, now," I had said, a little peeved.

"Maybe we can go to your apartment and drink all night," she had said.

My peevishness left me, stunned from my head.

"Is OK?" she had asked.

"Is great!" I had replied.

I strolled light-headedly through the neighbourhood made blue by the faintly glowing night. A wallen rustled through someone's garbage, and I peered at it to see if it was the one I knew. This one looked bigger, but I wasn't sure. While I had been kind of disappointed that the wallen I had met left so suddenly, I was in such a good mood now that I was sure that it would be back in my apartment by the time I was. Hopefully the droid wouldn't scare it off . . .

I arrived at the tree. I imagined telling my friends back home that I met someone under a tree. Lisa popped into mind.

LISA: Like a place called Tree? A bar?

ME: No, a *tree* tree.

LISA: You mean a tree like an actual plant?

ME: Yeah. They're really hard to grow in Octavia's atmosphere, so it's kind of like a craft. For ages I wondered why this old guy was always under it, then I saw him trimming it. He pulled himself up the trunk and shook the branches one by one. I also realized then that the tree looked a lot like an Octavian, upside down.

LISA: —

I cut Lisa off in my mind before she had the chance to say something rude or obnoxious. I looked towards the old man's house and, seeing no lights on, sat on the flat part of the coral where he usually perched. I smiled a little at my audacity. The roots of the tree actually went into the coral and I traced the lip of the entry point where wood penetrated stone, slid inside the . . .

When I realized it was turning me on I stopped touching it.

I started humming what I remembered of the Special Romantic Song. Then I cursed myself for not learning it — that would have been something to do when I was waiting for her to call. Of course, I wasn't thinking the thoughts of a lover then. I had been worried she had stood me up, that I had turned down a night of Matthew's sometimes appalling but always entertaining antics to sit at home.

"Sam?" Jinya said, her gently waving silhouette a little way down the road.

I got up.

"Oh! I didn't know it was you!" she said. "Because you sit down. I thought maybe it was Octavian man."

She was wearing a tan shift. "Your clothes remind me of the beach on Venus," I said, a little embarrassed by the flowery language.

She looked surprised. "Strange?"

"No, lovely."

We set off. "That is my favorite tree," she said as we left.

I thought of the root and the coral. "Me too."

A tip of her tentacle slipped into the space between my thumb and forefinger. "Not a tree on Earth?" she said.

"There's no such thing as an Earth tree." The tip of her tentacle slid away, and I didn't know if it was because I didn't squeeze it in time or if she never intended for it to be there at all. I bit the side of my cheek. "Only on old Earth moviedisks."

"No more?" she said, seeming overly concerned. "Too bad."

I shrugged, thinking about the planet of trees we had visited on our orientation, the heat and the constant prickling and the uneven ground.

"Do you want to buy some beer?"

She nodded enthusiastically and we made our way towards the store. I checked my pocket for beeds, and it felt like I had one or two of the big ten-beed beeds so I relaxed.

The store was empty except for an unhappy looking woman who barely glanced our way. I wondered what hopes she had had for the Special Romantic Day.

"Snacks," said Jinya, and I nodded and left her to it.

There were a lot of beer bladders hanging there but not a lot of selection. They did, however, have a few outrageously priced Earth-style bottles which I was nowhere near nostalgic enough to buy. I scooped a couple of big bladders of a brand I thought I remembered favorably and brought them to the counter. Jinya put a small pile of snacks on the counter.

The woman started ringing them up and looking us over. I couldn't see how this could look anything but bad — beer, night-time, Special Romantic Day, a horny offworlder — but Jinya looked entirely composed and relaxed.

"Is that enough?" I asked, kind of joking — it was a lot of beer.

She looked at it and answered seriously. "Is good."

We grabbed a few bags each and left. I watched the counter girl go back to her magazine, and was struck again by her misery.

"She is sad," I said.

"Yes," Jinya said. "No man. Too bad." She laughed again. "My teachers ask me, 'Where do you go Jinya?' 'I go to meet a friend,' I said."

We were walking down the last stretch and I realized that instead of passing us, the saucer behind us was slowing. I turned around and my stomach twisted quickly as I recognized the twined snakes of the police crest. The dome shucked down.

"Hello!" the fat policeman said, waving his tentacles. "How are you Sam!"

I got a smile out of my emergency reserves and slapped it on my face quick. "Hi!"

He looked at Jinya for a second too long. He looked back at me, and I noticed his eyes were swimming a little, maybe with the stress of thinking of more English phrases. "How are you?" he repeated. He looked at the beer bladders.

"Great!" I said, feeling my smile ready to give out. In my anxiety, I almost started speaking in Octavian, but I had a sudden fear that he would tell someone official that I was fluent.

Another saucer approached. He looked at it, then at us. "Criminals, maybe," he blurted, then he sealed the dome and flew away.

"He is not a good English speaker," was Jinya's only comment.

I looked around as we neared my apartment and was happy to find the area deserted. My droid was still cleaning away around the open door — everything else was clean, I suppose, so the dirtiest air was coming in from outside.

"Is dangerous, to leave your door open," she said, as I shut the door behind me.

Yes, I thought to myself, *criminals.* I looked around for the wallen. "I was hoping my friend the wallen would visit."

She laughed at this. "The wallen is your friend?" she said.

"Yes," I said stubbornly, giving up the search. "Last week he did not come to visit. I miss him."

She put the bag on the table. "He escaped. Wallens are trekerous."

"What?"

"Trekerous." She looked at my puzzled face. "Not good friends."

"Treacherous."

"Right! In Octavia, many years ago . . ." she began.

"I know the history," I said.

"Yes. A wallen eats food and then goes away. Not good friend."

Well, it might have something to do with the fact that you eat them, I thought. I looked at Jinya's calm face, and felt suddenly unsure. What the hell did I know? Maybe they *were* bad friends. Maybe hitting kids *did* make them learn better.

Jinya was setting out the bladders and the snacks, I was happy to see, on the ground instead of at the table. I hunkered down, thinking hard.

"*I think teaching English makes everyone the same. It's bad.*"

Jinya tore the top off of a red package festooned with English phrases like "good and delicious!" and "snack!" on it. Golden spirals floated out. "*We need to know English to do business well. English is important to the Octavian economy.*"

"*I know,*" I said, desperately hoping to get beyond the party line, "*But people like Earth movies, and food, and style too much. It makes a danger to Octavian culture.*"

She nodded, tweaking open a bladder. "*Octavian culture is important. But modern ideas are good too, like* jetatag *for women.*"

"Jetatag?" I repeated.

"Equality," she said.

That gave me a bit of perspective on why she found it appealing. "*One reason I came here was because I wanted to see a different culture. But I am helping make your culture the same as ours. It's very boring.*"

She laughed. "You are right." She took a pull from the bladder. "You speak Octavian too much. You are bad English teacher."

"Thank you," I said, getting into my beer, again wondering if she was using me for my tongue.

She hit me, giggling. "Is not good. Is . . . insult!"

Her giggling was a warm rain, melting my suspicions and leaving me pure and clean.

"*Where did you learn 'culture'?*" she asked. "Difficult word."

"*Octavian newsfeed,*" I said, feeling a little proud. I'd gotten to the point where I was learning by context.

"Your Octavian is much better," she said, seriously. "Great."

I thought back to my conversation with 9/3 and wondered how great she would think it would be if it meant that Octavia lost its cultural protection because of it. "Maybe. *Tell me about your parents.*"

"My parents?" she said, a little thrown off by my shift in conversation. "They are very good." Although we weren't finished our "good and delicious" snack, she opened up another that bragged about having pickles from Jukwong. "My mother's very funny. Very hilarious! She is very loud. My father is too quiet. Strange, you think?"

"Interesting, I think. *On Octavia, it is strange, but it wouldn't be strange on Earth.*"

"Yes, I know. Very different. On Earth, women sex women? Is true?"

I nodded. "Yes. Everyone sexes everyone," I said, liking the new verb. "My mother's lover was a woman. Jane. They broke up. My mother is loud too, but she is not hilarious."

"My mother sing songs in the morning. Too loud!" She curled two tentacles and guarded her earholes with them. "'Mom, we're sleep!' She says 'La La La!'"

I smiled. I didn't know if my mother could sing. Jane could, though, and the thought made me sad. I watched Jinya hook a few rings on her tentacle and raise them to her lips. She was humming, and making a light popping sound with her suction cups to accompany it. She saw me looking and looked down at the snacks.

"I eat too many snacks. When I study, too too many. Sometimes I stay up all night and just . . . tea . . . snacks . . . read . . . make jokes. You know?"

I knew.

"Sam, we should stay up . . . all the night. OK?"

I nodded, because her silver eyes made it immeasurably appealing.

And I almost made it. Hours later, after she had told me of her dad's pearl diving accident and I had described pug as best I could, we had come to the end of the beer and the snacks . . . but not the night.

Over the empty snack skins of our party, amazed at how little dark circled her eyes, I asked her if I could kiss her.

Her silver eyes became round mirrors. "Kiss?" her lips said.

I nodded, feeling defeated already. I looked to see if there was a tentacle within reach that I could hold, but they were circled around her.

"Sam," she said. "When do you go to Earth?"

"Seven months," I said immediately, having done the math.

"Is not good," she said. "In seven months . . . I be so sad. *Miserable.* You know?"

I knew all too well. I got up and felt my head spin. I gathered the garbage and got rid of it. I went back and found I couldn't sit down, my heart was too heavy and I was sure that if I sat I would never rise again.

"I'm sorry, but I'm exhausted. Very tired," I said, so childish-feeling I was unable to meet her eyes. "I think I'm going to sleep. OK."

She nodded, still unbelievably perky. "OK. I will stay?"

"Of course," I said. "Wake me when you want to leave."

The droid came alive and started to clean the crumbs around Jinya. *"No!"* she said to it with a laugh, as if she was scolding a child.

I fell into bed, leaden, not even bothering with the curtains. I lay there, listening for any further sounds from Jinya, feeling like one of the Armored in a sepulchral embrace. And then I went to sleep.

" . . . there room?" she asked. I looked up, and moved over.

"Sure," I said, giving her some of the white comforter.

I looked at her head on the pillow for a moment and I guessed she was finally tired too, and felt a bittersweet feeling that she had decided it was safe with me.

After a moment, she turned on her side to face me, a tentacle or two brushing up against human skin unnaturally sensitive. Eyes closed, her lips were inches from mine. Then they weren't. It was a dry kiss and her eyelids didn't even flutter. If not for the tentacles gently stroking my arm like underwater reeds, I may have not tried again.

Her lips moved slightly apart this time, and her nostrils moved.

Again. And again, and I felt them move this time, and I brought a hand up to stroke the side of her face, her earhole. She moaned.

I touched her headcrest, soft and hard and finely rippled, and rested my cheek on her shoulder. I moved my hand down the front of her shift and was gently rebuffed. "No," she said, as if half asleep.

An hour later the morning light woke me. I pulled the white comforter over our heads and looked at her some more. Bathed in white, luminescent, I tried to remember what she had looked like in the bus station, when she had been merely pretty, and couldn't. The impossible beauty of her at that moment was to be the image that would haunt me forever.

"Thank you," I whispered, kissing her cheek.

She turned her head to face me. "You are very honest when I ask you when you go. Most offworlders would say 'Baby baby, I'll take you with me.' "

She saw the good things in me, the things that mattered, and I felt unreal and chosen. It was suddenly there, taking the form of a lump in my throat, making my nose tingle. "I . . . love you," I said, before it went away.

She buried her face in the crook of my arm and I felt her sigh.

Seven months.

FIFTEEN

It was weird to see a droid completely still. By this time, it was fully constructed, and we moved along beside it as it slid along on the conveyor belt.

I tried to remember a time I had ever seen a completely still droid. That was the thing about droids, they were always sweeping, moving, lifting . . .

"*Ag!*" said Jinya's brother, yanking his tentacle from under my foot.

"*I am tremendously sorry,*" I forgot his name. Oh fuck— "*honored brother,*" I said, just as he was beginning to look at me.

"*It is less than nothing,*" he said, while moving away from me.

"You are too clumsy," said Jinya, poking me in the ribs.

"You're right," I said.

"*No English,*" said her brother, and I couldn't tell if he was joking. I didn't want to apologize again, so I watched the droid. It must have been nearly done, but I had thought that a dozen times already and then there would be a metal coating added or a screw tightened—

"SELF-DIAGNOSTIC!" the droid blared, becoming a blur of motion and flashing eyes. I leaped back to avoid its whipping metal tentacles. Jinya also jumped back at the same time so I luckily avoided squashing her tentacles.

"Wow!" she said in English. I said the same in Octavian, and this won a small smile from her brother.

Emboldened, I asked him, "*Why* diagnostic"?

"*The droids test themselves,*" he said, looking at me queerly. "*English word.*"

I wanted to know why it was an English word, not what it meant. I nodded sagely, deciding the answer wouldn't be worth the effort of clarification.

The droid, finished with its flailing around, rolled off the belt and away. We walked around the end of the belt and it was a relief. I had never walked with Octavians in such close quarters before. In fact, I was surprised we were allowed to walk in the small gap between the conveyor belt and the wall. I was pretty sure the same thing would be illegal for safety reasons on Earth.

Not that there were any factories on Earth, besides the image and photon shops. Which was why I asked Jinya so many questions about it that eventually she asked me if I wanted to visit it.

I had, a few years back, been fascinated by a clip I had seen of a jetpack factory. Not just because I was obsessed with all things jetpack, it was the noise and the movement and the mirror copies of the gleaming object. They didn't have self-testing, obviously, but that was even better — I remembered telling Lisa that I had found my dream job until I found out that they used nearby Ikkilians to test fly 'em. Stupid horse-heads, how—

"SELF-DIAGNOSTIC!" blasted through my thoughts. I jumped again, smiling apologetically as her brother looked back with raised eyecrests.

He said a word quietly to Jinya that I didn't understand, who linked tentacles with him as they walked along ahead of me. *"He's too sensitive,"* he said. She slapped him on the shoulder.

I pretended not to hear.

We caught up with our droid, who was now on another belt busily building a box around itself. Up ahead I saw that the belt led up the landing ramp of an industrial saucer like the one I'd seen in the cucumber fields, only shinier.

"Before I saw same saucer for cucumbers," I ventured.

Her brother looked at me, nodded. *"It's good for cucumbers. Terrible for droids."*

He didn't elaborate, only watched the droid assemble the box as it moved towards the lip of the belt. It didn't look like it was going to finish in time, and it also looked like it dropped into nothing, and for some reason these possibilities made me nervous. I wanted the factory to work properly, flawlessly.

I suddenly realized why it wasn't good for droids. *"Square boxes, round saucer,"* I said.

He seemed to notice me for the first time. *"Poor use of space,"* he said, nodding.

"Inefficient," I said, using one of the impossible sounds. I threw it out there, pretended I was watching the box and didn't notice his surprised face. It was gratifying to see his mild surprise — he had been brusque with me, not rude but a little dismissive, and so I guess I wanted to impress him.

Octavians usually hated me or loved me on sight, because of what I represented. I knew that it was a tricky situation. As I was an offworlder "friend" of his sister I expected to have to win him over. I would have found ingratiating behavior not just weird, but a little nauseating.

Hostility would also have been upsetting, although the way Jinya had insisted that we go to the factory led me to assume that it would be OK. It was actually better than OK — I instantly liked him for being an engineer who didn't give a damn about me, going about his business without a thought of Earth.

Well, other than an English word blared every 25 seconds.

The box finally went over the lip. A few seconds later there was a splash. Was the saucer flooded?

I looked at the two of them, but they didn't seem to be disturbed by this.

"*Why did it*" I didn't know the word for splash so I just made the sound with my mouth.

Jinya laughed, and her brother smiled. "*It's normal*," he said.

Jinya repeated my splash sound. "We say *poosh*," she said.

"Poosh!" I repeated dutifully, then looked seriously at her brother. "*How long have you been an engineer?*"

"*Ten years*," he said.

I thought about complimenting him on how young he looked, but adopted his no-bullshit attitude instead. "*Is it interesting?*"

He looked at me and nodded. "*It's a small factory so I get to do a lot of jobs. Some are boring, but some are very interesting.*"

Encouraged by getting two entire sentences out of him, I prodded. "*Like what?*"

He blinked slowly, a surprisingly handsome grin growing on his face. "*Sometimes the droids malfunction. Most of the time they are too responsive. Any sounds make it move strangely.*"

"They dance, Sam!" said Jinya, her face glowing.

"*We stand around and sing traditional songs, and clap. It is very hilarious.*"

"*Songs like 'Bubbles Over Plangyo'?*" I guessed.

"You know, Sam?" Jinya said, astonished, pulling on my arm.

"*No,*" he said, "*It's too sad. Happy songs,*" he said, singing a few notes and pop-clapping as an example.

"I see."

"*Tell him about the time when you were a hero,*" Jinya urged.

He shook his head, and went back to the belt.

"There was a crazy droid," Jinya said, her tentacles rippling like they did when she was really excited. "And . . . he ran up to people and hit them!"

"Dangerous," I said.

"Very dangerous! Everyone went away. But the droid break everything. So, elder brother shot it in the eyes."

"With a zap gun?" I asked, aiming my gun-shaped finger at her.

"No . . . before, you know?"

I shook my head. Her brother was peering under the belt.

She licked her lips in concentration, and the moistness of them drew me in instantly. "The gun that makes droids."

"Oh, the bolt gun," I said. It had fired the small metal plugs through metal with a violence that had also made me jump.

"Yes!" she said brightly. "Bolt gun. He used it to kill the crazy droid. Very good, I think."

He was walking back towards us. "He is very brave," I said.

"Yes," said Jinya, looking proudly at her brother.

"*No English*," he said gruffly, grinning.

🪐

On the bus back to Plangyo I felt the stress in my bloodstream dissolving into small ineffectual particles. It was a bit of a surprise that there was so much there, it having built slowly on the way there — even if Jinya had made it sound like no big deal, just something interesting to do, I still knew that it was quite serious to meet a family member on Octavia.

I looked at her briefly, making like I was looking out the window, taking in her peaceful face like a sedative. Her brother had a similar look, but not her sudden bursts of excitement to balance it — with him I felt observed and found slightly lacking. Or I did at first. Now I told myself that by the end, he had warmed to me.

"I like your brother. He is . . . diligent," I said, willing her to say something about how he liked me, too.

"Yes. Very diligent," she said.

I watched the countryside slide by. I could see a loading saucer far away, made normal-sized by the distance.

"Too serious, though," she said, shaking her head. "You are very different."

"I'm serious."

"No!" she said, squeezing my arm. "You are foolish. Very foolish!"

I looked at her fondly, smiling foolishly, my lips within kissing distance of her forehead.

"Is better," she said, then let go of my arm and wrapped her tentacles around herself, chastely. Which was lucky for her.

The familiar first signs of Plangyo — the police station, the sauna, the restaurant — passed by. I could read them now even though the fancy lettering made it difficult, but since I had first known them as a pattern of colorful shapes they remained that way.

We careened into the bus station and got off.

The bus bubbled away. "I must to class," she said.

"I think I'll go home to study," I said. "Because I am very diligent."

"No, you are foolish!"

We made further arrangements and I left, feeling a warm happy feeling that I was at a loss to explain. I imagined writing Lisa about it: *I like it when she calls me foolish.* I could hear her groaning thousands of parsecs away, and I smiled on.

I was headed in the general direction of the grocery store when I felt a tug on my leg. The tentacle belonged to a youngish looking man who sat in a round shallow saucer like the one we had used to move the toilet.

"*Four of my tentacles are dead,*" he said, his head lolling.

"*That's terrible,*" I said.

He let go of my leg. "*A bus hit me on the road near* Kindah."

"*I live near there,*" I said nodding. "*It is very dangerous.*"

"*A bus hit me in the head,*" he said. He smoothed back his headcrest with a tentacle and showed me a purple scar that wasn't nearly as disturbing as the milky eyes it arched over. "*Four of my tentacles are dead.*"

I looked around, at a loss. There were a few curious people on the street watching. I took out some beeds and handed them to one active tentacle. He held them for a second and then they fell, all but one landing in his dish.

I didn't bother picking the stray one up — it had rolled away, anyway — and walked on.

I stopped at a cart where a guy was selling small muffins and ordered a bag.

He snapped open his black iron moulds. At the same time, he used the covered tips of four tentacles to flip the fresh tiny muffins into a bag. It had the feel of a magic trick, although he looked bored.

"*Is he a beggar?*" I said to the cart guy.

He nodded. He looked over at the dish-boy, then at me. "*You are generous,*" he said, squinching the bag shut and handing it over.

I paid. "*Thanks.*"

He nodded and started refilling the moulds with goo. I walked away, pulling the bag open, and decided I disagreed with the guy. I think I was more motivated by not wanting to look like a heartless Earthling than by genuine empathy. I munched away on the sweet muffins, which Mr. Zik had told me were shaped to look like a fruit which I'd never seen, and I was almost half-way through the bag before I got to the store.

I did a quick shop, and the counter girl tallied up my items but stopped when she saw my spicy pickled onion.

She looked a little flustered for a moment, the pickled onions in her tentacle, then said "No."

I raised my eyebrows, which seemed to almost terrify her. Then she noticed another employee coming from the back of the store.

"*He wants to buy chikim but it's too hot for Earthlings,*" she said to him in a whiny voice.

He set down a box and pointed to the chikim. He mimed eating it, then waved a tentacle in front of his mouth.

"*I know it's hot. I love chikim. It's delicious.*"

She broke up into laughter and his jaw dropped. "*You speak?*" She hit the other employee.

"*I didn't know he spoke Octavian,*" he said crossly, picking up his box.

I apologized, and paid for my groceries.

"OK!" he shouted as he walked down an aisle.

The door shut behind me and I heard a new gale of laughter, its quality perhaps a little harsher and meaner.

On my way home I saw a moviedisk rental store and popped in.

I smiled at the guy at the counter, and he smiled back. He was on his wristphone. "Chikim?!" he said incredulously.

I couldn't hear what the other person was saying, but evidently it was hilarious. I looked at the rows of moviedisks, my ears burning. The bag of chikim hung obviously from my hand.

I glanced at him. He was looking at me with a smile.

Did that girl from the grocery store call here after I left?

He bleeped off. I picked up a moviedisk randomly and looked at the slowly moving image, an Octavian with a helmet and a lance.

Were they talking about me?

It was a really creepy feeling. Then again, chikim was very popular on Octavia . . . it could have easily been a chance reference.

I put the moviedisk back and approached him.

"Do you have English moviedisks?" I asked.

He nodded eagerly and pointed to a wall. I went over to it, and he followed.

"Good," he said, poking at a roboman action flick, *In Zap Guns We Trust VI*.

I looked them over, still wondering, not really seeing them. I picked up an Octavian one by mistake.

"No, Octavian," he said. "You . . . spik?"

"*Yes, I speak Octavian,*" I said.

"Oh . . . very good," he said with pleased surprise.

Shifting my bags in my hands, I realized that the grocery girl would have mentioned my Octavian if that had been her on the line. I relaxed a little. I went to the English section, looking for that action moviedisk — it would be interesting to watch it now that I knew 9/3 so well. Some of the appeal of the roboman action hero is that he is completely pure, completely ruthless, and I wondered how that image would jive with the memory of 9/3 walking softly through the forest, cradling Hugh.

While looking for it, I came across *Princess Artemia*. I was a bit surprised to see it there — while it was readily available during my teens, it was hard to find now on Earth. The current take on it was that the tragic doomed romance depicted the Octavian female lead as an exotic prize for the Earthling hero — a xenophobic product of its times.

I put it back on the shelf, wondering if the actress still lived on the planet, what she did now.

SIXTEEN

"I am very sorry, Sam," Mr. Zik said when I walked out of the classroom, recorder-pad under my arm.

I raised my eyebrow and smiled, expecting him to ask me some tiny favor or let me know about a minor inconvenience. Mr. Zik was always apologizing.

"You have bleen replaced."

I looked at his somber face. The usual tangle of kids roared around us in their swirls and eddies, and for a second their noise was the only thing I could hear.

"What?" I said, seeing Jinya's sad face in my mind, me with a suitcase.

Mr. Zik evaded my eyes. "The school hired another English teacher."

When we reached the ground floor I suddenly wondered if it had something to do with my fluency. Why the fuck did I have to show off? Or maybe there'd been talk about me and Jinya . . .

We walked into the teacher's room and he pointed at the only other human on the planet. "You bastard!" I said.

Matthew turned around. He was grinning ear to ear, sitting at my desk and in mid-chat with Mrs. Pling. "Hey, is that how you greet a visitor on Octavia?"

"Sam is very rude," said Mr. Zik, sitting down at his desk. "Blastard."

"Did you put him up to that?" I asked Matthew. "Corrupting Mr. Zik. Mr. Zik, you are a liar!"

"Ssss-sss-ss," laughed Mr. Zik. Mrs. Pling asked him what happened and Zik recounted the trick in Octavian.

"How'd you find our little backwater?" I asked Matthew, happy as hell to see him. It was funny — I had been crestfallen about the idea of leaving Octavia, but the prospect of hanging out with an Earthling and reminiscing about Earth things was also exciting.

"I have my ways," he said, nodding mysteriously.

"You look brothers each," said Mrs. Pling.

I looked at Matthew's Asian features and shrugged. "All Earthlings look alike." I turned to Mrs. Pling. "*He is much more handsome.*"

She nodded in agreement.

I looked at Matthew. "I just said 'You are considered very ugly on Earth.' "

"Ssss-sss-ss. Let's go!" said Mr. Zik.

Matthew reached under the desk and lifted a shiny new jetpack made of

Squidollian glass with chrome trim. He nonchalantly slung it over his shoulder and we walked out of the teacher's room together.

"When did you—" I started.

A gang of students attacked us, putting out tentacles for Matthew to shake and yelling Hellos!

"The students are very excited. Now there are twice as many offworlders," said Mr. Zik.

"But how could you afford—" I started.

Matthew looked back at me, wiggling his eyebrows.

I gave up. "You bastard."

He flicked the chrome pipe, and it dinged beautifully. "Yup."

We walked past the gate and I immediately started addressing the children in Octavian. "*Leave us in peace you little monsters!*" They laughed at this because "peace" required a cheek-pop.

"Man, your Octavian sounds good!"

"It's not so bad. I've been getting private lessons," I hinted. "How's your Squidollian?"

"Crap. Not that I have any interest in learning it anymore."

We trudged along, losing kids to the gravitational pulls of the school and the corner store. I waited for him to elaborate.

"My girlfriend got married last week," he said. "My dad told me."

I looked at Matthew. He looked back and shrugged.

"Yeah," he went on. "My dad was flipping out over us going to Pleasureworld 33. He actually called. My girlfriend must have told him. He was blithering on and on about how Pleasureworld was the most evil place in the world, yadda yadda yadda, and then he stops and thinks to mention, oh, your girlfriend got married."

Mr. Zik looked back. I thought he was going to say something but then he didn't.

"Then he says it's a good thing anyway because she's Squidollian —"

"Oh, fuck," I said, disgusted.

"Yep, typical. Then he's back on how dangerous it is for me to go to Pleasureworld," Matthew said. "So I just flicked off the vidphone."

"Good for you," I said. "How could it be dangerous? He's just xenophobic."

I pointed out a store to Matthew. "That's where I buy my chikim." We reached the main street and, behind Mr. Zik's back, I motioned to a window with shadowy round things hanging from strings. "Tell you later," I said to Matthew.

We walked a bit further. Matthew shifted his jetpack to his other shoulder.

"Little heavy, eh?" I said, eyeing it.

"Oh no," he said, holding it out for me.

I hefted it. It was admirably light. I wondered how it handled . . ."Take this away," I said.

Smirking, he did. "Yeah, I figured that since I didn't have to rush back for her, I might as well put a down payment on one of these babies. I'll have to sign up for another year to pay for it, but I'll be living in style. No more buses for this bucko."

I grimaced. Then my face did a total inversion.

It was my wallen! Rooting there in the alley!

I looked at it closely, to make sure — yep, little gray-black stripes on its shell . . . I walked over to it cautiously.

Matthew stopped and called out to Mr. Zik, who hadn't seen me stop.

The wallen turned towards me, its tail straightening and curling. I got close and crouched. It floated to me and bumped into my shoe once. I touched the top of its shell, the strange feel of its surface inspiring a tender feeling in me. His big eyes followed my hand, and I moved them in a circle to see him track it. They rolled around comically.

Matthew and Mr. Zik had approached behind me, and the wallen caught sight of them and scooted away. I walked out of the alley, feeling mean.

"You see, Matthew," I said, loud enough for Mr. Zik to hear. "Octavians aren't the only people on this planet. They share the planet with these other creatures, who are intelligent and peaceful. But because of an old war grudge, the Octavians *eat* the wallens." I threw the word "eat" over my shoulder at Mr. Zik.

Matthew raised his eyebrows, and I let his shock feed my indignation. "I think it's barbaric," I said, trying not to let my guilt at saying this in front of Mr. Zik overcome me. I thought back to the shadowy corpses in the window.

"He is right," Mr. Zik said.

I looked back at him. Mr. Zik looked unhappy, his brow furrowed. "It is Octavian tradition," he continued. "But it is blad, I think."

My mouth swung open.

"Sure is," said Matthew, "but you kill them first, right?"

"Yes," Mr. Zik said, "we bleat them to death." His head sunk even further. "Very blad."

"The Squidollians ate their enemies alive," Matthew said conversationally.

I was as annoyed at his blasé attitude as I was buoyed up by Zik's shame.

"Well, they don't do it today, do they?"

"Of course not!" Matthew said. "They ate them all. So at holidays they eat a kind of rice paste in the shape of the froids." He grinned. "The oldsters complain that it's no substitute," he said conspiratorially to Mr. Zik.

Mr. Zik smiled weakly.

☄

"You are dreaming," said Mr. Nekk.

I looked up from the thing I was pretending to read. "Yes, I'm daydreaming." Usually I discouraged speaking English during the workshop break by walking around the room or sometimes I would talk Octavian. Not often, though, because Mr. Kung would correct me in an insufferable (and often redundant) manner.

"What do you . . . daydream about?" asked Mrs. Ahm. "Girls?"

I smiled mysteriously. I had been thinking about Jinya, the way her lips set and the nod she gave after she said *You are honest*. But I wasn't about to give them the whole story like that.

I checked the time. Break-time was over, anyway.

"Have you been to the Sculpture Garden?" I asked.

Both of them had.

"Do you like it?"

They looked at each other and nodded. But nothing else. That was strange, with these two it was hardly ever this difficult to get them talking.

"Why?" I said, smiling a little to encourage them.

"It is very artistic," said Mrs. Ahm.

"I agree. There are not a lot of artistic places on Octavia," I said. "My friend Jinya took me to the Sculpture Garden and it was fascinating."

"There are not a multitude of art on Octavia," said Mr. Nekk, rather agitated. "Blut it is bleecause of war."

"Who is Jinya?" asked Mrs. Ahm.

"The Octavian pleeple are very artistic . . . very creative," stated Mr. Nekk.

Mr. Kung burst into the room. He looked like he'd been drinking, but I wasn't sure. "Very sorry," he mumbled. He looked at Mr. Nekk and Mr. Nekk told him in Octavian I had accused Octavians of being unartistic.

"Who is Jinya?!" said Mrs. Ahm, her excitement rising.

"She is a friend," I said. "Do you think Octavians are artistic?" I asked her.

"Yes," she said. "Some."

"We do not have time, bleecause of war," Mr. Nekk told me. I was amused and intrigued by his vehemence, which I had sparked entirely accidentally.

"War," repeated Mr. Kung.

"Mr. Kung, do you like the Sculpture Gardens?"

Mr. Kung looked desperately at Nekk who grudgingly translated for him. Today, I felt a kind of fondness for Kung.

"Jes, interesting," he stuttered out.

I nodded and went back to Nekk. "How has the war affected art on Octavia?" It was something I was interested in, and obviously Nekk was passionate about it. It would have been a good conversation, if not for the fact that I was intent on sabotaging it.

Nekk laid two more withered tentacles on the table, a sign of intensity — in bars I had seen guys launch at each other from this position, though I doubted sick old Mr. Nekk would be doing that.

"After the wartime, Octavia was very ploor. There was no time to make an art. Like in the movie, *Hard Years*. Have you seen it?"

I shook my head.

"It is very good," said Mrs. Ahm. "You should look at it."

"Watch it," I corrected.

Miraculously Kung had followed the conversation and he said to the others that I wouldn't be able to watch it because it was in Octavian.

"Well, I'll get my girlfriend to translate," I said.

"Girlfriend?" said Kung immediately.

"Last year, I try to learn to dance," Mr. Nekk said. "Because Octavian dance is very wonderful and splendid."

Didn't Octavians get stiff when they got old? I suddenly didn't care about the girlfriend hinting anymore — this was better. I looked at Mr. Nekk's pinched lips and tried to imagine him spinning, turning, whipping into a frenzy.

"Is Jinya your girlfriend?" Mrs. Ahm asked, finally.

"Are you a good dancer?" I asked Nekk. I had never seen Octavian dancing before, so I imagined him stuffed into a tutu and doing pirouettes.

"I am a terrible dancer," said Mr. Nekk, and he actually looked sad. "If I had children I could teach them, but I am blarren."

I didn't correct him.

"So no one will keep Octavian art alive."

Mrs. Ahm leaned over and gave him a playful little push. "I think, today, that Mr. Nekk is too unhappy. Young people like to dance."

Ah, I wondered to myself, *but do they dance Octavian-style or Earth-style?*

*

Intergalactic Cool Youth obviously ruled this planet.

On my way home from school that day I stopped in at a store dedicated to teen idols and saw their faces everywhere. There was Shy Guy and his bashful grin; the outrageous poses of Wild Guy; Wit Guy's splayed tentacles and hilarious hat; Sexy Guy's hypnotizing gaze; and the almost visible unpredictable electricity of Mood Guy. I loved them all, in my own way.

Their music blared out at me as I walked down the aisle. There were bins full of tiny crystal statues of them — probably manufactured by the slave Neb planets, given the detail — and I had to suppress an urge to bury my hand in them up to the elbow. Each member had his own bin and his own color. I unobtrusively returned the one or two stray I.C.Y. that had emigrated, just for the visual pleasure of seeing each bin a clean solid color. I took one at random, thinking that I'd give it to the little rock-headed girl if I could do so without making everyone else jealous.

There was a blue holo of them in concert that caught my eye, and the price-tag made me laugh.

"*It sings,*" said the attendant who had mistranslated my laughter as *How wonderful, exactly the price I wanted to pay!*

She pushed a button and the base of the sculpture began playing the song that was playing on the loudspeakers, only quieter. I enjoyed the effect of the same songs playing at once, and pointed up at the speakers.

"*It's a very popular song,*" she said, with a cute smile.

I immediately compared her to Jinya — she was almost as attractive, and her headcrest was very stylish.

"*I'm looking for a poster for my girlfriend,*" I said, which wasn't entirely true. I *was* getting it because she had said that my walls were blank, but that wasn't the same as getting it for her. Maybe I mentioned her to make up for my wandering eyes.

She nodded, and walked me over to a selection. I followed, watching her move and telling myself maybe it was normal to compare women of the same species, because they were similar after all.

I looked through the posters and found one I liked. It was a shot of all the

boys hanging by their tentacles in what looked to be an ancient Earth jungle —
I liked it because it was unlikely for all kinds of reasons, and it had the silver
English words "Because Intergalactic Cool Youth" almost obscuring the picture.
The one where they all were pointing eight zap guns each at the camera was also
really good. I bought them both.

Jinya's laughter flowed from the bedroom. It made me smile as I poured the
Zazzimurg tea. I put the pot back and picked up the cups, enjoying the warmth
of them — my apartment was cold, and I didn't really know why. I hadn't figured
out the heating system entirely.

"You are very foolish!" she said, standing in the doorway.

I handed her the tea and shrugged. "Why?"

"Intergalactic Cool Youth poster is for Octavian schoolgirls!"

I walked by her, stepping over her tentacles, and went to look at the poster.
I had hung the jungle scene above my bed. I set my tea cup on the bed stand too
close to the edge and I saw it starting to tip.

It would have been futile on Earth, but on slo-mo Octavia I was able to grab
it and only a blurp of tea got over the rim. I was able to feel surprised that my
instinctive reactions were attuned to being here — that I had even bothered
grabbing for it — before the blurp hit the ground.

"Clumsy, too!" she said, sliding into my bed. "Is cold."

I watched her getting cozy, her tentacles rippling under the covers, and
suddenly didn't mind my apartment being chilly. But I stood there for a moment,
sipping my tea and looking at the poster as if it was a piece in a museum.

"Don't look!" she said. "Is foolish!"

"Where are they?" I asked, pointing at the jungle.

"Is not interesting!" she said, hitting the cover.

"I went to a planet like this," I said.

"Earth?"

I looked at her, a little surprised. "No. When I was training to be an English
teacher I went there."

"I saw pictures like this from Earth," she said.

"They are very old pictures," I said. The idea of the creeping green taking
over the cities made me shudder a little.

I finished my tea and set the cup down. I sat on the bed, flicked off my shoes. I sat there for a second.

"It's very cold," I said, as if that was the only reason, and got under the covers.

I lay there for a second and then turned on my side to face her.

"I know it's for schoolgirls," I said. "It is very interesting to me because I.C.Y. are always happy. Our pop music stars pretend to be tough or angry."

"Yes!" She turned her head, but I was too close, and she turned her head back shyly. "I.C.Y. are always cheerful. Too cheerful. Is not real."

"I like sad music, too," I said.

"Sometimes on the bus, I listen to sad musics. I watch the ground go by. . .I think about old friends. . . or a boy. . . or my grandmother. . ." She smiled a sweet smile that pulled my heart like taffy, looking down towards the foot of the bed.

"Me too. On Earth, when I am on a bus and it is raining, the water hits the window. The water makes pictures on the window. It's very beautiful."

"Oh Sam! Do you know 'opatio'?"

I shook my head.

"Down far in the caves, it is like water."

I presumed she meant how the atmosphere became as dense as Earth pools at a certain depth.

"My father is diver. For Octavian pearls."

"I remember."

"When I was a children he took me to the opatio. All around, the air is very deep? Thick! The air is thick."

She made a hard-to-breathe face and I nodded.

"So when you move, it is like pictures. In the air! Very surprising!"

I imagined the cave that we had explored. Further down, on a ledge that we couldn't see, stood young Jinya and her dad. He spun his tentacles out suddenly and ripples emanated towards the four corners of the planet. She threw her tentacles up and the ripples travelled up, up, up until they washed over me a decade later.

I smoothed her headcrest and kissed her cheek. She closed her eyes, and slipped a tentacle into my hand. I turned her head towards me and kissed her lips.

I pushed up against her and planted a kiss on her earhole. She made a little *oh!* sound and squeezed my hand. I slid one arm behind her neck and let the other slide down over her body. Her shirt buttons gave me a little resistance, but she didn't, her eyes silver slits. Up and over her breasts, over her tummy, and — with a little thrill — into the alien part of her, where legs should have been but

179

weren't.

Stroking the part where her waist became tentacles, I picked one and held it at the root, then slowly drew it up. Her suction cups plucked at me as my hand travelled the length of it.

"Are you nervous?"

"A little," she whispered with a giggle.

"Don't worry," I said. "Just tell me when to stop."

"OK."

I kissed her neck, still holding the tentacle. The tip twitched a little, and I kissed it. I thought back to the times I had looked at Jinya's tentacles with lust and felt desire surge up. Then I took it in my mouth and sucked it, feeling the suction cups along it try to latch onto my tongue.

Jinya laughed, but it was a ticklish laugh. I let her pull her tentacle out and it went with a slurp, and it writhed there in the half-light, glistening.

"Very strangey!" she said after a moment.

I shrugged, feeling a heady mix of horniness and shame. "I'm a strange guy."

She was caressing me with four or five tentacles, one or two of them in the danger areas — not that it was likely that she knew where those were.

I knew more than her in that respect, thanks to Lisa. But not much more. She had spent most of her letter discussing whether or not Octavians were descended from humans, or vice versa. Whether they were octosapien or not didn't hold too much interest for me, since I figured it was a line of study hugely biased depending on your pro-monkey or pro-octo agenda. Finally, the last line read: "Oh yeah — the females do have a meaty hole which is roughly compatible with the human specs. Still no hard data (so to speak) on the modern-day after-effects of couplings on the female."

I had to smile at the memory of Lisa's classy wording.

"What?" said Jinya.

I didn't want to admit that I was thinking about an ex. "Something funny happened at school today," I said, and it was true.

"What was?"

"I played a word game with the students. They had to come up with English words from their memory. I called the game 'Memory' and wrote it on the board."

"Yes! Games are good, because they very competitive."

"Yeah, you're right," I said. I had learned that the quickest way to get them to pay attention was to divide them into teams. It was a kind of black magic, though, and one side-effect was that the boys were a lot more engaged than the girls.

Jinya moved closer and put her head in the crook of my shoulder. "And?"

"Well, every letter got one point. I played the game in all three of my classes. The smart class, the middle class, and the dumb class. Who do you think got the most points?"

"The smart class?"

"Nope. The middle class had almost twice as many points."

She made the Octavian sound for *huh*? Her head lifted to look at me and I kissed her forehead quick. She made the Octavian sound for *oh*! and then slapped me lightly.

"Why?" she asked.

"They were . . ." I didn't know the Octavian for cunning, only *clever*. "Do you know cunning?"

She was laughing. "Yes! Like clever! How cunning?"

"The smart class came up with good words like 'apple' and 'school.' They were thinking very hard. But the middle class were cunning . . ."

She laughed again at the use of the word.

". . . because they found words on their clothing. English words like 'Galactic' because the brand of his hat was 'Galactic Trendy Boy Love'. And the funniest was when they used the name of the game, that I had written on the board. 'Memory. Six points teacher, six points!' "

"Too cunning I think!" she said. "They are not school smart, but they are cunning!"

"Exactly!" I said. Buoyed by this success, I went even more abstract. "I thought, 'This is cheating, because they are not using their memory. But cunning is very important. Maybe it is more important than English.' So I gave them the points."

"Oh! You are right. Because . . . they are not good at English. So maybe . . . they are business, or shopkeeper."

I didn't say anything for a moment, because I was overcome by this absurdly massive crushing gratitude that I was beside this beautiful, soft, wickedly intelligent woman. I felt love, but immediately I wondered how much of it was because of my isolation. Before it could be cut to pieces by the crossfire of my analysis, I told her that she was so wonderful.

She made a happy sound, drew a tentacle across my chest. It tickled, but I was smiling anyway.

"You too," she said.

Six months.

We were inside a massive mechanical clock, and everywhere munchkins were dancing.

On the cogs. All over the metal frame work. There was even a few writhing on the pendulum as it swung back and forth. I had no idea how they got aboard it.

I had never seen Montavians dance. I thought 9/3 had been joking when he told us where we were going. I looked at him now, and he answered my stricken look with a shrug of his android body.

"You complained that the last place we met was boring." He had adjusted his voice so it was plainly audible above the music without yelling.

Matthew was looking around and grinning like he had been told he had inherited a jeevesatron. He said something to me I couldn't hear. I cupped my ear.

"At least now I don't have to hear any more about what's-her-name!"

"It's Jinya, you bitter motherfucker!"

He made a can't-hear-you gesture and danced off.

I took a breath and yelled at 9/3, "Are all Montavian—"

9/3 put his hand on my arm. "You do not need to yell."

"Oh."

I looked over at Matthew, who was dancing to the tick-tock music like he had been born into it. He was looking around himself in wonderment. And he had every reason to — I'd never seen Montavians do anything but fix stuff and then go to the next place to fix more stuff.

But if Matthew was enjoying seeing their squat little bodies jack and bounce, they were equally amused by his grotesquely elongated limbs moving about. But this mutual appreciation was not to last.

"He is not broken hearted," 9/3 said.

I shrugged. "Yeah, he's taking it pretty well, I guess. Maybe they weren't that serious."

9/3 seemed to think that over. "It must be nice not to care," he said.

I looked at 9/3 and wondered about this queer roboman who took so readily to a human body. "You bent out of shape over some Montavian?" I guessed.

"No," he said, not elaborating.

I looked at a girl dancing nearby, ringlets framing her face, and couldn't help myself. "Call me xenophobic, but I just can't imagine having sex with a Montavian. They look like ugly Earth children. It's wrong on so many levels."

"Ha ha. That is mean, Sam." 9/3 looked at me. "Sex with Montavians varies from sex with humans in a negligible way — in terms of physical stimulation."

"Well, how the fuck did you get to be such an expert, Randy Andy?!"

He shrugged. "I have been experimenting."

I felt betrayed. "And? Your results?"

He paused. "The physical stimulation plays a minor role in comparison to other variables —" 9/3 started laughing. Then he pointed.

Matthew was dancing. Fast. Unnaturally fast. He looked like he was on fast-forward. Even the expressions on his face came and went with impossible swiftness. I started to get scared.

"He has taken too much," 9/3 said. "He has taken a Montavian chrono drug. Do not worry, it will be over soon."

Before I could do anything, a Montavian came up to 9/3 and started yelling at him. I looked over at the group where he had come from and saw a girl wave at 9/3. One of the men in her group pulled her hand down roughly and yelled at her, holding her wrist in his knot of a fist. She argued with him.

"What's he saying?" I asked 9/3.

"Do not worry. Do not interfere." I looked at the girl who had waved and wondered if this was an unexpected result of a previous experiment.

The Montavian took a swing at 9/3's balls and connected solidly.

"Ooof," said 9/3 calmly as he doubled over and fell to the ground.

The adrenaline hit my veins and I took two steps before 9/3's outstretched palm stopped me.

"Don't move, Sam. My pain receptors are off. This is a ritual."

I stood there, my fists hanging like useless weights off of my arms, as the munchkin kicked the hell out of 9/3.

Matthew materialized beside me. He was screaming. "What the fuck why aren't you doing anything fuck I knew you were a fucking fraud just like your whole fake pug crap —"

I swung at Matthew but he dodged easily, all hopped up. Then he was in my face screaming again and my second punch knocked him flat. His body was suddenly still, his frenetic speed paused.

Meanwhile, the Montavian was standing on 9/3's chest and rearing his foot back. He booted 9/3's head off and it slid to where I was standing.

9/3's eyes flashed. "I am fine, Sam. If he was serious, he would have used his tools."

I realized he was right. But the little bastard was serious enough, staring back at me with hate-filled eyes as he walked back to his group. His tool box, slung low, glinted a promise of nastier times.

We moved on the belt towards the rocketship. 9/3 carried Matthew, whose chrono trip was now slowing time considerably for him. His face was a freeze frame of shocked misery.

"I . . ." he said.

I was upset myself. I had let the rush get the best of me and hit a friend.

" . . . thought . . ."

9/3's eyes flicked at me. "That place was a little too interesting."

I tried to smile.

" . . . we . . ."

"Maybe you should retire the andy body for a while," I said, watching the fuel cars leave the launching pad.

" . . . would . . ."

"Yes," 9/3 said. "Again, I am sorry."

" . . . get . . ."

"It's OK," I said. "It was just a little disturbing, all at once."

" . . . married."

9/3 and I looked at Matthew. Tears were dripping off his face.

I looked at the silver ship and looked forward to entering the velvet blackness of space.

SEVENTEEN

On the long trip home, I kept falling asleep. But now I was home I stared at the ceiling begging it for unconsciousness. I kept running the scene though my head, kept punching Matthew, getting upset with myself.

I got up, poured myself a shot of ujos from an absurdly large bottle Mr. Kung had given me. The liquid spiraled out of the bottle but I had no appreciation for it. I wished my little friend the wallen was around and walked out to the living room, thinking about going to find the little guy. If he was still breathing . . .

The pug moviedisk was still sitting on the floor. I tapped it with the pad of my foot and it came on. The sudden light made me squint, but I stared at the fight anyway. It was the same clip that Jinya had seen — I hadn't looked at it since. I wondered what else Skaggs had put on it.

I sat on the floor with my monster bottle of ujos and decided I'd watch them all. As a kind of punishment.

As it turned out, there weren't any more fights, but I got my punishment. Next up was the newsclip. Rather, The Newsclip.

The visuals showed a pug fight. "These are the pugs," a world-weary voice intoned. The fighting froze and the perspective panned around to frame Jason, clenched teeth grinning with both fists in action. "They're a group of youths who don't bother with the vengeance vendors. They take a more direct route to settle the score." They zoomed in on Jason's face, the crazy intensity about the eyes that he got. "Parents all over the planet are asking: Where is it coming from?"

A young man sitting in a high-backed chair appeared. "Anger," he said, looking up and then away from the camera, as if on a topic that fascinated and yet troubled him. "Youth should be angry. There's nothing more socially healthy than youthful rebellion. My company just meets the demand." He looked back at the camera. "Pug's been one of our most successful subcultures, and the reason why is because the early participants believed they started it. That it was theirs — that's pride of ownership for you — and it was theirs, in a sense." He shrugged.

The fight started up again and the camera panned around for another subject. I saw myself get a glancing blow to the head that made my smile grow bigger. The scene froze. "Some of these young boys come from good families, and have bright prospects in life." It panned in on me, my clean cut hair and swollen lip, and my mother's net worth was indicated. "Why are they playing these dangerous games?"

Back to the expert, who shrugged his shoulder. "They don't think they're games." The expert, in comparison to the world-weary narrator, was downright likeable. "Pug was started out of a real inequality." He put his feet up on an unseen desk and settled his hands over his stomach. "I'd been demographing for a vengeance vendor, and there was a big chunk of pie that couldn't afford even the smallest slander package. And this chunk was teenaged. The client wasn't interested in thinking creatively so a friend and I went solo. We looked at the tension points and the soft spots and put the money in the right places — launched a cheaper priced medvac and got a few plants working full time, that kind of thing. But that was just the beginning. Then we had to wait. It was the waiting that was the hard part. Waiting and keeping it quiet. Damn, that was hard." The young guy rubbed his eyes as he said this, and looked tired.

"Some parents were disturbed most by this quiet," the narrator said as the young guy was replaced by three people.

"It was fine," an older woman said, "that he wanted to be in a subculture."

"We weren't against that," said a full-lipped woman.

The older woman looked agonized. "But what's wrong with the one we got him for his birthday? We were bacchanalians, so we thought . . ."

"He didn't want to be the same as his parents, we understand that," said a man, his droopy moustache rising and falling.

"Well, he could have exchanged it, then!" the older woman said, running her hand through her hair. "The kit's just sitting there! And the oils will go bad, I'm sure . . ."

The fight came back on and the perspective buzzed around, the camera loving us even as the world-weary voice dripped disapproval. "Whatever the cause, pug has captured the imagination of Earth's teenagers. When other subcultures have had to struggle to even stay on the market, pug has grown steadily with absolutely no support." This was indicated by a line graph superimposed over the fight, with the noise from the scene rising as the line did.

"It was imperative that there be no support." Again the young man, swivelling in his chair. "Which is not to say that there was no cash outlay. Coolhunters, media outlets had to be generously compensated to prevent it going public. We needed at least two years of simulated authenticity for it to grow to a harvestable size. It was a harrowing period of time — most subcultures are seeded and harvested in the space of a week, because the fashion and entertainment spin-offs alone make it profitable. But we wanted to do something different. Something edgy."

The next shot showed pugs lined up for the medvacs, chatting in the post-rumble camaraderie. Bathing their hands and faces in the machine's glow. The voiceover was still the young company man: "There hasn't been a spontaneous youth subculture on Earth for almost a thousand years. They were hunted to extinction long ago. But we did the next best thing."

The next few seconds showed a few pugs pulling on jetpacks, heading home. It followed one of them up, and froze, and an offer for home delivery of a pug DIY kit appeared. Then the music swelled.

Free to fight
Young boy's right
Punch your way through the night

Hard as it was to intellectually absorb the rest of the segment, it was the final one-two punch that put me out: the kit and the song. It was always a running joke among pugs, what would be in a "pug kit" — because pug would never be lame enough to have a starter kit, like ready-made subcultures did. Yet here it was.

And the song, the fucking song that I had raged through so many fights on, that song that I knew was cheesy but for some reason got me choked up . . . it wasn't mine after all, it was theirs from the start.

Question their right
Challenge their might
Fight, young pug, fight!

I wanted to, more than anything. But it was their idea. They wanted me to fight, so I had to fight fighting. Punching Matthew for telling the truth — for calling pug fake — was playing right into their hands. And when I crossed the line with him, why not Mr. Zik? Why not Jinya?

The moviedisk blinked out and left me in the dark. I reached for the bottle and knocked it over, then righted it. I wondered if the spill would damage the moviedisk.

I hoped so.

When I got up to go to bed, I heard the droid bustle into the room, sensing a mess.

The next day I was waiting for Jinya at Hello Tea Time! It had Victorian touches — a welcome relief from the ubiquitous cowboy flavor that half the Earth-style establishments on Octavia chose.

Trying to ignore a hole in my sweater, I focused on the newsfeed — flip-flopping with different meanings until I found ones that made sense, and having to do it before it scrolled away, was quite a challenge.

I pressed the lever for a stream of Earl Grey — they had gotten that right, at least, down to the stainless steel piping — and took a sip. A group of girls came in as I blew on the surface of the tea, a bit harder than I would have on Earth, and to less effect — no steam to wisp and tear at my breath.

But then, girls never looked at me on Earth the way they did here. The three girls had chosen a nearby table and were watching me like the exotic animal I was. I studied the patterned rim of the cup as I sipped, giving them a serious profile to review.

"*He is extremely handsome,*" said one in hushed tones, even though the tea room was almost empty. I pretended not to understand.

"*Eh, you're crazy. His nose looks like a cucumber.*"

"*Plangyo nose!*" said the third.

I tried not to smirk at this joke at my expense. I didn't take it seriously — my stately Earthling nose was naturally going to appear big next to the Octavian bump that passed for a nostril-holder.

I glanced at them as part of a survey of the room. They stared back — two really pretty girls and one chubby, less pretty one. They could be university age. I focused my attention on the table and waited to see what they'd see next.

The pattern on the table was the same as the tea cup. I had initially registered it as floral, but when I looked back something slightly unbalanced in it caught my eye. It looked like a fish or a . . . dolphin. That was it. A dolphin. And now the thing I had taken for a daisy looked more like an Octavian.

"*He looks like Pan Venrugie,*" said the love-struck one, and my lip curled involuntarily. That mediawhore? That baby faced bimbo? I clenched my teeth and waited for the other girl to laugh her out of the room, to give me my dignity back.

"*He does look a little like him,*" she said.

I couldn't believe it. "*That's crazy!*" I blustered. They looked at me like I'd pulled out a zap gun. "*I didn't look anything like that, that . . .*" I didn't have the words. "*Are you blind?*"

"*I told you he could speak,*" said the chubby girl.

"*Not very well*," said the other girl.

The one who liked me was stunned, her full lips slightly parted. "*So you heard—*" she dissolved into a shame wail, and she put her head on the table and piled her tentacles on top. Evidently it was not a habit all girls lost after middle school.

"*It's OK*," I said. "*You are beautiful, too.*"

Her big eyes blinked at me through the tentacle forest, and the wail paused.

"*Are you Mr. Sam?*" said the chubby girl.

I nodded, feeling like a celebrity. Yes, 'tis I. You have found me.

The chubby girl smiled. "*I used to go to Plangyo Middle School.*"

"*Was Laz Cha Zik your English teacher?*"

"Yes, blut my English is blad." The other two laughed.

"It's OK," I replied, my smile forgiving, "*I like to practice my Octavian.*"

"*You need to*," said Annoying Girl with a smile.

"*How is your English?*" I enquired mildly.

"Good," she said. The girls laughed. "Very good."

"She lying!" said Smart Girl.

The conversation continued down this path for a while. It turned out the other two girls were cousins visiting from Artemia   which explained why I hadn't seen them around before. The one who liked me had nothing interesting to say, and even the one who didn't like me had only her coy spunk, which got old really fast.

They drank their Zazzimurg and eventually left, and I thought about how different that conversation would have been at the time when I first arrived in Plangyo. Not knowing Octavian, our conversation would have been limited to "You are beautiful," "You are handsome," "I love you," and a whole lot of giggling. I would naturally have assumed the beautiful girl had a formidable intelligence. Not knowing they were related, I would have seen her friendship with the chubby girl as proof of an admirable willingness to choose friends for something other than accessory value. I would have never known that she was here on vacation, and spent a painful week afterwards hoping to see her in Plangyo.

I looked on that alternate universe Sam and it was so tangible, so predictable, that I found it hard to believe that it wasn't real. That I had found someone to love, and someone had found me loveable, on a planet where I was a freak — that seemed to be far more bizarre.

A group of kids came in, shocked into momentary silence by my presence.

I began to regret my decision to come here so early. I kept forgetting that a tea house here was not a café on Earth, where I was ignorable enough for it to be an introspective space.

I looked away from the kids and the door. A minute or two later, someone was tickling my shoulder.

I smiled and whacked at the tentacle poking into the hole in my sweater. It had to be Jinya, and I was ashamed at my slovenliness and happy she was finally here—

The old lady giggled and pulled her tentacle away.

I stared at her, stunned. I recognized her as the heavily made-up owner of the tea room. What did she want?

She pointed at the hole again. I nodded. Did she think she was telling me something new? I looked at it again, tucked in the loose threads as if it helped. *Fuck, there's no way that Jinya's friends aren't gonna notice this . . .*

The owner was making motions with her tentacles. Then she actually started taking off her blouse. I shook my head desperately, no, and she insisted, yes, and started trying plucking at my sweater.

Don't ask me why I just didn't ask her what she wanted. It was one inexplicable gesture after the next, and in my anxiety I actually forgot I could speak Octavian. 100% of my brain was dedicated to deciphering this crazy lady's demands.

At this point, her group of cronies were watching and laughing. She was frustrated by this point and muttered *"Take it off!"* to herself.

This was all I needed to remind me. *"Why?"* I asked her in Octavian.

"We will blachet," she said, using a word I didn't know.

"Eh?"

"Fix!"

Oh. I looked over at the cronies, and one held up some sewing.

I figured, it's not like I can look any stranger to these people. I pulled off my sweater. She whisked it away, staring at my chest.

I crossed my arms. I didn't know what she was staring at — the hair? My nipples? Out the corner of my eye I could see her making chest-high motions to her cronies. They burst out laughing.

I looked away. It wasn't so bad, just a bunch of old ladies. Luckily there was no one else in the tea room.

Then Mrs. Ahm came in with her husband.

I would have ducked but I was facing the door — I'd chosen it so Jinya didn't miss me. She said something excitedly to her husband and then waved to me. I waved back.

Mr. Ahm's eyes bugged out when I exposed my chest and I quickly refolded my arms. Mrs. Ahm didn't seem to notice until she got closer.

"Oh! Sam, why do you no clothes?" she said, her careful English scrambled by the shock. Her tentacles fluttered.

I looked over at the cronies bitterly, who were chatting merrily about something else.

"Why do I have no shirt?" I said, adopting my teacherly-corrective tone.

"Yes, why?" she said.

"It is a holiday on Earth. No Shirt Day. You know?"

She shook her head slowly, no. Damn. I was hoping she'd fake it, and we could help each other lie.

"It is a special day to celebrate freedom. Freedom from clothes. It is a symbol." I glanced towards the door, knowing Jinya and her professors were bound to walk through at any time.

Mrs. Ahm was nodding. "Very interesting." She explained briefly to her husband. He tried to put a blasé, cosmopolitan face on but failed. He watched my arms constantly, trying to catch another peek.

"Mrs. Ahm is one of my best students," I said to Mr. Ahm. He jerked his gaze up at my face guiltily. "Hello," he said.

"My husband is very bad at English," she said.

He nodded. "Blad." Then he put his tentacle out to shake. "Nice meet you."

His tentacle waved there for a second and I discovered I was as unable to resist this social imperative as I was unable to resist gravity. I gave it a quick squeeze and pump and returned my hand to its obscuring duties.

But not quickly enough. Mrs. Ahm's eyes were moons.

"Are you here for tea?" I asked.

"Yes," Mrs. Ahm said. "Tea." She smiled weakly. "Bye-bye."

They moved off to the furthest corner of the room.

If I hadn't had to walk right by them, I would have gone and grabbed my sweater back. As it was, I looked at my tablecloth and wondered if it would at least cover my offensive midriff. What was the deal with that? I wonder if Jinya would have the same revulsion? Oh fuck, she was gonna freak out to see me here half-naked, I had to do something—

The owner dropped the sweater on my table, and I pulled it on in a gasmask scramble. It was backwards, naturally, so I switched it around without taking it off. I thanked the owner profusely, pretended to look at the stitches appreciatively.

I chanced a glance over at Mrs. Ahm's table. Mr. Ahm was listening to his wife talk, watching my every move. He was probably a cop or something. I tried to remember if she had ever said anything about his job. It was probably illegal to be topless on this planet — I knew I had never seen an Octavian bare-chested.

I saw Jinya at the door and stood up right away. I touched my sweater anxiously, as if it may have disappeared. I left the beeds in the cup — which isn't rude, just a way to make sure they don't roll away — and walked towards her.

"Let's go," I said, worried that someone would yell out what a freak I was, or communicate that through some Octavian eye-language I didn't know.

"Yes," she said. "I'm late."

I laughed. "That's OK."

We left the building. It was bright out, and I noticed a group of my kids. They gave me a cool nod, and went back to chatting, a tall boy placing his tentacles behind his neck in affected languor. I felt a little miffed at their casualness.

The guy with the pastry stand did a double take and greeted me as I went by, and I happily reciprocated.

"You want?" said Jinya, stopping.

"No no," I said, pulling us on. "Just saying hello."

"Mm."

I stopped. "Do you want?"

She tilted her head and smiled. "Yes, but . . . too fat."

I turned us around and ordered a bag, counted out the beeds. "I'll eat the fat ones," I said.

The bus was pulling into the station in a shower of bubbles. We rushed to catch it. I pushed Jinya on first. "Hurry, you're too slow!" I joked.

She giggled but even her transcendent radiance wasn't enough to combat the annoyance of the sour-looking bus-goers, unhappy at being delayed by an offworlder and even less happy that he was with an Octavian girl.

We had to sit beside one particularly pinch-faced old ape who stared viciously at Jinya as the bus pulled out.

"Fuck, these people are old and ugly," I said conversationally, looking around and meeting the stares with a pleasant smile.

She slapped my hand lightly. "I agree," said Jinya. "This old man . . . too ugly!"

"He'll be dead soon," I said.

My grin angered the old coot. "*Who is he?*" he demanded of Jinya.

She smiled and looked down, silently.

"*I am Sam Breen. It is none of your interest. You are not her father.*"

The old man ruffled, his nostrils twitching. "*All Octavians are family.*"

"*All right, Dad,*" I said, using the very informal. "*Can we have some money?*"

I had been saving that one. Two old ladies behind him laughed. One of them turned and poked him in the earhole. He cursed her nastily, but she cackled on. Then she got up and headed for the door. He followed her and they got off the bus when it stopped.

"Husband and wife," Jinya said. "She is very lively!"

Outside he was yelling at her. She laughed for a while but when the bus pulled away she started the ugly-yelling too. I wondered what my smart talk would cost her in the end. No easy victories here.

Jinya curled a tentacle around my hand and I squeezed it, sliding the pad of my thumb across it. I couldn't be bothered looking around to see what kind of attention we were gathering. I flipped her tendril over and put my fingertips on the suckers, pulled them off, the light suction like secret kisses.

"So we will meet your English professor?"

"Yes! Yesterday, he come up after class: 'Jinya, remember tomorrow we meet. Mr. Sam is special case.' I say 'No! Just Sam, not Mr. Sam!'"

I smiled. "You teach the teacher?"

Delight flashed from her. "Yes! He very embarrassed. 'Oh, I forgot.' He is worried because you come, but also excited."

"He is worried because I am a native speaker?"

"You are an English Test for him. Your name isn't Sam, it is Test!"

We laughed and sat in silence for a while, but it felt good. It was a full silence, quite different from our silences earlier on when I desperately tried to think of something to talk about.

We were coming into the crest of the valley that the university was nestled in, the round white main buildings looking like spores on the beds of coral. The coral looked red from a distance, but as the road dipped down the walls were more purply-blue close up.

I had gone by it a few times with Mr. Zik, but this was my first visit. We slid by the small stores and restaurants that grow around any university and I looked at the occupants with interest.

The bus pulled in and we got off. It idled there, oozing tiny bubbles, the driver seeming to linger — I didn't blame him, Plangyo was dull in comparison. The station was polka-dotted by bright circles of young folk waiting for buses or for their friends to arrive.

As we walked through the small streets serving the university, I remembered how much I enjoyed being around people my own age. Small towns like Plangyo were filled with the very young and the very old — most of the successful middle aged people headed towards the cities, and the young folk lived in places like this. The occasional older professor was always accompanied by a few students, who looked like they were cheerily escorting the man out for violating the age laws.

I caused the usual commotion as I walked with Jinya, who pointed out her favorite restaurant (unremarkable looking except for the overflowing crowd) and the droid shop her brother's pal owned. Every minute or so she'd run into a friend, and they'd exchange quick bows.

I'd follow their conversation for a while, but it was so rapid and the content so polite that I would just wait until the body language turned towards me. She introduced me as a friend, and I always greeted them with the honorific which was funny and flattering to them.

I was happy to see that she acted no differently with them than she did with me. She would say something about the person we had just met, but it was usually pleasant, or tempered with something pleasant. "Not good English, but she is very cheerful!" was about as critical as it got.

I found it a refreshing change from typical Earth cynicism. I remembered how Lisa and I would cut people up into manageable pieces; push how far we could take being clever and nasty without being outright hurtful. Of course, the more clever our quip the more likely that it would get repeated, eventually to the person who inspired it. It was like building weapons and telling yourself you made them for their beauty, the sleekness of their design . . . I was glad and amazed that Jinya was so continually positive.

Well, until you leave, the nasty voice in me quipped.

"It is good that you greet properly," she said, looking at me seriously.

"Naturally." I looked at her and smiled, felt like taking her tentacle and then didn't. I didn't know how the general university population would see our appendage-holding, and the idea of her pulling away was too painful a possibility.

"Not natural for Earthlings. Thank you," she said, twining up my arm and giving me a squeeze that made a smile pop out on my face.

We went through a gateway made of the same white material as the domes — close up, it looked like it might be bleached, sanded coral — and we were inside the university grounds. A droid bobbed in front of us for a few seconds while it scanned and Jinya designated me as her visitor. I couldn't tell if it was armed, but it had eyes.

"There is some problem with student terrorist," Jinya told me.

We walked by a soccer field and a very suggestive fountain before getting to the smaller of the two domes. There was a cleaner droid on it, scuttling over the curved surface in a way I'd never seen a machine move. Sometimes the limitless manifestations of droids made me shudder; sometimes I thought the Luddix Federation wasn't altogether wrong.

I wondered if Jinya had even heard of Luddix. We went into the building and up two ramps, and walking through the curvy, angle-less white halls I felt like I was in the round vein of some giant snowman. I swerved from side to side, enjoying the feel of the slopes under my feet until Jinya hit me. "Be serious," she mock-scolded.

There was a professor out in the hall talking to a student. "*You must be more diligent,*" he was saying, his back to us.

"Hello!" greeted Jinya.

A weathered-looking Octavian with a turtleneck turned around. The student hurried off.

"Hello," he said, his eyes wide and watery, offering me a tentacle.

I shook it solemnly and greeted him in Octavian.

He looked like he wanted to say more, but then gestured us into his office.

He turned to me again, like he was checking to see if I'd vanished.

"I was very surprise to hear that there was a native speaker in Plangyo," he said with polished English. "I am gleeful to meet you. You are the first Earthling I have met. Are you surprise?"

I took the seat he offered, a long cushioned bench that Jinya also settled on. "I am surprised," I said. "Your English is excellent."

He laughed, made a deprecating gesture. "It's horrible."

" 'Horrible' is an excellent word."

He said a few words to Jinya that I missed and she nodded and left.

"*So you understand Octavian?*" he said before I could enquire about her sudden dismissal.

"*Yes, I can speak and understand much Octavian.*"

He looked impressed. "The government believes that the offworlder cannot speak Octavian fluently," he said, looking around the room.

I wondered if he was worried about being overheard. "Is it better to speak Octavian or English?" I looked around the room, too, and noticed a porkpie hat hanging on a hook.

"Whatever?" he said. He folded his tentacles. "Some words are easy in Octavian, but some are very hard. Because—"

I cut him off. "*I take your hand, I am full of happiness.*" "Hand" needed the *thoc* and "happiness" needed the *op*.

He laughed suddenly at this. His eyes narrowed and he leaned back in his chair. "It is very cunning." He folded his tentacles again.

He sat there for a second, nodding and smiling. I was at a bit of a loss. I didn't know what I expected — I had only thought it through as far as this, telling an authority figure. He had a lot of things I assumed he would — a wise look about the eyes, age — but didn't expect him to have a porkpie hat.

"I like your hat," I said.

He grinned, and reached out, popped it off the hook and fluidly passed it down a succession of tentacles until it was close enough to place it on his head at a rakish angle.

I laughed, and Jinya came in carrying tea.

"What?" she said, and then giggled at the professor.

"You think I am very handsome?" he said, his eyes wide.

"No!"

He sighed and grinned and hung it up with the effortless-lightning passing. "I am very sorry Sam, but I only have Zazzimurg tea. Before I had some coffee but it is all gone."

I hid my disappointment. "I like Zazzimurg."

"The problem with your Octavian is that some people will say it is not real, not genuine," he said, back to business.

"They will say it is a trick," I agreed. "Because I use my hand."

He nodded, taking his tea from Jinya with sincere thanks. I was glad to hear the politeness, since it bothered me that Jinya was expected to get the tea — even if she wasn't really necessary for the conversation.

"It is real, I think," said Jinya, handing me my tea. I took the kettle from her and poured hers. The professor made impressed noises about my politeness, which I denied.

"I agree. You use your hand, not a machine." He rubbed his chin with a tentacle. "But some Octavians will not like." He shrugged. "But it will make us more modern, I think."

I was about to protest the use of the word modern in a completely positive sense when the professor burst out of his reverie suddenly. "I have a bright idea!" he said. "My friend is a professor for Octavian culture. We can go to see him."

He started to refer to his schedule to set up a time for a meeting, and it felt good. I had begun to feel like this wasn't nearly as significant as 9/3 had hinted at, but now that we were arranging an appointment it felt like it just might be real.

EIGHTEEN

The yellow oval of gelatinous substance quivered slightly. I peeled it off with two fingers and popped it into my mouth.

"*It is delicious!*" I said and smiled at the cooking teacher.

"*It's not like Earth food, I fear,*" she said, offering one to another teacher.

"*It has unique taste,*" I said. "*Did you cook?*"

She chuckled. "*Of course! It would be foolish to buy it when it's so easy to make.*"

"Sam," said Mrs. Pling, and proceeded to tell me that it wasn't *cook*, it was *bake*. I nodded patiently and tried to remember how much I had appreciated her English conversation at the beginning.

It was interesting how my understanding of the psychic map of the staff room had changed since I had learned Octavian. How the pretty teachers in the back did nothing but gossip and giggle at the gym teacher's dumb jokes. How the dumb jokes of the older gym teacher went over much better than the younger one's, and how the younger teacher was clearly bitter about it. How he took out his bitterness on the gawky history teacher, who had an almost supernaturally relaxed attitude. How he was the only one that got along well with both the clerical workers and the principal. How the principal's slackness was appreciated by most of the teachers, since he was correspondingly undemanding of them.

The bell played its little tune and Mr. Zik returned. I let him sit down before I pounced.

"I am buying a ticket today for my holiday," I said. "I have to go to the travel agency."

Mr. Zik nodded. "We will go together."

"No, I can take the bus," I said. I wasn't just saying that. I knew from talking to my workshop students that my holiday wasn't just strange by Octavian standards — it was extravagant. I didn't want to involve Mr. Zik when it may antagonize him at some level. "I just need directions."

"I cannot give you directions, Sam," Mr. Zik said with a smile. "My map is in my saucer. So I will have to take you in my saucer." A student came in, showed something to Mr. Zik. Mr. Zik stamped it carefully and handed it back with a word of praise.

"My vacation isn't very important so I don't want to cause you trouble."

"It is no trouble. It is near my home."

I looked at him sharply. "And your wife won't be upset?" I knew Mrs. Zik prepared the dinner, which was usually the case on Octavia.

"I will call! Don't worry." He adjusted something on his desk that was askew. The bell chimed.

I got my stuff and checked to see which class I was teaching next. Oh great — the dumb kids. It had gotten easier since I could tell which ones were cursing me out, but it hadn't gotten easy.

"Well, thanks a lot."

"You're welcome, a lot," said Mr. Zik with a wave.

🪐

We luckily found a parking spot on top of a pile that was only four high. I was still amazed at how much more space-efficient saucers were — where there were 20 saucers here, it would have been enough space for four, five floaters max back home. Some of the best real estate in the universe was wasted to keep the floater companies in business. Stupid Earthlings.

And the mapping function was far better, too, getting us there lickity-split. Stupid Earthlings.

The travel agency was decorated in Stupid Earthling style, but since my planet's the one associated with space travel I suppose that's understandable. Just not likeable. The seats were comfortable, though, and had armrests. I was probably the first — and perhaps the last — person with elbows to use them.

There seemed to be a bit of a controversy as to who was going to serve us, so I took in the posters on the wall beside me. Most of them were for Octavian destinations, but one of them showed a gleaming spaceship rocketing through The Mysterious and Inexpensive Neb Galaxy! I studied the poster, which was cheaply made with the only moving image the unconvincing rocket fire, and decided it must have been made specifically for an Octavian market.

"No, it is a not-good place," said a smiling travel agent when he saw what I was looking at. I wondered if he would have said the same to a naive Octavian in a lower price bracket. My own smile was consequently brief.

"I'm interested in booking a flight to Pleasureworld 33."

"How long?" he asked, his tentacle wavering over his pad.

"Three weeks," I said, looking guiltily at the impassive Mr. Zik. He only got two weeks since he had to use the other week for more training.

I told him the dates and he gave me a price.

Mr. Zik let out a surprised whistle. It was a few more creds than I had counted on, but not too many more. Mr. Zik obviously thought it was pricey, and I smiled inwardly imagining what he'd think if he knew about my daily-increasing student loan.

"*It is not a special price for offworlders?*" challenged Mr. Zik.

The agent, wounded, denied it.

I looked at Mr. Zik and shrugged. "OK," I said to the agent.

"OK!" he chimed.

He scurried off to the back room so quickly I worried a little. I didn't want to bother going around to a few agents, although I would have on Earth — I just figured if I could do it quickly and easily, then it was worth it.

♢

An hour later, we were still waiting there. My elbows were getting sore.

I looked at the poster for Pleasureworld, reminding myself how good it would be when I got there. It was a beach party, complete with dancing, eating, and a pair of suns. It was a classy piece of promotion — it lasted for twenty fun minutes before restarting. It looked real, too.

My eye caught a pair of Earthlings who I'd missed the first time. The tiny figures snuck off behind a tree and started snogging each other's brains out. I watched, wondering if the poster makers had noticed it, and if so — why didn't they make it more obvious?

A pretty, distressed female was standing in front of us and I quickly looked away from the poster. The agent who had originally served us had — after apologizing about the delay to our less-and-less tolerant selves — started sending her out. The first delay was to check my legality with the governmental authorities. The second delay was to confirm my existence with the bank.

"*Blood*," she said, a lower lip trembling. She had a scalpel in her tentacle, which she stretched towards me. I pushed back my chair and she let her tentacles flop dead, defeated.

"*We need your blood for the machine*," she explained, which didn't make me feel any better.

"*To confirm his identity?*" Mr. Zik asked calmly.

"*Yes. To the bank. Usually we use oogma-print, but . . .*"

"*Oogma?*" I asked Mr. Zik.

He lifted the tentacle — the sex one — and I remembered how he had signed for the toilet with it.

Unwilling to attempt a penis-print, I grabbed the scalpel and nicked my hand. Still, it was pretty ridiculous — any Octavian who could successfully impersonate me deserved the honor. I handed it back to her and she ran to the back room, face screwed up in disgust as it dripped to the ground.

I sighed. "I'm sorry about this. I didn't think it would take so long. Oh! Did you call your wife?"

"Yes," he said. "But maybe I should call her again. "

He tweaked his wristphone and after a while a mousy woman with glasses answered. It was the first time I'd seen his wife, and I was touched by the similarity between them. I leant into the wristphone's vid range and called out an apology, and she seemed so shocked I felt silly.

I leaned back in my chair as Mr. Zik continued his conversation, and didn't look over at the stupid Pleasureworld poster — it better be worth it, but I knew it probably wouldn't be. I wished I hadn't let Matthew and Hugh talk us into going there when I would have been happier checking out planets nearby that weren't Ultimate Tourist Destinations. Maybe Jinya could have afforded to go then . . .

The first agent came out, his smile a shield. He mumbled an apology and passed me a small gold cylinder — it was awkward, because he didn't really know how my hand worked, and my impatience made it even more so.

There were the governmental twined snakes at the tip of it — perhaps that's why it had taken so long, I didn't know they needed that much official approval. I wiped off the sucker marks left by a very nervous Octavian and relented a bit. He stood there, twining and untwining the tips of his tentacles.

"*Thank you for your service,*" I said, using the honorific.

We started to leave and I waved my little cylinder at the female agent. "Bye-bye!"

A startled smile.

Mr. Zik tapped the saucer door, and it rose. "I am very sorry, Sam," he said as he climbed up.

I thought I'd misheard him. "What?"

He snapped into the chair and started the saucer up, his tentacles flying over the controls like he was absently playing a fugue to cheer himself up. "I am sorry."

"For what?!"

"Bleecause . . . they are Octavian. You will have blad impression of

Octavia."

"*You're brain-soft!*" I exclaimed.

"Ssss-sss-ss," he laughed ruefully. He puffed the saucers on top off, and slipped out of the pile.

"No, it's . . . I don't pay attention to them. You give me a great impression of Octavia. You've been an excellent host."

He tilted his head to the side, neither a nod or a shake.

I was seized by the desire to make it clear that I was sincere, yet I felt suffocated by the multiple layers of the habitual Octavian politeness. "Many Octavians, when they help me, are very loud. They say, 'Look at me, I am helping the offworlder, look at me!'" My voice spiked, because I was excited, I was figuring this out for the first time.

"Ssss-sss-ss," he laughed.

"But you are very quiet when you help me, or tell me something — so I don't feel like an outsider. I don't know how you say it in Octavian — dignity? Do you know?"

He nodded, and told me.

"That's what you give me," I said. "It's more important than fast service." I realized I had been leaning forward with the urgency of communicating this, so I leaned back in my chair

We drove on in silence, except for his occasional nose sound.

"What's amazing is how exceedingly fond I've gotten of that sound," I said, hefting the bowling ball. "It's sick. I'm getting nostalgic about people I haven't even left yet." I whipped it down the alley and got a strike I didn't deserve.

Matthew frowned at this injustice, watching the score tally up.

The autoscore was about the only concession to modernity. Everything else breathed the ancient art of bowling, as it had been played for millennia. I found it a little pretentious, but not nearly as bad as some places — they'd let you use your own shoes at a pinch. Which was good, because they only had Montavian sizes, the largest of which I could wear as an amulet.

"Yeah . . ." he said, after he took his turn. "I probably shouldn't ask you about Jinya, then."

I nodded and grabbed a ball. "I just have to forget I'm leaving in four months. But it looms there, you know? Always in the shadow of it." Crap.

Gutterball.

"Oh, too *bad*," Matthew said, jumping up. "Yeah, just enjoy the moment, I guess. Although . . ." He paused as I took my shot, watching the ball pick off a few pins. " . . . it's good to think about it. It can kind of sneak up on you. Fuck you up."

I looked at him. This was the closest he'd come to alluding to his breakdown at the club. I took my shot and wondered what to say about it. If anything. I wondered if Matthew was waiting for me to say something.

He took his last turn, seemingly focused on the game, watching the score after each shot. I found his competitiveness amusing — so Earthling. It annoyed the hell out of Hugh.

"Did you call Hugh?" I asked.

"Yeah, I left messages with both of them." He checked the time. "I'm surprised 9/3 hasn't shown up — we're practically in his neighborhood. It was kind of last minute, though. I just couldn't stand the idea of being on display for the weekend."

I nodded. It was hard enough for me, and I had a place with non-transparent walls to escape to. I picked a cherry red ball.

"Unfortunately, they've figured out how I masturbate," he said glumly.

"Yeah, I was wondering about that," I said after another strike.

"After my first week, I realized that they had no idea what human sex organs were or how they worked. So when I was in the mood, I'd walk around naked in my living room till a crowd congregated. There were always a few fine-looking women there for stimulus."

I laughed and got another strike, just because I wasn't trying. Matthew cursed bitterly in Squid, and I realized I had won.

We went to sit down on the row of multicolored chairs, which we had adjusted to our height. Matthew waved the waitress over.

"So what happened? How'd you get caught?"

"Well, it was fine at home — if I just kept it regular, they figured it was like grooming or something. But one day I was walking home and I see this beautiful girl having sex in her apartment. So being horny, I whip it out and casually started beating off. I wasn't, like, staring at them or anything obvious. I was just standing on the corner, old ladies were shopping and stuff, no one even noticed."

He shrugged. "But then one of the English teachers from my school came by. At the worst possible time." Matthew leaned back and impatiently watched the waitress help the only other group in the alley.

"Right when you —"

"Yep. So I've got this ecstatic look on my face. She was smiling at first, as if she thought I was so fucking happy to see her. She doesn't even live in town! Fuck, what a fluke. Anyway, the cum's just floating there because of the stupid atmosphere. And like an idiot I look down, and she notices it. 'Urine?' "

I cracked up, imagining the snaky semen wriggling, floating, the look of confusion on her face.

"But then — she must have seen me looking before I realized she was there — she looked over at the apartment, where of course they were still having sex, and figured it out."

"Holy," I said.

"Can't go anywhere now without people staring at my crotch," he said, adjusting his Speak-O-Matic as the waitress neared. He ordered some drinks.

He snapped it off as she left. He had a pendant version. I wondered how different my life would be if I hadn't lost it.

"Wanna try it on?" teased Matthew.

"*May wallens have sex with your mother's corpse*," I said cheerfully.

He had twisted the dial but only caught the end of it. "What about a corpse?" he said.

"You bowl like a corpse," I said.

"So you're still keeping at the language lessons," Matthew asked it like it was a subject that horrified and fascinated him. "I dunno . . . I have trouble remembering any words without connecting them with an English word. Like dichchimp -- 'thanks' in Squidollian -- I learned by thinking, 'Thanks for being a dick, chump.' But every goddamn word has to have this chain of words attached to it."

I shrugged. Despite the laborious and inefficient method, I doubted Matthew had stuck at it long enough to be worthy of sympathy. "Sucks to be you."

He was rubbing at his temple. "Every word, I have to make up some dumb connection . . . I gotta haul up the chain every time . . . but you! Damn you. Are you fluent yet? Bastard?"

"Not yet." I shrugged. "But if I keep at it, I think I may be the first one."

Our drinks arrived. Matthew paid the waitress and hooked his small glass of black soda. Mine was lime-colored, with a fizz. It was tasty.

He gave me a mean look over his glass. "Doesn't that worry you? That no one else's bothered?"

"Fuck off," I squeaked. Literally. My voice was several octaves higher.

Matthew laughed uproariously, then took a gulp of his drink. "Who you telling to fuck off?" he said in a rumbly boulder voice that echoed slightly.

"Hee hee hee," I laughed, mortified by my tone. I noticed the waitress looking over at us curiously.

"HO HO HO," he chuckled.

Another round of giggles, which I got under control. "Last time I let you order the drinks," I squeaked.

Matthew belched like an earthquake, and I nearly jumped out of my skin. The other group of bowlers looked over at us, the guy who had just thrown a gutterball standing there in the classic hands-on-hips munchkin pose of annoyance.

We looked like utter morons. I tried to stop my hysterical high-pitched hee-hee-hee-ing with my hands, and looked over at Matthew.

"What else's in the drink?" I said, feeling light-headed.

"Just the pitch juice," he boomed quietly, looking nervously at the argument taking place in the other group. "Let's go call the guys and tell them off."

I took stock of the munchkin pointing furiously at us and said really quickly, "OK let's go I don't wanna get in another fight."

It sounded so wimpy we couldn't help snickering as we left. I pictured the Montavian's tools flashing into action and that helped sober me up, although (if Matthew was to be believed) there was nothing unsober in my system.

We left the bowling alley and snapped (stomach flip!) into zero g. We pulled ourselves along the hallway, where a half dozen or so Montavians were headed to the alley. I was surprised that there were so few people on the little orbiting amusement, since I had heard that Montavians liked bowling — one of the few sports their tiny size didn't handicap them in intergalactic competitions. But I was surprised that this place stayed open —

"Great!" baritoned Matthew. He had found a vidbooth, and ducked into it. I looked at the icon, a dish with waves emanating from it, and realized I would never have figured out what it indicated. Matthew was already inside and looking at the instruction-laden panel. It was Montavian, and I looked at the angular characters with a feeling of defeat. *Why did everyone have to do it their own way?* I thought, the stupid lazy thought penetrating my carefully placed barriers of cultural tolerance.

Matthew was punching buttons.

"Do you know what you're doing?" I chirped.

"Nope," he said, and stood back. The vid snapped onto standby, and we were bathed in the green glow. I looked at Matthew in profile, and he was already smirking in anticipation of how 9/3 would like our voices.

"You're a good man to have around, Chan," I said as gruffly as my high pitched voice would allow, which wasn't very.

The vid snapped a connection, and the image resolved itself. 9/3 was working on this huge metal sculpture that was wider than the range of the vid, and came up to 9/3's barrel chest.

"What the fuck?!" Matthew boomed. "You passed up a night with us to stay home with your metal collection?"

9/3 adjusted something near his ear, I presumed because he thought the sound had to do with the vidphone. I piped up. "Yeah, dude, I had no competition bowling against this guy."

9/3's red eyes flicked once in confusion. Then, "Oh, you are drinking Montavian juice. Only children drink it here. Young children." He placed a ball bearing at a high level of the metal structure, and it started rolling.

"Does this sound like a kid's voice to you?" I squeaked indignantly.

"Ha," said 9/3 hollowly.

I looked at Matthew. Matthew shrugged.

"Have you heard from Hugh?" I said, getting sick of my voice.

"No. He left," 9/3 said, grabbing a whole boxful of bearings in his pincers. I knew, suddenly, what he meant.

"Left to come here?" Matthew said.

"He went back home," said 9/3, pouring the bearings onto the structure. "To the moon." I watched the bearings slide, sparkle, whiz. So did 9/3.

"Fuck . . ." said Matthew. "Did he tell—"

"No," 9/3 said. "I called him today, and his number was out of service. His school told me he left three days ago."

I was stunned. I had known how unhappy he was, but why would he leave without saying anything? I felt abandoned, and by the look of it that was a tenth of what 9/3 felt.

We watched the last bearings slide to the bottom. I could hear them clinking into a pile offscreen.

"Well, we're still going on holiday, right?" said Matthew. His voice was suddenly back to normal.

"I've already paid for it," I said, and 9/3 nodded. He static-sighed and used his pincers to bend one of the tracks by a small increment. The vidphone flashed for more money.

"Good," said Matthew, relieved. "Fuck him. He'd just slow us down, anyway. And you, my good roboman —" he said with a point and a leer, "You make sure you remember to pack your android body, 'cause you're gonna need it!"

He blinked no. "I am leaving that at home. It just makes problems."

Out of time, the vidphone winked out.

Matthew raised his eyebrows. "I hope he forgets to pack his bad mood."

As we left the booth I realized that originally, it was Matthew and Hugh who had lobbied for Pleasureworld 33. Now it was just Matthew, and I felt a surge of annoyance for him.

"Holy fuck!" he said suddenly.

I didn't say anything.

"God*damn* it!" he said, slapping his forehead.

"What!?" I said finally.

"Hugh owed me 150 creds!"

I felt a little bit better.

Later that night, Matthew tried to convince me to go down to Montavia to try and cheer 9/3 up. I didn't. I regret it now, but how was I supposed to know? Even with Hugh's departure proving how quickly things could change.

But consider the argument against it, without the benefit of hindsight: I would have had to take a rocket home from the surface, and it would have cost a lot more. I was sure we'd get wasted, and I knew from recent experience how dangerous that could be on Montavia.

On the other hand I could take a quick shuttle back to Octavia and be able to slip into my accustomed atmosphere in a few hours which I craved like a warm bath. (I'd never admit that to Matthew, of course, even though he probably felt the same way.) And I might be able to see Jinya tomorrow, before she went to her folks' place.

So an hour or so after talking to 9/3, I was on a shuttle staring out the window, seeing the shape of a certain woman in the constellations, silver star eyes.

I was leaning against the twined tree waiting for her to show up. I hummed a song by Intergalactic Cool Youth and watched the road. It was twilight, and I shot an occasional glance over my shoulder to the house of the old man who cared for this tree. A saucer whizzed by and lit up the house and then me, the twilight atmosphere rippling in its wake.

I previously had sat beside the tree, which had been a step up from standing beside it. Now I lounged indolently, possessively against it. My physical comfort was almost nullified by an equal quantity of anxiety, and perhaps even exceeded by it. So why was I doing it?

I decided I was doing it to look relaxed and cool. And how ridiculous was that, when Octavians relaxed in a totally different way? When their concept of cool was utterly different from an average Earthling's, which was different from a pug's?

A saucer went by slowly. I listened to the hum of its motor for any slowing, refusing to squint in the glare of its lights and looking as hardcore as possible. When it moved on, I blinked.

The whole scene had a distinct familiarity. After a second, I realized why. We would be waiting for the subway, going to London or somewhere for a fight, twenty or so of us warming up and goofing around. Most of us would squat down along the wall, leaving the seats for the normal patrons. A transit droid would inevitably trundle by, attracted by our motion and noise, and blind us with white light. No one would pay attention 'cause none of us had any weapons except the ones attached to our wrists from birth.

The only time there had ever been trouble was when Skaggs had filled his jetpack with a green solution that left this fantastic trail, and it turned out it was mildly toxic. The droid detected "tainted fuel." Seth had reared back and kicked the droid onto the tracks as the subway was coming in. After lasering the droid the train locked down and kept going, of course, and we missed our only ride to the Bolivia fight.

Everybody had been furious. Seth was finished after that. He couldn't walk down the street without being taunted by "Bootboy! Whither thou?" I had felt sorry for him at the time, but after the Pug Swindle news hit, he had a sneer and a jab for everyone.

As unpleasant as it was, I was glad I had a complete memory of the whole time. I dreaded the sappy sentimentalism that seemed to be an inevitable chemical process of the human brain. I wondered what Skaggs was doing now — selling pre-stained pug jackets to wannabes? That had a kind of mean, hard-edged appeal to me.

Jinya appeared out of the haze, stopping as she saw me, then moving faster. Her excitement made me smile, and I watched her approach, her silver eyes downcast.

"Sam!"

"*I like your headcrest,*" I said. She had done something new with it, and it came out in expansive waves.

"Oh! Too big . . ." she said, touching it with the tip of a tentacle. We walked towards my place.

"*Beautiful,*" I said. "*Did your exams succeed? I mean, did you succeed in your exams?* "

She nodded. "*I did fairly well.*"

We chit-chatted, mostly in Octavian — we'd agreed to talk in English until her exams were over to keep her in training. I loved to hear her talk Octavian — her English was cute, but didn't do her intelligence justice. It was her turn to giggle at my fumbled phrases.

I pulled out my key and unlocked my door. "*This week, your professor has been calling me a lot. I have been avoiding the vidphone,*" I told her.

We went in and my vidphone was flashing a message. Jinya laughed, and said a phrase in Octavian I didn't understand.

"You cause it, because you say it," she said. I nodded and repeated the phrase, then tried it out in a few situations: If I talk about bad weather, and then the weather becomes bad?

"Exactly right!" she said, her eyes bright. She put her bag down.

"I almost said, 'If I talk about rain,' but it doesn't rain here."

"No, on Octavia it only," and then she said the word for excessively humid weather. "But I have seen rain on movies. Is romantic."

"*It is only romantic in movies,*" I said. "*In real life it is wet, only.*"

She laughed and took out some bottles of ujos and some snacks.

"*Joy! An ujos party!*" I said. "*Because of the end of your studies!*"

"But, I can't get too drunken. I must go parents' house tomorrow," she said, glumly.

"*Maybe I will meet your parents, someday,*" I said.

"*Perhaps,*" she said, opening a blue package of Delicious Things. "*Someday.*"

I wondered at her reluctance, but also at my probing. Meeting parents on Octavia was the first step on the path to marriage. Considering I had four months left of my contract, why was I even saying these things?

I took a Delicious Thing as Jinya rooted around for glasses. I slapped the vidphone and the professor's face appeared, complete with hat. I wondered if he thought that would win me over. He seemed a bit drunk. He told me how great it would be if I called him. Jinya came in and gave me a drink.

"He is drunken!" she said, and started laughing. The professor was talking to someone offscreen, and then he pulled the speaker into range and wrapped his tentacles around him.

"Oh! Professor Long!" she exclaimed. "Octavian teacher!" He was, indeed, talking in Octavian, entreating me to call them. Then, partially because Jinya's professor was leaning on him so heavily, he fell over. With no one in the shot, the message automatically stopped.

Jinya laughed and went to play it again. "So stupid!" she said. "*I've never seen Professor Long so drunk!*"

I presumed this meant she had seen her other professors drunk before. I pictured them meeting to discuss me and getting so excited about it that they needed to talk to me immediately.

It was a little overwhelming, but at least they looked like fun.

"*That's why you should have a wristphone, so you don't miss calls like these,*" she said, quite seriously.

"*That's why I don't have wristphone!*" I said. "*I told him a week before that I would call him after the holiday.*" I didn't know what I was hoping to figure out in that time, but I figured a bit of delaying couldn't hurt. "*It's a foggy situation,*" I said.

She nodded. "Because many people are proud," she said. "*They don't think offworlders can speak Octavian.*"

In my worries about cultural protection and wallens, I hadn't even thought of hordes of irate Octavians out for my dry skin. Pleasureworld was looking better all the time . . .

The professors fell down again. Amazingly, she started it again, settling back into her seat with her drink and watching it like it was a movie.

By the fourth repetition, I was howling as loud as her, eyes brimming.

NINETEEN

We lay side by side on top of the coral reef, my face slack-jawed with pleasure.

Jinya laughed at me. "*A smile is no stranger on your face.* You know? Is Octavian phrase."

I looked over at her, the slight shift causing the rippling beneath me to change direction. "Oh my god, that feels so good. Earthling phrase."

She giggled. "I remember that one."

I laughed loudly, surprised at her bold reference to our interspecies experiments. My laughter didn't infect the old ladies waiting in line — in fact, their faces darkened as if they somehow had divined our lewd talk.

I sat up slowly, so as to not tear up any of the bright orange coral from the reef, enjoying the little popping sensation along my bare back. I pulled on my T-shirt and we moved on. I put a pair of beeds in the bulb the white-eyed ancient keeper clutched and we walked into the tunnel. He nodded his thanks.

"*He's blind, did you see his eyes?*" Jinya took my hand when we were out of sight. I kissed her forehead.

"*Blind but not deaf, daughter. I heard that kiss!*"

Her tentacle tightened around my hand and we started to run. "*Sorry, grandfather!*" I called back, hoping the tunnel's echo concealed my accent. I wondered if kissing in the Living Gardens was even allowed. We squeezed by two more groups of Octavians and a group of Squidollians, one of whom took a picture of us.

We emerged into another roofless plateau, but this one was much bigger. I stood at the tunnel entrance, entranced. The round hills of softly moving coral were infinitely garish and gorgeous at the same time.

Jinya tugged my hand and I let her drag me past the hills while the dozens of Octavians and occasional Montavians looked on. I couldn't help but admire her quiet courage, because I knew that she fought not only the disapproving eyes of strangers but also the inner voices of Octavians that she respected and loved.

In front of a hill, a purple one that was as high as my shoulders, we stopped suddenly. So suddenly that I knocked Jinya a bit. She made an annoyed sound and poked me in the armpit.

"*The color of this coral is familiar,*" said Jinya, looking at me. I shrugged — it was the shade of my first toy floater, but I knew that's not what she meant. "*My brother! His eyes!*"

I nodded, although I had been more concerned with avoiding the droid parts whizzing by on the belt at the time. Stepping back, it did look like a half-buried eye, if you could ignore the gently undulating fibers that grew out of it. Jinya touched the blindly groping fibers with her own fluid tentacle, and I was struck by the planetary affinity.

So of course, Jinya tore a strip off of it. The fibers on the entire hill stood up rigidly, a shock to the system. She ate some of it. She offered some to me but I refused it, looking around to see if anyone else had seen her.

"*I like it raw,*" she said. She saw my expression. "*Don't worry, it's not trained.*"

Evidently, the coral that had massaged us had been specially trained by the Gardeners. But the fact that it could be trained, and its reaction to being torn, made me uneasy.

"Hello!" said someone from behind. I raised a hand to give an obligatory wave and found myself waist-to-face with a beaming Montavian. "Are you from Earthling?" he said.

"Uh, yes," I said.

"We are from Montavia," he said, indicating himself and an even smaller person.

"It is obvious?" said the smaller person.

"Obvious, yes," said Jinya with a laugh.

He introduced himself — a long name that I immediately forgot — and his son. They worked for the government. We stood there for a moment, smiling at each other. I was intrigued — I'd never felt this kind of goodwill from a Montavian before.

"My friend teaches English on Montavia," I said. "He is a roboman."

The father nodded quickly. "Yes, I heard!" he said, touching a tiny ear.

"My friend saw . . ." the son said. "Uh . . . roboman at a building conversation."

I nodded. 9/3 took an interest in architecture.

"Restaurant?" said the father.

"Robomen don't like restaurants," I said.

The son and father took a second to translate. "No, you and you . . ."

"*Do you want to have dinner,*" I asked Jinya who was already nodding. "OK," I said.

"OK!" they said, chuckling. "Let's go!"

We walked away together. The son walked beside me and the father started chatting to Jinya.

"Yes, uh . . . robomen hate restaurants," he said. "Obvious!" He looked up at me with eagerness, his little legs almost a blur as he easily kept up.

I smiled and laughed, even though 9/3 actually put up with our trips to restaurants without complaint. Just like he put up with being disassembled by irate Montavians week after week. I couldn't put up with that shit.

I looked down at the son, who was biting his lip in an effort to think of English conversation. Dad and Jinya were chattering away ahead of us.

I had mercy. "How old are you?" I asked.

"I am 12 years old," he said. "But I am small."

I smiled.

"Every Montavian is small," he said, looking up. From my perspective, he seemed to be nothing but an impish grin and a triangle-blur of legs. "I am very small. Teeny?"

"Tiny," I corrected.

He nodded quickly, his face falling, repeating it.

"But you are very fast! And your English is excellent!" I said this loudly enough so that his father heard.

His father looked back and said something in Montavian that echoed broadly in the tunnel — it sounded foreboding, but most everything spoken in munchkin tongue did. The son's face didn't change.

"How long have you speak Octavian?" he asked.

"A few months," I said.

"Months?" he said. His pointy eyebrows got more pointy. I imagined that his father had been talking English to him in the womb, so I didn't ask.

"Why do you learn English?" I asked him instead.

"It's very important . . . for many things. Especially business."

"Do your friends speak English?"

He nodded quickly. "For school we must learn."

"Is it fun?"

He gave an adultish shrug. "One of my friends is very superb at English. We talk about . . .secret things . . . and some jokes. No one understands." He laughed.

The Living Garden may have been a boring obligatory family trip for an Octavian, but for me it was awe inspiring. Appalling, too, in a way, since it showed how beautiful the landscape could be through the whole planet, if the coral plants weren't killed off by saucer exhaust and general habitation.

I wondered if the Gardeners were angry about it. As we walked into the expansive eating area, I noticed several Gardeners moving around with bowls of food, passive and benign expressions on their faces. The food, I decided, was sprinkled with something that would slowly dissolve the eater's insides. Their smiles anticipated the time, twenty years from now, when the people they served would explode and the coral plants inside would be free, riotously free to grow wherever the body lay.

"What?" said Jinya, poking me. The father and son were looking at my crooked dreamy smile as well.

"I'm just hungry," I said, protecting my stomach from Jinya. And I was. The smell of the cooked seaweed was making me salivate. The father had secured some seats and was waving us over.

I settled into my indent and took out my fork. As if on cue, the son and father took out spoons with serrated tips.

"Fork, right?" said the son.

"Yes," I said. "I've never seen your utensil before."

"Pample," he said.

We sat there for a second, which I spent hoping that he wouldn't ask to try my fork, and then considering whether they considered their tool the superior one — Montavians were infamously arrogant in this department — and if they expected me to be sitting here ashamed by the inherent *wrongness* of the fork. Thankfully, silence reigned.

Jinya looked towards the bowl, which was making its slow way down the blindingly white table. "So hungry!" she said, and we all murmured agreement. It was hard to think of anything else, and I shifted my fork, imagining shovelling food into my maw, but then stopped lest I revive the utensil discussion.

A Gardener, barely out of his teens, flung dishes at us from his four precarious stacks before moving on. Despite the atmosphere, they came at us at quite a speed. The father reached up to grab his just in time. Then he proudly looked at Jinya, who hadn't noticed him doing anything unusual and just looked back. He looked down finally, obviously feeling silly, and I suddenly liked him immensely.

The food came — a simple fare of seaweed, rice, and boiled coral — doled out by Gardeners. I had never had coral — it was sweetly rich and had a weird texture.

"Do you like coral?" asked Jinya, watching the father eat it with gusto. Octavians always seemed surprised when offworlders liked their food.

"Yes, I love it!" he said. "On Montavia, we have . . ." he pointed to the rice and the seaweed, "But not this. It is illegal."

"Illegal means against the law," I corrected.

"I know," he said, nodding. "Illegal. Because it is not plant. It is an animal."

I stopped eating. "Animal. Like us?" I asked.

The father nodded. Jinya laughed. "Not like us. It is more . . . simple."

I took a forkful of rice, shaking it so the bit of coral fell off. I was seized by the urge to scrape the red and purple and yellow nubs onto the bright white table, but instead I poised my bowl over the father's. He nodded happily and I pushed the sad little things over the rim, where they floated down onto his rice.

"It is illegal to eat animals on Montavia?" I asked.

"Yes," he said. "Because of trading status with Earth."

"Octavia trades with Earth," I said. "Saucers."

"It has cultural-protection," he said. He used the words easily — they were phrases he used a lot, it sounded like. Maybe in his work. Jinya was looking a little lost, as was the son.

"Do you think cultural-protection is good?"

He shrugged, but he seemed to consider it. He translated to his son. He sucked on his pample a little, and then stood up — we were face to face.

"For me . . . my job, it is to make things easier between Earth and Montavia. We make a lot of money — is good. But there is a lot of Earthling things — like movies, and news — is very big, you know? Is everywhere . . ."

He sort of seemed frustrated, but I didn't know if it was by the complexity of the subject or by English. He tapped his pample against his knuckles thoughtfully.

The bowls came around again and I had more rice. I still had the taste of coral in my mouth. Everyone else, of course, helped themselves to another serving of the gruesome delicacy.

"Is difficult subject," said Jinya. "Protection helps this place. It gets money from the Earth Council because Octavia is unique."

"Earth's influence is bad," I said. I looked at the kid, and wanted to tell him that learning English was bad, too, but couldn't go that far.

"Sometimes . . ." the father said. "Maybe the young Montavians are angry, I think. But I like Earth."

There was a sudden click as I thought about how a planet full of young men must feel about being the munchkins of the universe. I thought about the look in the eye of the guy who disassembled 9/3. Were they even conscious of their smallness before the giants came? I wanted to ask him, but again, I couldn't.

"I like Earth," he said, reassuringly. "I love Earth."

"Do you go to Earth?" said Jinya, and the envy in her voice was heartbreakingly apparent.

Not long after dinner, the Montavians took their leave. I had been quiet for quite a while, so I made my good-byes especially heartfelt. The older Montavian had given me a lot, even if it was bitter medicine.

"I am upset that I cannot see the Lovemaking," he said.

Jinya put her tentacle to her lips. "Is a secret!" she said.

Their rented saucer bubbled away and I looked at Jinya with a neutral feeling that had more in common with indifference than lust. "Lovemaking?"

"Let's go," she said with a smile. "Is interesting!"

I followed her back into the Living Garden and into the tunnels. I was thinking about how awful it would be if she actually did want to have sex now, finally, when all she inspired in me was despair.

But what the hell did I want, anyway? A militant Earth-resister? Of course she thought Earth was great — it was like her hobby. Was she supposed to look at the loss of a few traditions that were probably really boring to her as some kind of crime? When it brought with it new, modern, liberating ideas? When it made her as a female — and as a female who spoke English — a lot more powerful?

"He is a very nice Montavian," Jinya said.

"Yeah."

"Or . . . you say . . . munchkin?" she said, giggling.

Sigh. Infecting her with the English virus *and* xenophobic slurs. I deserved to be left alone with a vicious Montavian with a set of sharpened tools and time on his hands. Fuck.

Not even the sight of the basin below improved my mood, stunning though it was. The basin was dominated by a single massive donut of coral reef. There was a bridge across to its center, where a few hundred people were congregated.

"What're they waiting for?" I asked.

She just started over the bridge. I followed, stepping carefully — there were wide gaps in the metal floor not intended for bipeds. Bright green coral pulsed a few inches from my feet. I thought that a glass structure would have been more effectively minimal, but perhaps that was too Squidollian.

At the arch of the bridge I let my eyes run over the colors blending into each other, running over the loop two times before my eyes were sated and content to rest in the center. I noticed that many of the people were Gardeners. They seemed excited, chatting amongst each other and stopping people from touching the coral.

Lovemaking. What could it be? Would there be some sort of a ritual? Would the Gardeners suddenly form a lusty oogma chain? They certainly seemed to be ready for something. Would Jinya slip onto my lap?

"What is it!" I said, when we got into the center. From here, the colors completely filled our field of vision. She grinned mischievously and spun around. Her silver eyes flashed with the coral's colors.

A young gardener, attracted by her enthusiasm, sidled up to Jinya bursting with his own.

"*Is this your first time?*" he said. He seemed to not register that I was there, which was a refreshing change. He was rubbing something on a chain around his neck, but I couldn't see it.

"*Yes. I have only read about it before,*" she said, with an immediate open enthusiasm.

"*Me too,*" he said. "*I have only been a Gardener for half a year.*" He proffered the pendant he'd been rubbing, seemingly as proof. It was a gray dolphin.

I glanced around at the other Gardeners, and noticed they were all wearing dolphin pendants in varied hues. But why were they wearing their enemies' image? I was about to ask when his eyes fluttered and he went limp and floated backwards.

Jinya made a concerned noise and leaned over him, touching his forehead with her tentacle, and I made a mental note: *when conversation lags, faint.* But he stayed out, and I began to look around for help, thinking about the Earth cure of splashing water in his face. I just wagged my hand in front of his face, pushing the atmosphere at him.

When I gave up, he came to.

"*Oh!*" he said, seeing me. He got up and bowed twice. "*I'm sorry. I've been fasting for ten days.*" He looked at me with such surprise that I began to wonder if, in his half-starved state, he had seen me at all before that.

"*It's too small to apologize for,*" I insisted, his wild eyes unnerving me.

An older gardener came over, one wearing a blue dolphin, and took him gently by the tentacle. He bowed to us and drew him away.

"Why do they wear dolphins?" I asked her.

"He is too hungry, I think!" said Jinya, concerned.

"He is trying to make you feel sorry for him."

She watched after him, and he disappeared into the throng.

An old but clear-eyed Gardener passed by, and I stepped into his path. I bowed and introduced myself. "*Why do you wear a silver dolphin?*" I asked. I was determined to get to the bottom of it.

"*I am old,*" he said, turning away abruptly to pull a child away from the coral. He stared at the parents, who looked down and entangled their squirmy spawn in a bramble of tentacles. Then he left.

"Why is it shaped like your enemies?" I asked Jinya, frustration creeping into my voice.

"*This place is the old border. That's why the garden is so fresh. Beyond here the dolphins used to live.*" She said it absently, a childhood school lesson.

"*It is for remembering the war,*" I said.

"*Before, the people who lived here were soldiers. Now they are gardeners.*"

No more enemies to fight. I imagined these slim men in combat with the dolphins — flailing arms versus battering ram heads? Or did they have weapons? These were things every Octavian knew, things they never thought to mention because it was like telling someone that Earth once had seas and forests. Everyone knew that, everyone had seen the old pictures of ancient Earth as a blue-green marble.

It was twilight now, and some people had settled down — some old grannies had brought their own disks to sit on, collapsible ones. They took grandchildren in their laps and cooed to them, the smaller smooth and larger wrinkled tentacles twining and moving familiarly.

When Jinya and I were in bed together, she would hug me with one or two tentacles in a simulation of a human embrace. In the middle of the night, though, I awoke to find myself truly held: encircled by eight arms.

I sat down and leaned back on the palms of my hands

"When are we going back to our hotel room?" I wanted to know.

"*Relax. After the Lovemaking.*"

"I don't understand," I said, painting my face perplexed. "You want to go back to the hotel for Lovemaking?"

She poked me under the arm. "No!"

"You want to do Lovemaking here?" I said, pointing to the ground.

She poked me in the kidney. "Shut up!" she laughed.

"I don't understand Octavian, I think," I said innocently, and the Gardeners began to chant.

The people that weren't already sitting sat down, and turned their attention outwards. The Gardeners remained upright, making sounds that may have been Octavian, but I didn't recognize them.

The coral was really starting to move, and at first I thought it was in response to the chanting, but it started to pulse faster and the Gardeners sped up in response to that. It was a little bit bewildering, and Jinya gave my questioning looks nothing more than a sly smile.

The whole circle pulsed even faster — the colors almost blurring with the speed, the shouts of the children, the Gardeners lifting their tentacles — and then a huge wash of haze came over the whole coral reef.

A white, milky, almost silken substance emanated out from the coral and spread into the atmosphere.

"What the hell?" I said. Jinya just giggled.

Next to us, a grandmother pointed to the coral. "*Sperm,*" she said to her grandchild. She pointed to another spot. "*Eggs.*"

The Lovemaking. Ah.

I looked around at the crowd, who were watching the juices flow out of the hot and ready coral. Pointing at the shapes it made. It was floating down to the ground, and no one seemed like they were going to move.

Were we going to sit here and let the spunk settle on us?

One of the Gardeners started to leap into the air, impatiently. Even at this distance I recognized the wild eyes of the young man who had talked to us earlier. His leaps were pretty good, actually, aided by his waving tentacles.

Eventually, he reached the descending cloud, and started inhaling it. I winced and hoped the old man who had helped him before was nearby and would stop him. Then the other Gardeners started leaping.

The white gossamer whooshed into their mouths like spaghetti strands.

I looked at Jinya.

"It is good for stamina," she said. "High in protein."

Some of the kids were already sitting on their parent's shoulders. I watched the cloud descend and wondered how long I could hold my breath.

🪐

Ever since that family trip to the Ice Fair on Pluto I'd always sworn I'd never go into stasis. But ten hours after leaving Octavia, the jelly was beginning to look pretty damn good.

The three of us lined the walls of the Pleasureworld-bound rocketship. 9/3 was offline, his perfectly circular eyes gray as the rest of him. True to his word, he had not brought his android body.

Matthew had the sensemask pulled on, his grin curving so often that I was sure it was porn. I glanced down at his trousers and decided the lack of tenting suggested a comedy instead.

On the other hand, I had been dealing with a boner like Neb pig iron for the past ten hours. Most of the people across from me were wearing sensemasks, luckily, except for an old Octavian who was more worried about 9/3. I couldn't wear a sensemask. Soon as I pulled it on I was back in the hotel room with Jinya, her writhing around in a way only a creature with flexible bones could, her tentacles slipping over my ears . . .

I turned around in my harness. Oh why did I drink that coffee? When I knew? I looked at 9/3 enviously. I leaned over and flicked the side of his head, and it donged comically. His eyes lit green.

"What?"

"Teach me how to turn off like that," I said sullenly.

9/3 paused. "Watch very carefully," he said, and his eyes went dead.

The harness was pressing against my crotch in a terribly deliriously nice way.

Jinya had let me touch her there. It was insane the way we had rubbed each other up and down, how the sounds we made and ways we moved let our bodies find each other's spots. We weren't even the same species, but we *knew*.

I was literally dizzy with lust. I punched the button for water and sucked at the hose until my mouth went numb with the cold, my own tongue reminding me of Jinya's thin sharp one. I noticed a stewardess climbing down the rows.

"Can you put me in the jelly?" I asked her.

She looked confused. She had a half dozen pillows under her tentacles. She was very attractive, had the same color of eyes as Jinya, the same sympathetic smile. I wanted to take her somewhere private and fuck her brains out.

My face must have looked pained. "Are you sick?" she asked.

"Um, no. Can you put me in stasis?"

"Sorry sir, only when ship is docked." She offered me a pillow.

I accepted it, resigned to my fate, and she pulled my straps tight. The one south of my hips had been particularly loose. "Mmph!"

"Too tight?" she said, curling a tentacle between the strap and my business.

I smiled weakly. It was all I could do.

She loosened it bit. "Have a good sleep," she said, with a dazzling smile.

I was worse off than before. I watched the stewardess move away. My mouth was dry again. I didn't know why Octavians didn't bother to cover up the place where all their tentacles met — that slippery nexus. Where, I knew now, it all happened. Where a tentative finger sliding across could draw forth the sounds that swirled in the ear, drowned the brain.

"What the fuck is wrong with you?" said Matthew, the cloth sensemask in his hand. "What are you staring at?"

"I don't want to have sex with anyone on this trip," I said desperately, incoherently.

He shrugged. "Suit yourself. It's not like you gotta get your passport stamped LAID before you leave the planet. Now me," he said, pulling down his beverage hose and taking a pull. "I plan to break a few records."

"They have records posted?" I said. It was an interesting, if slightly grotesque idea.

"Personal records," he said. "I wouldn't want to compete with that guy over there." He chinned to a large-eared fellow who was snoring with his mouth open.

"Seriously," I said.

"So did you have a good time at that garden place?"

I nodded. "A little too good."

He gave me a serious look. "Is she fixed?"

"Fixed?" I said.

"Yeah. A friend of mine told me that his brother went out with an Octavian for a while, but she was a widow, so she had been fixed."

All this time Matthew had had inside information? "What do you mean, fixed?"

"Their word for it. Squidollians and Octavians have this thing that they die after they give birth. A hormone is released. They lose their appetite, and eventually starve to death."

"I heard that," I said uneasily. "Always? Like what if someone . . . feeds them?" I thought about having to encourage someone to eat, everyday. Someone who didn't really want to eat.

"Not if they've been fixed. Then the hormone isn't released. Squidollians are fixed at birth now. But Octavians still have to get their parent's approval. It's pretty conservative, not like modern Squidollia."

I thought back to last night with a flashbomb of guilt. But we hadn't, I told myself.

At least, I didn't think we had.

More flashbombs went off as I imagined Jinya at her parents place, listlessly moving the food on her plate around. Her mother's concerned look. Her brother's dawning realization . . .

"I don't think she's fixed. There's something awful about that word." I said, annoyed. "It's like if they don't have mating patterns like humanoids they're broken. Why is Earth the standard for the universe?"

Matthew rolled his eyes. "You sound like my dad. What's wrong with Earth? You'd rather have your girlfriend die?"

"You're an idiot," I said, pretending it didn't splash terror in my face.

The Squidollian stewardess came by. Despite a characteristically flat, extended head she was quite attractive.

"I was wondering why there is no Pono tea," he asked her, actually batting his eyes — for my benefit, I can only hope. "It's my favorite. Squidollian tea is the best."

She frowned. "Is not popular. Is not a galactic beverage," she said briefly and whisked away.

I smirked at him. He shrugged. "It usually works."

"Did you talk to your dad before you left?" I asked.

"No way. His last messages got weirder and weirder. I ended up erasing them without even listening to them. I don't know," he said with a concerned look. "He was always nutty, but I'm afraid he's lost it. Which is too bad."

It was an interesting difference between him and me. We both disliked a parent, but he was moving into a phase of pity, almost sympathy — I wondered if I'd ever feel that way about Mom, that detached. I remember how she had reacted when she found out I'd been a pug: *Well, if it interests you that much I can call a few friends of mine who are in subcultural design . . .*

Trying not to think about it — I didn't need any more adrenaline running through my system — I asked Matthew about his dad's warnings.

He rolled his eyes. "Oh, it was stupid. One sounded like a doom and gloom horoscope, and then he was on about his conspiracies . . . he sounds like he needs to get his brain soaked again, the last treatment's worn off."

I thought about the story he had told me about his last vacation. "Did he suggest we meet up with his Unarmored friend to hang out on the rings instead?" I teased.

"That was real. I —" he saw my smirk and stopped.

"Go on," I prompted.

"Fuck you!" he yelled.

9/3's eyes lit up. No one else reacted.

"Our ship's been hijacked by Unarmored terrorists," I told him. "We're headed for the Neb galaxy. Right Matthew?"

Matthew was smiling and biting his lip and giving me the finger.

"I have informed Roboworld that this ship has been hijacked. We will be intercepted and destroyed in two hours."

Oh. "I . . . was joking."

"I know. 'Unarmored terrorists' is an oxymoron," said 9/3.

"Did you clear it with Roboworld, this trip I mean?" I asked.

"Of course," he said. He started a system check: his pincers twisted, his elbows bent. "I was surprised they cleared it."

"Maybe it has something to do with your function?"

His arms lifted, as much as they could in his bracket. His head swivelled. His eyes cycled: red, green, white, off.

I gave up waiting for a response. I admired his silence. It was intriguing to think he might be called into action suddenly. Matthew involved in intergalactic espionage was ludicrous; with 9/3 it was something you suspected all along.

Of course, perhaps he would be called into action to eliminate a threat to Octavian sovereignty. I had trouble imagining him lasering me, though. I looked at 9/3's square head, the weld marks like scars along the edges. I'd never looked at the welds before, and I wondered if they were different on each roboman. I lifted my hand to touch them.

9/3 moved it away. "What are you doing," he said, tonelessly.

I realized I had been about to, well, stroke his face. "Nothing," I said, ashamed to admit I had been thinking of him as an insensate object. Then again, why would he care? Why did he move away so suddenly?

"Man, the first thing I'm gonna do is get me some real food," Matthew said, his eyes wistful. "Number two: get me a beer that I don't have to squeeze out."

"What's the diff?" I said, exasperated at Matthew's Earth-centrism. "It's the same rotting barley."

"Yeah, but," said Matthew, "there's nothing like a cold bottle. Even a can. But a soft bladder? All I can think about when I'm drinking on Squidollia is how I'm squeezing one bladder into another bladder . . ."

I laughed, glad to see him chipper again. It was good that one of us was excited about it.

"Number three—" he said, staring off into lewd space.

"You'll go for a refreshing swim," I said. "Right? Submerge yourself in water for a change?"

"Ha ha," said 9/3.

"What are you going to do?" I asked 9/3.

"Pleasureworld is geared towards humanoids," he said. "It should really be called Meatpleasureworld."

We laughed hard, shocked as always by 9/3's irreverence. The stewardess climbed by, smiling nervously at us.

"But there is a small oilpool that has my name on it."

"Well, your serial number," Matthew piped up.

"Yes. 'Has my name on it' is a colloquial English expression," 9/3 mock-explained.

That started a series of English teacher in-jokes that lasted until the stewardess came around to tell us we were landing soon. I looked out the porthole at our destination and thought that it wasn't going to be so bad after all.

☄

I was wrong.

☄

I was sitting in front of the desk, watching Matthew grow. The window was massive, covering most of the wall I was facing. I was surprised that a planetary emergency ship like this would have niceties like a good view.

Matthew was now twice as big as the rocketship we had come in on. It stood beside him like a younger brother. He looked pretty scared, focused on staying still and upright.

A young man came in, his recorder-pad embossed with the Earth Council crest. I hadn't seen that in a while. I hadn't missed it.

He extended his hand, gave me a quick pump. "OK Sam," he said, sitting down behind the desk. There was a bit of the air of a doctor about him. He saw me staring at Matthew.

"Maybe we should move to another room," he said, his voice concerned.

"No," I said quickly. I had spent the first ten minutes after we had been netted and dropped in the ship feeling completely blind and almost delusional. It was better to see what was happening, how it was happening.

"Now we haven't got very much time here," the young man said, staring at his pad and holding a tuft of his blond hair in his hand. He turned his sharp eyes on me. "Matthew is growing exponentially. There's a chance we can get him back to normal if we can get some critical information from you."

I nodded, looking out at Matthew. Giant naked Matthew. He was looking at his hands and arms with the same puzzled expression that he'd worn when we'd first gotten off the rocketship. *I feel weird* . . . he had said, and I almost missed him saying it in the roar of the beachfront, the screech of the gulls.

"Now 9/3-0001 has said that the two of you were quite close."

I nodded, trying not to show that I realized that he had used the past tense.

"We need to know anything he may have mentioned about Saturn or Jupiter. Anything. A comment about a trip there, a family friend who worked there, anything," he said, the look of concern on his face a little too labored.

I sat silently. Did they have any intention of getting him back to normal? Or was this some kind of trick?

His wristphone spoke. "Target is on the move." I watched Matthew turn slightly, carefully, squinting at something in the distance. The side of his foot knocked a concession stand slightly askew. He glanced down at it, appeared to consider bending down to right it, then didn't. He moved his pale shoulders uncomfortably.

He realized that the word "target" had shut me up. He sighed, his voice a little harder. "Look, it looks like he was foetally modified for a site-triggered mutation. There were a handful of them that weren't accounted for after the war. Quite alarming, but not terribly dangerous. But a few of them also carried an atomic payload."

I wondered what Matthew's dad was doing right now. Was he eagerly watching the newsfeed for reports? Was he holding a bottle in a two-fingered grasp and crying? Was he going about his normal day, oblivious? What kind of man would condemn his son in the womb?

I looked at Matthew, who was obviously exhausted. He was as tall as the mountains pictured on the promotional poster, and the top of his head was getting wispy with clouds catching in his hair. He wasn't appreciating that, but he was nervously watching the ships going by to net another load of people, as if he suspected they would soon be turning on him.

"I need to know if he was on Jupiter or Saturn. This is important, Sam."

The window flickered and I realized that it was a viewscreen. I looked at Matthew and had the sudden realization that this wasn't Matthew at all. It couldn't be. Who ever heard of people growing up to the clouds? It was absurd.

"Sam, I need your help here."

Did he think repeating my name made him more trustworthy? It didn't even look like Matthew. His nose was different. I started to smile, amazed that they had almost tricked me.

"Are you OK?" he said. Anger and concern fought for control of his face.

"I'm fine, now," I said, smiling bigger. They had the fake Matthew crouch a little as he approached the cloud line, playing like he had trouble breathing. When he was leaning over, he started to smile, then leer.

He was staring at his crotch. He said something that I couldn't quite catch.

The young guy's wristphone spoke again, but I missed it. I was watching the fake-Matthew stand up, to his full height. His shoulders were wreathed in clouds, but his face was clearly visible. He lifted his arms and pumped them in a victorious way, repeating what he had said a second before. This time I could read his lips clearly.

"My cock is huge!"

Well. It was Matthew, after all.

I looked at the young guy and he was frantically speaking into his wristphone. He was looking at me and holding his hand out as if to pull the answer from me.

"Saturn," I said.

Outside, looking woozy from a lack of oxygen, the real Matthew collapsed onto his knees. The land around him jumped from the impact.

"Goddamn it, that's the continental plate busted," yelled the young guy, gritting his teeth as he stared at the scene. "We have a no-payload mutator here, folks, act accordingly."

He grabbed his recorder-pad and strode from the room, slapping the door locked as he went.

They left the viewscreen on to let me watch Matthew be carpet-bombed, to see the little puffs flower between the bony knobs of his spine.

🪐

9/3 was the only other occupant of the shuttle. I was still in magnashackles but he, of course, was not. I was marched into a chair and then the guard sat me down hard.

"Enjoy your flight, scum," the guard said with a lazy grin.

The shuttle door hissed closed too quickly for my spit-gob to reach its target.

9/3 looked at me and sighed. It sounded just like the door closing and I smiled a mean smile at 9/3's expense. Blood and sweat dripped a stinging cocktail into my eyes.

The shuttle softly pushed away from the prisonship.

9/3 got up and rattled through the emergency box. He took out a medvac.

"Why are you so stupid, Sam?" asked 9/3. He trained the ray on my face.

"Leave me alone," I said. "I'd rather bleed."

9/3 ignored me and continued, moving from my face to my hands. Then he went and returned the device. He sat down, heavily.

"I have not been in a shuttle since the day we went to the forest planet. The four of us." He sat perfectly still, perfectly boxy, not looking towards me. "That was a very special day."

I stared at him. I wished I was back on the ship being beaten by the guard. The guard was someone I could hate. It burned pure, but with 9/3 it was all pops and guttering.

I felt a perverse gratitude to the guard for being a focal point. Now all I had was 9/3.

"So I guess you're headed back to Roboworld, now that you've fulfilled your function," I said through gritted teeth.

9/3's eyes blinked no. "What do you mean?"

"Well," I said. "You were sent to spy on us, right?"

9/3's eyes flashed red anger, then back to white.

"If you hadn't told them who I was, maybe they wouldn't have confirmed that he was safe to kill." I excluded my own part in it, though it sat in my brain like an implant. "Maybe they could have . . . shrunk him." I had an image of Matthew, normal sized, with pools of skin around his ankles. It was an appropriately stupid image, as I realized how unlikely it was.

"In a planetary emergency, I have to report all pertinent details to the authorities and Roboworld," he intoned.

I flared up at this. Just more hiding behind procedures, just-following-orders bullshit. "Well, did you tell them that you fucked Hugh?" I yelled, straining against my magnashackles. "Did you report to Roboworld that you were defective?"

The word hung there like the piece of shit it was. I was ashamed but determined. I willed 9/3 to get angry, ground my teeth together and psychically flung my rage over him like waves of radiation.

His eyes flickered several different colors at once, landing on red a few times. There was a sound of static that came from his voicebox that was nearly inaudible.

I stared through the window. A star crawled across it. I wished I was burning in its core. And then my fierceness was gone.

I checked my aggrometer to verify. Yep. The needle was dead.

9/3 went offline.

When I fell asleep, I saw a squirrel gathering food and stopping at a sound. There's a new river on Pleasureworld 33, rushing over rocks and around trees. A red river that flows from a head cracked open on a mountain, where the gigantic boy's parted lips leak endlessly, bubble and leak.

TWENTY

"It was very unusual to inhale the eggs and sperm of another animal," I explained to my workshop teachers calmly, a week later.

"It is Octavian tradition," Mr. Kung said. "But boyfriend-girlfriend no. Just wife."

"Fertility," said Mr. Nekk. "Is very important to Octavian families."

Mrs. Ahm nodded seriously.

"Boyfriend-girlfriend . . . strangey," said Mr. Kung, crossing his tentacles in case I missed the meaning.

"After marriage, OK."

"The Gardens are an Octavian treasure," I said, deliberately using words Kung wouldn't understand. "The colors are amazing."

"Why did you not go to Pleasureworld?" Mr. Nekk asked.

"We changed our plans," I said, with no intention of going into it. The Pleasureworld chain had used their clout to kill the story. I continued quickly. "I have some bad news."

"Bad news?" said Mrs. Ahm, always the quickest. "What?"

"I am moving to Artemia. My language skills will be tested." Jinya's professor had set it up, after an excited meeting. I wasn't convinced that it was the right thing to do, but I figured I could clam up at any point.

"That's terrible," said Mr. Nekk.

"I'm sorry to hear that," Mrs. Ahm said.

"Too bad," Mr. Kung said. "We go drinky?"

🪐

"Did you tell the teachers about the . . . accident?" Jinya asked while we lay in bed.

"No. I told them about the Living Gardens. And about the coral orgy."

"Orgee?"

"Like . . . sex party."

"Yes! Coral sex party!" she said, laughing against my shoulder. It felt wonderful, and I almost smiled.

"Sam?"

"Yeah?"

"Are you sad that we don't sex?" she said. "Humans like to sex."

I thought for a second, tracing the spaces between her suckers with my fingertip. "Yes, but . . . you are sad that I am leaving, right?"

I felt her nod.

☄

The next day was my last day.

"Artemia tomorrow?" said Mr. Zik, getting ready to leave for class.

"Yep," I said, waving at my cleaned-off desk. "All ready."

"I can drive you," he said. "In my saucer."

I thought of what that meant to him — the harrowing request he'd have to make of the principal, the sixteen hours of travel — all for an offworlder who was abandoning his post.

I got up and hugged him, gently holding his stalk-of-corn body.

"Ssss-sss-ss," he said. "What?"

☄

I ended up walking to the bus stop alone. Jinya had school and besides, we were going to meet in the city soon.

It was a short walk to the station, but long enough for my melancholy to build. I walked by the tree and nodded to the grandfather and the dumb, rock-headed girl. She climbed down from the hill and started walking beside me. I looked back at grandpa but he didn't seem in the least concerned.

I hadn't seen her in a long while — ever since the test I monitored, maybe that long. "*Shouldn't you be in school?*" I asked, but with a smile.

She just answered my smile with one of her own. She reached out and took one of my lighter bags.

"Thank you," I said.

"Yellcome," she twisted out after a moment, the first and only English word I'd hear her speak.

We walked through the town together, pretty empty at this time of morning. A scooter buzzed by on a delivery, and I wondered what it would be like to be that blank-faced boy. I willed myself into his head, his life. Did he have any worries about what he was doing, what effect he was having? Or did he simply weigh his decisions by which held the most beeds and the least trouble?

My suitcase was getting heavier by the step but the station was within sight. I checked my time. I was all right. We cut through the small market and an old lady called out.

"Come help me!"

I stopped and looked at the old lady in the booth, her tentacles bristling with cucumbers. I was trying to figure out what she wanted when the rock-headed girl shook her head and showed her the bag of mine she was carrying.

The old lady nodded and went back to stacking Plangyo's favorite vegetable.

When we got to the bus station and sat on the bench, I was surprised by the amount of memories that had accumulated there so quickly. There was the spot where that little chump had sung I.C.Y. to me, the day Jinya and I met. This was the place that every one of my trips on Octavia had begun and ended.

I looked around at the ticket vending machine and the two or three other mid-day travellers. From my spot on the bench, I could see the hills in the distance — never terribly impressive but now even less so that I'd seen the incredibly fecund Living Gardens. Not much to be fond of, but I was sad to be leaving anyway.

I remember how defensive I'd gotten when Matthew had visited. "My station on Squidollia is twice as big as this. This is pathetic."

"Yeah, well," I had retorted. "I'll bet we have twice as many hideously old women waiting here at any given moment."

The rock-headed girl sat beside me, her eyes disinterested. But I guess it beat stacking cucumbers. I wanted her to ask me why I was sad, to divine with a child's insight that something weighed on me, and to want to draw it out.

"Why are you sad, teacher?" she could say.

"Well," I'd say, and then decide to tell her. *"A good friend of mine died."*

She wouldn't say anything, then, because what could you say that wasn't stupid or trite? That's why I hadn't bothered telling my teachers. It was bad enough that the memory of it kept backing up like a brackish sewer, draining only to bubble up again, without hearing people fumble through empty phrases.

Ha, Matthew's voice mocked me, *big bad pug hopes a kid will make him feel better. Aw.*

A bus came for somewhere else and picked up two people. I watched its backside as it moved away.

The bubbles from the exhaust were caught in its wake and thrown up, an answer to the song.

Bubbles over Plangyo,
Where did you go?

I heard Mr. Zik singing in the sing-song room in my mind. I hummed it, since I didn't know the words, and looked at the rock-headed girl. She had her little painted stone friends out, playing with them contentedly. She was humming too.

TWENTY ONE

The charliebot was polishing glasses, and I was getting them dirty.

"Fill'er up," I said, staring in front of me. The charliebot stuck out his hose and let me have another. He didn't say anything. They don't when you're drinking at an optimum rate.

It had been a year since I left Plangyo. The spaceport bar was exactly like every other one I'd been to. The light just bright enough so that you can see the pretty bottles sparkling, an offer of the rough stuff. It was the same as every other spaceport bar in the bloody galaxy, although sometimes there's more people.

Today, it was just me and the charliebot. Goddamn trash can.

"Whattaya lookin' at, bud?" it said.

"Shut the fuck up, metal man."

The charliebot kept polishing. The door slid open.

The guy was dressed in a gray body-suit, with a collar he probably thought was pretty damn stylish. I sneered at him.

"Gimmie a gin-and-tonic," he said, in a scratchy voice.

I snorted. "Sounds like you need a drink, buddy." I slammed the glass on the bar. "And so do I."

He looked at me, a weak little smile on his face. "Where you coming from?" He got his drink and took three quick sips from it.

"Octavia," I said.

"Well, welcome back to civilization," he said.

I laughed and raised my glass. He clinked it.

"You know, I had a . . . thing with one of them once," he said. "A *digital romance* they call it."

"You were lucky, guy," I said bitterly. "She didn't get her fuckin' tentacles around you." I breathed heavily, feeling bile in my throat and not just from the drink. I washed it down with the rest of my beer. "Didn't get her hooks into ya . . ."

Then I whipped the glass into the row of liquor bottles.

"Goddamn sea monkey!" I bellowed, clenching my fist and thumping it on the bar. The guy in the body-suit laughed, a dry clicking laugh.

He offered his hand. "I'm Kevin."

I shook it. "Sam."

"You're gonna end up owing quite a bit for that, Sam," he said, watching the charliebot tally it up.

The door slid open. An Octavian walks into a spaceport bar . . .

"Oh, great," I said. "They're following me." Then a crafty look stole over my face. I knew a few tricks. I got up and waved the Octavian to a seat beside Kevin.

"*Welcome,*" I said in badly accented Octavian.

I got the charliebot to pour the Octavian a drink. He was young and reminded me immediately of one of those cheerful morons from, what was that stupid pop group? Whatever.

The charliebot went back to tallying up the smashed bottles.

"*A friendly Earthling, how unusual!*" exclaimed the prettyboy.

I shrugged, pretending I didn't understand. It would be easier that way.

The charliebot finished. "You owe the bar 150 credits."

I pointed at the prettyboy.

"*You owe the bar 150 credits.*"

I sat down and smirked at Kevin, who was laughing.

"*That's an expensive beer!*" he exclaimed. He lifted the glass and looked at it. Through the glass he noticed the smashed bottles.

I ordered another round of drinks for Kevin and I.

The prettyboy looked at us and seemed to figure it out. He set his beer down and started to leave.

We were in front of him in the blink of an eye.

"*Go back and pay the bar,*" I said. Kevin nodded.

"*You tried to rip me off,*" he said. "*Get out of my way.*"

"No speak Octavian," I said, sneering, and now he knew I was lying. He tried to push us out of the way and Kevin swung at him.

The Octavian took the punch and wrapped Kevin in his tentacles, squeezing with all his might. I started to pull him off until a well-aimed tentacle poked me in the eye.

I reeled back, hand over my eye, and refocused on the fight in time to see a powerful twist of a tentacle snap Kevin's neck.

When he fell with Kevin, I ran at him and aimed a boot at his head. I missed, and felt a tentacle — maybe two — wrap around my lower leg.

Oh fuck.

I went face first into a table and grabbed the edge in an effort to get up. I just succeeded in toppling it over. But the tentacles were gone. Prettyboy was making his way for the door.

I got up and lifted the round table and swung it at him, laughing as blood ran down to my chin. At the last second, the Octavian dropped on his back, caught the table with all eight tentacles, and swung back.

It connected solidly with my skull and knocked me back a few steps. The prettyboy hopped up and, when I was still dazed, strolled up and gave me a light push in the chest.

I fell backwards, knocking over the entire bar. Every bottle in the place shattered.

The prettyboy looked at me coolly and waited for the charliebot to announce the damages: 2575 creds. He looked at me on the ground, my hand twitching, my mouth still twisted, and shrugged.

"*That round's on him.*"

Then he walked out.

"*Cut! That was perfect!*"

I got up. *Lucky it was perfect*, I thought as I spat out the blood packet, *that was the third take.*

Kevin was still lying there. "Oh — get up, Kevin. Scene's over," I told him.

He bounced up. "He just said 'perfect,' right?"

"Yeah," I said. "Learning the language, eh? Good."

The door slid open and the guy who just thrashed me came in. "*You're a great actor, Sam!*"

"*Thank you! I was happy to work with you, too. You're the funniest member of Intergalactic Cool Youth.*"

He beamed and pulled his lips out with six tentacles and crossed his eyes.

I laughed. It *was* funny. I explained to Kevin briefly who he was and he was appropriately impressed.

Around us, the set was being cleaned up and taken apart. The director hustled in, patted me on the back. "*You were right about the charliebot. It was more realistic.*" He had originally wanted to use an Octavian bartender, but I convinced him otherwise. He was big on realism, this director — except for the fact that there were no spaceport bars with atmosphere where an Octavian could stand upright. But unless Octavian action-comedies became a big export, I figured we'd get away with it.

Kevin was shaking hands with the director. "Very good," the director dredged up, and Kevin stuttered out an Octavian thank-you.

"*With an accent like that you don't have to worry about your job, even if he is better-looking,*" the director told me as he zipped off.

Kevin looked at me. "He's always on some stimulant," I said, in lieu of translating. "They get black dots in their eyes. That's how you tell. Never trust an Octavian with pupils."

"Well, thanks for getting me the job," he said. "It was fun."

We walked over to the food table. "The part was actually written with you in mind," I said. "I work with the scriptwriter, and when I found out there was gonna be another human on the planet I figured . . ."

"So you have some say in the part you play?" he asked.

"It's the only way I'll work on a project," I said, feeding my face. Getting beat up made me famished!

"So why don't you give yourself a better part?" he said.

I munched on, a smile growing on my face. "Why indeed?" I said cryptically.

Kevin waited, his eyebrows raised.

"Let's go," I said finally. "Drinking all that fake beer made me thirsty. Let me buy you a bladder of the real stuff."

We stopped at my place first, to wash up. When I was in the washroom, Kevin said he liked my apartment.

"It's OK," I said. "I have my eye on this traditional house on the outskirts of town, though."

"Oh, I've seen those. They're beautiful," called Kevin.

"Yeah," I said, *everyone but the Octavians think so.* I thought back to the fight Jinya and I had had over it, and sighed.

I left the washroom. Kevin was peering at the decor which mostly consisted of a bunch of pictures of Octavian landscapes and my glass jetpack. "That's an unusual clock," he cracked, nodding at my aggrometer wristwatch. It had been pinned to the wall ever since the strap broke.

"Yup," I said as I checked to make sure I had everything.

We left, Kevin looking at Matthew's jetpack again but not asking any more questions. I was kind of glad. I had thought that I was beginning to feel OK about the whole incident until I was at an offworld party a few weeks ago. It was one of the first times I'd hung out with a bunch of Earthlings for almost a year — it was a year since it happened — and at first I was having a good time. But then, in the dim light of the bar, I saw Matthew's silhouette. But of course it wasn't really Matthew — didn't even look like him — but the lurch in my chest showed that I was still expecting him to show up. Show up with his evil grin and make fun of what I was drinking, or ask me about my students, or tell me how much he needed to get laid . . .

Kevin sensed my mood, and we walked in silence to the place just around the corner. "Hello, Sam," said the owner, a woman in her late forties. Her handkerchief was bright yellow, which was like her. "*You bring me new customers, eh? Doesn't he like the Earthling bar?*"

The Crossed Snakes was a no-frills eatery, unless you counted the owner, which I did. "*The Earthling bar is too expensive,*" I said, although actually it was the way they liked me to sit up at the window, a living model, that put me off it.

She cackled, and took our order. I got my usual — vegetables wrapped in a fried rice paste — and the same for Kevin. "*And two regular beers,*" I added, not wanting to presumptuously order large.

"Handsomebloy," said the owner, holding Kevin's shoulders. "Where you?"

"*Blusan I am hometown Octavia,*" he pushed out in a rush, looking at the owner for understanding. Some of the patrons laughed.

"Bloosan," she said, nodding.

"Bloosan," he repeated gamely.

She left us, and Kevin exhaled. "Man, I feel like an idiot. Everyone's watching."

I didn't bother looking around. "Everyone's always watching," I said.

Kevin wasn't listening. He was staring at what I assumed to be a group of giggling schoolgirls. I glanced back. It was a group of giggling secretaries.

Kevin's trance broke. "Was I staring?" he said. He ran his fingers through his hair. "I mean, they're not wearing any pants!" he said, desperately. He looked back again. "There's no one like that in Blusan. All we got are noisy little boys and sitting-disks."

"Sitting-disks?" I said. The food arrived, clattered down by the surly daughter of the owner.

"Yeah. 'Blusan is famous for sitting-disks.' "

I nodded. "My town was famed for its gray cucumbers." I dug in, eating with my fingers. Kevin used his fork.

He looked back at the girls.

"Best thing to remember," I said, doling out advice despite my better impulse, "is that any relationship is going to affect them a lot more than it affects you. You probably won't live here all your life. She will." The dumplings were hot and good, and I dosed one mouthful with a squeeze of beer.

Kevin took a pull at his beer and nodded. "That makes sense. They weren't very up front about that stuff at the orientation. What have . . . I mean, have you —"

I cut off his struggles with a merciful raised hand. "Yeah." I was glad he was unsure, unbalanced — he should be. I had been worried that I would finally get an Earthling neighbor and he would be a bonehead. I looked at him, decided to tell him the story.

"Hello Sambreen," said one of the pretty girls, her light blue eyes shining with mischief, which was my favorite shade of light blue. I waved as they passed out the door, and my attention caused one to collapse on the girl in front of her. She said something as the door closed.

Kevin looked at me quickly. I knew how he felt, every incomprehensible phrase seemed to promise the code to understanding Octavians. "She said, 'He's famous.' " I stretched out against the wall. "Everyone human's a superstar here," I said. "Even worse if you can speak Octavian."

He shook his head. "They said that you're really gifted, the people at orientation."

That was gratifying, in an entirely unexpected way. "Well, you don't see them getting me to speak at orientation, do you?"

Wonneel walked in with some guy in a toque, talking out the side of his mouth as was his perpetual habit. He spat his tobacco in a stream out the door before it closed. The owner nodded to him.

I raised a hand to Wonneel and he gave me a wan smile.

"Yeah," I said looking back at him. "They're not exactly proud of me. I was a better student than teacher." I smiled, more at myself for being so vague. But when you had a year to get to know each other, what was the rush?

Wonneel came and sat down beside me. *"Who's the new kid,"* he grunted, eyeing Kevin. *"Can he speak?"*

"Nope. Kevin, Wonneel. Wonneel, Kevin."

Kevin looked a little freaked, and I saw him scrambling through his mental drawers for the Octavian greeting. "Hello," he said finally.

Wonneel stared at him for another few seconds then turned away, the embodiment of dismissal. He was the only person I knew who wouldn't return a "Hello!" and I loved him for it.

"You get home all right last week?" Wonneel said, aiming a stream of tobacco juice at a dish we'd emptied.

"*I heard I left just in time,*" I said.

He gave a rueful shrug. An old man in the back was kicking up a fuss, cursing out the daughter. "*I want wallen, you brat!*"

My lip curled. The owner whisked by our table. With an eye on her back, Wonneel pulled a small container out of his bag and passed it to me.

"*You know it's illegal, sir,*" the owner said to the man, her yellow kerchief bobbing.

"*Thanks,*" I said to Wonneel, who was watching the fight. "*Get you back later.*"

"*This is a modern place. That's old-time food. Unhealthy!*" she said.

He waved them away, disgusted, went back to his cups.

Wonneel shook his head. "*There's no respect for the old,*" he tutted.

I raised my eyebrows on this selective reverence. Wonneel would sooner lose an eye than his seat on the bus to an oldster.

"*Can't refuse an old man his meat,*" he said, and got up and went over to the old guy.

"How do you know him?" Kevin asked.

"He was an extra on a film I was working on," I said, watching as Wonneel said something to the old man. The old man listened and then, after throwing back his ujos and throwing down his beeds, unsteadily followed Wonneel's slim figure out of the restaurant.

"Yeah, he played an Octavian gangster," I said, finishing my beer.

"He kind of looks gangsterish," said Kevin. "Sharp features, dark eyes . . ."

"Uh huh," I said. I yelled for the waitress. The daughter poked her reluctant head out, and I ordered more beer.

"So do you always act in action films?" he asked.

"Not always . . . comedies, too," I said, thinking about how Wonneel was always disappointing, but at least he was consistent. Also, less seriously, that I should get a cut of his new business, since I was the one responsible for the demand.

"What did you play in the last comedy?" he said.

"Um . . . That was *Loafer's Revenge*. I played Loafer's Earthling sidekick." I smiled, remembering it. "I had this thing that I hated black noodles, but I kept getting served huge heaping dishes of it."

Kevin looked at me, confused.

"Well, black noodles have a kind of sexual connotation . . . it's a bit of a pun . . ." I said, shrugging. "It's funny to Octavians."

"Huh," Kevin said. Then he leaned forward and poked the table as if trying to pin down his point, a particularly human gesture. "But isn't there any chance to play a part that isn't a bad guy or a sidekick?"

"Sure there is," I said. "One script I saw last week had a part for a charismatic and earnest rocketship captain from Earth who has an affair with the daughter of a prominent Octavian family. Leading man stuff."

"But . . ." Kevin spread his hands. "What? You didn't get the part?"

I chuckled. "The part was written with me in mind. They can't afford offworld actor rates. When I turned it down they just made it a Squidollian captain — less controversial that way, anyway."

"Was that what put you off? The controversy?"

I corralled my thoughts. I wanted to make this good. "One of the reasons I left Earth was that I didn't like it there, especially the way society revolved around money. But when I got here I realized how much Earth had already infected Octavian culture — it's come to symbolize modern life and progress — and I realized I was kind of a representative of the whole planet."

Kevin nodded sombrely. "It's a big responsibility."

"Now, my first inclination was to play parts that were heroic and noble, but I realized that that was just me wanting to be liked. And Octavia's already got enough of that crap beamed at them. So I decided I was going to play parts that evened out that singular view of humans-as-heroes by playing the exact opposite." I paused for a squeeze of beer. "Greedy bullies and idiots."

Kevin's jaw literally dropped.

I had a long laugh. He was a great audience.

"So . . . you're doing it . . . deliberately?" he said.

I raised an eyebrow. "Crazy, huh?"

"Well . . ." he said, looking into middlespace, brow furrowed. "I mean, I think *I've* got problems with the Earth Council . . ."

I nodded, let him talk for a while.

"But it's like . . . sometimes it's necessary. I mean Octavians were still eating other sentient beings until a couple of months ago."

I smiled ruefully. Yeah, the Earth Council had got a lot of mileage out of that. Someday I'd tell him the whole story. "There's lots of good things about Earth," I said, picking at the food. "And Earth culture. But the problem with it replacing alien cultures — beyond the fact that it makes for a boring universe —"

Kevin nodded at that.

"— is that, after a generation, no one even remembers how those other societies were run. So there's only one template for a society, and there's little room for debate or change when there's no real-life examples of people doing things differently."

Kevin nodded, raising his eyebrows in a kind of *maybe you're right* way. He squeezed the remainder of his beer into his mouth with a frothy squirt.

It was unsatisfying — I'd have preferred he argued. I filled the glass with beeds and got up. "Octavian tradition. Never stay in one place for more than a drink."

He got ready to go and I grabbed my precious container. "Almost forgot," I said. "If you ever get desperate enough for coffee to trade a week's wages for one of these," I said as we walked to the door, "Let me know."

It was already dark outside, but not dark enough to hide the owner's daughter in the clutches of a young tough-looking boy. Tentacles retracted guiltily. *"Boyfriend?"* I asked.

She denied it.

"You're kissing a stranger?" I enquired mildly as we walked away.

"Keep your jokes to your movies," said the boy to my back.

I smiled, but was a little stung. Not everyone accepted that my asshole Earthling personas in the movies weren't my own. Of course, the slight venom a few Octavians felt for me was nothing in comparison to what it may have been had my part in the "modernization drive" been revealed.

The actual testing of my language skills had been a joke. I had expected a room full of Octavian experts that would listen and judge. I had been terrified. But the reality was, as usual, entirely more banal and entirely more horrible.

After I arrived in Artemia, a representative from the Earth Council had shown me to a room with a desk. He had the same boyish haircut and doctorly manner as the guy on Pleasureworld 33. He tapped his recorder-pad and asked me to make the impossible sounds. I thoc'ed and op'ed for him. He hadn't even smiled, just nodded and left. That had been it, and about three months later, the Octavian government instituted a series of unpopular laws in the name of modernization. I had tried to ignore most of it, guilty and unsure, although Jinya had shown me one editorial cartoon depicting a plague of wallens overrunning the streets.

I stuck my hands in my pocket as we strolled down the street, which were, at the moment, wallen-free. I took a route through the flashier parts of the city, where saucers tried to behead you and flashing lights tried to blind you.

"No one says hello here," said Kevin, watching a chain of girls turn sideways to slide by us. "I almost miss it."

"Most urbanites have seen bipeds before," I said, looking at a snazzy hat in the window display. "There's a small tourist trade."

We turned down a series of successively smaller streets until we came to the alley. It wasn't even flattened, really, just a path worn in the coral. At the end of it was a small entrance with a glowing eye above it. It pulsed different colors. Kevin looked at it before he went in, but looked more excited than frightened.

"*Oh no, they're multiplying!*" Ilnok said, throwing up his tentacles. I introduced Kevin to the old husk, and we followed him to the far end of the small bar. One of his students was working there.

"Where you from?" demanded Ilnok.

"Kenya," said Kevin.

"*You speak English?*" I said, surprised.

"No in Earth. Where Octavia?" Ilnok pressed Kevin.

Kevin told him.

Ilnok nodded, mimed sitting down and then made a sucker-pop: really good.

We nodded. Blusan's sitting disks *were* really good, not that our big asses could possibly appreciate it.

Ilnok turned his attention back to his student. The student was oblivious to our presence, dipping the tip of his tentacle into a small dish of pale red pigment.

"*The colors remind me of the Living Gardens.*"

"*I went to the Living Gardens last week!*" Ilnok said, animated. "*It's too expensive now that the government doesn't fund it.*" He shook his head.

I nodded, glad that guilt didn't have a particular smell to give me away. I resolved to buy a few more pictures from Ilnok later this week.

The student smeared the pigment on the cloth, adding a hazy pink line to the landscape's horizon.

"Oh," said Kevin. "It's a flat picture. Of a reef." He cocked his head to the side. "Huh."

I nodded. "It's a uniquely Octavian art form. They call it 'smearing'.."

"Uniquely?"

"Well, humans can't do it," I said, waggling my thin fingers. I looked enviously at the thick, dextrous appendage adding definition to a saucer in the distance.

"*How's Jinya?*" asked Ilnok.

I shrugged. "OK."

Ilnok rubbed his forehead, leaving a yellow mark. "OK?"

"*She didn't get a teaching job this year*," I said. "*She was hoping to move here.*"

He looked surprised. "*Very competitive,*" Ilnok said, doubt in his voice. He reached down and lifted the student's smearing tentacle up. "*Lightly.*"

"*They liked her English. But I think they didn't like her boyfriend,*" I said, guilt and frustration welling up. "*Some things I said about the school system were reported on the newsfeed.*"

Ilnok nodded, his cloudy eyes regarding me sadly. He was partially blind.

"Wow," said Kevin, as the student used his suckers to roughen up the texture. The student looked up at this familiar word and smiled, slightly embarrassed.

It had been a long few weeks after Jinya was rejected. We didn't see each other at all: she had been busy, looking for private teaching jobs, and I had been working long hours on a movie called *Intense Believability*. The gritty drama had been a good backdrop for the agonizing I had done, deciding and undeciding that it would be better for her if we broke up, assuming in the silence following her rejection that she was cursing the day she met me.

Then she brought her parents to meet me on the set. Her mom had beamed at me benevolently and called me "son" . . . and I burst out crying. On Octavia, crying is extra-dramatic, because the atmosphere causes tears to linger. I figured the drama was excusable since I was an actor now.

"It's OK," I summed up for Ilnok. "*Next year will be different.*"

🪐

9/3 was sitting at the lunch booth, his android arms crossed and leaning on the counter. I smacked his shoulder as I seated myself at a stool.

"What's the occasion for the andy body?" I said, wiggling my eyebrows.

"You are late."

"They gave me trouble again," I said, shrugging. "They didn't believe I was meeting someone on a way-station."

"They can not restrict you from travelling within the sector. Just leaving it. I would like an orange juice, please."

The squat droid swivelled to me. "Same as him."

We had to buy something if we wanted to sit there, and I was sick of bowling. I liked this place because everyone was in a rush and ignored us.

"Yeah, I told them that. They're just not used to dealing with suspected terrorist-accomplices at the Artemia spaceport."

"Have you requested a case update?" 9/3 was convinced it was just a bureaucratic oversight.

I shrugged. "Nope. Haven't had any contact with Earth — other than occasional messages sent to Lisa — since they refused to let me visit." My overwhelming feeling had been a perverse joy at my official exile status. Not only was I free of any obligation to visit, but there was a satisfaction at finally qualifying as dangerous. Ever since pug had been unmasked I had been unconsciously seeking it, and it fed me.

"They will clear your name soon," he said in an extra staticky monotone I had come to recognize as unsure.

"Whatever," I said, meaning it. "If I don't go back, I don't have to pay my student loan." Not that that was a real concern, anymore. I had the savings to pay it several times over from my acting work.

"I had a dream about Matthew," 9/3 said, and my first reaction was: *Robomen dream?* I'm such a goof. "He was growing on Pleasureworld 33. Then he said, 'My cock is so big.' "

I laughed, and he looked at me. "It's just funny to hear you say it. Go on." Our orange juice came. It was orange, and it was juice, but it just wasn't orange juice.

"But he didn't have a cock. He had this large toggle switch, covered in skin."

"Eww," I said, sipping at the juice despite myself.

"And he stopped growing. He was turning the switch on and off, and the sun was controlled by it."

"Both suns?" I said.

"No," 9/3 said patiently. "Just the small one. He wanted to turn off the big one — for some reason I knew this. And Hugh —"

"Hugh was there?" I interrupted. I hadn't thought of Hugh in months, and idly wondered where he was, how his angel search was going.

"Do *your* dreams make sense?" he said, his eyes flashing red momentarily.

"Go on," I said.

"Hugh told him that he had to click the toggle switch to the side to turn off the big sun, so he did. That was it."

"How did Hugh tell him that? I mean, how did Matthew hear him?"

"He was standing on the part of the ear right beside the hole. We all were."

I shook my head, impressed. "Man, that's a fucked dream."

"I know. Ha ha ha."

Jim Munroe lives in Toronto. He was managing editor at *Adbusters* before writing his first novel, *Flyboy Action Figure Comes With Gasmask* (Avon, 1999). His website, http://NoMediaKings.org, has info on do-it-yourself publishing as well as a video game or two.